NEWTON'S NIECE

Derek Beaven lives in Maidenhead, Berkshire. His first novel, *Newton's Niece* (1994), was shortlisted for the Writers' Guild Best Novel Prize and won a Commonwealth Prize. His second novel, *Acts of Mutiny*, was shortlisted for the 1998 Guardian Fiction Prize.

Also by Derek Beaven

Acts of Mutiny

Newton's Niece

DEREK BEAVEN

FOURTH ESTATE · *London*

This paperback edition published in 1999 by
Fourth Estate Limited
6 Salem Road
London W2 4BU

First published in Great Britain in 1994 by Faber and Faber Ltd

1 3 5 7 9 10 8 6 4 2

A catalogue record for this book is available from the British Library.

ISBN 1–84115–011–8

Printed in Great Britain by
Clays Ltd, St Ives plc

For
Philip
and
Lyn

Dross

'You're sticking me back in it.' The bland little consultation space, the beige of the chairs, the rust of the curtains, the hard paleness of the walls began to unweave. Their presence gave way; even the cyclamen on the ledge failed. I sensed tears needling my eyes. But I pressed on in an effort to describe the reciprocal image of my feeling: 'There's a room. I have to go in.'

'What's in the room?' Brendan's voice penetrated as if through a stretched film, a membrane.

At length: 'So many things. I don't know which are true.'

I smudged away the tears and murdered the memory of the room. Brendan and the July Saturday morning came back into focus, but not before another distinct and separate trace flapped in from the past. I was ten. I was holding the lid on a curious glass jar. I had just dropped a swab, soaked in poison spirit, through its neck. The magnified, common, beautiful, garden tiger moth panicked briefly at the bottom of its prison. I held the jar up to the panes of an old sash window, to see sunlight strike the bars on its still faintly moving wings.

I didn't tell Brendan about the moth. What was the use? None of it made any sense then.

He shifted in his chair and glanced at the clock. It pleased him to measure his sessions with a battered Fifties-style travelling alarm clock, illuminated in green with radio-active paint. It glowed in the dark, he said. Generally, I felt comfortable with Brendan: he had a worn but perky air about him. His spectacles grabbed on to the concern in his face and tucked into spills of comb-resistant hair, so that when he nodded their gold arms ticked away in a sign of genuine warmth. But I was annoyed with him just now. I was distressed and couldn't show it. If I'd turned to jelly at work and come to howl it out in front of him, or dashed my head against the wall to burst the build-up, he might have registered. But the wicked injunction that had been laid on me prevented the disclosure even of symptoms –

1

although I think something inside was smuggling messages out in the hope that he'd catch on.

He didn't. He was on the wrong track. But even if, by some miraculous accident of speech, he should have come up, there and then, with the very names that were beginning to haunt me – Barnabas Smith, the two Benjamins, and Isaac Newton – they would not have triggered my violent rage or incandescent recognition; not then.

And this was the end of another session; troubling my sensitive eyes against an invisible barrier. Brendan put an arm on my shoulder and saw me to the door. Confused by this gesture, I thrust myself back into the hot street. For my true companions at that time were creatures of nightmare and poetry: I'd given up the attempt at teaching and was working by day as a cleaner in one of those terrible old mental hospitals, one of the last. By night, antique half-birds and, yes, moths, came to hold converse with me – products, perhaps, of my imagination.

The steering wheel felt sticky. I left Slough with the sun on my roof and headed towards the motorway intersection, hoping my rusty Ford would bear the rigours of the M25. And, as always, perhaps, half-hoping that it wouldn't. Mid-journey the peculiar breathing started again. I found myself panting, and wondered what it was that should manifest thus. I hung on to my faint suspicions and the concrete perspective ahead; they kept me going.

The Ford held together. I got crossly on with my shift at the hospital. It was in the children's block, the chronic section – poor damaged souls.

There's a subtle comfort in working with a mop and bucket, a kind of atonement that keeps a nagging voice off your back. I could begin to make inroads against the tide of chaos; even if the dirt was ingrained, it was not Victorian, as it was in the main building. The children lived in a separate Unit – built in the Sixties as a square, unlovely and functional contrast.

I mopped restlessly down corridors, and privately across wards, behind cabinets or under beds, some of which contained speechless and tragically handicapped occupants, their wasted limbs stretched out in a sort of not-sleep. Tied, I suddenly thought, to their beds. Seco, my workmate of the day, left me alone. By lunchtime I'd reached the foyer at the main entrance to the block. It was a sensitive area. I hated having my work messed from all the coming out and going in while it was still wet. The coast looked clear. I needed only a five-minute window to get the whole floor done and dried.

Four minutes later the expanse of grey tiles shone sweetly with a fast-evaporating film of radiance, until the glass doors swung open with a flapping of white coats, and two pairs of medical soles left their thoughtless imprint on my wet floor. My blood seethed. It was the thin boss doctor, the callous one who soon after all this would be prosecuted for running a negligent ship, and one of his henchmen. As they charted their course, clipboards waving, between the double doors and the wards, I caught a snatch of their conversation.

'Of course, she's painting again,' the henchman was saying.

'What? Ms Jay? More slogans? More Action Now posters? Ha, ha,' his laugh more like a cough. 'Anyway, when?'

'No. Real painting. She's been up in the Art Room since this morning. I'm told she asked to have the dark room set up. Someone brought her some negatives. Alright to let that go on?'

'If she knows what she's doing. Bit of a special case. She'll be OK. Everything's more or less screwed down, I'm assured. Don't want to cross her again and have to sedate. Or risk the not-eating game.' They stopped to glance at a notice-board.

'Copying the photographs. Domestic reminiscence. But with each one some preoccupation seems to gain in strength. She's . . . well, strikingly intent.'

'Ah yes. Characteristic. Give a bit of leeway. However I don't think we want to run the risk of over-stimulation. Don't want her drinking the stuff. Silver, what is it . . . iodide? Or am I hopelessly out of date? You never know, if the press gets hold of it. Ask a nurse to pop up every now and then.' Moving on, their voices attenuated.

I caught: 'The cocktail as usual, then?'

'For the time being, I think so. Don't you? Just increase the . . . ' They turned a corner and disappeared from view, severing the name of the drug.

I rammed my mop into its strainer and twisted savagely. Then I applied myself to the smudges and footprints even though I could see through the doors, approaching fast, a posse of chattering nurses likely to ruin everything. But I knew who the doctors were talking about.

Saphir came from the girls' wing to complete the damage.

'That's not my bucket is it, Jacob?'

'No.'

'It'd better not be, that's all. Wait till I catch the bastard who's got it. Seco. Where's he bloody gone?'

She swung off with panache. She covered her legs with a black *shalvar*, and managed to make even her cleaner's overalls look expensive. She was a medical student doing a Summer job. Her pretty black braids, seen from behind, touched my recollection somehow. But my memory was shot to pieces – I'd learned that, at least, from my sessions with Brendan.

Later, after lunch, and when I'd finished my share of the washing-up, Seco the Italian grounded my bucket and forced me to be composed. He sat me down in the little scullery, insisting I take one of his Marlboros. Technically he had seniority. He said I should learn to relax – like him; and not to work so hard – like him.

'You gonna bust youself. Take it easy for Chrissake.'

But if I stopped my scrubbing I felt threatened, today more than ever. The cigarette tasted like its own ash. When it was finished I moved towards my mop.

'Sit down. You want another? Why you're so keen? This place is a dump. A dirty dump. Iss gonna stay that way no matter how much you do.'

I waved away the second cigarette. 'No thanks, Seco.' But I sat down again with him; and felt . . . panicky. My breath shortened and the scullery, its stainless-steel certainty slipping on the instant into doubt, receded with a sick faintness that reminc᷄ d me of Brendan and the morning.

Before I could make a fool of myself I grabbed on to the remnants of the conversation. That woman the doctors were talking about – 'Ms Jay'. I'd seen her. She connected something, somehow, but not from now. From before . . . whatever that meant. She *reminded* me . . .

'Where's the Art Room, Seco?'

'I donno. You interested in Art? In Italy we know what is Art. These folk here just make . . . what you call it . . . splashes. Like mud. They too far gone, mate.' He wound his finger significantly at his temple. 'Waste of time. They don't know one end of a pintbrush from another.' He looked out of the window and gestured towards the main buildings. 'Iss over there somewhere, anyway. I donno.'

'How could I get over there?'

He looked at me as if to wind the finger again.

4

'No. I mean this afternoon. Now. This shift. I need an excuse.'

'Just go. Go over to get chemical. For you bloody toilets. Say we run out.'

'Yes, but Mr Prime'll check. He'll come over with me.'

'So tip what we got away. Down the pan.'

'Ah. Yes. Good idea, Seco. Thanks.' Doing violence to the drains.

'No problem. You have another cigarette. Then maybe we start.'

Sun slanted in through the reinforced windows. Heaven splashed over the taps, bright steel. We finished the washing-up, Seco and I. The torrid July day made us sweat in our overalls. Our rubber gloves stuck to our hands as we put away the cutlery, made all the work-surfaces acceptable, and trundled the heated trolley wagons back to their parking stations. Seco called another time-out. I was on edge. We'd exhausted the tales of his taxi-driving in Rome a week ago. We had not much left. Seco – whose name, because of what he claimed was my impure pronunciation, reminded me of the sharp taste of wine – let his smoke drift out into the sunshaft. Sitting on his stool, he kept watch through the windows for any of the managers venturing nosily to visit us, across the heat-drenched lawns.

'*Eccolo!*'

'What?'

'Mr Prime. He's come out.' His cigarette was suddenly at the 'ready' position, angled back, palmed with the quickness of an old hand.

'Where?' I peered across the grass to the office door. A small grey-haired man in a coat of authority was poised, clipboard in hand, on the brink of paying us a call. But he turned further than our direction, and marched off towards C block, which was a kind of vast *terrapin* hut, to inspect the geriatrics.

'OK. No worry,' said Seco.

In the dining-room beyond the serving hatch, the male nurses were finishing the last of the difficult ones, poor children in their bruised crash helmets, or gleaming, rigorous callipers. At last Seco threw his cigarette down. Its remnant melted fine geography into a floor tile.

'It's arright. We mop here first. You control that bucket. I this one.'

'Seco . . . ?'

'*Si?*'

5

'I'm not feeling . . . I don't think I can . . . '

'What?'

I stopped. I held on to the mop handle. 'Never mind. It doesn't matter.'

'OK. Whose turn the toilets, yours or mine?'

'Mine. I think I . . . '

'It's OK. I take the machine. I scrub the dining floor. We finish here, OK?'

'OK.'

The toilets over here were unlike the crazing art-porcelain originals of the old building. There everything was excessive and mad, in a fantastic Pre-Raphaelite way. Here they were kickproof steel. When I first started the job I was confident that I could take them all on, block by block, and restore their shine; in, say, a couple of months. Now I knew by a sort of intuitive calculus that their rate of moral decay would forever just outstrip my labour; the backsliding fungus and slime had its old ammoniac eye on my workrate. I could never win. Yet I hung on to the delusion that if I worked still that little extra bit more furiously, a spurt might at last put me right with them.

Following Seco's advice, I checked the store cupboard and found only one and a half industrial standard containers left, which I put by the door of the toilets to compose themselves for their journey downwards. Then, armed with my other chemicals, I entered, prepared to begin.

Appalling! An opera of neglect. I hadn't seen them for a couple of weeks, having been assigned elsewhere by Mr Prime; and yesterday Seco had *volunteered* to do them. But I'd left them gleaming last time. My colleagues could have held the fort at least.

They were disgusting.

'Seco!' I accosted him.

'*Si.*'

'Have you seen these?'

'*Dio!* Terrible!' He tapped his teeth.

'But didn't you do them yesterday?'

'Sure.'

'Then how did they get like this?'

'These folks got no idea how to crap.'

What could I say? All my hopes, all my works, all my days: a personal waste. I set to furiously. I did not speculate then as to why it

6

could be that I was hurling myself, with such intensity, into such a humiliating task, in so ruined and appalling a world.

A Chymical Toilet

It *was* the pits of the world – Cloaca Mundi, a kind of hell – inhabited by those for whom there was no hope of release. In the toilets you found the evidence. Some biological devil was at work. He made it his business to dehydrate the colons of these innocents so that they were mostly costive, and you might mop cruel khaki rocks about the floor, their sharp edges sometimes bloodied from a final passage.

On odd occasions a witty anomaly would appear in one of the corners: a starfish, or a dead wren. Always on the stand-easies grew encrustations which it took hours to remove with even the most powerful chemicals – a testimony to years of skiving cleaners. I speculated on the human interiors whose fluids had marked the deposited limescale. They'd given it such drama and so flamboyant a coloration. Satan had here his stony monument, and the story of his penetration into this world found here its only inscription. Well, no, not its only inscription. Some of them daubed: formless, wordless, lonely brown fingermarks on the walls of cubicles. I recognised the father and mother of all expression: without language; without design, representation, code; without signification of any sort; without hope of being heard – perhaps the damnedest and most tragic artistic cry.

I thought of Michelangelo painting the Sistine Chapel. We write our own story on the walls of our world; we project ourselves on to our account of the past – and the future. I did not think of Isaac Newton stitching his own version of things with meticulous and mathematical care into the very fabric of the universe so that scarcely a mouse could wriggle out from under those skirts.

Occasionally a naked madman lay unconscious on the stone floor. When I saw my first I'd thought he was dead. I went over, pulling off my rubber gloves, and knelt by his head. The memory of a star reflected in a pool of blood had flitted in, and out, of my mind. From where? From what? Then I'd noticed the fitful rising of his back. I took the details to one of the bored male nurses.

'It's alright,' he said. 'He's OK. It's the heat.'

7

'But he's lying on the stone.'

'Just leave him. He's OK.'

Unable in my condition to recognise negligence, I'd gone back and mopped around the terrible exhibit.

I began on the walls. Working my powders into a biting lather, I sought out the villainy of the place. I restored a fallen glory square foot by square foot, dodging the bouncing corrosive splashes that leapt off the tiles and paintwork towards my eyes. Inhaling God only knew what combination of active vapours, I mopped; I bucketed, seized with a grim enthusiasm. And the treasures of the floor and walls went raw into the jakeses from my brush and dustpan: sludges, geodes, hair, dead insects and arachnidae, a rubber glove and tainted paper waste, a mouse's skull and tail, a set of used plasters, dust and tomato, the ghost of a prophylactic and several other unnameable matters. I didn't flush.

Time rubbed on in my frenzy. I hardly noticed. Until suddenly I was assaulted through the high-stationed open windows by an infernal roaring and clanking. Then the frosted screen of the sky was blotted out. I identified the rattle of a huge diesel; presumably it was an apartment-sized delivery juggernaut parking close up next to the glass. So I found myself dark within one cubicle, scrubbing and deafened. It was a mechanical and stinking dark, and gave rise to non-visual sensory streaks: a trace of recaptured taste, and, with my hyperventilation, a recalled *other* smell mingling in my nostrils with the present fume. My lips pulled back from my teeth in a frightening , grimace. I stilled them automatically.

Even as I tried for calm the cubicle floor grew unsteady. The seals and grouts sweated. Something hurt violently in my head, and something else was illuminating the wall in front of me. I swung round to look up and back for the source of the rays, but there was only noisy, noisome dark, and the shouts of men outside. But when I regained my balance and turned back, forms *were* cast on to the surface in front of me. I tried to erase them from the wall of the cubicle with my scrubbing: bright transfers which began to declare themselves as lewd cartoons. They animated their moments, unrolling themselves beyond my brushstrokes. Still in my ears was the unstoppable roaring of the engine.

They held an initial fascination, these workings. They glowed and ran and re-expressed themselves. They scudded across the wall of the one cubicle and led me beyond, hiding themselves in the pipe-work where my brush couldn't reach. I panicked again with that wretched desperate feeling in my stomach. They were mine. They took me fast and crazy round the whole place, dabbing and scouring. The more I tried to dash them out the brighter they became, some too obscene, others too gorgeous – episodes from the history of my world. They defied cleaning powder and led across roughnesses of plaster, the dull drum of coated metal, the ridged slide of tiling, back to my original cubicle. She was there, that woman the doctors were talking about. Her long locks gleamed over water. I stared across a lake whose surface was immense. It was as though I stood upon a cliff. The moon's reflection – the moon itself – whirled in incredible rings and gears. It winked. It was loose in its chapel with water and tides.

I moved into action once my stomach had finished heaving. Put-ting off the need to drink, I groped to empty my whole container of powder into that bowl, and then, as my eyes normalised to the persisting but ordinary gloom, went on to all the others areek with their abominable soups. Next I made them ready for their final flush by stirring and diving with my brush, lest the huge energy of the event I'd just witnessed should eructate again out of the U-bend.

The lorry moved away while I was finishing the last. The rattling of its diesel drew off from my little lavatorial cave and the sun streamed in.

When I opened the cubicle door I saw there were great sweeps of foam where I'd brushed. Powder was everywhere. My rubber gloves felt claggy.

I wanted to leave it all behind there and then, but merely poking my head out into the corridor brought back the shrunkenness of the fallen world, and the wretched taste in my mouth. I'd seen too much; it had to be expunged. There was nothing for it but to mop the walls properly this time; to squeeze out in the bucket all that revelation.

In a while, though, more stable and beginning to relax, I recalled the whole ulterior purpose of today's entry into the toilets: the Bleach! That was no problem. My canisters tipped up conveniently over the well of the moon and stars. How simply the stuff gurgled down as if to give my whole vision a longed-for chemical white-out.

Now I could legitimately make my way over there. Standing by the last bowl, I cast an idle eye over the legend on the yellow plastic container I held in my hand:

NOT TO BE USED IN CONJUNCTION WITH OTHER LAVATORY CLEANERS

I mustn't share it with Seco? A joke? And then the mocking air went green and clutched at my eyes with caustic fingers. I gasped – the worst thing I could have done, because it made me gasp again. Instead of getting out I found myself coughing stupidly at the mirrors over the wash-basins, trying, as I gazed at my reflection, to make sense of the greenness and painfulness of things, and the seemingly relentless malice of the day.

Seco appeared at the door.

'Eh, Jacob! Saphir says . . . ' He sniffed, choked, coughed, shouted, and yanked me from the faint green cloud. 'Santa Siberia! What! You do a Devil's fart?'

We coughed and retched our way out – out along the corridor by the dining-room, through the foyer I'd mopped that morning, through the double glass doors and right into the rose garden, where he fell to roaring hysterics. And while I comforted my eyes and jerked up a bit more corroded spittle from my insides, he pirouetted among the rose-bushes. Thus among their gaudy blooms, he shed his urbanity and shrieked with laughter. The sun flashed on his sharp Roman teeth.

'For God's sake stop laughing and get me a drink, you bastard!'

'OK OK. I get for you. You lie on the grass. What the hell you doing in there?' And he coughed and giggled all over again. I stretched myself on the corner of the dry lawn. 'Eh? What was it?'

'What's so damn funny? I could have been killed in there.'

Seco's eyes narrowed and his grin froze. 'I save you, mate. You got no gratitude with you bloody toilets. I'm Secondo. I'm second son – Lucky. Lucky for you, eh?'

'Yes. Sorry. Thanks very much. Now for Christ's sake get me a drink. Please.'

'That's better. Otherwise I take you back to you damn toilets and I kill you.'

While he went off to the scullery I lay back. The sun worried the prickly-watery feeling in my eyes. My chest hurt from the gas, my stomach from the retching. I shifted a bit to my side and gazed over the mass of the asylum. Against the tough heatwave-blue stood the observation tower – what else could it be, that great fat Italianate finger, widening at the top to accommodate a windowed look-out under its pinnacles? The whole thing was a celebration of imprisonment, in two colours of brick topped with its gilt pyramid of a roof. It watched over the colony of suffering as if with a magnificent eye; or perhaps was a mere deserted symbol. Either way the effect was that we all policed ourselves, uncertain whether God was really watching from above.

A thought struck me as Seco was returning with the drink.

'Christ, Seco. Supposing some of the kids have gone in. They'll damage themselves, poor little sods. And I'll get the sack. Were the windows open?' In a mixture of altruism and self-interest I leapt up, swallowed the water and dashed back into the block. A speechless boy was on the point of entering the toilets.

'No, no, no, no, no! You go to toilet – you die!' said Seco, slitting his own throat with his forefinger and pointing to the door to emphasise the danger. A look of terror came over the boy's face as he turned to flee in tears.

I pushed open the door. Thanks to the open window which had allowed me to be so mysteriously oppressed by the lorry, all was well, beyond a faint bleachy smell. A teenager with a palsy was struggling to coordinate himself at the urinal.

The Tower of Bedlam

Holding the yellow canister – my passport – against my grey overalls, I stood windily at a high spot. The hazy blue of the clear half of the sky was air-brushed on to space behind the stucco of the gallery frames: no glass in these slot-thin outer arches. I'd finished the climb and was standing facing a pointed door. It was the entrance to the Art Workshop.

A surprising location: to my amazement I'd been led to the very top of the tower at which I'd stared as I lay painfully on the grass beside the children's block, waiting for my glass of water. The ascent had started by means of a grand staircase, intended mainly for show, clinging to the inside of the tower's walls. This had quickly given way to a series of wooden flights which led up from stage to stage. I'd waited for Polly to catch up with me at each one, but had been too impatient to enjoy the vistas over the woodlands of Surrey. There was a layer, as it were, of industrial machinery, and what looked like storage tanks for the oil-fired heating system. Finally, punctuated by a few mysterious doors, there came a spiral in which one lost track of number before emerging high up at the open gallery. In this institution the entitlement to Art Therapy, if Polly's geography was correct, was clearly dependent more on physical fitness than on psychiatric need.

'There! In there!' said Polly, recovering her puff and opening the door. She pointed through the arch at what could almost be described as a bower. I peered in, past the faded timetable of classes pinned to the oak. Who would have thought that this exalted place with its lightflood of ivory and its breezy hangings of unswept gossamer would be the place? I might have wandered about fruitlessly in the shrieking maze of corridors had it not been for Polly, whom I'd met in the dining-hall; as I had on my first day in the job, swimming towards me with her outstretched arms and big wet kisses, full of the Lord's innocence, sighing into my ear: 'You're my only 'eart, darlin'. My best 'eart.' Kiss. Squeeze. 'Ooh you're my 'eart, sweet'eart. Look at you!' Hug. Kiss. Bristle scratch. 'One true love (deep breath, long aspiration) hhheart.'

Polly, in her maroon slippers, with her three gypsy teeth and black beard – I didn't know the clinical name for her condition, no more worldly-wise than a toddler – was one of the ugliest and most spiritually open beings I'd ever met. She rejoiced my heart. And she'd taken me conspiratorially to this eyrie where they 'do pain'in'. Only she wasn't allowed to paint. "Cos I carn pain' nothin!' she happily stated of the foul prohibition. 'Nothin. Aint no use me pain'in. Cos I carn pain' nothin. Ar, you're my true love 'eart, aint you, darlin. Carn pain' nothin, me. But you. Ar, you're my . . .' Kiss. 'Pain' me a pitcher, darlin.'

I stood in the arch with a certain apprehension. What was I doing after all? Why was I intrigued by the mention of a woman and her images – to the extent that I should have tangled with chlorine and then made this bizarre climb? I suspected a dissociation; had I run up here in an urge physically to separate myself from an accumulation of pain? Did I expect her to inform me; to ease the intensity through some sympathetic current? Was it hope? I'd seen her before in my duties, going about like other patients. 'Ms Jay' didn't appear mad.

Her face was urgent, yes, but her body looked as if she were cold – as if there would be no more summers for her, nor for the missing shape she appeared to cradle sometimes, down in the straggle of her long brown hair. Sometimes too in her ceaseless drift about the place, I'd seen her pause, her lips moving privately, while the twitch of a smile hovered about them – as if she were answering the whispers of a ghostly lover standing behind her. But she hadn't touched any chords in me – not then. And my revelation down there in the toilets had spilled too much too soon. I was resisting it; who would not indeed? So it was that something at the back of my mind drove me on all day towards what ought perhaps to have been a gentler discovery. For the forgotten and the forbidden constantly seek to be brought to light. I ventured in.

An almost untouched relic of the Arts and Crafts era, it might have been used for an interior by Holman Hunt – the Virgin's Studio, mawkish, but a distillation of the pure. There was an arrangement of old easels, tables and stools. Certain Victorian values were enshrined here. The discreetly barred larger windows which ran all round between the oriels at the corners had stained borders with emblems. One of them was open, unhasped and swinging slightly, the only moving thing. I could see through it dark cloud-heaps gathering over the western horizon. But the studio was unoccupied.

On newspaper on a cupboard top nearest us stood a collection of crude uglinesses in clay, left by sad hands lovingly to dry. I wandered past it, uncertain what to do. In the centre someone had been sitting very recently at the main table. Brushes stood in a jar of cloudy, greenish water, and the house on the paper, with its wonky perspective, had pools of colour still wet on its lawns. Beside it was laid out a photographic print, monochrome, enlarged, clearly the source material for the work: a big, old house, in front of which was a car and a tiny family almost lost in the graining. A plastic cup of coffee stood nearly full, steaming faintly.

'Ar, nice,' said Polly, picking up the painting so that the greens trailed in droplets down over the bright blobs and dabs that were herbaceous borders. She put her head on one side. 'Ar, nice.'

Behind us, on the wall of the arched entrance, one corner and much of the space had been partitioned off and labelled 'Do Not Enter When Light Is On'. The warning light *was* on; but the dark-room door wasn't closed. Perhaps that was where she was. I put my head in. The tower's windows had been faced off with boards; in the murk I made out a sink, a photographic enlarger, and, on the bench nearest us, a white porcelain tray in whose chemical a darkening image lay. Polly pushed by me and took the thing out, dripping.

'Tha's 'er, look. See! Tha's 'er. Ar.' It was a formal portrait. 'See!' said Polly, pointing with her finger into the overexposed emulsion. Half out of the door, I held one edge. The image, taken in happier times, restored her youth and confidence. That face ... An excitement tugged at my heart from beyond the sudden rational grasp of who she was. For now I could place her at last: a woman from public life. Her name was Celia Jenner.

We hadn't noticed that there rested on the corner of a desk a cigarette with an inch of ash beyond the burn. I laid down both the enlargement and my canister and made as if to put it out; the ash fell off as I picked it up. 'Ms Jenner!' I called, not quite sure what to do. Was there a toilet somewhere up here? Or down a stage, off the stairs perhaps?

'Ms Jenner!' I knew why the doctors had described her as a special case. It had been a heavy political story. She'd taken the rap for a financial scandal in her party, a homelessness project, had it been? A striking and distinguished academic, she'd moved into the public eye, and found herself manipulated. And then a breakdown; I remembered the papers now. The tabloids had claimed she couldn't hack it, of course, but there must have been more to it. Much more, to put her in this state. And no private clinic – still a woman of principle.

Polly called as well: 'Muzz! Muzz! Where you gone, Muzz?'

I looked again at the haunting photograph – so like. A pair of birds suddenly appeared in the room and proceeded to flap crazily against one of the barred windows: martins, with white fronts and thin tails. They had a frightful urgency. Polly grabbed on to me and the cigarette spun out of my hand on to a stack of loose artwork.

'I don' like birds!' She clutched at my overalls. 'I don' like 'em!' She screamed as one launched itself in our direction. 'Aaaah! They'll get in my 'air.' She pulled me across the room as protection. An easel toppled.

'It's alright, Polly. They're as scared as you are. Just keep calm.'

But she was in no degree calm. 'Get 'em away! Get 'em away! My 'air!' With one hand she covered her head; with the other she held very firmly to me and yanked me to the door. 'Help! I don' like 'em! Polly don' like birds! Fuckin' birds!' She now had the one hand over her offending mouth and had started to cry with the extremity of her distress and guilt. But she still hung on.

I got her outside the door and tried to force her to let go, because I'd seen flames starting where the cigarette had fallen.

'Don' go back! There's birds!'

'There's a fire, Polly.' Everything, absolutely everything, had gone out of control. But in turn tears sprang up for me. I had the room. It wasn't Victorian – no, earlier. I have to go in. A man in a full wig holds a stick. There is a child. Something unspeakable takes place. Eyes like the eyes of a monstrous owl are so close, so frightening. Here are coats with many buttons. Men have wide hats. My mother's breasts are pushed up by the squeeze of a curious dress. It is a voiceless, horrible knowledge that somehow it all makes sense at last; but it is impossible.

I scrabbled with Polly's wrists. Whenever I got one grip off she'd grab me again, with surprising strength. We wrestled for the door-way – I could hear the crackling sound inside. I must get in there to stamp it out. At the same time I knew that trace from the past was important. Both worlds fought for the freakish moment. Even up here in this unsullied haven I have brought my chaos and created a destruction. My ankle felt the splash of wet; the stone floor under us turned dark, and I saw the drips at the hem of Polly's skirt. She wailed in embarrassment, but she didn't let go. We twisted round in that outer gallery again. 'Polly! Don't you see? Polly!'

In a flash, there is a yard with horses; the copulation of dogs; the story of a wolf. Upstairs, in the house, there is a wig, a window, a coat with its full skirt hung on the chair, a woman's dress waiting, pain which can't be screamed. Hang on to something – it will end. It will be over before I die. Tied to their beds. Downstairs my mother plays the spinet. Outside, the grind of cartwheels and the thump of hoofs: inside, the peculiar breathing, panting, riding. And if I speak my mother will die. 'Polly!' I wrenched free and sprang into the room.

The Lull

There was a livid sky now. Driving the Ford back to Walton after I'd worked out my shift, I watched through the windscreen the heavy cumuli that had been building from the West ever since I came down from the tower. I'd said no word of my efforts with the fire; not to anybody. Polly was incoherent. I certainly hadn't told Seco. I'd changed my overall and kept my distance, even when he tried to chaff me to good humour, and called me over to enjoy from our scullery the spectacle of the emergency services, and the chance to down tools. So, of course, he knew no more of my activities than the chlorine incident.

'Eeeh, Jacob! *Vieni qui!* We sit down for a smoke, yes? You an' me. No one's bother us, eh? It's OK. No more gas. No problems. Look at that lot – commotions, eh? Why don't you just relax ever? You find the Art Room, yes?'

All seemed lost now under the quickening wind. I drove along by the Cowey Sale. Great bruising thunderheads massed above the ugly bridge, and darkened the meadows. The river was ruffled, yellow and purple.

I turned through the town and, reaching home, crunched on to the gravel patch where I was allowed to park. On a gust I smelled, like a dog, the hot drift of rain to come.

My quarters were close: a cupboard for a kitchen and two poky cabins so cramped in the roof space, with their sloping ceilings, that you couldn't pass from one to the other without straddling the void of the top step. Now, as I bridged it after coming up the stairs, I felt again that today had taken it upon itself to peel me open. It was the most fraught day of my life as yet, and still it had not done with me, though the sirens and 'commotions' were past. I didn't sense how completely the walls of my world were cracking; what leaks had appeared and what flood threatened. I put it down to stress, Seco and Saphir; fumes, images and blurred deeds. I rested against the Baby Belling for a moment and took a grip on the angle iron which supported the house's cold-water tank.

But the smoke was still on my clothes. On what passed for the landing I tore them off and dumped them into a black bin-liner. Then I returned to the cooking space to wash in the sink.

Outside there came the first grumbling note of the storm. Far below, the front door banged. Mrs Dangerfield, my landlady, left for her rendezvous of the evening. My hands smoothing soap to soothe my forehead found bristles for eyebrows. They'd been scorched off. I felt upwards to my hair, searching the headache for a little tell-tale bump, but there was nothing. I dared not look in the glass for signs of charring in case I should seem a clown, a buffoon, a Grimaldi. Thus by increasing associations, signs and traces, the god of my past sharpened the edge each time before laying to his work at my hairline.

I would have welcomed an anaesthetic: alcohol, pills – alas I had none; companionship, the soothe of rain even. A pulse of lightning split the view from my tiny kitchen look-out, touching my gaze cruelly with its intimacy, until the echoes of the discharge died away. Dry and still lay the broad garden and the twin apple trees that grew out of the halfway hedge. Behind that, through the little pathway, waited the untended vegetable patch; and right down by the far fence beside a rush of periwinkle, the shed with its overwinding of creeper almost audibly rotted. A lush, dank, heated, Summer garden, it lay unmoving, waiting for the storm.

The bedroom looked out over the same garden. On the wall there was a vestigial mantelpiece and the traces of a fireplace; while on the mantelpiece itself much to Mrs Dangerfield's discomfiture sat my two skulls. I'd named them Entropy and Gravity, but I didn't know how I'd come by them. Standing naked at the window, I felt they were conspiring behind my back. A tree of electricity welded roots to neighbouring Weybridge. Almost at once the ruptured air hammered at my eardrums and rattled the bedroom window. I felt myself shiver as I finished towelling myself dry.

The very verdure of the garden was alert, still, and charged to shudder up at the sky. I opened the window and smelled, in the humid air under the grey, an energy in each green tendril. There; that was the present, waiting to continue; but I would not bear it, and turned to my bed. Perhaps exhaustion might disconnect me.

Again the air roared over the room, the house and the town. Almost in synchrony, my past chopped at my head, and the ache flared. Excruciated, I turned on my side to where I could see from the bed my clothes lying not far away, in their open black plastic bag. I thought I could smell the waft of char. The two skulls grinned, and then appeared to listen, I fancied, for a new note: a tentative patter that quickly swelled to a drumming din against the tile and timber immediately above me. Outside, the sky was emptying at last as if it planned to wash us all away.

Sleep came suddenly, and then dreams, as if pain was the developing chemical of an entire holographic film; as if a surgeon entered the shatter of my brainpan and started rebuilding every structure brick by illuminated brick. I conceived in that enlightenment a meta-Byzantine edifice full of images beside which the asylum itself, with all its old painted nooks, its dusty corners, alcoves, recesses, curlicues, cusps and mouldings, was an inhibited matchbox. Memories like moths came to life, stirred from far off in the rain, and headed for my bedroom. They passed the glass of my window, aligning their molecules with the molecular spaces in the structure of the panes, and entered whole and flapping, as big as storm birds.

When I awoke from that torrential sleep I had the key to it all. Now I understood why it was it should have been blotted out; for who could have lived with all that? Either forget, or go mad. Yes, with the bucketing along of time there had been no rest; no place for drawing breath, to order, to transcribe and to persuade myself.

But now I determined through my tears to begin this ragged chronicle, describing nothing less than a bulging, three-hundred-year-old universe, full of the echoes and resoundings of all knowledge, of all time and space, of all the stories my unusual flesh was heir to.

For I knew why the two skulls were on my mantelpiece, and who was the guardian of the Elixir of Life which my Uncle Isaac made with my help and by accident after twenty years of crazy research in his laboratory in Trinity garden. And I believed I had the first hint of why I tried to find Celia Jenner, and how I acquired the name of Jacob, and who were the Hatted Hummers. And of whom Saphir the Indian reminded me, of the Batavian Thorn, of Inertia and its cure, of the melting of my heart, and of the horrible speeding up of time.

So I took to my other little garret room, the one at the front, in the morning after the four elements celebrated themselves. Outside my dormer window the great oak tree by the Hersham Road, full of its waking Summer beauty, stirred in the cleansed air. The little caterpillars on its leaves set to their task of covering my car in sticky blobs. The sky was rich with day. One sodium streetlamp was still on, red, and reminding of the night. I sat at my desk to begin the story, which you will not believe.

First Things

My mother brought me in. I was dressed well in cleverly designed restraining garments; my coat, for example, gave the illusion that I stood habitually with my arms folded. They were in fact secured by the sleeves. I was fourteen. There'd been a bloody civil war and a bloodless revolution. The mathematics of gravity had just been published, and the universe had been told that it was dead. I had no speech but I could sing. I sang to him. To my Uncle Isaac. Church songs and street songs, psalms and farm songs; the old revolutionary songs my Granduncle Ayskew said he'd learnt in the army, that I didn't know the meaning of:

> Let us with a gladsome mind
> Make away with all we find.
> Church and King will ay endure
> Till they take the common cure.
>
> Here's an Earl and here's a Lord,
> Harlot's hair and Spanish sword,
> Church and King will ay endure
> Till they take the common cure.
>
> All who seek to heap up gain
> While men landless do remain
> They their profit shall endure
> When they take the common cure.
>
> Let them think on Charlie's axe
> Ere the next ungodly tax,
> For His mercies ay endure
> Taken with the common cure.

I piped, but my voice was breaking, and not just because of my age. My fit of rage was beginning to give way to the other emotion, hopelessness. Soon the restraint would hardly be needed and I could be sat in a corner without danger to myself or others. My mother used the fact that I could sing to shore up the lie she told herself that I was normal. She liked to give out that I was her young gentleman protector on the journey from Northamptonshire. And whenever she, flushed and carnal, came to Cambridge on one of her various *negotiations*, leaving me in my Uncle Isaac's rational care, she would first stand me in the centre of that charred and reeking chamber and have me sing. Why was it that I sang? Somebody once referred to the vocal art as licensed screaming. The negotiation that Autumn, I think, was with a Mr Trueman.

My mother was very persuasive. I see her now with her strict coiffure and her distinguished features, which were only belied by a moistness she managed to secrete on her lips even as her *Purity* eyes engaged you. Ordinary men melted; my Uncle Isaac shuddered.

So many years ago. I said you would not believe. I hear my young voice again, knowing and unknowing. It is not the voice of a stripling hero of fiction. I lack the clear skin and bold dash of a handsome Johnny who within a year or two will escape the hangman and sail off to Virginia in search of a fortune. I have the feel and looks, beneath my mother's grooming, of what I can only describe as a wolf. My teeth are too often exposed and there is a distinct howl to some of my high notes. The skin of my face is blotched from the various scratchings and attacks I have made on it. I register and understand what goes on around me but I do not take part, being racked with waves of rage and fear which make me pant, and occasionally growl. In my sullen phases I know I am collapsing inside. I can read well and write; for I may be uncontrollable, and inadmissible in society, but I am not stupid. Far from it: I have had enforced leisure for study, and my father is a clergyman. Now I remember it, he lies at home, dying, and my mother must be concealing her anxiety about income.

It was an Autumn of quiet red celebration. Low sun illuminated the Cambridge brick and stone so that it glowed brighter than the blue sky it cut into. That wonderful light struck inward at the casement, but I could not let myself feast on it.

My uncle, at fifty-one, claimed a total indifference to music or poetry in any form, but nevertheless made a point of shooting pained looks and drawing in his breath when any of my notes came out flawed. So the singing ritual pleased neither of us. He too was 'in his fit', and as she denied mine my mother over-acknowledged his, casting my music as a species of psychological bandage. She said it 'eased him' to hear my assortment of canticles and bawdry. She particularly toadied to him now that he was famous and no longer the other embarrassment of the family; and we were facing destitution.

Isaac's dis-ease at the time was that he was laid low with an unusual melancholy. It was a bleak and restless frenzy. His bowels griped him and he went about a little stooped with his hands clutched across his belly, as if his body were feeling the loss of a child. But his look remained undemonstrative. As for the proof sheets of a special reprint of his *Principia* that Mr Halley sent, he could hardly bear to see their impressions. I grasped him intuitively, but could not articulate then what I can describe now – that he was at the mercy of what he had striven so hard to exclude from the whole universe: human feelings. He was experiencing a reaction equal and opposite to Monsieur Fatio de Duillier's Platonic teasing – that sly, Swiss and mathematical little *chienne*. Mr Newton's great brow was greatly knitted in a Type of stifled despair. Each icy orb promised to melt into a tear. But could not.

For politeness' sake he thanked my mother shortly when I'd finished. Every time, after I'd performed, he'd refer to me as a young siren, and laugh cynically. I disliked his jokes; they were wounding. Then he begged leave to cast himself down in the little cluttered bedchamber. I recall my mother following him and fidgeting in its doorframe. It was a frame only, because Uncle Isaac had taken off all the interior doors, including what used to be Mr Wickens's, to aid the supply of draught, and to ease all the coming and going.

She said: 'Well, is all agreeable to you, Ize? He has everything he needs in the basket, and I've done some baking for you. And Mr Anderson sent the wine. And Robert sends you his best wishes and blessing in Christ.' She lowered her voice to a mutter. 'There are his cords for the night-time under the package of his linen. Which reminds me I packed some of my own which I must take out directly. Linen, I mean. It's the last day or so of my courses and you can imagine . . . ' She drew breath and then whispered on. 'Regarding what I wrote to you about his . . . ' and here she only mouthed the word and I could not see her lips, but I knew she said *devil*, 'you will see what you can do, won't you?' She continued in a normal voice: 'But I believe I've seen to everything and he'll be no trouble. Is there a screen or corner where I can . . . ?' She looked round and then back to him. I saw terror come into his eyes. But she was driven, tactless, itching to be changed and off. My dear mother: an unknown; a variable.

She left. I sat. He wrestled with his misery, ignored me, and at last was empowered to continue his Quest for the Philosopher's Stone – the riddle of *Matter*. It was the only thing he could bear to do.

I knew from previous visits that every bit of his space and time was pressed into the service of this great activity. He either worked here or in the laboratory – a tiled shed the College had caused to be put up for him in what was known as Mr Newton's Garden. There was a large iron furnace up here in the fireplace as well as the one down there, and scattered around both rooms were a number of secondary structures he had made himself, that bubbled and smoked at various times. Papers and books lay about inviting combustion.

I did not feel safe. But then I never did.

My mother would be with Mr Trueman for a week's holiday, hoping, I surmise, to clinch some relief for the family's financial crisis from this comfortable city businessman, in addition to that from my uncle's sense of family duty. It was the week in which we made the Elixir. Yes, it was accomplished. Newton and Co. (and an odd company we were) succeeded in the ultimate goal of alchemy; but it was never made public. Of course not. It was never sent up to the Annals of the Royal Society, whose august fellows later conspired to deny for centuries that their sainted Mr Newton even so much as looked at an alembic, let alone suffered from a primary obsession with the warped and solitary art of the *Puffers*.

And he'd had practice enough – after the twenty years he made his *chum*, John Wickens, help him fire and pour and puff and skim and slake, coming and going with the great scuttle full of seacoals, the nets of ores, ingots and fossil turds; crucibles, pelicans, tongs; bags and boxes of God knows what; until they both had hands as black as print and not an eyebrow between them.

But he did not achieve it by any rational means, as he'd have liked. It occurred because of *me* – and by *accident*.

*

My uncle had his own ways of dealing with me which were different from my mother's. He had no intention of attempting to exorcise my devil according to *her* wishes – I believe his new fame had suggested to her that he had some special power over the moon and thus could do something about my version of lunacy which my father could not. She had no more expectations from *that* religious quarter.

But Uncle did not hold with priests or ritual of any sort. When I made the noise and gestured to him that I needed to use the chamber-pot, he undid the concealed tapes that turned the sleeves of my green coat into a straitjacket and let me loose. He had a cane on the ledge over the chimney-breast should my sudden rage call for it. His only general precaution was to lock the main door to his rooms.

I went into my doorless sleeping space. This bedchamber was, like my uncle's own, off the main room, and it was empty for the very good reason that no one now in the College dared to share his noisome, explosive centre of activity. John Wickens, his close and only friend from the time they were both undergraduates, had left him two years ago, to get married; and was replaced in due course by an H. Newton who was not related to us, and whom I was glad to see the back of when my uncle dispensed with his services earlier that same year, 1693.

When I had finished he came and saw me clean myself up. Then he held my wrist with one hand and brought the chamber-pot in the other so that he could empty it as we went down to the laboratory.

His garden was immaculately kept by a gardener whom we passed on the way. It was a maze of pretty paths between which were beds of a great variety of unusual flowers that I wished I could destroy.

In the laboratory I was left to myself in a corner and immediately began to seek manual comfort.

'Leave off that, you young dog!' said my uncle, looking up from his work at a crucible he had in the tongs. 'Or you'll feel my cane across you! I'm about God's work here and I want none of your impurities.' In my family I lived among lies and contradictions. Although I knew different about him, my odd uncle was held up to be a creature of the most absolute temperance, virginity, and, dare I say it, gravity. He even believed this himself. My mother and the College certainly did. He'd once quarrelled with another alchemist – Vigani, I think his name was – just because he'd told a lewd story

23

about a nun. And yet I had earlier evidence that he suspected himself possessed and was tormented by the suspicion. The lies of adults were one of the reasons I could not speak. Their aggression was proportional to their denial. He came over and tied my right hand to a ring in the wall.

It was in the *Corner of Fermentation*. This corner of the laboratory had as its heart and nominator a great *hot-box* full of horse shit – a device used in those days before thermostatic heating elements by many a *chymical projector* for incubating any processes which needed generous room temperature over a long period. Sunk into the steaming rancidity of the *hot-box* my uncle had left a large vessel – a sort of glass bath – and in this vessel there was nothing except a grey, scum-plagued liquid.

I made noises at him equivalent to: 'Are you using this at the moment, Uncle?'

He looked up with a certain suggestion in his eyes that he was sorry for the way he'd corrected me and saw in me the image of his soul.

'What? Eh? What do you want? You can't do any harm over there.' Then he turned back to his torture of the metals.

With my free hand I could reach various piles of objects that lay about the Corner of Fermentation. It was, as it were, the slag heap of the operation – a dumping ground for sweepings, or for remnants of the process, or for forgotten things from former parts of the obsession.

I decided on a vaguely rebellious whim to drop everything shiny or attractive from the slag heap of bits into the bath. I looked at the prettier amalgams and lumps of pure metal. I thought of Elizabeth, whom I loved and could not come near. I thought of the curious composition of her name, and the way the sounds might be made in the throat. These were the sounds that denoted her. Remote breathy compositions: El-iz-a-b-e-th. I thought of jewellery and murder and beautiful women with soft breasts with whom I was not in love. I thought of these metals lying upon the flesh, their sharpnesses just grazing the tender nipples. Then I plummeted them. I had no idea of their rarity or chemical composition or the fact that my uncle must have had them supplied from strange sources and then worked them, in incalculable ways, according to his books and recipes. They were an assortment of metallic substances probably never before or afterwards assembled so closely in one small dump, not counting the other shards and offcuts, stone chips, curios, corals, crystals, dried offal and organs, pastes, bladders, potions and gums which he was too preoccupied to notice me adding in once I'd lost scruple for the seriousness of my project. Thus into that glass bath went some very far-fetched chemical company. Soon the faintest steam began to lift from its surface, and the tiniest bubbles to appear at its rim. This was my first and momentous attempt at experimental science.

Things Whereof a Man Cannot Speak

In the evening the mathematician Nicholas Fatio arrived, unannounced and knocking at the locked door. He regarded me with intense curiosity. I regarded him with suspicion, while my uncle was put into a complete fluster such as I had never seen in him before. 'It's the son of my half-sister Barton,' explained Isaac. 'He means nothing. His mother left him here for some days. She has some business to transact. It's a regular arrangement.'

When he had sat the man down he bundled me into my sleeping space and tied the tapes that crossed my arms again. He would have made me stay there out of sight but that the other man appeared in the doorway and started asking questions and opening a conversation. My uncle explained that I was dumb. 'He is . . . distempered. His mother gets exhausted with him. There is a need for . . . unusual measures.' But he did bring me to sit near, if not with them, in the main chamber by the furnace.

I had been sometimes stared at and mocked if I went into the streets, but next to my Uncle Isaac my looks must have achieved a slight advantage. He never dressed up or received company – he rarely washed, combed his hair or lurched as far as his wig, so preoccupied was he with the race against matter and, currently I guessed, the impossible disorder Fatio had already caused to his carefully cauterised feelings. Fatio had striking, somewhat petite features, a fashionable get-up, and unusual manners which I took to be French. In my experience no other like this had ever appeared in his chamber – *such* a young man of mode. I had never seen one. Behind my mask of exclusion from everything I gawped; while Isaac hastily and apologetically cleaned his face at the bowl, changed his coat from the one which was all burnt and spangled from molten metal, and made an attempt with a periwig.

Acknowledging myself half-animal I was very responsive to atmosphere. I picked up the ghastly tension in the air between the two men, although they preserved a brittle politesse, seeing that I occupied the third corner of a triangle. I was not exactly a public to their privacy, but I was, as far as they knew, sentient. As a result they were more open than they might have been in front of another, but yet cautious, and embarrassed. And still Fatio seemed to want to include me in the meeting. I felt there was some final passage of feeling, some *quod erat demonstrandum*, that one man *wanted* to engage in, but could not because of me; and some teasing defence or private cruelty that the other could *better* engage in because of me. So everything in the room felt more mad and distraught than ever.

He had brought no servant. Since Uncle rarely troubled the company in Hall at that time, they made a meal of some sort with what my mother had left and other scraps of food they could find. Isaac wouldn't untie my hands but fed me pieces and a little wine. The other man joined in, laughing, and pressing the food against my lips when I already had a mouthful, to provoke me and see me snap. Nicholas Fatio drank the most wine. He'd been away, he said, since their former break, which had left him so desolated, he claimed. He'd taken a second *tour*, and had also visited his mother in Switzerland. He was now recovered and had called in for good fellowship, and to show there were no hard feelings. And to learn of the progress of the Great Work, to which he reminded my uncle he had contributed so much in former months.

As he came to feel the effects of the wine, and because my uncle seemed to have become almost as incapable of speech as I was, he began to grow rhapsodic – to fill the painful vacuum in the room. The *tour* was a great cure for the distempered soul. He recommended it to us both in his curious English. He was casual about it all – a much travelled man. But although I might have flown at him and bitten him had I been untied, or have scratched at my own ears to drown out the sound, I could not but listen and be overcome by the descriptions he made with his words. They threatened and compelled me as much as the stories I'd heard as a little boy when the children were eaten in the forest. From the *camera obscura* of my mind I saw, through his words, and through his memory, the exotic,

damned, Papist lands to the South; the vineyards of Provence standing in the baking Summer heat, the enchanted white-walled cities
and palaces; the pitiless Alps where the air bit and purified the
lungs, and where wild mountaineers used women as currency; and
then Italy herself, where no surface went unpainted, and where fornication was an Art. Seeing me half-snarling but listening, Monsieur
Fatio engaged his wit. I believe I was the earpiece of a powerful
Amplification. For me the Duomi were pressed all over with gold
leaf; for me the cloves of European garlic opened like culinary sun-
flowers, ravishing the imagination of my brutalised taste with new
and magic meals; for me the floating wonder of Venice reflected
itself and its smell in the clouds.

A College servant knocked. We were all silent as he lugged in a
box of logs. It was well after dark. He cleared some utensils and left.
My uncle pressed Nicholas to stay the night. He accepted. But where
was he to sleep, seeing that Monsieur Newton already had company? Isaac offered immediately to turf me out of my room: 'He can
sleep on the floor.' Fatio experienced an access of nicety concerning
the prior rights of family over friends: 'But no. It is not to be dreamed
of, Maître.'

Uncle made a sort of gasp and offered his own room. Monsieur
pursued him with a knowing eyebrow. Uncle became uncannily
silent.

'No, no. *Pas du tout.*' Nicholas would couch himself on his cloak
between the Desk of Opticks and the Athanor of Alkhimia.

'Take my bed, man. For God's sake.'

'Pray, Maître, do not trouble yourself. I would not dream . . . Why,
there is no man in all Europe whom . . . ' and into fragments of
French or Latin, or whatever, as was his fashion of compliment. And
so, heavy with implications, they played out their game of offer and
refusal, until Nick Fatio won, as he was bound to do, being the more
calculating of two mathematicians.

Therefore, after some geometrical discussion which I was not
equipped to follow, we all retired at more or less the same time, with
the newcomer promised to stretch out by the furnace in the main
chamber on the horsehair-stuffed seat, after he'd taken some more
wine. My uncle found the night cords my mother had left and bound
my wrists to the two head-posts of the spare bed, which was the

configuration in which I had slept on my back for as long as I could remember.

Some chiming clock of the city and a pressure against my mouth woke me at about two. I opened my eyes to the almost pitch-blackness of an abominable assault. A male smell under my nose. Faint pallor of linen suggesting the presence of a part-clothed torso. His voice above me whispering in a foreign language. Fear mapped me to the bed. Something automatic made me try to scream but I had no voice, only a poor rasping in the throat. And my mouth had opened, which was the worst thing it could have done. Invasion; the thing stuffed back and forth in my head; the taste; the revolting sensation of being gagged at the very back of the palate, while held down by superior force. But for some reason I couldn't bite, and the violation continued, against my will but beyond my control. Why couldn't I bite? I felt waves of panic. My breath was knotted into my grimace, my neck locked rigid. I was sure I should die. Until I found myself at last panting through my squashed nostrils, like the choked dog in the farmyard. But it wasn't enough. The torso was all over my face. Not enough air to survive on. The fight for air. I would not survive. Could not. All my chest and throat contorted in the effort, the drag for air. A point of black pain expanded in a rush towards me, until it enveloped me totally.

Then I was out of myself and looking down from the ceiling in the small-hours murk which only a window's faint moon-and-starlight illuminated, at a larger person over a smaller one's head; whose hair was held down by a fist, and whose trunk thrashed between tied cords. I saw my knees rear up and catch him so that he grunted, withdrew and tried to wrestle me over on to my front. Great heaves of longed-for breath filled those lungs. In such dark, however, he clearly hadn't grasped the fact about my strung wrists; my body wouldn't turn. I watched myself twist and hurt. Then he gave that up and returned to the mouth, penetrating it and jerking on his violent weight. Why did I, that sufferer below me, comply? I watched the asphyxiation build up once more. I watched my renewed thrash.

Maybe a minute. He shuddered and came off. And again I saw the desperate lungs permitted at last to inflate themselves in relief.

I remember having a discarnate idea which seemed, incredibly, to exist everywhere around us both. I would sing. I would.

I did. And that was what now in *fact* filled the room with a powerful and almost tangible vibration:

Let us with a gladsome mind

I felt myself, as I returned to my body, swallow the stuff that was in my mouth. It was a reflex. And now I *felt* what I had only *watched* a moment ago – the great gulps of air rushing down my throat between each phrase of the hymn.

Praise the Lord for he is kind.
For his mercies ay endure
Ever faithful, ever sure.

I was squinting in the darkness into a startled face which itself had just made a sound: some little feminine squeak which mingled with my last two lines. It reminded me of a creature I'd once seen cornered – a hare which somebody had tried to make a pet of. He moved at once to escape but the noises had aroused my troubled uncle, because I heard him hurry round to my doorway. There was a crash of breaking glass followed by a cry of pain and a rational curse. Then his dark bulk appeared in the frame, and I could sense him peering in. Fatio turned and was clutching at his breeches, trying to tie or pull them up – I don't know which. My uncle roared in a roaring whisper:

'Villainy! Whoredom! Fornication! Caught in the net! By Christ Almighty!' And then he burst into tears.

Fatio claimed first in French and then in English that he'd been in search of a chamber-pot, being blind drunk, and had tripped over my bed in the dark. Then he too burst into tears and fell to grovelling at my uncle's feet, licking them and proclaiming his own mathematical limitations in an attempt to smother the memory of the incident in all of our minds.

'Maître, you are the foremost mage of all Europe. An intellectual Volcanus. Before which I humble myself, like the savage who knows no salvation, in abject Abasement. You have anatomised Light and thus have delivered us from our Darkness and Error; you have interrogated Change itself and given it Number; Movement, the Divine, you have glimpsed the limit; Prophecy! Gravity! The Moon! And you are trying for the Stone, and shall see it, yes, yes, draw even the constellations from their spheres and peer into the immortal Mind itself. It is that *Faculté Incroyable* which has so drawn me to you, has enforced my presence here, to be with you and none other. You must know that as soon as ever I heard of you I suffered that force you alone have justified – impulsion from a distant Attractor: I was drawn; I was conjured. And still I am drawn back to you here after you have bid me depart and I meant to be absent for ever.'

At last I could close my mouth. Something vomited back from my stomach. I spat up and growled and spat up again over myself and bared my teeth in shock. Inside I was weeping but no tears would come out of my wolf-eyes. The dark bulk of Uncle Isaac knelt down to break his hindering clasp. He put his arms around the snivelling one, and then took his, Fatio's, luxuriant, curling, blond hair and jerked it back in a tragic gesture.

'Not Mars with Venus, neither. Not betrayed with Venus. Nor even the messenger boy of the Olympians. But, to my eternal shame, Cerberus.' Visibly demonstrating a profound agitation, he picked him up like a child and returned him to the horsehair. I understood nothing that had passed.

No more was said. I doubt if any of us slept much more that night, but there was no more migration of place. In the morning I was freezing in my own sweat.

And no mention at all was made of the dark offences of the small hours. A servant brought food. We ate. Then I was tied to the desk, shivering and panting by turns. My neck and shoulders were filled with cramps. Newton kept sighing and staring at the furnace. Fatio began to shave, then he gave up. He proceeded to unpack his saddle-bag. He claimed to have a homunculus in a bottle. From Egypt, he said. Furious, my uncle went to cast it out of the window, hurling up the sash in preparation, and saying:

'Nay, Sir. We do God's work here. At least by daylight.'

That was the sash by which I gassed the moth in the curious jar when I was ten, four years before.

The homunculus sat also in its curious jar. It was a little septic foetus, cushioned on its placenta, and hermetically sealed, by some glassblower, in a vacuum. Nicholas prevented its fate:

'*Maître! Non! Non seulement est l'homoncule fort précieux, mais encore pourrait-il être le truc même qu'il nous faut.*'

My uncle hesitated. And then:

'Pray, Sir, get thee behind me. For years I've sought the justification of God in the secret of these metals and in these,' he indicated the walls full of leather-bound volumes, 'testaments. And I have sought freedom from the Fiend – at least, as I said, by day. The homunculus is but an emblem – a figure of rhetoric. It is not a literal requirement and refers to a state of the metals. As such this is an obscenity and declares in its horrible shape the continued presence of the evil one. My only hope is to maintain the restricted path. I shall try to keep up my shattered honour, sir, and my reason, as I am a gentleman and a Protestant; otherwise it shall not be done. When you return,' and I could see his disciple's sweet foxy eyes receive the hint that the straight path was compromised even as it was declared, 'take care that you not bring that abortion with you.'

It was enough. The Swiss collected his saddlebag and blanket, and affirmed that he would go out into the city to find a barber to attend to him. He did not return that day. My brain ran again and again on what had happened. I was wound up in a kind of shock, because there was no grounding of it. And most of all I wondered why it was that I'd submitted. It made it somehow my fault: I deserved all I got. I was already half-brute. What else could I perform upon myself? But a pure thought rose off that frenzy like the coil of a vapour, and lodged itself in a corner of my mind. I'd read of calculated killing. As I came of age that morning I realised what my brain was for. When he came back I would find a way . . . This thought I lodged in a safe place.

In speculating about where he might have gone I saw some point in making contact with the world of humankind – I would need to think their way in order to out-think *him*. I rummaged my random learning for any impressions as to where such an adult might go during the day, how he might exist while out of my sight; but the heaps of ideas remained as chaotic as the hotchpotch in the laboratory. With hindsight I reason now that he was meeting some contact: that he had gone back with the damned abortion to the Masonic Gentlemen's Club or the Papist Intelligencers, or the Parisian Rosenkreutzers, or whichever bent spy-ring was paying him. So Uncle Isaac and I had a couple of days to ourselves. As the morning went on *he* ran his fingers through his hair and studied and got up to look into whatever he was cooking on the furnace. *I*, tied to my ring, and losing my clarity, attempted with my free hand to saw my arms with pieces of shiny rubbish before dropping them as ingredients into my primal soup.

The Portrait

I look back through memory's peephole. This laboratory, the place where I learnt my science, has no modern counterparts. No long mahogany school benches here; no gas points nor curving slender taps; none of those tripods and burners, and cupboards full of flasks; none of the distinctive microsensitive balances, preserved in glass cases; nor instant electricity piped down red cables from a suspended matrix. Not here either the functional fluorescent hum of the research lab, with its white coats and computers. No spectacles parked on the bridge of a painstaking nose. No female student glued by the eyelids to a microscope. Not a decerebrate cat in sight.

In fact he kept home for an intact and enormously well developed tomcat who used to snuggle up by day near whichever of the furnaces was alight. I had always disliked the cat, but at least it went out at night. Mr Newton's cat was an amatory legend of the college, if not the city: a feline Don Giovanni who had his own cosy hell to return to through one of the draught holes in the skirting. He would also follow my uncle up to his chamber and slip into a haven hotter still. And that was the place of his body-building activities. Simply, he ate most of my uncle's meals; for, as I said before, Isaac rarely troubled the company in Hall, and, if he remembered, ordered food to be sent up to him. But because his custom was to become totally absorbed in his project of the moment, he'd take merely a bite or two before another idea struck him, and then he'd dash back to his metals or his notes or his instruments. So the cat profited.

But in the garden room – the laboratory – there was usually no food, and the cat went there for solitude and repose. From the outside, the laboratory looked like a little negative mimicry of the College itself, which was built in a square around a magical fountain. So the laboratory sat in my uncle's private garden as if in a tiny quadrangle. And if it looked oddly shaped and hardly able to compose itself under its tiled roof, this was because its ground plan was an exact and secret replica of Solomon's Temple. Moreover, the garden –

which in my memory looks like any number of formal ornaments of the period, with its mathematical division into four quarters and its little intricacies of flower beds – this too had its secret. For it was a representation of Eden, being planted with medicinal herbs from all the four continents we then knew of, each in its geographical set, and watered by special Rivers of Paradise that Uncle had ducted from the roof of the chapel, so that when it rained he might as Adam, or Solomon, or Jesus look out over the unfallen book of Nature. Apples, even, that Newtonian fruit, grew neatly pruned and disciplined along the walls on either side of the entrance. It being September, those that there were on the little trees glowed with ripeness.

Inside, and viewed from the Corner of Fermentation, this laboratory was what *we* should call a study cum sitting-room cum garage, albeit in Biblical configuration. It had three elaborate fireplaces, built around a central chimney. There was also a clock on a bracket and the remains of the tall water-pressure cabinet with which he'd played a density joke on a carpenter. On the stone floor there were three tables and some oaken chairs all covered with books and curiosities. There was one of his famous telescopes on a stand, and a number of other mechanisms in brass and leather which I didn't like the look of then, and can't put a name to in the recalling. Two pendulums made like delicately swinging miniature cupboards hung from the roof timbers. And he'd built a mobile close stool to save time. But above all there were his tools and his vessels. Everywhere lay the implements of a master craftsman: chisels, pliers, saws, tongs, ladles, scribers, grinders, a treadle lathe, bellows, gauges, rulers, compasses, hammers, drills; and everywhere else there were crucibles, flasks, coppers, cannikins, leathers, leads, cauldrons and tubes. For he'd become above all a wonderful artisan; the apotheosis of all those energetic and 'Puritan' young men from the skilled trades who for decades before the civil war attended lectures and evening classes in practical arithmetic, geography, navigation, weights and measures – in short, mathematics – because they wanted to take destiny into their own hands. And thought they'd done it when a precisely ground cutting edge traced out a significant locus that terminated in some royal vertebrae.

But these young men married and were mercantile. If they somehow supplied a context for his activity they don't explain his origins or singular obsessions, the most fraught of which was alchemy. What motivated Mr Newton, Professor Newton even, to this solitary passion of *Prima Materia*? I, seeing him at that time through my wolf's eyes, could tell something: that he was a stunned being.

It suits our view now to look back and see him as a superior brain. Having lived quite long and seen many, I wonder if there *is* such a thing. In those days anyway it would not have occurred to us to think so. As samples of tissue go, brains are all much of a muchness. If we'd had the word maybe we would have seen ourselves then as *aerials*, that might through grace receive God's messages. We resonated; we were attuned; we rode down signals with the angels. Intellect, and its dysfunctions, were visitations we permitted, were granted, or had imposed on us. And some of us were thought to have been instructed by devils.

In any case, what could be more intelligent than language itself? I have my own reasons for resisting the cult of Genius. I say my uncle merely made himself proficient in the codes that were newly developing then, and cross-fertilised them for the sake of his overriding purpose: to get back all the control his birth and treatment had stripped him of, and to blot out everything else.

His father died before he was born. He was delivered, so my mother told me, a little bloody foetus that no one expected to come to life. They put it aside to be dealt with later. It lay, cold, and further out than the remotest galaxies for half an hour or more, which it might have experienced as longer than an ice age. At first, no one noticed it had started to move. Eventually the bundled mess in the corner turned into a baby, and they began with surprise to push pap into its mouth.

When little Isaac was no more than an infant, his mother, my grandmother, married Rector Smith, for financial security, on the condition that she left the child at Woolsthorpe. Rector Barnabas Smith, almost the squire, did not suffer the little children . . . Isaac was only allowed to make visits, brought over by his grandmother. Was this bar sufficient motivation for his whole later career? I doubt it. But I tell you this: as soon as he was old enough he tried to burn down their house.

He was an angry, isolated boy, though not a complete wolf; strong enough to suffer no fools and find few friends. He made models – windmills and other curious engines – from being inquisitive and much alone. He sought with miniatures the secrets of power and control. And when he was fourteen he forced himself to make friends with the girls at his lodgings in Grantham where he'd been sent to the Grammar School. But that didn't last, since they were out for more, it seemed. Love and so on. So he became difficult and solitary again, because the womb sang of interstellar distances, rejection and all he could not speak of.

Then circumstances put money his way, together with a sponsor, so that by a train of associated events he arrived at Cambridge, and was as lonely and powerless as he'd always been. The great Alma Mater fornicated and drank and prayed and idled her way along, leaving him little, hurt and open again, unnoticed in this corner for a year. He survived, convincing himself that by austerities he might become pleasing to God.

God in his turn took several more months to be convinced by Isaac's mortifications; then responded by thrusting in his way the submissive and equally lonely Wickens, who had a friend who owned a copy of Descartes's *Geometry*. Reading Descartes, Uncle Isaac saw his chance to grapple something back in face of whatever it was that had happened to him. It was a great secret tool that could put power into his hands. A Language of Shapes.

When he came up to Cambridge, Mathematics was a nothing – it was all but forbidden, or at least irrelevant to the business of cramming the heads of the future incumbents of the Church of England, like my father, with thirty-nine articles. The prescribed education my uncle found tedious; he wouldn't and couldn't do it except to pass through the hoops which would keep him there – and offer the time and space for his secret vice: Mathematics. Mathematics as subversion; Mathematics as terrorist barrels under the House of the universe – or his stepfather's house as it was to him when he was a boy. Why else would anyone bore themselves with the study of Mathematics unless there was a significant payoff – world-shaking power, revenge, and personal, Godlike, self-esteem?

But at first the Descartes horrified him. He could make nothing of it and went to bed in despair that he should be overcome by another's words or diagrams. However, on the next day he went to it again and stayed up late by candlelight until he was four pages in. And so on. And this was his method, driven by day and by night and by an intensity of anxiety and desire, to give up all company or

35

other solace in order to stabilise his sense of weakness, his cosmic helplessness, and the violence of his lust. It was this single-minded dedication, as I remember him admitting to someone much later, which was his character. 'I keep the subject constantly before me, and wait till the first dawnings open slowly by little and little into the full and clear light.' He forced himself, and was forced, to think on the matter in hand to the exclusion of all others. And so it was with all God's and Mother Nature's intimate secrets: her petticoat Light, her fluxional Change, her capacity to attract, her Mirror the Moon; and His eternal Motions.

By night ... but by what right, you ask again, do I so assault *Genius*, that most treasured of latter-day concepts, which enables us to label other folk as lesser lights and use them accordingly in our monstrous schemes? Wasn't he a Cambridge Professor at twenty-six or whenever? Listen. The Lucasian Professorship was equally a nothing. It's true that he'd invented the calculus. He did this because his mathematics was entirely self-taught, and from only the most modern, analytical treatise of the times. So his thought was undamaged by any educational process. His boldness, arrogance and persistence paid off. Dr Barrow and Mr Babington slotted him into the Professorship. Dr Barrow, who was Lucasian Professor before my uncle, passed it across to him even as he stepped up the next rung of his own career ladder. It was a hobby-horse: they were the only two men in Cambridge who knew a surd from a tangent, anyway. Do you think students crammed the halls to hear the great 'Dr Newton' expounding the conic sections? Do you think they hung on his syllogisms as if he were a second Abelard? No one came. It was a purely financial arrangement, for which he must deliver a certain number of lectures. Every so often, then, Isaac read out some pages of his notes to the walls of a room and then went back to work. So they were able to pay him. But you see that he had then, and has always had since, shadowy backers in his doings, some human, some magical. And that is part of the mystery. But I know all this because I was there and saw what drove him.

Listen and I will tell this also before the Elixir is made. He had his eye on me.

I've indicated how I spent the time after the night of Fatio's attack. The first morning I was more or less left to myself in the laboratory.

My uncle worked. Elizabeth's face appeared to me, at times weeping, at times blank, once terrible and mocking; so that I wrenched her beloved picture from my mental eye and returned to the material present. At one stage I tried to entice the cat to come within range so that I could torment him. Perhaps he picked up on my bouts of shuddering; because he seemed well aware of the intended violence, and stayed just out of range, purring and smiling. However, as I said, I was gradually evolving a mentality of revenge, which reduced my emotion at the time, and sent the image of the night into its own locker. To some degree. And this is a repression, which, as I look over my account, I realise is a precise term. For I repressed what I knew and had grasped, so that here I'm able to recover it, to remember it as a concept, and to set it down. But I also realise that *at the time* I knew in another way what it was that had made me feel so wolflike before, and why it was that, though I hated my rape and was tied, I had accepted it. *This* knowledge I cannot now recall, though I try and try, even stubbing my pen at the paper in my frustration. I'm only aware that then, that morning, I did have the key both to the inexpressible experiences that had formed me and to the repressible one which had begun to change me.

My uncle may have noticed something was different, for at midday he thawed a little and I was untied. He had brought pieces of bread and meat. He seemed to acknowledge that he had some duty of care towards me. I must be fed even if his life had become ashes. It dawned on me how I should act; I grew very submissive and helpful. I made noises about assisting him with the work. I tidied up some of the mess. I controlled my face and stroked the cat. So we passed the day, at the end of which he nearly smiled on me, and asked whether the cords were really necessary. I shook my head and looked sadly down.

On the next day, after a morning's alchemical labour, we went out to a nearby house to buy a pint of soup in one of his cans. We'd become a social unit. My arms remained untied. I nodded to my acquaintance, Slack, the Porter, as if all were well.

Isaac went up to his chambers to prepare the soup, and left me, so great was his trust in my new demeanour, to mind the furnace in the laboratory and sand clean a few vessels, some for a new step in the work and some to eat the soup from. My mother would have imagined he'd done wonders with my devil. I saw to the fires, worked with energy and finished quickly.

And then I crossed the garden, climbed the stair to his chambers and padded in with the pair of scrubbed-out iron bowls, whose insides had curious patterns left by melted metals. I came upon my uncle standing on a stool against the wall, holding a brace and bit. He looked round with a start and got down.

'My portrait,' he said suddenly, as if to explain himself, although through the years I'd got well used to the oddest of activities. 'I am, it seems, become famous, boy,' he said, looking at me guiltily. 'They want my likeness and are sending a limner. I thought I should be ready to hang the picture.'

I made a singing noise.

'But of course he won't leave the picture here,' he said, out-thinking himself. 'Or only briefly, perhaps. Ah, no. Probably not at all. Of course. You caught me in a moment of folly, my boy, and the drill bit has gone right through the wall in any case.'

Into my bedroom? I moved to put down my bowls and get a brush to sweep up the mess.

'Forgive me, boy. I'm . . . not myself. Foolishness.' And he turned his head away, leaving me feeling embarrassed and uncomfortable. No one had ever asked my forgiveness. 'I'll use it for something. That rack of polishing pastes wants mounting somewhere out of the way.'

I looked thoughtfully at the soup and my bowls.

'Yes. I forget about food, sometimes. I suppose we've got to eat, haven't we? But don't touch this cucurbit. I've got something important going and it has to boil continuously. Use the lower hook, here. No, not that one. And don't whatever you do . . . ' etc.

The soup cheered us both up. In the afternoon we returned to the laboratory where he said he had something very delicate to do. I read; which is to say that I looked at the diagrams in one of his Alchemical books. I could make no sense of their inscrutable Latin.

But the Alchemical illustrations were intoxicatingly curious. I could see now why men became obsessed with the mysterious quest. Not that Isaac was that kind of romantic. His aim was to demystify the whole corpus and win the game. His great gamble was that, hidden behind the flounces of fantasy, the Green Lion, Virgin's Milk, Tailbiter, the Mysterium Conjunctionis, the Net, and so on, there was some genuine key to matter carried down from Mosaic times or before, and therefore stamped with a Biblical authority, as if God had delivered Nature to us in a brown paper package but supplied the instructions in Japanese. For he was caught on the notion of God the Artificer. He had to be. His whole position was that there was a Master Mechanic behind the whole creation, who had worked expertly in the construction of a neat little engine for us, which was clear and rational, if complex. But, since its creation, whores, devils and whoremongers, and Papists dressed as whores, princes and whoremongers had used the blueprints to wipe their backsides. He blamed the inscrutable nature of inherited wisdom thus to avoid offending God.

Now had he not believed this way, as in my cloudy way I did myself at the time, because it was in our family and the tradition in those parts, then he must have become a mere fornicator or incendiary. But more and more he felt himself led towards the role of *Favoured Apprentice in whom I am much pleased*. Which disturbed and motivated and thrilled him the more success he had. Why, I'd seen him with my own eyes searching the Scriptures again and again, and I realised later that he was checking and rechecking for the timescale of the great winding down, the Apocalypse and the second coming. Not for vanity, but to see whether he *was* the . . . you know; because it would affect his plans, his conduct. Should he speak out now, or should he wait? Should he denounce the Church of England as a harlot and start rooting out the money-changers – he'd researched the proof – or should he keep quiet? Of course he did speak out on King James – with some success. I was much younger, and didn't know what the Glorious Revolution was. But everyone had been suddenly very proud of mad Uncle Isaac, and he was made an MP. But then even after the *Principia* there still remained the tantalising matter of the metals; and the fact that this so resisted solution suggested that indeed the time was not fulfilled. And then there were the shadowy backers, about whom he never spoke, and who supplied him with materials and manuscripts.

I looked at the strange images, finely engraved. A man stood in a boiling bath with a crow on his head. A peacock in a bottle in a garden of paradise. A crucified snake. A man having his head split open with an axe so that a beautiful virgin might emerge fully clothed from the incision. A king and a queen pressing their naked bellies together as they drowned in a river. Tools of revenge?

So the day passed. Then more soup and a meal sent up from Hall. Sure enough there was a new rack of jars neatly mounted on the wall. And the Autumn evening fell into night. He had placed a screen across the door to my bedroom. Thoughtfully. My heart warmed to him for a moment. I was getting used to the liberty of being my own attendant and sleeping without cords. I took in a copper of warm water. By candlelight I went naked and stood in it to clean my body. Then stretched up and felt my own breast there in the flickering glow to see whether Fatio's knee had left a mark. Of course there was none, in spite of the sensation I had. Was it *his* hungry eyes I felt on me? There was a crash from beyond as if my uncle had bumped into something.

I found the lens in the morning when he had gone out to enquire about something to do with a horse and Mr Locke. I was clearing up our breakfast when I saw that the stool was broken. It was a pretty little stool, the one he'd been standing on to drill the hole. I looked up at the rack of jars, thanks, as I now know, to Mr Locke's Associative Theory. Among the jars was a little brass cylinder. I dragged over a chair and stood up to examine it more closely. It was an exquisitely made eyepiece, its brazings bright and new. From this level I could also see the hole in the wall behind the jars. I placed the eyepiece into the hole, drawn on by the train of ideas. It fitted exactly. I applied my eye to the lens and the whole of my bedroom leapt into view.

Love's Limbeck

'I'm ready to attempt Projection,' said my uncle quietly, as if it were an everyday sort of thing.

'But, Maître,' said Nick, 'I had no idea you would embark on such a thing. If I had known I would never have left you. I would have been here, with you, by your side at such a time.' And then he continued in a Swiss Latin which lost me. But I knew the falseness and flattery of it from its tone.

It was a grey, squally day. The air was full of droplets; they blew finely against the casement windows, then dried again – a faint cold precipitation of Winter in our jar. *He* had just arrived. My Uncle Isaac and I had spent all the previous afternoon preparing the furnaces – all five, in both rooms – which he had constructed himself; I'd never felt so involved – in anything. My uncle was keyed up, and kept moving from one place to another, checking the colour of this one's glow, supervising the firing of that, or the rich boiling of another, giving me instructions and then taking the tongs or the bellows out of my hands. 'No, no, no, not like that; like this. See? Stronger. Not that strongly. Let me. Here.' And there was the occasional 'Good', and just the occasional 'That's right.' So despite my discovery of the lens we still had a good time together, sweating and chuckling, both so excited about I didn't know what that we neither of us touched the food sent up. The cat bloated.

Some of the pictures in the books had shown a man and a woman standing on either side of a brick oven, she wearing a moon and he a sun. I fancied myself absorbed into the magic of the curious process, as playing a part in a masque. My mother had once allowed me to stay to see a masque in Cambridge. In the figure of the magical heroine I'd allowed myself to suspect that there was a condition of life unlike my own imprisonment – my imprisonment in the male body of a wolf creature. Now I allowed myself in thought to escape into this masque of earth and fire, full of roar and hiss, strenuous lift, and dip to your partner. I tasted salt sweat whenever I licked my lips. Then, when it was late, and we'd banked up the fires because we were exhausted, and the amalgam in the larger crucible was skimming with a faint crinkly green, like the burnish on a housefly, while the last concoction in its glass needed to cool down for some hours, I slipped out of my clothes and into bed too quickly for the lens; to fall nearly asleep, nearly elated.

But Nicholas showing up next morning changed the whole atmosphere.

'It is not a position I would naturally have occupied,' said Isaac.

'Pardon me? Position?'

'The position of Projector. It smacks of sorcery. Quackery, charlatanism,' said my uncle. 'I told you we do God's work here. We proceed along rational paths. The grand drama is not my way, Mon sieur Fatio. What I've been seeking to do, as you, Sir, must know . . . For it's I who've brought you to this converse with matter, and opened your eyes a little – though you imagine yourself already an adept, and once sought to betray me in London with the . . .

friend . . . you wrote of, claiming to have made a production of the medicinal Stone to sell! Yes indeed, Sir, I know you what you are, since I went there to London to find out all and expose the traducement.' Fatio's face turned white. 'But we shall say no more of these things,' went on my uncle, his voice trembling. 'What I've been seeking to do is to bring logic and order to my subject. Mine, Sir. I have made it mine enough.' He looked up at the shelved volumes, and at the open ones, and a sudden rage lit up his face. He brought his fist down on the desk quite unexpectedly and a whole case of stoppered bottles threatened to smash themselves against each other. 'It is an art hopelessly . . . forgive me . . . Papist! Cartesian! Hookish! And Athanasian!'

These thundering epithets were my uncle's oaths. They were the areas in which he saw the greatest evidence of the underlying whoredom that clogged up the works of things; and showed moreover that Descartes had become for him almost the Antichrist, together with his other *bêtes noires*; which was surprising in the light of what I said before, and had occurred because he'd realised that in the wake of *I think therefore I am* his necessary God was rapidly disappearing down a Cartesian vortex. You should imagine that in these Words lay twenty years of utter frustration at the labyrinth the whole subject of chemistry represented to him.

'Of course, of course,' said Nick, soft and startled, unwrapping from its basketwork protection a large glass object – not the homunculus – which he had brought.

'However, things have come to a pass,' said Isaac, taking the object without comment as if somehow its production were pre-arranged and the conversation merely for the benefit of some audience beyond the immediate action, 'which seems to demand that the arcanum of the Mysterium is attempted. Under properly controlled conditions,' rolling these phrases grandly off his tongue to intimidate the other man with his intellectual authority even as he took the key ingredient. 'For I don't see how else we might know the complete ins and outs of the curiosity referred to so often, and so grossly, in the tomes.' He jerked his head again towards his shelves.

'You mean that never before have you . . . ? You haven't . . . ? You've never tried . . . ? Never done . . . ? In all these years?' said Nick, allowing the sexual innuendo to build up in all these silences while maintaining a look of wide-eyed scientific innocence on his foxy little face.

'No, Sir. I have not,' replied my uncle firmly. 'I've been seeking the Net, the Atomic Theory, a matter of weights, truth and values, not questing vainly after fools' promises.'

'Ah. *Bien sûr. Bien sûr*,' the Swiss nodded.

'But today Philosophy demands this ultimate. I tell you, Sir, something I would not confess to any other. To none other.'

'Monsieur Isaac, what is it you have to confess to me alone? It is a boundless honour you do me with this intimacy. What is it, Maître? What?'

'It is . . . I have of late, Sir, entertained more than ever my . . . my dark suspicion.'

'Suspicion, Isaac?'

'A terrible suspicion. A suspicion that . . . that I am mocked.'

'Mocked? By whom? Ah, Monsieur . . . !'

'Do not interrupt me, Sir, I beg you. Mocked by . . . by all this. By my own Art. By these metals. By . . . but it's of no account. I've been under such strain these months. It is nothing. Of no account. Take no thought for a moment's lapse. Come along, boy, we must take the vessels down to the greater Athanor.'

And he led us down the stairs in a curious parade of three, bearing strange gifts out to the micro-temple where we should generate the divine child. But Nick wouldn't give up.

'Mocked, my dear Monsieur Newton? How is this? My feelings for you, Maître. Maître, my love . . . and respect for you.'

'Sir! The Athanor.' We entered the laboratory.

'Isaac!'

'Don't tempt me, Nicholas. I've had such sorrow at your hands. Four years I have known . . . Don't mock me now, Sir. I'm about to do a terrible thing because of you; and this . . . creature,' indicating me.

I felt my eyes widening and my lips peeling back from my teeth.

'You! Yes, you . . . !' suddenly turning on me, his demeanour madly changed, and then breaking away with his head in his hands. 'The satyrs mock the lame smith even as he attends to his fire. But you two shall be initiates and I shall burn the corruption out of you as I've burnt it out of myself and these metals.' He flicked at his mercury-white, disordered hair. 'No. Forgive me. That's unjust. For my hard heart reaches out to you both in . . . it is such a knocking

43

in my breast . . . ' tears sprang to his eyes and he could hardly breathe to say the phrase, ' . . . in love. There. It is a word I have given to no one else before this moment. You are the chosen ones.'

I think we were both aghast.

'But my mission!' he went on, turning away as if to cover the lapse. 'Don't you understand how important it is that I should be utterly . . . But of course you couldn't. Although I thought perhaps, Nicholas, my dear . . . my dearest . . . friend, that you might have . . . Never mind. Listen, both of you.' He took from his bench a great leather book and exposed the pages to us. 'The work of Alchemy is said to be a Christian work, a Platonic fulfilment of . . . of love. What we do in the fire, according to these writers from the past, from the dead, is to purify the flesh of the world. And I? I've sought only to understand. I've sought to understand what it was that lay behind the trumpery and lewd filth it was all dressed up in. What was the star regulus, the dove, the eagle, the Babylonian dragon, the Green Lion, the menstruations and ferments of the actions of the Sal Ammoniac, the royal or uncommon sperm? What were they? Find them, said my soul. Uncover their truth. These I would, by my pure . . . my nearly pure life lay at His feet, saying Father, so hath your servant performed.' The book fell open at its title page: its *Tableau de Riches Inventions*. I saw the representation of an eagle flying. Far up in the sky, it was attached by a string from its beak to a sealed vessel below. My uncle went on: 'And yet He kept all from me in this matter. For years. For years! But what does He ask of me now? To be drawn into the very flesh of these emblems even as the old writers describe? To find my passions, even *my* very flesh, set . . . set alight so that I may not separate myself from the business I . . . we . . . do. God mocks or instructs . . . Or the Devil does!' and he heaved a great sigh, 'and this grotesquerie that we embark on now is what I must do to put Him to the test as He puts me; saying, very well, let us try whether we can all burn away the faeces of carnality, for this glass may be the vessel, but so is this body and this room and this unusually quadratic College in which we find ourselves locked up together. In our own torment. Oh I am all broken in pieces.' He paused and stared from the brick of the small furnace, to Nick, to me. Then he picked up his thread again, 'Could it be that even as I attempted with cool head to construct the sense of the wretched books, they have with their cold pages constructed me?'

Outside the laboratory the wicked East Anglian wind was getting up. Sure enough, a storm rumbled in the distance. We raked out, woke and refuelled the main furnace, and then bellowsed it until it was roaring, with a terrible white incandescence inside its walls. Into this heat we lowered, Fatio and I, according to my uncle's instructions, the conical crucible that contained part of the work from yesterday. Within a short while I saw the clay grow a kind of transparent orange. My uncle set on top of this an alembic, which I gathered was to collect a distillate as it ran down a long tube, which he wound round so that the nozzle entered the orifice of another furnace. This we also renewed, and installed in it a bath of iron which was spiked by its feet into the clay of the floor. To my amazement, he poured into it the contents of my great fermenting bowl – the one I'd filled with bits at random. He muttered to find so much trash at the bottom of it, but seemed to believe the decanted soup was satisfactory for his purpose. Then, he took Fatio's sealed glass which I'd brought down from his chambers. I had a chance to inspect it closely. It was egg-shaped. Coming from each end of the egg were metallic projections fused through the shell, which was intricately silvered and obscure. It seemed designed to stand by itself in a fitting in the base of the iron bath, so that the thick wire coming out of its top stuck up towards the chimney.

Over this Newton and Fatio together lifted a ceramic cover to marry up with the iron rim, but not before they'd threaded a fine chain through the top. For the first time I noticed that this chain hung down from the interior of the chimney. Its dangling end was so designed that a little biting clip could fasten on to the wire from the glass egg. The whole apparatus now seemed complete, with the egg nested in its cover and seated in its ironware, but it remained to them to feed in the downpipe from the alembic and make all the seals up with fireputty.

'So,' said my uncle, 'the hermaphroditus must be roasted over the coals until he's ready to give up his star semen. This essence rises up with desire and we draw the spirit down this long condensing tube so that it fertilises the Queen here.' Then he went over to his work-bench and took one of his notebooks. He motioned us to sit down.

'Twelve years ago I felt I was on the verge of solving the riddle of the metals, but it merely drew me on to torment me and left me weeping and bereft – as indeed I find myself now. Had it not been that I wrestled with *Heavenly* Nature and overcame . . . '

'You speak of your *Principia*, Sir?'

'I do, Nick. But this earthy trade came near to wrecking me. I felt as though I should die with grief. Listen.' And he began to read from his notes:

'May 10 1681 I understood that the morning star is Venus and that she is the daughter of Saturn and one of the doves. May 14 I understood the trident. May 15 I understood "there are indeed certain sublimations of mercury" &c as also another dove: that is a sublimate which is wholly feculent rises from its body's white, leaves a black faeces in the bottom which is washed by solution, and mercury is sublimed again from the cleansed bodies until no more faeces remains in the bottom. Is not this very pure sublimate sophic sal ammoniac? May 18 I perfected the ideal solution. That is two equal salts carry up Saturn. Then he carries up the Stone and joined with malleable Jove also makes sophic sal ammoniac, and that in such proportion that Jove grasps the sceptre. Then the eagle carries Jupiter up. Hence Saturn can be combined without salts in the desired proportions so that the fire does not predominate. At last mercury sublimate and sophic sal ammoniac shatter the helmet and the menstruum carries everything up.

'Two years later I made Jupiter fly on his eagle.'

'Sir, I had no idea you had achieved these things,' said Fatio. 'You told me nothing of it.'

'Yesterday I completed the retracing of those steps, ready to put everything to trial today as I told you, in the light of what I now suspect.'

'That you are mocked? I still do not know what you mean, Maître.'

'That it is not possible to separate off the Me from the It. The Us from the That.' And he pointed to the fire. 'It is my worst fear – that what goes on in there depends on us, and on what goes on out here. It is that which I put to the test today.'

I looked out of one of the windows. It had started to rain heavily on to his Biblical garden. A man stood outside. Great drops bounced on and battered at the opium poppies, and at the stranger's wide, black hat. We, inside, were both awestruck by the solemnity of my Uncle Isaac's tones.

Projection

Could he predict the weather? I don't know how he was so confident there'd be a thunderstorm overhead that day; and not just a late Summer drift either, but a full blaster from off the North Sea, with proper maritime impulsion in it. Perhaps some Intelligence was looking after its own, or perhaps he had some secret since lost. Why not? There must be such things. Unless he called it up . . . I just preserve the image of him in my mind's eye, up there on the chapel tower with Charles Montagu (for that was the name of the visitor) in the pouring rain with the great kite soaring into the whelming grey above him, and his hands looking disproportionate because of the huge ceramic gauntlets with which he was controlling the string. A thin rope, separate from the kite's actual string, ran from the top of the laboratory chimney up to heaven. I began to understand what was being done, and something of its danger. However, no member of the College seemed remotely to concern himself with Mr Newton's eccentricities. Occasionally scholars in cloaks, or servants, or deliverymen passed across as much of the open space as they had to until they could get themselves under cover again. They hardly looked up. Maybe they were used to him. I was not used to this.

Popular wisdom ascribes the origin of this kite activity to Benjamin Franklin. I imagine the masonic tradition which hovers around so much of early science carried the technique to him, but he certainly didn't invent it. It occurred to me that this was what I'd seen darkly illustrated in the *Tableau de Riches Inventions*.

But Fatio too was impressed at the sight. And we could make out the miniature aqueducts Uncle had made from the chapel deluging the water from above on to the courses in the garden. Four tiny rivers rushed in Eden. Lightning ripped the clouds in the distance behind the College roofs. As the thunder boomed, Nicholas hurried me out of the rain to the interior of the laboratory. The storm was coming nearer. I ran to catch up a poker and stood with it next to the furnace watching him while he was latching the door. My lips snarled away from my teeth. I measured his skull, then turned the weapon sideways, while still regarding him, until its point stood in the hottest part of the fire. It was a defensive action, you understand. My plans for settling him were not nearly advanced enough.

47

'No, boy. I mean you no harm. It was all a misunderstanding. Besides there is much to be done. Projection, boy. The great work. We are chosen. We must . . . co-operate.'

Once again I was unable, as it were, to bite. He had the craft, it seemed, to rob me of my will, so that I was confused about what was real, what had really happened and what had not. He acted as if there were no matter between us, and I had difficulty holding on to the truth of my memory in face of that mesmeric exercise. How could this be? It was a mystery; nevertheless there I was, snarling, but morally disarmed for the time being. He actually touched me, moved me to a station where I could pump the bellows; and I went, mute and obedient, to work.

The fire roared and whitened; my face scorched. Thunder again. He was moving about behind and around me, checking the apparatus with a light risky touch, as if to have hands close to that focus was to court death – which, of course, it was, for who could tell exactly how and when the kite would catch hold of God?

Something was going on in the apparatus. I speculated on that egg Fatio had brought, which was sitting in the juice of my fermentation bath, opaque, pregnant. How had the man happened to bring exactly what my uncle expected? How was it that the whole apparatus seemed to have been designed around it? What was Projection? They had spoken of the snake Uroboros. I imagined a horrible creeping thing of the earth trapped in that glass prison, as my soul was trapped in me, live, poisonous.

And so I expected any moment that the momentous would happen. But seconds stretched into minutes, and, while there was the rattle of rain and the surge of wind and a constant rumbling from all around, nothing roared down the chimney; although occasionally some water penetrated its fall and hissed into the heat. I ran to the door and unlatched it. Fatio looked up and made after me, but all I had in mind was to look up again at Uncle Newton. There he was, alone and soaking on the tower in the puffy wind; no, there was Charles Montagu too, struggling with a safety rope perhaps. Uncle Isaac, near-exhausted it could be by now, working at the string to keep the kite high, staggering about in whatever space there was against the leads; and there it flew, still up, far away, in danger of disappearing into the actual cloudbase. Fatio pulled me back within by the arm. I hated his grip, but submitted. Backs against the wall, and well away from the central furnace, we sat down on the floor to wait.

He was calm, as if his nerve allowed by daily discipline for this scientific extremity. I had to admit he was calm. The apparatus shuddered in its excessive heat. He took out something from his coat pocket that looked like a musical instrument – possibly a high flute – and then began to take powder from a box he drew from another pocket. I didn't see the details of the little ritual that went with the preparation of his smoking mixture, but I understood what he was about when he took the crazy chance of striding quickly to the furnace to get some end of charcoal to light it with. Then he was back near me against the wall.

He puffed a while for his own satisfaction, inhaling in short breaths from the pipe. Then he passed it to me – it was wooden, a hard, dark wood, inlaid with yellow amberish material and fitted with metallic rings.

'Keep puffing, boy,' he said in his accent. 'If you don't keep puffing it will go out, and one of us will have to dare to go near the fire again.' He laughed. 'I have seen it done once before, but I would not tell *him* that. At least, I have seen it *tried*.' He laughed again. I sucked anxiously on the pipe. At once a bitter-sweet fume choked me. I made noises which came closer to speech than I was used to, apart from my singing. Hard smoky consonants were forced from my throat.

'Again! Again! It will do you good. It will cure you of your . . . impediments.'

I snatched some down into my lungs as I had seen him doing. I coughed. He moved closer and held it for me in my mouth till I had no choice but to breathe in a good quantity. Then he took it back and smoked at it himself a moment or so. I wanted more, for my wishes were altered and my discretion suspended in a way I did not understand, so that between us we got through it and I learned how to bear the smoke and cough less.

However, the last pulls hurt me and I stood up. But my standing was unlike any standing I'd made before; it was a lurch into a vault, and the vault was full of my feelings and childhood – I did not recognise them but knew they were mine. I looked down, it seemed an immense distance, to the floor. My feet were the feet of a wolf, a story-book wolf, grey, thin, feral; I felt the coil of my wolf thighs above the narrow ankles, strung up like clock-springs. And there were my hands, intricate with grey fur, from which the sharp nails protruded. Suddenly the room was alive with the language of smell winding its detail through the long passage that led from the end of my subtle nose to my brain. Nick's smell, sickening, evil; my own, amplified incredibly and full of the tones of unhappiness. Traces of Uncle Newton lifting and curling almost visibly from every object in the place; and the sharp odour of cat. Then I knew again why I felt half-animal and why I could not speak; and the space was peopled with horror. I know I knew it then, I say. But it was not graspable in the way I name and describe things to you now, and so as I write I weep almost with frustration that I can't get it back. But I do remember what, drugged, I *saw*.

'And if by the help of such microscopical eyes, a man could penetrate further than ordinary into the secret composition and radical texture of bodies . . . ' so wrote Mr Locke as I was to read in aftertimes. And the description fits also the effect of my directing my visual attention to what, in those expanded seconds of dislocated time, my nose had noticed first. Surfaces unstitched their finish. Their microstructure revealed itself; things indeed lost their proper names with their boundaries and I became a connoisseur of edges and gaps. Now these gaps became vortices, threatening, and, as I said, peopled. Worst of all I remember here, I saw in my vision the central mystery of the apparatus at the focus of the room. What was that white-hot crucible but a chamber of volcanic torment? There, strapped to a griddle, a two-headed two-breasted naked monster of man and woman endured for eternity. But as I observed, and possibly as a result of my act of observation, its flesh sublimed from its body and its bones darkened to a char, then whitened into a crumbly ash – and it was gone up, into the miniature vault of the alembic, searching its path out of one system, and down as feculent distillate into the next. Where I followed it.

Yes, the sun man (who despite his beams wore a dark wide-brimmed hat like Charles Montagu's that I had seen through the lattice in the first rain) and the moon woman stood up to their thighs in a primal sea. And in the sea, my sea, were the grains of all meaning, and the essential chemical spirals of all fish, beasts, plants and people, looping and squirming over one another, enquiring of me how they should combine. But there were also the metals, some clearly radiating. I could see their emissions which were stark and dangerous like the warnings certain animals carry on their skins. In the sea too there were faint streaks of blood – mine, perhaps, from scraping at my arms.

Between Charles and the woman floated the egg, now transparent to my altered sight. It did indeed contain the snake, but it was a snake that shimmered with an unbearable bright scaliness, while its part-human face gripped its own wilfully penetrative tail. The jaws were bound shut with a thin twist of cord so that the tail of flesh was locked in the mouth. It looked at me with a pleading complicity. There was shaking, either its or mine, I couldn't tell. Perhaps it pleaded for release – or to be left unnoticed. I could not continue to look.

My body was seized and spun round. I knew what was intended, and hated it. At the focus of the hatred was a figure. It was not Nicholas, although part of me grasped that he was its inspiration. And it had got at me, leering and terrorising, in an appalling slowness of feeling. I struck out, again and again with all my force, desperate to grind or smash that awful presence away, that mask with eyes and tongue, that wigged man in a room holding a stick. I wanted only to empty the eyes out, to shut fast the jaws with their nightmare bite on that hateful tongue poking, poking out of and into its hole.

The room erupted in blue light and fire. I screamed.

A Shift

A blurred rectangle of sky. By degrees it assembled itself into its panes of glass, held in the lattice of their joinery: the casement window of my uncle's chamber. The moth window. And I lay on a horsehair couch, hardly conscious of anything else; adrift, in fact, on the impulselessness of my body. The window filled my whole attention. Pale clouds, crinkled here and there through irregularities in the glass, were tinged by a weak, filtered sunshine.

A face next to me. It was my uncle's. He looked reverential, some-how, and worried. A sense of dusk. A pewter vessel with a spout that jutted towards me was raised in his hand near my face.

51

'Do not try to move. This is to drink.' I sipped from the spout. It was something slightly bitter but warming, some herbal concoction. Of course I did try to move. I lifted my head.

'I can lift my head,' I said, in a high tone of absolute amazement. And what I meant to be amazed by was not the movement but the voice. I had spoken. How strange and different my body felt, before sleep overcame me again.

A doctor in a wide coat – a full man with a full wig. But not *the* man.

My mother. The window. The doctor said of me: 'She is out of danger in my opinion. Of course there will be a need for rest, and I suggest a . . . change of lodging? Not equipped for . . . young woman . . . impressionable age. Family of course. Still . . . ' And he was gone.

I levered myself up on the couch and found myself wrapped in a rush of linen which laced at the front. I wondered if I had died. 'Mother.' My voice came out again with that breathy high sound. She looked at me. I don't know what there was in her face. Distance? Discomfort? Dislike?

'Aye, it's my child alright,' I heard her say, 'but bewitched or unbewitched I don't know.' My uncle came into view. 'What am I to do, Isaac? What am I to say? I came up from Robert's rectory with a manchild, though I grant you a knotted one, and now must take him back in skirts.' She looked at him and then at me. 'What am I to do? A girl! It's a miracle, but a damned one. A cranky one, Isaac, and I can't take it in.' She began to breathe too quickly and sat herself down on one of his bleak chairs, while he hovered behind her, wearing his wig for protection, perhaps, but uncertain whether to touch her shoulders by way of comfort. 'I can't take it in. Should I cry and praise the Lord. Should I throw my arms about him . . . her, and weep on . . . her *bosom*.' I saw her wince as if with disgust. 'It's too much, Isaac. You've gone too far. Too far. How can this be God's work?' And she did begin to snivel, and to shake a bit. 'What shall I tell people? Robert? Family? People in Bridgstock? Oh, I shall be hanged, Brother. Do you realise? It's me they'll hang. Godfearing folk like they. They won't like this. They'll find a way. Or drowning! I shall be drowned!'

My uncle turned to the window as if to escape this imminent flood of disaster. On the window-ledge, I noticed there now stood a human skull.

'My dear Madam,' he said, trying for a mode of address which would cover the deep awkwardness he felt in the presence of female feeling. 'Sister Barton,' he said. 'Hannah. Need anyone know?'

She stopped her cramped crying and looked up, licking her lips. Two tears left their traces down her cheeks. Then she looked at me. 'Can you hear me, child?' she said.

'Yes,' came out my little breathy voice. 'Yes. I can hear you, Mother.'

'You've changed, boy. Or been changed. Do you know that?'

'Yes, Mother. I can speak, God be praised.'

'Now don't give me any of that. Get up. Get up and look at yourself, boy.' But she recollected herself: 'That is, I'm sorry, if you can indeed get up, child. I would steady you, but I . . . I . . . would rather you tried on your own.'

How different I felt, swivelling my legs in their linen until I could place my feet on the floor. How curiously released. My uncle ostentatiously kept himself turned away, and coughed slightly to inform us of his propriety. Nick was not about.

I pushed down with my left hand on to the head of the couch. Yes, I could stand for a moment or two. All different. The same. Yet all different. Loose, soft.

I had escaped, I thought.

You will not understand me when I say this. You will especially not understand me if you are a woman. There is surely no woman alive today who is not aware that in all the authorities women's condition is generally held to be more exploited than that of men. Now. And worse in the past. But in my particular set of circumstances – unusual, I grant – and among those with whom I lived, I *believed* that to be suddenly female was to be suddenly delivered from, I hazard, unwelcome attentions.

And so it was that, having been miraculously changed by the projection experiment, I entered on a phase of life which seemed to promise better things. Yes, I began my new season.

Somehow, perhaps, it's our musculature which holds memories. By a change of my outward flesh the record of my darkest past was switched off, suspended. It was a blank. As blank a sheet as the linen

I wore. Well, blankish – bearing only the painful trace of the week of the projection. Thus I began life as a female. There only remained a shadowy knowledge of the rape – of someone I no longer quite was – and a plan of revenge. Enough to bear, but too little to render me a wolf-girl. So the awkwardnesses were all gone, the stiffness and cramps in the legs, the heavy entrapment of my heart within its ribcage, the wily animality of my neck. This particularly I noticed: my head ached, but seemed to float above my shoulders without effort of mine. It was liberating to my thoughts and feelings. I was light. I felt cleaner. Innocent.

Then I sat down again, being still weak from the shock of the explosion in the laboratory. I had no recollection of how I was borne from there to here, nor of how long I'd taken to recover and 'develop' into my new shape. I had no knowledge of whether my uncle saw the experiment as a success – whether this had been the intended outcome, or some incredible catastrophe. I could vaguely remember a blinding flash.

I put my hand to my head, as one does just on to the hairline above the brow, because, with the dull ache throughout, this seemed to be the place to smooth it out. I disturbed an itch, and found a small bump, as if from a blow right to the centre, midway between hairline and crown. The itch was the remains of a scab on the bump. Its pieces flipped down in front of my eyes as I scratched; one landed on my nose. The bump was hard and painful to the touch, but in spite of this there was a compulsion to poke at it as I worried the scab – until I felt drowsy again and organised myself to lie back.

As I did so there was a knock at the outer door, which was opened without pause for reply. I heard my uncle's voice: 'Charles. How glad I am to see you. Come in.'

'Returning to London. Today, Isaac. I shall see you soon? Madam,' he acknowledged my mother.

Isaac made a hesitating sound in his throat. 'Going back already? It seems you have only just arrived.'

'This politicking,' Charles laughed. 'It takes up all a man's time. And to make a final survey of your tender patient's condition.' He came into my view, the man in the garden on whose wide dark hat the first few drops had spattered as on the opium poppies. Hatless now, not tall; urbane and smiling, dressed soberly in very good cloth, he moved between me and the window. As I looked back at him I felt the burning embarrassment of the piece of scab sticking to my nose, and dashed it away with my hand.

'Her eyes are open. There's hope,' he said. 'Your servant, Madam,' to me. My gaze stretched in astonishment. He looked searchingly back before turning his attention once again to my uncle. Very searchingly. To Isaac, he said: 'You'll be most welcome, my dear fellow. I look for you earnestly.'

'You have thought of me? Of my situation?' said my uncle. 'As I described it to you?'

'Of course I have, Isaac.'

'I'm doubly indebted.'

'As I to you. London.'

'It may answer after all,' said Uncle Isaac. 'But in what capacity?'

'I am a man of influence,' he smiled. Tiredness overcame me. I lost interest and drifted off.

At my next waking I found myself dressed in clothes I recalled all too clearly, including the restraint coat. My heart dumped into the pit of my stomach with a terrible sensation – as if one has not escaped a nightmare by waking after all. My escape had been the dream.

But no. As I came to myself more and more I realised that the painful wolf self had remained transmuted, and that I was still light – merely *wrapped* in my former style. There were no mirrors – apart from those little optical pieces he had. What was I – to look at? I pressed at the fronts of my coat – soft bubs under the tough, lined, wool facings. Their slight tenderness to the pressure was mine. I stuck my hand between the legs of my breeches, then into my pocket, then round from behind. Then my mother came into the room. I put my hand up to my small, smooth face.

My mother did treat me differently. She was in awe of me. But the plan was, as my uncle had said, to continue to pass me off as the boy she arrived with. Until when, she wanted to know. How long could such a deception be sustained? Surely *things* would come to light. She was in fear for her life. Isaac told my mother that he would apply himself to the matter with his best attention.

I held my first real conversation. It was with my uncle, after mother went out to see about our journey. Neither of us knew how to begin. I decided it should be me. 'I have no need to sing, Uncle,' I said, looking up from the bowl in which I was dipping my bread.

'What shall we call you?' he replied. 'Or more particularly, what shall I call you, since when you return home your conditions of life are to appear unchanged?'

'Am I to see you again, then, Uncle?'

'I think you must. I am much shaken, boy, I . . . I mean . . . I . . . You see I cannot name you. I am shaken all to pieces. Every certainty has evaporated, exploded rather. I saw . . . nothing. Well, indeed I saw a great marvel. I saw the heavens open and . . . I saw what I had been waiting for. I was jolted back to the edge of the roof despite my precautions. The very air broke apart. Charles held me. He saved my life I believe. The voice of it . . . Ah my guts churn over now when I think of it.'

He paused. 'Listen. For my sins I am known about the world – O wretchedness of publication, a vile prostitution to the public gaze – as the man who captured God's language, who understood His workings, His secret movements. My *Principia* explains everything . . . except the matter of the metals, the Chymistry, to which I also sensed myself close, so close. But now all that has . . . gone up in smoke, quite literally. I understand nothing. Nothing. Because of you.'

'How because of me?'

'It is a question of who we are. I . . . Yes, I am resolved. I see we are bound together. I will tell you things I have told to no man. And because of your changed condition you are still no man to hear it, I suppose. Well, it became clear to me as I grew into my Cambridge self that I had been specially chosen, specially marked out. It would be a fool who did not recognise this. You understand me?'

'No, Uncle.'

'Do you not know what I have done?'

'You have turned me into a woman.'

'No, no, boy . . . woman. I mean what I have achieved. In the world of Art, Philosophy and Mathematics.'

'No, Uncle. I can read, but I have only read my Daddy's Church books, and what I could occasionally steal from Grandad Smith's shelves, and from Ayskew's library room.'

'Like myself as a child.'

'And the books in your laboratory, but only the pictures, not the language. I know nothing of the world of anything.'

'Then I'm wasting my words. But I want to inform you – why, I

56

don't know. Why I should feel compelled to speak to you of myself and my Art, I do not know, I say. It is like an instruction; whose origin, as always, could be either from above or ... below.' He brought his fist down on the table, suddenly, and his face became anguished. 'Shall I never be free of this ambiguity, this mockery of all I do? You were a monster, and are now a miracle. You're an escape from reasonable law. To make you rational I should have to claim myself as the Christ, the only miracle-worker, which would be an abominable blasphemy in the light of what I see now. Damn you! You return us all to the abyss, the abyss of superstition. My project is thus in ruins and you are a walking fairy tale. Surely you see this. You cannot be so blank and recondite as you appear. What is it that you are? Amphisbaena. Ha! No. So I tell you once again that God, or someone else too horrible to mention, spoke to me in my ceaseless labours of the wretched *Principia*. I published, and he has proceeded to destroy me ever after. For what? For my Hubris? For my heart? You tell me, tell me what should I do. I can't. Boy! Whatever you are! Female thing! Tell me!' He became suddenly very agitated, but I was not frightened of him.

'I don't know what it is you wish me to say, Uncle.'

'No. I shall teach you. I shall visit. It will be safe: I am unlike most men. You will be my Protégée. I shall tell you ... what it is that has ruined me. And between us we shall survive this terrible event.'

'On the window ledge. That skull.' The clay-coloured relic grinned at the room.

'It's a gift from ... Mr Nicholas. It's for you.'

We, my mother and I, left Cambridge on one of Mr Trueman's carrier vehicles, which happened to be going West. She marked my face like a beard shadow with burnt cork, to mar my new beauty. Further to preserve appearances my mother tied my arms by their secret tapes, which was a zaniness, because the whole purpose of the secret tapes was to keep up the illusion that I was normal while travelling. I suppose it made her feel she had some control, particularly when Mr Trueman was there in the depot shed while the wagon was loading and they were saying their farewells. I saw them embracing and touching behind the angle in the wall where the counter ran, his hand thrust into the folds of her skirt.

Then we were bumping out of the city of my transformation at the slow pace of horses, moving off into the dung-smelling countryside. My mother sat up with the driver. Wearing a black hat I sat at the back with my legs dangling over the tailboard. My gift-skull hung from my neck in a net bag which bumped and rolled on my lap.

It was a bright day after the morning mist had cleared – one of Summer's last throws. The St Neots road ran in lurching ruts while we curved between hedges, or struck across great reaches of stubbled fields, or plodded through villages. Other folk went about their sunlit business without sign of emotion, but the sight of ragged children playing and fighting round a pond triggered me to tears. Elizabeth. Elizabeth. And my tears ran and ran, not with the choking of sobs, but with a kind of permanent rinsing, so that I looked out over leaking elms, smudgy churches, and swimmers. I had the sense that at the back of my mind the other life was being catalogued; we might say now like an expanding video of lewd cartoons, played in another room, from which odd snatches and ungraspable flashes reached me. Or you might say they leaked through to me, because they made me cry even as I didn't apprehend them. They were assembling and sorting themselves, I think. Their only bright clarity was in their summation: my resolve to destroy Monsieur Nicholas Fatio de Duillier, which had been a turning-point, if you recall the decision I made to out-think them all. And I knew that I was able to be still, and to wait.

So where, I ask now, had the wolf-boy's cramps and twists gone *to*? Where were his snarls? Perhaps he was in hell. He had been displaced into another frame of being to await his time; but I think I also knew then that he could touch my thoughts, and that only by his aid should I make good my revenges.

'Well. What with your uncle's contribution and my endeavours we're out of the wood for the time being, as far as money goes,' said my mother. 'Thanks be to God.'

His Creation

While I finished growing up, he paid me visits. First, soon after the Incident, I had a letter of his to announce the programme:

'Here,' my mother'd said. 'He sends an enclosed for you. You may count yourself pretty fortunate.

'*Events which I do not specify on paper, child, have led to great alter-ations in my life. You have known me but a short while, and in that while you have seen me only as the thing I was; which the world now acknow-ledges was not a nothing indeed but a seer of new worlds and a maker of new contrivances. Nevertheless there are reasons why I must change my state. Where I saw so clearly and for so many years into the meanings of my researches, I find now my vision is muddied; perspectives have shifted, faculties altered.* I'm sure he expresses himself very courtly,' put in my mother, 'but most of his writing sets me at a loss. *You will, perhaps, not understand what I find myself compelled to write* – indeed, and to the point at last,' she said. Then she continued making out the intricate shapes on the page, '*to you here – suffice it to say, child, that I must go on in an entirely different way. Things are not what they were with me; I shall never find my former self again, I think. A parcel of books will arrive for you shortly by my direction. You are to read them. When I come I shall hope to find you perfect in them. I hope you keep up your duty to my sister your mother, and are of service to her in her bereavement. We are all in God's hands, to whose mercy you may be assured you are commended by*

your Unkle

Is. Newton

'There. He's decided to make something of himself at last.'

He gave me books indeed. Many, many books. I read them. I was the second woman in his life. The first was his mother, whose death he had overseen, nursing her illness himself until the last – though whether from love, guilt or social obligation I never knew. Every other representative of my current gender he seemed to regard as an advanced example of upholstery. But I was indeed his Protégée; I was one of the two chosen people.

I knew it wasn't love, on either of our parts, but a kind of double-tracking, which we both acknowledged without question. It puzzled me. I felt it must somehow serve us, though in a way that I was entirely unaware of. But then what was I to do with my beauty and my brain in darkest Northamptonshire? Marry? I had offers.

I hadn't stayed in the clothes of the wolf boy. My mother got over her fears. Having seen the advantages of a talking female as opposed to a snarling male, she weighed up the bigotry of the community against the sense of achievement she might get from putting one over on them; and chose to have it given out that she was sending me away North to distant cousins. These were good folk, she said, who were willing to harness her son's unreclaimability to ceaseless heavy labour, in return for a social chance for their pretty daughter. She flattered herself in the comparison, for though we were Rectory we weren't rich, and the locality must have conceived a grim impression of the fictitious North Country cousins. Nevertheless in due course mother and *son* travelled off on one of Trueman's trailers, even though the affair was technically over; and a clever sleight of hand was achieved between two out-county inns, in time for mother and *daughter* to meet a return transport.

Of my father? My father lived six weeks after my return from Cambridge. It was some indeterminate disease that wasted the flesh of innocent clergymen and demanded to be flushed through with brandy. He died in delirium when the brandy ran out. He called us in as he lay dying, my brother and sister and myself. He blessed my brother, and kissed Margaret and me. He said he'd always been so proud of his two girls but poisoned worms and now woodlice were tunnelling in his legs. He screamed. Uncle Benjamin Smith, who was staying with us as he so often did, came running upstairs to see what was toward. His wig flapped as he flung into the bedchamber. But his haste was redundant; his brother-in-law had passed on.

Thus I was acknowledged, and was called Catherine Barton, and learned how to live among people.

'You've read the Fermat? And the Wallis?' he said.

'It's too hard, Uncle.' I sat at a desk in our house. In front of me a rare copy of John Wallis's *Arithmetica Infinitorum*, the Arithmetic of Infinites, lay open, on top of a specially made copy in my uncle's hand of Fermat's *Varia Opera Mathematica*. It said:

$$\frac{0^2 + 1^2 + 2^2 + 3^2 + \ldots n^2}{n^2 + n^2 + n^2 + n^2 + \ldots n^2} = \frac{1}{3} + \frac{1}{6n}$$

'As *n* becomes indefinitely large, the ratio of the area under the curve to the square enclosing it approaches the limiting value of one third,' he said. 'I spoke to you about limits when I last came down, didn't I?'

'Yes, Uncle.'

'Well, then. Have you been idle?'

'Of course not.'

'Then what do you find hard?'

'It would help if it were in English,' I said.

'Ha! You must stick at your Latin. Without it you're lost.'

'Yes, Uncle. But why is it so important that I learn the mathematics? I don't take naturally to it.'

'Do you think I took naturally to it?'

'You must have done. You find it all so straightforward. To me it's infinitely crooked and tangled. Why does it matter?'

'It matters because . . . because . . . because of the event that we never speak about, and which must not be spoken about – you understand that, girl, don't you? It must not be mentioned. Ever. To anyone.'

'Yes, Uncle. I understand that.' I wondered which event he meant.

'Well I hope you do, for I'm wrecked if you say it. You don't want to wreck me do you, Catherine?'

'No, Uncle,' I replied. Wreck him? How could I wreck him?

'Well, then. You must learn this because I must be sure of you. Tcha! You must understand these things. I must share them with you. I must include you. Your mind must be formed according to these designs. It's to protect you, Catherine. It will protect you from becoming idle, frivolous and wanton, as your sex are most likely to. It's to protect you from Eve's faults. I must have you *with* me. Do you understand? It is imperative.'

I sighed, and looked again at the Wallis: a sea of Latin with numbers and diagrams afloat on it. 'Yes, Uncle. I understand.'

But in a few years money once again became a serious problem.

It was my mother's suggestion in all innocence – if I can attach that word to her – that we apply to Uncle Isaac in London to see if I might be something domestic for him. She played into our hands. I was to be *with* him literally.

He paid for everything. I arrived one bitter March afternoon five years after my transformation, by the West Chester coach which ran up to the metropolis on Watling Street. He met me at the Three Cups Inn just outside Westminster and checked first of all that no one had tampered with my bundle and wickerwork hold-all, and my net bag with Nick Fatio's gift-skull in it. Then he looked at me. 'Well, Catherine,' he said, 'we recluses are both moved into the fashionable world, at last. What do you think of the great city?' I'd never thought of myself as a recluse; I'd never voluntarily sought Northampton-shire. But perhaps he had a point, I thought to myself as I looked around me.

'It's more than I could have expected,' I said. What comment could anyone pass who came upon that place for the first time from nowhere? I'd probably seen more people in the previous quarter of an hour than I had in the rest of my life. Cambridge was as nothing beside this. And I felt cold through and through. But I was pleased finally to be here, because it felt as though my destiny were being fulfilled. The last few years in the Midlands, during which I was learning to be human, and female, had brought me up against the tightness of village life – of life in general. The holiday of feeling light was soon over. The wolf self lay primed and potent at the back of my mind, half-known; half-impossible. He was excised from discourse; so how could he have existed? Yet I felt him in me. And how soon did the dealings I had as a female – at church, at market, in the network of visits, or just in casual conversations in the street – yes, the very language I swam in – imprint on my movement, my expression even, all the things I might *not* do, the places I might *not* go, and the feelings I might *not* have. They laced me tighter than my stays. And in this my mother was not, I think, my friend, as she purported to be, but the chief agent of my oppression. She liked having me to talk to around the house, she said; better, she claimed, than my sister. She could see her young self in me, she said. So we developed a mother–daughter relationship of sorts – a relationship grown out of the air, without soil. But in fact she policed me. I played my part, and didn't know why I was so often on edge, or thrown down in spirits, since I supposed she must love me. She said it was my womb, and taught me how to bind it up with clouts by monthly necessity.

'How does my womb imprison me?' I asked. She told me it was the curse of Eve, and not to mention what was disgusting to God. Am I designed for no more than this? I thought.

At night, when my stays were off, when my sister, who lay next to me, was asleep, I tried the womb for whatever was the female equiv-alent of that sticky release which I sensed had so often soothed the wretched wolf-boy to sleep, and was part, somehow, of his con-ditioning. But although my own hands could experiment at will, and imaginary lusts could stir me and have me search my body's secrets out, there was no end available. No inner softening. No rest. Arousal became its own prison; and there were times, whole seasons, which indeed grew longer as I grew older, when I held myself stricter than a nun to fend off the frustration of my own desires. And love? My thoughts were all alchemical, like the King and Queen in the river. I conjured Elizabeth, whose family had moved away. I conjured the love and nakedness of the worthy women of Bridgstock and their drowning husbands, who groped blindly at their breasts.

What then could I accomplish? I had the revenge constantly before me, and when I once dreamed, that, dressed again in my coat, I actually performed it with a garrotte, my spirits lifted and I became almost buoyed up for several days. I started to plan, and speculated on other methods. But rural routine soon stifled the fantasy, while my dreams returned to bad but vague; and being now female I was denied even the opportunities for slaughter which the men had. My father had shot birds, or followed hares with dogs. I disdained to wring the necks of farmyard chickens and had no quarrel with the smooth innocence of the ducks on our pond.

In spite of my uncle's letters, his books and his educational visits, I lost belief sometimes that the hope of moving on could ever be fulfilled. Yet he must be instructing me to some purpose. I did study. I even worked at the mathematics, but without much cheer or success. Well, not in his terms. And I wondered how Christ might make me free, as Mr Witham, the curate, said He would when he stood behind me for my organ lesson, catching and releasing his breath. I felt moreover there was some other important matter I must prepare for. My destiny; my purpose. I mean beyond my purpose of revenge. I remembered my first conversation, and my uncle's anguished uncertainty over Who it was that had set him up.

So, yes; I was pleased to get to London.

His house was in Jermyn Street, a pleasant location as befitted a man of some distinction. It was made of sober London bricks, and, like much of the new London, was in the so-called Dutch style; the roof was tiled. It stood out dark against the setting sun. I was so glad of the fire in the first room. Heated wine. Supper. Like me he'd acquired some sort of social touch in the intervening years; the dishevelled projector had been laid to rest behind a fine suit of clothes and a regular wig. He showed me round.

The interior of the house was all done out in red: drapes, beds, sofas and seats. At the time I was amazed; with hindsight the phrase whorehouse taste leaps to mind. It was such a contrast with the rooms I'd come to know at Trinity – as if a child had been asked what colour it wanted most in the world, and been indulged. But the furniture was good – obviously; much more luxurious than anything I'd seen in the country. Better than the Smiths' house, where Uncle Benjamin, Isaac's stepbrother, was now squire. I unpacked in my room, hanging up my few outfits, and stuffing the wolf-boy's breeches, coat and hat into a small chest. He'd got me a good bed with four posts. Here in my bedroom there was another decorative dimension: expensive frilly white lace. And the drapes? Red. All red. Was this really *his* choice?

If it was, then he'd been overfulfilled in another matter, as I learned in growing used to London. That was of gold: he commuted each day to the Mint at the Tower of London, where he saw to the coinage. He took me to see: vast furnaces, noise, bellows, the brilliance of liquid metals. A grand scale of activity beyond the conception of the most obsessive souffleur. I felt here he was in his element at last. Can you imagine the fruition to an alchemist of the ceaseless pourings and runnings, pressings, millings and stampings of purest gold and silver; the quiet beauty of the metals ever set off deliciously against the clamour and filth of their surroundings – for the place was driven on horse power and full of shit.

To be truthful, this was also my early impression of London itself, except for the great concourses and squares, and those were plagued with pigeons. I'd expected it all to be easy. But the city leaned on you with its unconcern, its hardness. No new season offered itself here. In the streets I was alone in a throng. I even missed that stifling camaraderie of the village women as I began to learn how to live in this callous jostle. It took me weeks before I could stomach the sheer concentration of people, with their dogs and their total household excretions. A smoky, smelly, muddy, milling, wintry place.

In the Jermyn Street house I was comfortable enough, though. I was indeed something domestic; I was his housekeeper by virtue of my sex. What else could I be?

A man and woman and their daughter lived on the top floor and did the cleaning and maintenance and some of the cooking for us, in return for their keep. Their name was Pointer; we called them by their Christian names, Tony, Mary and young Pet. I had nominal charge over them, but in practice they were entirely self-sufficient as to how things should be done for Mister Eye, as they called him. Having by now been introduced at one or two other houses less obsessively furnished, I framed a second hypothesis about our red frilly décor. Perhaps it was Mary's uneducated taste. Perhaps she'd been given a free hand by my lofty uncle to set about making the place an elegant London address, without having any sense of elegant restraint.

While I was a newcomer, Mary and Pet fussed around me. 'Oh, Mistress Catherine, you'll 'ave suitors by the dozen, you will. Look at her eyes, Pet, and that pretty mouth. You'll have to look alive, Missy, as the sailors say, 'cause the young men here are all up to the chances if they can, aren't they, Pet? She knows! I know myself! But if you keep your wits about you, dear, you'll be all in the clear and have no end of a following. Won't she, Pet? Just you make sure they keep their hands out of your pocket. Such a pretty shape, my love. You don't have to put up with anything you don't want. Till you decide you do want it, that is. Eh, Pet?' She nudged her daughter for the joke and then returned to me. She seemed to want to touch my hair and adjust my caps and my dress. And then she was full of advice on society seamstresses and milliners. Good ones, it turned out.

Pet, who had soft eyes but was rather plain, didn't seem to resent her mother's enthusiasm for my looks. They both giggled and sparked themselves up at the prospect of love opening a lively market outlet in the house.

Love? Love? The city had love on its lips; it pressed the word into the currency of every encounter; it worked at love. But it was compulsion – as mechanical as the Mint, and as sweated. What was it that kept these people at it, toiling and moiling, breeding and hoping? And they were compelled to wear their love, as it were, on the outside. I was amazed at the openness, the show. I had never, except in the interchange between my mother and Mr Trueman in their farewells at Cambridge, seen love acted. Here I saw the rich kissing or preening in St James's Park. It was thought nothing that powdered men who found me walking there in company they knew should slip a hand across my bosom, even as they looked into my violent eyes and left me alone. As the Spring hastened on and the weather warmed up, whores sat out at the street alehouses with a crescent of painted nipple showing above the basque, sipping their cans and talking with tradesmen; and smart gentlewomen shopping near the Abbey aped something of their style. Men walked with their arms round their wives, or mistresses. I saw other people whom I met at my uncle's lean dinners roll eyes at each other; I met folk who were engaged in intrigues; I heard salacious talk at times in passing; and there were the Sunday mornings when rhythmic gasps and creakings came from the top floor of our house as the Pointers enjoyed their lie-in. One week I met a woman who was famously in love. She came to the house on some Royal Society pretext. When her man appeared at last in the hallway she flung herself on him with an almost tangible rapture. Despite my own passionate compulsions, I was terrified. And sad. Love? What was it? Sex? How? There was a place, Pet told me, somewhere in London, where a woman did headstands in a booth so that the passing wits and gallants could attempt her with thrown coins. Why?

In May I saw a man forcing two boys into a coach by hitting them with a cane through the rents in their rags, and when I got home I was shaken and sick.

My uncle and I were manifest public virgins.

He took me to the theatre. By the close I believed not only the actors but the audience to be false. Again I tortured myself as to the meaning of this place.

'These people, Uncle. What on earth is it they're doing? How does it keep on going?' I watched them. Daily they flooded along the streets about their various businesses; they lied, double-dealt and cheated; they apparently exchanged coinage, credit, and body fluids with very little prompting; they laughed, festered and grew old. They clung to life until they died. They appeared content with their orbits, eating, drinking, smoking and paying. Their story was private – I found no real way in, nor did I wish to; for I knew it was lacking in something, as I was myself. It was his city, his creation – as I was myself. Whither more naturally than here should we gravitate in our sadness? Commercial London. He was Warden of the Mint; Charles Montagu had fixed it for him, and all the universe had died.

Nevertheless I was also glad; for in this bleak description I recognised my own purpose, and began work on my Project. Which was to find the gaps in his.

I often thought about Nicholas. Perhaps he was somewhere in London even now. Perhaps he lay at night in some house in the streets I passed through every day, and was within reach, so that I had only to bend my intellect to his discovery in order to make all good. At such thoughts I felt my pretty lips lift away from my pretty teeth, found my pretty nails pressed against my own pretty cheeks.

'Do you ever see Monsieur Nicholas, Uncle?' I asked one afternoon when we were entertaining. His hand holding the new decanter shook momentarily so that some of the wine splashed over the side of Charles's glass on to the oak table-top. It started to run down the imperceptible gradient of the wood towards Sir Christopher Wren's lap. Henrietta Bellamy caught the little stream in time and headed it off until she could get hold of a napkin. Later Etta and I stood side by side at the mirror in the drawing-room to which we had gone while the men of science compared notes.

'Etta. Is it easy to be married in London?'

'Easy? What an odd thing. As easy as anywhere, Kit.' She teased at a stray of hair behind her ear.

'No. Being married. Is it an easy thing?'

'Edmund is a jewel. I love him. He makes *everything* so easy, my dear. Positively delicious. Why is your hair always swept up, Kit? Don't you wish for a change?'

In reply I took hold of her right-hand index finger and raised it to the centre of my brow, then just above, until it touched the concealed bump under the front wave I wore. She pushed at it of her own accord. I felt still the sharp pain whenever it was disturbed.

'Ow!'

'My dear. You're deformed. I've found a flaw in your beauty.' She bent to kiss my cheek.

'Only a little deformed, Etta.'

'I wonder if my hair would go in your style. On you it looks . . . stunning sometimes, Kit. Sometimes I think you have no conception of your looks.'

'Am I a mess?'

'No. Quite the contrary, dear. You're always well turned out. It's that I believe you know nothing of your effect on others. On men. On women, for that matter.'

'No? What's my effect?' I dabbed at myself in the mirror again.

'It's useless my telling you. I can hear by your tone of voice. Your effect. You know. But you don't know, do you?'

'Etta. Did you see my uncle's hand shake as I mentioned the name Nicholas?'

'No. When was that?' Delicately she re-applied a patch to her cheekbone.

'When you had to mop up the wine.'

'Oh. No, I didn't notice. I was talking to Wren. He was just leaving. Should I have?'

'That was something, Etta, that you know nothing of. It was a gap.'

'A what?'

'A gap. I see these moments. They are special. I call them gaps.'

Pawnee

That Summer of 1699 a schism in the Royal Society led to informal scientific demonstrations taking place at our house. We set up a rival outfit. The true cause was my uncle's hatred of Dr Hooke, whose vainglorious mediocrity, he said, lodged by the barb in the institution's flesh, so that twist as it might it couldn't shake the accursed, old duffer off. What my uncle's faction actually *did* in these evenings was not so much different from the authorised meetings.

'What is it that you have there, Mr Van de Bemde?'

'A pint of slugs, Mr Gregory.'

'Are they live slugs, Mr Van de Bemde?'

'Not at present, Sir.'

'I'm afraid I must be going. My deepest apologies, Gregory, Newton, Gentlemen.'

'Let the record show that at the time of Sir Christopher's departure, the slugs were dead, but their juice is still applicable.'

'So recorded.'

I showed Wren out and escaped to my own bedroom. I'd coped with the gassing of the hedgehog in the bell jar, and the nerve poison from Batavia. But the dog had been too much. I noted that my uncle hadn't liked it either, but he'd let them carry on. Food for my dreams: the way the gentlemen sat round unmoved while it cried and twitched. And now the man with the slugs. I who plotted revenge had motive, but how had these creatures offended? Should the gentlemen not anatomise their enemy Hooke?

Yet these were enlightened, modern men. They'd rebuilt the country and the city out of a legacy of war, disease and chaos. They must have good reason. Gaps. Where were the gaps? What was it that would get behind such sober, influential folk as these Londoners?

In my commonplace book I made a note of the chemicals for the gassing, and of where they were kept. And of the Batavian extract.

My uncle had showed me his notebook written from both ends. He'd got its prodigious supply of paper from his stepfather Smith when he was a boy, and it had served his whole career. It showed how he'd started when he was a young student. He'd put: '*Amicus Plato amicus Aristoteles magis amica veritas.*' Then '*Quaestiones Quaedam Philosophicae*', which I rendered, having learned my Latin lessons, as: 'Plato and Aristotle are beloved to me but I'd rather know the truth. Certain philosophical interrogations.' And he'd gone on from there. Through motion and conics and optics, to God, the creation; even to the soul, and sleep, and dreams. His thought was free. I wrote therefore:

'Certain questions of a young woman wishing to know the truth'
Then:

'1)   Jesus said, *I come not to bring peace but a sword.* Is this the razor of the anatomist?
2)   Is God well pleased? Has He indeed come down again? Is that Him? Downstairs?'

Then, frightened, I shut the book so that no one should see it. But of course in my bedroom my confident self knew that no one could really be watching me. God was more remote to my mind – if He existed. I was as advanced as that! Beyond Locke even! Despite the terms of my *Quaestiones*.

I tried again:

'3)   *If the Son therefore shall make you free, ye shall be free indeed.* In this work I shall be free. Though I am in the world, I am not required to be of it. What is it to be free?

4) Is it a bold thing for a woman to devote herself to study and experiment? Is it an unattempted thing? Am I the first?

5) If motion in this age of progress and wonders is determined as my uncle has shown, how shall Christ intervene to bring comfort to the tormented? Are we but bodies ceaselessly continuing in our right lines? What forces are impressed on us? Hunger? Disease? Lust? Blows? Blades? Have we in us *inherent* forces? What is Love?

6) These lovers sport in the public eye. But in private, when there is no one to see, what is it they say and do? What feel?

7) Why will not my passion discharge? Is a woman's body inferior to a man's in this? Is a woman's *mind* capable of discharge?

8) Why does my time hasten away, faster than my uncle's clock, so that I am always afraid? Are these the last days?

9) Why am I so frightened of my words. . . . ?

10) What forces have I reacted to, so that I should once have been', and my pen hesitated, 'of a lupine disposition?'

I shut the book. Not much for the start of a *Principia*, I thought. I felt I had done something shocking.

Having hidden these deliberations, I went out of my bedroom and walked to the end of the passage until I came directly in front of the steep back stairs, which continued their upward oak pathway to where the Pointers lived. This was the place from which I contacted them about household matters. We usually shouted up. I'd never yet intruded upon their flat, although nominally I had the right. They had an air of security.

I called quietly: 'Mary! Pet!' There was no answer. I called again, then hoisted my skirts and stepped up, hanging on to the rope and placing my little shoes sideways on the well worn, almost vertically raked flight. At the top I stared around in the dark, waiting for my eyes to adjust. There were two doors in front of me, at right angles to one another, and an extension of the little landing space that led off to my left.

I knocked on one of the doors. No reply. I opened it cautiously. Darkness. And the other – dark too.

Down the whole flight of the back stairs, I searched for a spare light in the kitchen, from which the Pointer family was equally absent. They must have gone out on some family jaunt; I didn't know what these London people might do at night. Perhaps he'd given them some expenses to blow. I sheltered my candle up again, right up to their privacy, and looked in for the second time. It flickered on a sparse, easy domesticity. There were the embers of a fire. Here was the parents' bed, made, normal. There were the careful wife's shelves of knick-knacks, a chest and a press. I noticed Tony's gardening boots and galoshes; Mary's stays and stockings drying over a horse. A covered chamber-pot. A washing bowl. Blue blinds drawn over the little casement. Pet's child drawings on expensive birthday paper propped over the hearth.

In the other room, their parlour, there were chairs round a little table, and the sofa that Pet must sleep on was covered and turned back ready, with a pillow at the wall end. My eyes took in baskets, a coal scuttle and irons. Knives were on the table, and unwashed plates with the pieces of a loaf on them; a newspaper; a Bible; candlesticks; a rack of plates; a collection of unglazed jugs and metal ones. A corner held a pile of mending and a wig-stand on the floor with an old wig of my uncle's on it, presumably awaiting some sort of repair. In the air there hung the odour of the folk I lived below: food and must and smoky body smell. I sensed my own separateness from this close, human place.

I picked up one of the knives and went back to the bedroom. Putting the candle carefully down on the press, I lay on the marital bed. My mind ran on the possibility of some alternative demonstration. That I should hoick my skirts up to my waist, spread my legs, and cut my wrists open perhaps, waiting to be found. I poked the point of the knife into the candlelit flesh of my left wrist, teasing up a peak of skin.

Was that a sound? I got up, alert, grabbed the light, then tiptoed back to the entrance of the parlour. No. No one was coming. Near the door I caught my hem and hurt my toe on a heavy cobbler's last which stood on the boards. I noticed the ends of the wig trailing on to the floor. I stole the great drapy thing and took myself back down to my own room, suddenly powerfully aware that these lacy red appointments were nothing to do with Mary; that they must

71

spring from my uncle's design and from nowhere else. I had the flash that they were designed for me.

One morning I walked with Pet to Etta Bellamy's house up further towards Hyde Park, where I was invited for tea. I had my suspicions that Etta was pregnant. I wondered who else there might be at the house, in case I should not be able to ask her. To my surprise there were lots of women there, a few of whom I knew. Etta was nowhere to be seen. I left Pet on the edge of the gathering with someone else who was a maid, then made my way toward the kitchen. A middle-aged fair woman called Margery came towards me carrying a tray of cakes.

'Where's Etta?' I asked. 'Hello Margery,' getting my addresses in the wrong order.

'You're going in the right direction. Hello Kitty.'

It was a few steps down at the end of the passage into the kitchen. Etta and a number of other people were in the midst of the swelter, managing the supplies for the entertainment.

'What is it?' I whispered, getting near her free side and blotting her forehead with my pocket handkerchief.

'You'll see. Don't ask all these people, either. I've left you in the dark. For a surprise. Nothing ever surprises you. I'm determined to.'

'Are you pregnant?' I asked. It was horribly bad manners. The question just came out. Sometimes I made these social gaffes. I can't even remember if that word was current then. Probably I asked was she breeding, but it seems in memory the natural sort of language I would have blundered with.

'Are you mad?' she replied.

'I'm so sorry. I don't know what to say now.'

'It's alright. Go up and wait in my saloon with all those other gossips.'

We drank expensive China tea from expensive little dishes. Etta played the society hostess, which is what she was. We rustled and fanned. We ate the cakes. I sat daringly on the floor as did one or two other younger girls. More status-conscious older women squeezed themselves on to the various seat levels. Pet and the ladies' maids had to stand at the sides.

'Now,' said Etta. She opened an interior door. Through it, after a brief pause, walked a young girl whose skin was like fine leather, whose black hair hung in huge braids, and whose clothing was stiff, like leather too, in the form of coat and trousers covered with beadwork wildlife. 'I introduce to you – Pawnee,' said Etta. 'She is an Indian Queen from Virginia, or thereabouts.'

'Good day, ladies,' said Pawnee, in impeccable English. 'I hope the time of year finds you all well.'

Etta aimed a whisper at me. 'Are you surprised?'

I was surprised.

'A gap!' laughed Etta.

'A gap indeed,' I said.

At my uncle's house I said to Pawnee and Etta: 'Do you know how when you are grown up the weeks and years seem to pass more rapidly than they did when you were a child?'

We were sitting in the back room looking out of the double doors at the sun on the goose-pecked grass between the honeysuckles in the yard.

'I know what that is,' said Pawnee. 'The world is speeding up.'

'Of course it isn't.' Etta contracted her nostrils; it exaggerated the fineness of her noble nose for a moment. 'Why should it?'

'Why shouldn't it?'

'Well I hope it's not, for my children's sake.'

'There. I was right,' I said. 'Rude but right. Sometimes when I know things I blurt them out. I can't help it, it seems. But admit it, my dear.'

'You are preoccupied,' she replied. 'Edmund is very skilful.'

'What's that? What is skilful?' The other two both laughed.

Etta choked out: 'Edmund is, Kit.'

And Pawnee added: 'Let's hope the world doesn't speed up on him, then.'

'My world is speeding up,' I said. 'I'm frightened.'

'Nonsense,' said Etta. My uncle's fine bracket clock chimed the quarter.

'This is a prismatic sextant, Charles, in a new mode. I finished it last night. You'll be impressed with the notion, I believe.'

'Isaac, your ingenuity. It's very fine.'

'Take it. With my esteem. Oh, and make sure you show it to someone when you call at the Admiralty. What a pity Cherry Russell's no longer quite placed.'

'Isaac. I'm overwhelmed.'

'I'll teach you to use it.'

'You don't subscribe to this Millennialist hysteria, then?'

'It's not according to my calculations,' said my uncle seriously. 'And if we are to adjust our calendar the false prophets will find themselves mightily confused.' Charles laughed.

Round the fire in the back room on an evening when the red curtains were drawn and only a few candles were lit, I said to Pawnee: 'I was once a boy. I was changed by my uncle into a girl.'

'I was once a polecat,' she said. 'Were you ever anything else, Etta?'

Etta came back into the room, from which she'd been half out, putting on her mantle. 'I must get home. Could you tell Tony I'm ready, Kit. Are you ready, Pawnee?'

'It makes it difficult to know who you are,' I said.

'It's not difficult for me,' said Pawnee.

'Why not?' I asked. 'It's very difficult for me.'

'What do you mean, was I ever anything else? Tony!' Etta leaned back out of the door and shouted up at the top flight. 'Tony!'

'Etta was a bird,' Pawnee said, thoughtfully. Her skirts rustled. She was dressed now in normal clothes; the native rig was just for the surprise. 'A beautiful crow with dark shiny feathers. She flew high above the forest looking for babies and earrings, until there was a great fire, and the forest went away. Then she flew higher and higher. Edmund too was a crow. He found her in the tent of the sun; her wings were bleeding. Dark, dark blood. There were two drops. One was me and one was Kit.'

'What's so difficult for you, Kit?' said Etta. 'Are you talking about Charles Montagu?'

'Everything,' I said. 'And my time is speeding up so much. So much.'

When they had gone I went in to join my uncle. He was occasionally drunk – ish. From the solitude of evenings when no one came.

'What do you think of me, Catherine? Do you think I'm greatly changed?'

'Greatly, Uncle.'

'But not so greatly as you, eh, boy? I have maintained my gender.'

'Have you, Uncle?'

'What d'you mean by that?'

'Mean?' A pause, during which he took another glass of the brown fluid he had in front of him.

'D'you know what it is I do? What I did today, for example.'

'No, Uncle.'

'I found a series of mistakes in the accounts submitted to me by Mr Blackwall, my Superintendent of Works. I took luncheon. I interviewed a Person of Quality who thought he was interviewing me. And I saw to it that a notorious coiner was committed to be hanged. Catherine!'

'Yes, Uncle.'

'Well, do you hear me, or not?'

'I hear you, Uncle.'

'And you say nothing?'

'What would you have me say?'

'You have no comment at all.'

'Am I not conformable? Do I displease you? What should I say?'

'That I have nothing left of my former . . . frenzy?'

'Your devil has left you, Uncle.'

A pause. 'You speak mighty directly, when you speak at all, Catherine.'

Another pause. I could find no words that would fit him.

'Don't you find me strange, Kit? I leave the universe alone. I could wish I'd always left it alone.'

'Don't you find *me* strange, Uncle? Strange beyond belief?'

I wished he smoked, so that there might be a substance to these intervals.

'What do you think of Charles, Kit?'

'He's a great man who is fabulously rich and runs the country almost. And he makes you feel cheerful with his visits. He is your friend.'

'Do you think he looks handsome, Kit? Why don't you sew or something of an evening? Etta Bellamy embroiders. Didn't my sister teach you to sew?'

'She tried, Uncle.' His face eased into an uncertain smile.

'Ah.' Then again: 'Well?'

'Well what?'

'Charles. Do you think he's handsome?'

I'd lost the grip on my sex. I wondered if, being a little the worse for drink, he was going to make some appalling confession regarding his feelings, and to ask for my opinion – or my blessing.

'Yes. He's a good-looking man, in an unconventional way; although he's smaller than you,' I ventured carefully.

'Well?' he said, looking pointedly at me. I glanced down and smoothed my skirt. 'Are you blushing, Kit?'

'You needn't confide in me, Uncle. Shall I make you some coffee?'

'The Devil, Kit . . . I beg your pardon. But *you* don't have to play the coy virgin with me.'

'Isn't that what I must play, Uncle?' With the merest trace of an intention to wound.

'Not if you'll have him, Kit. I grant you he can't consider marriage, even though he's free now. Sadly. But he thinks a good deal of you.'

I felt dazed, as though I were a sycamore seed, newly fallen from the tree.

That night in my bedroom I realised the true significance of my uncle's choice of décor. He wasn't just the civil servant he claimed to be. He had a new project which had actively outstripped mine. He was way ahead of me. It *was* a whorehouse – a laboratory whorehouse – and I was the whore.

Mirage

'Catherine!' My uncle's voice called me from my bedroom. I checked my hair and face, leaning over my dressing-table, holding my shell-backed hand-mirrors ludicrously poised behind my ears. My head hurt. My belly hurt. My skin was tender. My breasts were sore. And I'd woken feeling too hot. I tipped some scent water out and rubbed it on my wrists and temples.

'I'm coming, Uncle!'

I'd been working at my project the night before: the last point, the one about the Lupine Disposition. How difficult it was to make myself look at it, and yet how it nagged at me and made itself of all the most important Question. How its meaning vanished out of my mind just when I thought I had the next move and was about to put my ink on to the page. What *had* made me feel and act as that monster? Why that animal in particular: wolf, dog, what have you? An accident of birth? A fault in my incarnation? I see myself wrestling then, as I wrestle now, with the recurring words of the room, the man, the wig and the stick.

'Catherine!'

They were just words, leading to an impossibility, which I'd attempted to displace with those reasonable alternative explanations even as I jabbed my cut quill on to the paper in the frustration of non-recall. The words led to an impossibility, because everything I knew in the world said the opposite so loudly: that God was watching over us, that parents took care of their children, that Adam and Eve had been naughty and were deservedly expiating their sin throughout history, that the Church taught the truth through clergymen on both sides of my family, and that my Uncle Isaac had blessedly transcribed the word of the Creator for the New Age. What matter that as far as I could see, as I've said, Isaac's version, his creation itself, was a deadness in a glass jar against whose hard outside God's knuckle might knock in vain? That seemed to bother nobody else. They all seemed mightily satisfied with it, and could get on with their businesses the better for it.

'Aren't you ready yet!?'

'The merest moment, Uncle. My earrings. Then I'll be down!'

'Do try to hurry, Kit!'

Well, I'd been speechless then, yet I could sing. How could that happen? *Let us with a gladsome mind.* I made myself go back to that moment when it had seemed an inspired idea to give forth those words. In the body; out of the body. Out of the body, of necessity. An intelligent escape – from memory too? Had I done it before, and was that why I hadn't bitten – because I was inured to such acts, schooled? I had been pulled back in by the act of singing while the evidence was still, I swallowed involuntarily, tangible, and the perpetrator a distinctive stranger. I shuddered. Was that why I remembered only this one time? It was dangerous to think this way. Someone might get hurt; die even.

I scurried down the main stairs, scrunching a fistful of brocade in each hand to clear the skirts from where my shoes were treading. I had on my best blue shoes.

*

Charles was in the saloon. He had his back to the fire. He was quietly, almost casually dressed, as he often was when he called on us. But his wig was an imposing affair, designed perhaps, like his shoes, to increase his height: a great man. My uncle hovered near the door, while Pet stood with a tray for coffee.

'Here's Kit,' said my uncle. 'Sit down, Kit.' I sat in a chair by the wall under the landscape of Greenwich Park. Looking down at my blue shoes poking out as evidence of my legs, I felt painfully self-conscious. The fire made it too hot. Although it was November, there was a freak mugginess to the day.

'How are you, Catherine?' Charles said.

'Well, thank you, my Lord,' I lied, feeling the room sweat.

Charles laughed. It was a private joke. He'd not made much secret of his angling for a thorough ennoblement, but it was as yet only a royal promise.

'You look bright. And in good form,' he said.

My mouth was dry. 'I feel a touch out of sorts. Maybe I'm starting a cold.'

'Pull up a chair yourself, Charles,' said my uncle. Charles placed himself smoothly opposite me. He smiled. Pet put the tray on a little table before the hearth.

'You're relaxed enough, man,' my uncle observed, 'for someone who's lost everything.'

'Lost everything?' I said, startled for a moment out of my discomfort.

'Everything,' Charles smiled again. 'All my political career, at least.' He snapped his fingers and reached out for his coffee. 'For a week or two.'

'Charles has resigned,' explained Isaac.

'But that was months ago,' I said.

'The Exchequer.' Charles pulled at his lace cuff. 'Yesterday I threw in at the Treasury as well. As far as lordships go I'm no longer the First of the T.'

'But the recoinage!'

'Yes, Catherine. Everything leaks away, even despite your uncle's massive endeavours. Or gets melted away, I should say. And government's always a fickle thing. You drudge for years to rescue the country from its recurring propensity to fall to pieces, and what thanks do you get?' He looked at my uncle. 'But your position's assured, Isaac. And I don't care so much about mine. One could do with a rest; or a change. The death of my poor wife.' He looked back to me. 'Time,' he said. 'Time for one's own concerns.'

I thought of the mistresses he'd had, or was alleged to have had. And of the antique Duchess, married for sheer advancement, who had conveniently died last year. A man who was attractive to women, thirty-eight, with power, rank, money, in excess. Looks? How should I know? Good teeth? Mostly. Height? No. What exactly would be required of me?

'Ingrates!' My uncle exploded quietly and subsided. Then, like a grumbling Etna, he gave out some more blasts: 'Bank of England . . . currency reform . . . East India Company . . . Exchequer Bills . . . General Mortgage . . . Could I begin to list . . . Ingrates . . . national saviour . . . d'you hear, Kit?' Charles beamed and then looked modestly down.

'Window tax,' I muttered.

'Kit!' Shushed my uncle. Charles laughed. Uncle Isaac said he'd go out and see what on earth was keeping the girl with the coffee refill. What was she doing with it, he wanted to know. The door clicked meaningfully behind him. I looked at my nails, and then across the space at the dull London day outside the window. A dozen chimneys leached grey into grey. I drank from the coffee dish which had lain so far untouched in my lap. The hot, sweet stuff helped. When would he start?

'Time, Kit,' Charles said slowly.

'Time. Yes.' I looked steadily at him for a moment, and then away.

'I've a word game. You must help. We're in a house of numbers, so I'll make a metaphor to suit. When I give out you must continue.' We had played such games, but now I felt my head swimming. He said: 'In our world of mathematics, time is a line I might draw on a sheet of paper. A pathway. Two. As many as you like. Some lines intersecting, or curving together. Some, thanks to your uncle, whose rate of approach can be notated, even predicted.' The coffee I'd drunk lay queasily on my stomach, but I fought the feeling down because I wanted my wits about me. I wanted to do the right thing – for all concerned, including me; but I couldn't for the life of me think what the right thing might be. Charles went on: 'How many young women could I speak so to?'

'Of analysis?' I said. 'Or of fluxions? Hardly to me. Did your wife appreciate mathematics?'

'I don't know,' he said. 'I never asked her. I never seemed to have the time. Which of course may also be conceived of as . . . a train of dots – moments – each infinitesimally small; adding up to . . . this. Us. Now. No, now. Gone. Now. How they escape us as we try to catch them.' He gestured as if to pluck the time as it flew. '*Carpe diem.*' Then he spread his hands to indicate our presence in the room, with the fire and the coffee table and the window. 'Are you for lines or dots, Kit?'

I couldn't think. Usually I'd have come up with something sharp. 'I can't tell,' I said lamely.

'You're not yourself, Kit. What is it? You don't call me Charles and make me feel merry. You don't cut me down to size.'

'Lines, Charles,' I tried, flagging up a smile. 'The fire. Surely it's very hot in here, don't you find?' I really did feel thoroughly uncomfortable in myself, and he'd hardly said anything about the matter in hand, with his elaborate address. He went to open the window for me.

'Come here and get some fresh air. You look poorly, my dear. My dearest. Kit.' He put his arm on my waist. I froze. I didn't know how to act. 'Our lines first crossed when you were ill at Cambridge. You were fourteen, I believe. How old are you now?'

'Nineteen.' Were my teeth chattering?

'I pray you're not ill again now that we curve together. Heavens, these are hard lines. A shared locus. Asymptote. No. The game defeats me and you shall have to help me out. Help, Kit.' His hand played with the gatherings at the top of my skirt, his fingers just pressing in to find the flesh of my hip. I wondered sweatily what figure he'd have used if I'd said dots. But the game had defeated *me* from its outset. I think it was something he'd composed and was hoping to pass off as spontaneous – a word-screen to hide behind. Yes I really did feel as though there was something more wrong than I could put down to emotional stress. Had Pet laced me too tightly? 'I'm sorry,' I said. 'Let me sit down.' But before I could do so a wave of nauseous faintness swept over me and I fell – or would have fallen had he not caught me in his arms and held tightly on to me. I recall his forceful hand next to the fabric roll at my buttock. It was at this moment that my uncle returned to the room.

I remember finding myself in a carriage – a specially hired one, I imagine, because I don't think we owned one at that point – sitting opposite Pet. I remember there was singing coming from beyond the window – no doubt some balladeer at a public house. It was a country scene as I looked out, and Pet said to me: 'Don't touch your face.' She intercepted the hand I was involuntarily raising as I stirred from my drowse.

'What?' I said.

'Your face. You mustn't touch it.'

'Why not?'

'Madam. Miss Kit. Your illness.' She looked at Pawnee.

'Ah!' I said.

Once the worst of the temperature and delirium had begun to abate they'd lost no time in shipping me off to better air. My uncle wrote to me at Mr Gyre's farm north of Oxford, also alarmed for my face and suggesting cow's milk for the remains of the fever.

> *I am*
> *Your very loving Unkle*
>> Is. Newton

I am very comfortable here I thank you, my dearest Uncle Isaac. Charles's man saw to everything and the people, and then returned to London, having ridden beside the coach all the way and made sure that we were provided for most generously in the journey. I am well enough recovered to write, and to be up and about in the house; which is very well kept up and quite large. Mrs Gyre has been most kind, as have all in the household. I want for nothing and am not permitted to exert myself. They make sure I rest after meals on a settee in front of the fire. Indeed the weather has been very cold, but the airs are fresh and no doubt do me good. I shall be writing to my mother and to my sister Margaret to tell them not to worry any more on my score. Pawnee and Pet keep me company and play me at cards; and make sure that I do not give way to scratching! Which I can assure you is a hard thing to do, as the pocks are very provoking until they fall off. We go out for strolls beyond the herb garden when the sun shines. Pet is very taken with the life in the country and the Landscapes that are to be seen; she is wide-eyed at having so much of an horizon, and thanks you very much for the gift of the coat. She wishes me to send her love and duty to Tony and Mary and that she is quite well, and so I would beg you to pass this on. Please also pass my love and best wishes to Etta; I believe her vomitings are usual and will pass. I hope you are recovered from your cold in the head and that the temporary setbacks you mentioned are now resolved. It would please me to know when you would have me home.

Your obedient Niece
and Humble Servant

C. Barton

The moon had shone into my bedroom where a last drench of fever was flushing through me. I'd opened the window to get the freeze of the air on to my skin, and then I'd seen my moonlit self in the mirror. I'd sat with my shift off my shoulders poking, scratching and squeezing at the pock scabs on my face. I don't know whether I'd wanted to rid myself of them or to scar myself, my dangerous beauty, for life.

But now it was Spring. I was recovered. My uncle had insisted that I stay out of the city until I could be reckoned safe. It was strange to have been ill and to have been, in a sense, mothered by the people around me. Women's arms embraced me as if I belonged. The old house was relaxed and safe in a way that I'd never known before. The place had no hooks, no sense of dark memories. The look of the timbers didn't make me feel unaccountably tense or churned up in the stomach. They were just the timbers, and it was just a country home; for which the mistress cut flowers as soon as there were any to be had, and the corn figures and drying herbs hung up comfortingly in the big kitchen, where unless there were visitors we mostly took our meals informally, all together. I say 'all' since there was an assortment of children and a couple of aunts of indeterminate ages, together with an old servant and a sort of housekeeper woman. Of course, I reasoned to myself at other times, it could well be that Charles was paying them to be good to me, as perhaps he was, since someone must have arranged all this. Nevertheless, overpaid or not, I couldn't help sensing a genuineness in their treatment of me, that both pleased and threatened – I had no practice in receiving it.

My separate bedroom looked out over the wooded April scene I came to love; there, lambs and kids had begun appearing in the paddock. Yes, I still had the bad dreams, the twisted nights and

82

violent preoccupations, but they receded into what you might call proportion; they didn't matter so much.

Pawnee said: 'Mrs Gyre has a gardener who has a niece.'

I said: 'Yes, Pawnee.'

'She is a niece you should see.'

'Why?'

'You'll see when you see her. Come on.'

I followed her down into the old hall, and then out via the kitchen halfdoors. A week of warm weather had dried the mud and muck of the yard. We went beyond the new brick and timber sheds where the carts and wagons were now kept.

'There,' she said. 'Good morning, Tempest. That is what he's called. I told you I'd bring Mistress Catherine Barton. He thinks I'm a gypsy, Kit, pretending to be resident and probably up to no good.'

'I beg yours, Ma'am,' said the gardener, seeing that I was English-looking, and dressed as well as Pawnee.

'I'd suspect him of blushing if his cheeks weren't more tanned than mine anyway,' said Pawnee. He grinned and started to spit. Then thought better of it. This wide-jawed grin held my attention. He had no overbite – his teeth met edge to edge all round. The girl with him looked up from the weeding where she was kneeling. I turned away from the curious teeth and found myself staring at her instead – with a peculiar sense of recognition. Where . . . ?

'Well?' Pawnee said with a certain air of triumph. The face was the face I saw every morning in my mirror. She was my double.

'Heavens!' I said. And like a mirror image her eyes widened at the same time as mine – I guess as the impulse of recognition affected her too. She was, at a hazard, about seventeen. She straightened up and then reached out at a head of the rose-bush, as if to smudge away a parcel of aphids. 'Can you tell me your name?'

'Lucy'lizabeth, Miss.'

'I have a confession, Kit.'

'A confession?'

'Now that you're better I can tell you.' Pawnee sat with me on my bed, holding my arm through hers, while morning sunshine flooded in from the outside world. With my free arm I put down the crust which was all that remained of my bread. 'It's this.' She held out a little twist of paper. 'This was sent by your uncle.' She released my arm.

I unscrewed the twist. It contained a powder, blue-purplish in colour, with a few grains or crystals of white. I smelt it as if to gather something of its significance. 'Am I supposed to eat it?' She passed me a letter.

Madam Virginian

I believe I am at the end of my wits with distraction concerning my niece's illness. I am relapsed into a state of mind I thought never to see again. I despair for her and would come to the country myself to doctor her condition did I not suspect my powers are subject to an alteration at present. I write to you alone with the paper herewith and must trust you, though I know little enough of you indeed, to be my niece's true friend in this, and to keep utmost confidence regarding this letter and the powder. All the world now knows the vile accusations that have been levelled against me of late, regarding my niece, my friend, and – I hardly know how I shall write this – her position in my household. I cannot get out of the house. There is a throng of spies and intelligencers in the street. They conceal themselves but I have smoked them. The powder is the only thing that might save her, and in saving her, save also her beauty. Give him the half as a decoction and have the remnant made up with a kindly oil for his face. Leave on over the pocks. It must not be washed off. Let it fall off rather or grow away. Do as I say. It is the Stone. It is some of the fruit of the damned miracle, which I recovered at the time. Tell no one, as He may have spies that have followed her even to Woodstock to see her nakedness while he is engaged in it. As to the charges they are false. I never engaged myself *with the* women. *These are damned lies put about by a spaniel of Hooke's. I fear I am not well, Madam, yet she must have the powder. She must not die now. Burn this. They must not know.*

Is. Newton

I re-read the letter in amazement. I'd never had the chance to see into his illness before.

'I didn't apply the remedy,' Pawnee said. 'You've mended miraculously enough. Your skin is unblemished.' As she smoothed my hair back from my forehead she pressed on the little painful bump so that I felt the sharpness of it.

'Lucy Elizabeth. You see I'm convalescing, but I'm not infectious, so you won't be in danger of the smallpox yourself. We can talk while you put these linens away for me.'

'Yes, Miss.'

'You've made me think, Lizzy. I need you to tell me things. I need you to tell me what your life holds for you.'

'Miss?'

'What's going to happen to you?'

'I don't know, Miss. I don't think about it.'

'D'you think you'll get married?'

'Bound to, Miss.'

'And have children?'

'Bound to, Miss.'

'Is that what you want?'

'Yes, Miss.'

'With all the attendant dangers?'

'You mean I could be dead before I'm twenty, Miss.'

'If you put it like that, Lizzy.'

'If they couldn't get the baby to come out.'

'Or after indeed. Some women . . . What choice do we have, Lizzy? If we love the man who marries us.'

'Or gets us up the stick. Pardon me, Madam.'

'It's nothing. Have you been in love?'

'I may've been.'

'Have you felt loved? Are you myself who is unspoiled? What is it like to be loved?'

'I'm sorry, Miss. I don't conceive you. What d'you want me to say?'

'I don't know these things, you see. I believe I'm a strange sort of woman. I live with a guardian. How should I know things?'

'Are your folks dead? Your Mammy?'

'Yes. They are. Quite. So in asking you I feel I'm asking in private: a magic mirror. Here I'm lighthearted. Can you believe that? It is a special place. If you saw me in London you'd not know me. There I'm usually troubled, but here I find myself closer to . . . I hardly dare say it because if it were said it might be taken away directly. Well-being. Perhaps it'll only last one more day. One more day flicking away still faster. I see these flowers you've brought in, so clearly. So bright; how couldn't I have seen such beauty before? I daren't trust this. I have to go back. Soon. I wish I might stay here, Lizzy. I wish . . . I need to hear what women . . . I am a woman now, and shall have to go back to my . . . my fate. Does your mother love you?'

'Yes.'

'Your father?'

'He left.'

'How does it feel to you to be shown your own likeness? We are twins, Lizzy, apart from our difference of precise age. What's your notion? As if from your side of the glass.'

A pause. 'You scare me, Miss, I ask your pardon. Can I go now?'

'Are you a virgin?'

'Sort of.'

'Is there some young man already?'

'Handy. Handy enough.'

'How do you . . . manage that?'

'We lie together downstairs at my mother's till he has a house. We don't do it all up. Just . . . you know.'

'Do you love him?'

'He's only a country boy, Miss. He don't have London manners. You wouldn't think of him.'

'But you. Do you love him? This love is why we venture our bodies.'

'I reckon I must do.'

'I . . . No. I . . . A man will have me.'

'What's his name, Miss?'

'His name? Charles.'

'How old's he?'

'Forty. Nearly. A Restoration baby, Lizzy. And now a London man. A powerful, rich, political man, and I don't know the first thing, Lizzy. I don't know what I should say if I can't . . . if I can't . . . to stop him if I don't . . . Help me, Lizzy. But you can't. You can't, can you?'

To Mrs Catherine Barton:

Kit, dearest, I am on fire for news of you. They tell me you are alive. I prayed that you should be spared. Confirm by your own hand that my prayers have been answered, and you will lift the devastating anxiety that possesses me on your account. Forgive the familiarity of my address, but is there not already an understanding between us? You must have discerned at our interview so tragically terminated some measure of the depth of my feelings for you; I cannot believe that we two are not in some sense by this time

*beyond the artificiality of opening politenesses. Kit, we know each other and
what we are about; write as soon as you can that all is in truth well with
you. I would be, dearest,*

your ardent and ultimate servant,
Charles Montagu

The Suitor

Pet went back before. Pawnee and I travelled after, with an armed
guard, courtesy of an admirer.

'You're well, Kit. You're beautiful, by the grace of God. You're
rich in most people's terms. Why do you frown? We're nearly at
Colnbrook. If there was going to be an attack it would have come by
now. There's no cover here for them to hide in.'

'I'm not afraid of robbers and ravishers. I told you that. I'd use the
gun – on myself, if necessary.'

'Kit!'

'Or on us both. I'd find a way.'

She didn't speak for a minute.

'Is it Charles, then?'

'I can't bear it, Pawnee. I'm their prisoner. I know it.'

'How's this? Your uncle loves you I think. They both care for you.
You just torment yourself with your suspicions of them. I see no
reason, except they're men, and all these European men are beasts in
their own normal way. This I know for myself. But it isn't as *you*
think.'

'These aren't *just* men. Now you're like the voice inside me that
tells me constantly I'm wrong or bad or ungrateful. Perhaps I am.
Perhaps you're right.' I paused and looked out of the coach window,
where the meadows stretched flat to the heath. We rumbled on the
rutted Bath Road.

'What'll he expect of me? He'll expect a real woman.'

'You are a real woman, Kit.'

'He'll want a mistress. I shall want, ha! to fall in love. But I can't,
Pawnee. Not with him. Not with anyone, perhaps. I can't. I'm a
wreck. I'm maimed. I'm maimed in my deep self. I cannot let him. So
then what'll he think? I told you I was once a boy. I haven't got the
right feelings. I haven't got the right responses. When he gets close to

me, no matter how compliant or helpful – or female – I shall want to try to be . . . and Pawnee in part I do want to be normal now. I do perhaps want to be like everyone else. To be quiet and happy as we've been.' A surge of feeling took me by surprise. I hit the coach-work with my fist so that my knuckles bruised. Then I denied my pain. 'I'm so . . . distorted.' Then I tried to shudder myself into great, heartbreaking sobs. But only pitiful trickles squeezed themselves out of my eyes. I wished I could drown the Thames, but I was locked and blocked. 'If he gets near me I'll have to . . . stab his neck. Cut him somehow. Pawnee, what's wrong with me? I'm possessed, aren't I? I'm a monster the Devil made in the moon. That's what my mother used to say.'

She leant across and put her hands on my hands on my thighs.

'Why does it matter? Can't you refuse him and go on as you are now? As you and I do. An honourable spinsterhood. Yes, people do, so why not you and I? Plain girls of good family do, and so do good girls with no money. For years. They live and live. They sew. And you; you're a wise scholar woman. You've got your project, you said. What do you want with a man? Yes they are rascals. They spread pox and pregnancy. They blame us. They beat us. And then they leave.'

Charles's man saw me to the Jermyn Street front door where my uncle embraced me. I inspected him for signs of the distraction he'd shown in his letter to Pawnee. His smile was tight, as if he was making the effort to be of good cheer. Mary and Tony embraced me cautiously. And so I settled back into the red; I re-established myself in the richness and lace of my bedroom, where they had hung the portrait of Charles beside the chimney-breast. There were fresh flowers in two jugs, and a new outfit of clothes laid on the bed. There was a silver save-all candlestick. New sconces had been fitted on the chimney-breast above the fireplace, on either side of a pretty little convex mirror in the Flemish style. My skull had been left where it should be, I was pleased to see, and a shelf had been put up to receive some decorative China plates, on which were four exquis-itely perfumed wash-balls. An opened parasol in Japanese lacquer. A little jewellery box. A porcelain container beginning to sprout what looked like very expensive foreign bulbs. I took it all in. I re-entered my determined universe.

*

Charles came to call. He was shown up to my bedroom by Mary as if it were an established thing. Nobody seemed to bat an eyelid, least of all me. I read these relationships of polite force.

'Kit. My jewel. You're safe.'

'Charles.' He seized my hands and pressed them to his lips. I didn't ask myself what was this assumed intimacy, nor on what it was based, nor what I had done to arouse it.

'Dearest Kit. You're as beautiful as ever.'

I looked down. He sat; as one who felt no stranger to the room. I sat too, in the chair in front of my dressing-table. I was in technical déshabillé – in that the finishing touches weren't on yet.

'They tell me so.'

'I'm so glad to see you. So happy.'

'And I to see you, Sir.'

'I believe you are. Kit, I believe you feel for me. Am I right?'

'Charles. As much as I'm able to feel anything, I feel for you.'

'And you are flesh and blood. Therefore I take heart. You don't lie to me. Although you torment me, you are honest and honourable.'

'Torment you? How?' I was astonished.

'You must know.'

'Know what? What have I done to you?'

'You've robbed me of my heart. You've had it out of me with the oyster knife of your eyes. Now I bleed Venus's salty fluid.'

'That's disgusting.'

'You haven't stolen my humour. But your eyebeams impale me, seriously; I can't sleep for thinking of you. I can't eat. It's all the fault of your exquisite form. I blame you, Kit; your skin, your hair, your cheeks, your absolute gestures, the low sweetness of your voice. I'm on the rack of your feminine perfection.'

I stood up. 'Come. This is a game. Where does it lead?' I was twenty, politely losing patience. When I was a boy, I remembered for a flash, I used to think it was my fault. Turning my back, I looked out, over the yard and to the park beyond.

'You're very direct. You're unlike other women. At least I've never met one like you. You say these outright things and I'm nonplussed. It puts me beside myself.' He came over to stand behind me.

'I'm different, I know it. I can't help it.'

'No. I don't wish you any other way. It's part of your beauty.'

'My beauty. Yes.'

'You say them with that bewitching half-smile.'

'And . . . ?'

'And I'm overthrown.'

'Do you like that? Do you like to be overthrown? Be honest with me, Charles, if you want to secure my respect.'

'What do the poets call it? Sweet torment. Delicious agony.'

Feeling him touch my shoulder, I slipped sideways to escape, catching a glimpse of myself in the mirror as I passed it.

'Did you love your wife?'

'I married for career reasons.'

'Did you come to love her?'

'Why do you ask?'

'Because for someone who could bid to understand the economy of a whole country, and wished patriotically to serve – I put the best construction on what I know of your past – even for a man who hoped to make a dazzling success in politics and wanted resources, marriage with a rich old woman is remarkably cynical. It's stage comedy stuff, Charles, I believe. Was she . . . beautiful?'

'You can't interrogate me like this, Kit. You realise who I am?'

'Very well. I shan't interrogate you like this. What do you want of me now?' I took up the sash I planned to wear. 'You have a reputation about the town, I'm told.'

'Who tells you this? What reputation do you mean?'

'That you have pretty young society women for breakfast, and pretty young whores for supper.'

'You believe this?'

'Let's merely assume there have been other women in your life. What do you do to them?'

'What do I do? . . . What do you mean what do I do?' He got up and stalked to the corner, where he sat under his portrait.

'Charles. I want to know what's expected of me. Here you are in my bedroom. Don't you grasp my . . . my situation? My reasonable uncertainty?' I felt myself smile suddenly. 'Reasonable, Charles.'

'For God's sake, Kit, I love you. I'm the uncertain one. Do you understand? I have fallen in love with you.'

'But what does that mean for me? What am I expected to do? Exactly.'

'Don't you have . . . some feeling for me? Kit, I'm supposed to be a busy man. A public man. And I'm . . . crucified. Forgive the reference.' He put his head in his hands to hold the frustration.

I heard myself sigh as I put down my sash, although my teeth were now clenched tight. I wished I could force myself out of my body; out of the room. Instead I started untying the bows at the front of my bodice. After a while he looked up.

'Good God. What are you doing?'

'Undressing.'

'Stop. Stop it at once. Do yourself up. By God's blood you'll see me under. Are you a whore? How many lovers have *you* had, Madam? And I thought I was assured of your absolute chastity.'

'You were what? How were you assured?'

Charles looked lost. He said: 'I've known you since . . . when was it? . . . Ninety-three?'

'Known me?'

'Known of you.'

'Had an eye on me?'

'Have you had lovers? You must tell me.'

'Lovers,' I said scornfully. 'How would I manage that?'

'Then . . . ' He turned away. 'Blood! You tie me in knots!'

'What do I have to do? That's all I want to know.'

'I . . . Excuse me.' He left.

Balance of Power

I thought I might have gained a week. In fact I gained a year.

After the interview I tried so hard to make sense of his sudden departure. Was this some sport? I suppose I was so blinded by my fear of men in general that I was slow to credit one with any hint of subtlety – either in action or reaction. At my most extreme I put it to myself that, being such a man of importance, he might just have remembered a more pressing appointment, and taken himself off without much ceremony. He'd be back to complete the encounter at any minute, any day. But this was a spook thought. In reality I'd seen his face, and knew from my saner reflections that what had actually rattled him was my undressing. Well then, expecting to be resisted he'd been put about by my compliance. The object of the experiment hadn't given the anticipated answers; so the projector had gone back to his desk, and was reworking his hypothesis. I'd have a week at a guess. Yes, it would probably take him a week.

It was something to do with doubts upon my virginity, a condition about which men were known to be famously excitable. He'd read my frozen submission as knowingness.

But why should signs of experience have put him off in any case? Surely my helpful gesture would have reassured – lessened the awkwardness of the encounter – ensured a smooth passage and heightened the pleasure for him.

I racked my brain. Was he concerned about doubtful paternity? Because he sought children? Immediately? There and then? Ridiculous. My mind ran round and round the curiosity of this business; this sudden discomfiture of the male.

Perhaps he feared an infection? But men visited whores. Charles himself had a reputation. True? Or lies in the Tory press? Whatever, men didn't expect exclusivity there. And what was the difference in my own case? What would he say to that?

He would say Love. And he did.

I know not what to write, Madam, and yet write I must. You have turned my soul about so that I cannot eat or sleep, nor hardly attend to my business, which is severe at present notwithstanding the setbacks I have lately suffered. Much is demanded of me by this uncertainty in the world, this international Crisis, even though I am out of my Office; yet I cannot give time and thought to all these pressing, needy matters. And party men come to trouble me with this turn and that turn: without limit are the policies, lies and scandals that are put about by those who seek to ruin every achievement of our Revolution. That I should have been outrageously traduced and hounded from a distinguished Ministry; this was as nothing. Those who have power to change whole nations, and use it, must expect calumny and betrayal. All such attacks (and I am monstrously set about by this generation of jackals, their parasitical hacks and political blisters) have stung me not at all, since I have been protected round and armoured by my thoughts of you. My early, soft and constant admirations of you, my anxious fears for your life, my tender care for your safety, and my anticipations of joy at your return, all these made me invulnerable; and (permit me the sudden variation in my figure; I have not wit left now to make all smooth) led me to dream of a safe haven in your arms awaiting my outrunning of the storm. But where am I now? Landed indeed on your home ground, yes; but overthrown at the first hold like an unapt voyager who ventures his strength at a inland Fair. And why am I thus brought to disorder? I know not. It is You. Of that I am sure, because my thoughts run on you by day and by night. But, Madam, I cannot come to you again. I do not see your colours. Invasion? You have invaded my heart and, Madam, done there your absolute mischief. In truth I know not whether you are angel or witch, nor can I tell what is my right course with you. So that in the very telling you of my enslavement to your Beauty, I defeat my own intention; which is to stay further removed until such time as I may know myself myself again. Therefore, you shall find me strange if we must meet, and though I long to see you, I shall seek to force the sphere of my activities far from its lovely Centre; or I fear for my wits, Kit. Thus with pain I own myself still your

Charles

Here was one fraught soul, struggling with his words; my uncle was another.

'Have you read this, Kit? The consequences! It is appalling!' Everyone had jitters to a certain extent, because the Prince of Bavaria had died and the Spanish succession, I remember, was tumbled into a new query. The great European powers agonised on the brink of another all-out war. We'd just upset our soldier King Billy with the disarmament issue, and the Blue Guards had marched back to Holland. Lacking Charles's authority, and with Minister Somers under attack too, the Commons was a shambles; nothing could be decided upon. The Stock Exchange plummeted. Everywhere people talked of invasion by the French Papists, or the Irish Papists, or looked for underground Jacobite terrorist organisations. The Jacobites put about counter-stirs of a neo-radical threat. Levellers and Diggers under your beds. Then there were the Scots, who woke up that year to discover that they'd invested most of their national wealth in the delusion of a mercantile colony in Panama – the Darien scheme – a private-enterprise bubble set up by a friend of Charles's which had burst utterly to pieces. They weren't well pleased.

Against this background, and with the anxiety of my illness, my uncle had indeed suffered a relapse into his paranoiac melancholia. He was now Master of the Mint. Sometimes he couldn't go there, but sat all day, sunken and sighing, in his great chair – except for nervous breaks, when he'd creep to the window and poke his unwigged head round the drape to tell whether there were spies posted. If anyone knocked at the front, he'd stand with his shoulder against the saloon door, ready to withstand the forces of the Enemy, should they try to burst in and have him. The Enemy was unspecified. Two things I gathered from his slips of speech: one, that They, or He, would blazon it out that he'd had dealings with lewd women, which he hadn't: or two, that the press would tattle his religious deviance, which was dangerously true.

'Charles, Catherine. Where's Charles? Why doesn't he come? Why doesn't he call? I've sent to him, but he puts me off. What have I offered him to be insulted like this? All the affection between us these years! Pah! Nothing but trickery and ill-usage. Take a note, Catherine. Send to him straight.' I fetched some paper and a pen. 'Tell him he's no more than a puffed-up little rogue. That's the man exactly. Which of *my* pockets has he had a hand in while he's been my guest at my table? Ha!' He grunted this out violently. 'Filcher! Yes, Filcher! Ha! That's about right for him. It seems the papers are true after all. I call him out. The man is a toad. A damnable little puffed and croaking toad. Tell him I call him out, Kit. Wherever he pleases and with whatever instruments. Send it, Kit! Send it straight!'

'Yes, Sir.'

Because of me this crazed communication never left our house; but also because of me, no Charles called to comfort him. Sometimes he wept sentimentally. 'Charles. Charles. My one, my only true friend.' Sometimes he turned his tall figure on me.

'I never laid a finger on *you*. *You're* not the true disciple. It was your fault. It was your own fault. The disease was God's punishment. And you can thank Him about your wretched face, not me. Go on. Thank Him. Down on your knees, boy. By, I'll thrash that look out of you.' And I had to go down on my knees there on the rug in the saloon, while he watched and watched me; until Mary's knock rescued me from the stillness of our joint trance.

On good days, when he'd forgotten all this spleen, and he had liberty, he spent hours closeted up with his attractive young friend Hoppy Haynes (at least that was what Pet and I called him – his true name was Hopton), poring over Biblical prophecies and patristic texts from his shelves; trying, I guess, to sort out the Timing of the Last Days. But on several later occasions, when he was back in a bad fit of agitation, I had to send to the Mint and have Hoppy hauled

94

over to our house. He was the only one who could calm him down – though I don't think he sang to him.

And then there was the business of Sarah Stout.

That summer the Tory rat-pack was still making hay with this perfect scandal. One of our party's up-and-coming stars (I say *ours* – you see me learning to live among my people) whose name was Cowper, I think, MP for Hertford, had a brother called Spencer. Yes, Spencer Cowper. Sarah Stout was the daughter of a well-to-do Hertford Quaker family; she became passionate about Spencer, who was already married. He was a barrister, and so he travelled the circuit. And avoided her. However, soon after I came to London, he'd been in Hertford at the Spring assizes, and had business reasons actually to call on Sarah to deliver some money. The next morning her body was found in the weir.

The anger generated by this monstrosity, in the family and the locality, led to a curious Quaker–Tory alliance. The Tories saw their chance both to threaten our man's seat and to generate a truly spicy London story, which would run and run. Spencer Cowper had been arraigned for murder. His trial was due to come on.

But we were more closely involved. Dr Sloane, secretary to the Royal Society – his name was Hans; a very famous doctor – was called as one of the London witnesses for the defence; because the case turned on the instability of the girl's mind, and the defence was suicide.

I listened with concern to the conversation between my uncle and Dr Sloane as they sat in our room preparing the groundwork for the hearing.

'Have you not heard? There are crowds here in London declaring for Cowper, and crowds declaring for Stout. Have you not been about on the streets? Or to the coffee houses?'

'Forgive me, Sloane. My distemper.'

'What's the matter, Mister?'

'I don't publish it. Something of melancholic spirits.'

'My services?'

'I treat it myself, Sir. And Kit.' He looked over at me where I was at some writing or other, keeping my head down. 'What are the facts of the matter?'

'The facts of the matter are these: a good-looking, forward, unstable girl designing on the career of an able young man. She makes away with herself, and the family look for blood. There was something wrong with her; they've had to accept that.'

'Something wròng?' my uncle enquired.

'*Hysterica passio*. Abnormal obsession. Suicidal impulses previous to the death. These cannot really be in question.'

'Impulses of what kind?'

'She threatened to throw herself out of the upper window. This was witnessed. She took care to be restrained. Other incidents of a theatrical nature.'

'And the obsession?'

'Likewise acknowledged. The known sexual levity before she conceived this extraordinary physical desire for the young man. A letter from her to him is admitted. Her feelings clearly well beyond the female . . . gamut. Then there's the religious excitement and . . . '

'Religious excitement?'

'The girl was no doubt tightly governed by the Brotherhood she grew up in. This has been, in my observation, often a source of . . . maladjustment in that sex. She publicly called out on a man in her community. She made herself, shall we say, an exhibition. It might be said she courted notice; and courted her own disaster.' I looked up at my uncle's ashen face. The subject disturbed him.

'And you're called to Hertford? In what capacity are you to witness in the trial?'

'The corpse was found floating. This, by the simple-minded local physicians the Tories have suborned, is said to indicate that the girl was alive when she entered the water.'

'So she would have been if she had drowned herself.'

'But the Quaking family assert that suicide is unthinkable for one of their members. So they claim the strangulation was only partial before the body was committed to the weir pool. The case is a morass of contradictions. There were no marks on the neck. Nevertheless the charge of murder was laid. They have even bought in common sailors to testify. Although to what exactly we shall have to wait and see.'

'The thing is a nonsense,' said my uncle, unsteadily. 'What do you consult me about?'

'I wished to check my opinion about the floating with yours.'

'A body in water would be subject to the force of gravity,' said my uncle, 'but so would the water. It's a relative density problem, and dates back to Archimedes. It would depend upon the quantity of air left in the . . . corpus.'

'But we are not in the capital for the hearing, Newton. Some of these people remember swimming witches. To them water is God's instrument of divination. It may declare evil. It may exhibit the guilt of a murderer by floating up the innocent relic to the eyes of the world.'

'Superstitious folly!' exclaimed my uncle.

'But there it is,' returned Sloane. 'All the world are not yet men of science.' He placed his big fingertips together. 'Then,' he went on delicately, 'if it isn't about the water, there remains the genuine question of the difference between human substance and the inanimate creation. Whether the laws that apply to Matter apply equally to . . . Us. Murder is a crime against Nature herself.'

'I cannot help you, Sloane,' said my uncle after a pause. Outside, the hot Summer blue had converted itself to inky heaps. It started to rain very hard. 'I cannot risk myself in this embroilment. This wretched female threatens to pull us all into the vortex. Do you see I am ill? No, I think you don't. I wish I could help, my friend. Kit will tell you I am not myself these months. Today there's been some improvement, but it is subject to variations. I desire you very earnestly not to mention this about, Sloane, on your honour and as we are friends. But I can't risk myself if there is this . . . ' he hesitated for so long, 'uncertain element in the case. Forgive me. Forgive me. But you'll be alright. I gave my poor opinion. You must see to it that our young friend is acquitted. We are threatened in this.'

Ostensibly he meant the Whig Party. I forced the nib of my pen against the paper until it split. Then the quill itself buckled. I picked up my things and left the room.

That night I lay in bed with Pawnee. I felt an amazement which alternated with anger. I should have liked to talk it all out with her, but it was a half-formed incommunicable anger. I, like London itself, found myself torn between the claims of the victims in the case. Supposing the facts as given to be true: a young man has business in a difficult situation and walks honourably into it with a couple of colleagues. The next day he finds himself inexplicably thrown into jail, to sweat for a year under the shadow of the noose. Terrible. But the girl! What echoes of my own state did her story start up within me. I didn't hear the differences; I heard so loudly in my own mind the note of her charged activities. All that. I knew, I knew, she was trying to speak, yet couldn't. There were no words for what she meant to say. I didn't know them either, yet I knew so well how desperately, how impossibly she'd been driven. I recognised her; and I recognised in all that the two great men had said, the unmistakable certainty of the closing of ranks. Everyone and everything around this dead girl, the waving of arms, the calls for blood, the rallying round, public furore, political exploitation, represented a diversion from the truth of the matter, so automatic as to be utterly unquestioned, and utterly horrifying. It was a truth I did and did not know. That night I dreamed I was in the weir, and that Cowper was acquitted.

My uncle took a severe turn for the worse. He began to believe it was he who was to be put in the dock – because he had published, he said. Because he had published his *Principia*. He thought it a strong possibility that he would be sent for directly, and that things would go against him, and that he would be hanged at Tyburn. He was immobilised with this, panting in fear, by day and by night, until the shambles of a trial was over and Cowper was acquitted, as in my dream. Then he grew stronger. But the girl was dead.

I nursed him. He, in time, recovered – or at least got back to normal. Our year went on and Charles stayed away – even from London a good deal of the time. What influence I'd achieved by doing almost nothing! By undoing a lace, it seemed. I wrote in my project my speculations about Charles's loss of impulse and fall from power. I wrote Sarah's name several times, with spaces between. These voids were the only way I could signify what I somehow knew but couldn't express. She presented her own gaps. Perhaps you'll wonder how I followed up my insight as to the singing and the memory. I tell you I put it from me. No, I'm not angry with you. Just reckon will you at my uncle compelled so to invent an emotionless universe that he spent all those years in the making of it and all these in the maintaining of it. That was his solution. And if mine is by definition the opposite of it do you think I go in there easily? Then Pawnee and I were taken up with the ripening, delivery and coddling of Etta's baby. Etta survived. She too was acquitted.

Mirror

'Captain Kidd brought me here,' said Pawnee, 'and I don't want to be reminded of him living. But as to his death . . . ' It was the Summer of 1701. The papers were advertising the hanging of Kidd in Execution Dock. He'd been extradited from New York the previous year – and that had been another of the Party's worries; but I won't go into that now. 'I'm not surprised he turned out to be such a despicable criminal all over the world,' she continued. 'If he's to die I want to see it done. I'd do it myself. Our women know how to control the dying of a man. I'd begin with needlework. I'd sew his balls to his tongue.'

Charles's stand-off was mitigated in the spring by a new tactic, which showed he'd regained something of his self-confidence: he'd placed a coach at my disposal, with two men and a gun. He'd survived the attempt to impeach him, along with Somers and Cherry Russell, the great Admiral, for his part in the peace-making plan of all Europe, the Partitioning of the Spanish Empire. They, the Tories, had accused him of selling out England's commercial interests. Charles! In the Commons the impeachment succeeded. In the Lords, where there was a small Whig majority, it failed. He'd been made Baron Halifax of Halifax – or some such title. This meant that, having survived their time of trial, the four great Whig leaders, Somers, Russell, Wharton and Charles, could operate on government together. They were all in the House of Lords, where the real power still lay, although the Commons held the purse-strings. They got exactly what they wanted. Hence the coach; with arms on the door. It was a great gift, and would have been a great temptation to a regular virgin. But I was not so much open to temptation as confused, as I've said, about what on earth I was supposed to be feeling. For two months I refused to use it, and the coachmen, Tom and his younger cousin Graveling, spent their time trying alternately to seduce Pet. They both claimed success. One claimed Mary as well. These things I overheard.

But to please Pawnee I relented, and we drove to the hanging, where the insignia on the doors of the coach secured us a fine view, courtesy of the Admiralty. Together, through the window, we watched the strangulation of the piratical old rapist who'd been entrusted with making the seas safe and instead had made them ten times worse. It was a moving and horrible sight; Pawnee found it gratifying, while I was overcome with sickness and the memory of Nicholas. I told her of him. I said there was a man whom I myself would have to see to the death of, but that I was now too liberal and feminised, and doubted whether I still had the stomach for it.

That night, 'Of course it would be a most unchristian thing to do,' Pawnee lectured me. She had been very well brought up, and knew the difference between judicial punishment and a private hit. 'But an intoxicating one. You might leave it to me. I might do it for you, Kit, if you believe you've lost your nerve. Or we both could bring it about. But if the truth were to be told I'd regard it as *your* duty. I had a husband in America. Whom I loved.'

We lay together in my bed as we did when she stayed over. I believe it was past midnight, but my mind still ran on the subject. 'It will be very difficult.' I said. 'Nevertheless I *shall* kill him.' Pawnee turned over towards me, nestling her cheek into my shoulder. The word Elizabeth flashed into my awareness and then out again. The odd perfume of Pawnee's clean neck and powdered braids moved me. I put my arm around her as I lay on my back, looking up at the flicker patterns the last inch of candle made on the ceiling. My hand rested through her shift on the soft flesh of her waist. Her breasts were only a few dangerous inches from my fingers. My body stirred; the wrong body. I thought of the hanged sea-dog. I knew my unutterable loneliness.

But then the eerie sensation came to me that we were not quite so alone as I thought. I felt observed. I was convinced. It was a compelling intuition.

'He sees us, Pawnee.'

'Who? God?'

'No. Well . . . That's as maybe. I don't know. I mean *he* sees us. His eye is on us.'

I got out of bed and took the candle from the save-all. Shivering slightly, I inspected the wall opposite, for my bed-head lay towards the exterior of the house. I held the candle stub up to the portrait of Charles.

'What are you doing? Kit? Is it a spirit? Take care. Keep still.' She came out of the bed and took my shoulders from behind; I felt her peering past my ear at the wall and the picture as if to share my enquiry. 'There are lots of spirits in this street. I see them often. Your uncle has seen them I think. You don't want them in your bedroom. Show me, Kit.'

'It's not a spirit, Pawnee. It's him.'

'Who? His Chancellor of the Exchequer Lordship? Turn him round. To face the wall. Take his coach but take him down if he troubles you.'

'He does trouble me, but the him I mean is my uncle. Now where should he be at this time of night?'

'He's gone to bed. He wished me goodnight in the corridor.'

'Then where is his eye?' I examined the frame of the picture, the carvings below the mantelshelf, the crack in the plaster that led like a long forking spark in the red wash. Then I looked up, trying to make out in the uncertain light any tell-tale flaws in the moulding at the ceiling's edge.

'His eye? Mr Newton's eye? I don't understand. I don't understand you at all, Kit.'

So I turned to face her. The candle flickered between us, lighting up her strange face like the icon I'd seen put up for a curiosity at Mr Locke's.

'I told you I was once a boy.'

'You told me.'

'As a boy I was different. Dangerous. Not normal. They had to tie me up. When he – my uncle – lived in Cambridge he drilled a spyhole in the wall.'

'A spyhole?'

'To . . . look at me.'

'He couldn't bear to look at you in the ordinary way? You were too ugly?'

'I believe I was . . . not a good sight. But this was to catch me undressing for bed.'

'Ah,' she said. 'I see.' She looked at me, her brow furrowed in concentration. 'Where can we be in this room that we know we are not seen?'

'I can't guess. He's so clever,' I found myself whispering.

We grew more rooted to the spot. She whispered back: 'Is he a sorcerer? It may be he has a mouse in the skirting, or a moth in the curtains of your bed. And these would relay to him what they have seen and heard.'

'No. He hates all that sort of thing.'

'But he changed you into a woman!'

'That was different. That was the projection for the Stone.'

'Not sorcery?'

'Not in the way you mean.'

'How was it done then?'

'I can't imagine. But . . . ' I was exasperated – not with her; with him. 'Who can tell what is and what isn't? I thought once that having become a girl it would all be different. I thought he just quite liked me. And that we should be together in London while I . . . grew into my real self. Became the person I was destined to become. Pursued my revenge.' I sat down on the bedcover, where she sat too, and touched the stray curls of my hair. 'But I've begun to grasp that being a . . . female, I've become – well, massively significant to him.' She traced the curl down the outside of my ear and the curve of my neck. I felt the tips of her nails. 'Pawnee. I am an object of his further projection. I hate it. And if it's to be here – I mean the spyhole – which I believe it will be – it must be – it'll be some contrivance of lenses and prisms.' I turned myself back to my impassioned scrutiny of the walls and fittings. 'It has to be here. Somewhere.'

'Or mirrors!' She gestured up at the convex glass on the chimney-breast.

'Ha!' I said. 'Or mirrors!' Could mirrors also pry? I jerked my wrist and the hot wax splashed over my fingers. I dropped the stump, which went out on the floorboards. Darkness.

'He can't see you now.' I felt her hands steal under my arms and cradle my breasts, through my shift, in each palm. I caught my breath as my mind raced. I became absolute intellect. All I could think about was that the mirror was mounted against a cavity, and that if it were some magic eye the viewer would have to conceal himself up the chimney. Impossible. A good try, but impossible. What about some hidden telescope in the opposite wall, focused on the mirror and concealed by the top rail of my bed? But that was an outside wall and the viewer would have to be up a ladder in the night air. Impossible. I allowed the hands to drift me back to the bed; sliding my feet tentatively in the dark. The focal point of a convex mirror was virtual. What would be the optical implication of that if one wished to mount a prism such that the rays . . . At the foot of the bed the hands unclasped in order to press me round by the arms and buckle me backwards into the sheets. Of course, the principle employed in the construction of the Newtonian, or reflecting, telescope involved the examination of a real image by a magnifying eyepiece of the astronomer's choice . . . Something was insisting my garment over my head. My arms were up above me, compliant. Perhaps a combination of prisms might duct the light beams round a series of corners so that the hypothetical viewer needn't in fact be up a chimney or ladder but might be somewhere else. The covers were pulled over me. Naked skin was pressed all along the length of my body. A hand was trying to push itself under my shoulders. Another touched my nipple with its warm palm. The breath of lips fell on my cheek. But then there arose the problem of the focal length, didn't it, and in any case the image was still unreal.

'Pawnee,' I croaked out. 'I don't know who I am.'

But there was no reply in the lightlessness.

Ruth

There followed a gross, premenstrual day, although I was nowhere near due. I couldn't look at Pawnee and so she left me to myself and went to Etta's. I could not settle nor eat with any conviction. My uncle also kept out of my way, and I heard him telling Charles's man, who came to call, that I was out of sorts. Eventually I shut myself in my room, and read some fiction, that business of fabricating lives; but as it grew dark I began to be more and more *focused* on last night. I glared up at the convex mirror.

When it was truly night I went and got two candles, lit them and placed them on the mantelshelf. In their light I faced the mirror, reached to unlace myself and pulled down my bodice and stays. I held my sore breasts up at the eye, squeezing them and wincing, and pushing them towards it.

'There, damn you,' I muttered. 'Take a good look. If that's you. And if you're looking.'

Then I put out one of the two flames, taking the other on a small search, until I'd fished out of the bottom of my oak chest the wig I'd stolen, the restraint coat, and the old breeches. Within half an hour I was creeping down the back stairs to the kitchen with a purse of coins in my pocket. By the scullery rack there was an old hat of Tony's. I dragged its ridiculous shape on to the top of my disguise and left. Then I came back for the spare key.

The woman stood under somebody's lantern by the last wall before the edge of the park, lamp-lit and moon-washed. The sentry-boxes stood empty; the Princess of Denmark was at Windsor, still mourning the loss of the hydrocephalic Duke of Gloucester, that single little token she'd hoped to salvage from the wreckage of her womb.

'What'll it be, Sparky?' she said as I came up to her. Then she looked more closely. 'Christ, what have we got here? Where do you keep your cash, soldier?'

'How much?' I tried to make my voice sound grating and low.

'Depends what you want.' Her face was pasty and painted. I gave her a guinea.

'Jesus!' she said. 'You got any more where that came from? You can marry me for that, I don't care what sort of a nosebag you look like.' She put her hands against my lapels and swam her face towards me. 'But I don't kiss, alright?'

I was an inch or two taller than she was. I pulled her against me and forced my mouth on to hers. She wrenched away and eyed me carefully. There was still light enough, really, now that we were away from the wall, but the moon offered no colour. Half crouching, she pulled something out of her skirts. I thought it might be a small kitchen knife. 'Fucking hell,' she said. Then turned, ran into the park, caught her skirt and stumbled towards the long grass. I threw myself after her – it was her attempt to escape that did it. She fell. I stood over her. The hem of her skirt was up round the backs of her knees. Just as I bent down and yanked it further to disclose her naked backside she struggled up on to all fours. I covered her with my self. My teeth were at her neck. She thrashed over, more to escape from my teeth, I imagine, than from anything else I was doing. I collapsed on her front. I tried to guard against her arm but felt the knife's point jabbing ineffectually at my coat – even so, my other hand forced its way under what minimal protection the twist of her skirt left her there, seeking to violate the hair and clamp of her thighs with my fingers and nails even as I still bruised away at her with my hips.

She cried out: 'Alright, Charlie! Alright. You've paid your money. Don't rip the bloody goods.' She was breathing fast and frightened.

'Do what you want and get it over.' Her face slumped to the side, resigned. 'Only use a suit will you. For both our fucking sakes.'

'A suit?' I said in my false voice.

'A suit of armour. Oh for Christ's sake, haven't you got one? Here.' She fumbled in her pocket, then held out a small disc-like object.

'Go on then.' She parted her legs and with her free hand hoisted up the few inches of skirt fabric still covering her front. 'Go on. I'm freezing my filly.'

I came to myself. Kneeling, I worked my grip out along her thin arm towards her wrist and pinned it to the ground so that the knife was no longer a threat. She looked upwards glassily; her eyes were wide and star-illuminated. 'Well?' Used to living on the edge of sexual violence, she wanted it over, the tension released, the bull cowed. I was paralysed for what to do, still holding her wrist to the ground. Moonlight flicked off the knifeblade. 'Oh let me go. I won't try to cut you.' She released the knife; I released her arm. 'You want me to put it on? I hope you ain't put marks on my neck.' She had become subtly mistress of the situation, reaching for the buttons of my breeches, opening the flap, starting to slip her hand inside, as she looked up at my face at last. At the same moment I realised my wig and hat were no longer with me.

She made a little scream, and pulled her hand out. Then the whole atmosphere changed. She relaxed. 'Well. Now I've seen it all. Gentleman Fanny, the female cannibal.' She looked me coolly in the eye. 'Don't reckon you're much to be frightened of, dear. Where's my knife?' She pulled down her skirts and stood up, turning her back on me, hunting about in the moonlit grass. She found the knife and stowed it. I got, trembling, to my feet. She had a hand stuck through the placket of her skirt still, delving like a schoolboy. 'Ohhh! Where's that fucking guinea?' she muttered, standing still, completely ignoring me, and bodysearching herself. 'No!' She stamped her foot. 'No! It must've fallen out!' She dived down into the grass again.

'I'll help you look,' I managed to say. It shone silver-lit gold at my feet. 'Here.' I held it out to her. 'Not worth what it was. Twenty-one shillings, since the recoinage,' my voice quavered.

Once again she seemed unsure. Watching me very cautiously, she stretched out for it, took it, held on to it, looked round at the park, and seemed to decide against running; as if the extent of space was too great to offer escape. She checked her dress instead, looking

behind herself – 'Hope we didn't choose any dogshit to roll about in.'
Then, turning back at me, she decided to play the moment out. 'Well,
what is it for you?' she said. 'What were you hoping to achieve?' she
mocked my society vocabulary. 'Like a bit of the same side, do you?
Twenty-one shillings?'

'I don't know,' I said. 'I don't know who I am.' It sounded ridiculous. I felt ridiculous.

She came closer, reaching out, touching my hair, framing my face.

'Fucking hell, you're quite the goods. You could have a rich nob
after you. You could, you know.'

'I have,' I said. Her painted face was gaunt.

'So, what . . . ? How . . . ?' She shook her head, despairing of me,
uncomprehending. Eventually: 'What did you want to do to me?'

'When did you last eat?'

She laughed. 'What sort of eat?'

'I'll buy you food. Now. Some place. Where shall we go?'

'Here,' she stooped to collect my wig. 'Hold still.' She rearranged it
over my hair, tucking in the strays. Then she found the hat and stuck
it on top. 'Are you going to bite?' Her cheek was near my cheek.

'No,' I said. 'Not now.'

'Take me out then, Pussy.' She put her arm through mine, trusting.
It was all ridiculous, quite impossible. 'Somewhere where they can't
afford candles, though. What a bloody sight we must make.'

We promenaded through the London night, intimate wanderers. She
told me her name was Ruth. I told me mine was Henrietta. We
crossed the river. I paid the boatman; we pretended to be courting in
the back seat while the little boat swung and dipped on the tide.
Ruth smelled of musky resin mingled with the sharp odour of her
own body – a reminder of fear, perhaps. I don't know what I smelled
of. Confusion swirled up in my body again – you'd call it now a
sexual confusion. What did I want from her?

As we climbed steps at the far bank, her nearness made me ache,
but the oddity of our situation coloured all with caution. The district
was both dark and busy; it was the other side. Under a coarse sign
we turned into a cheap pot-house, which was, as we'd wished,
poorly lit. As I ordered her a meal it occurred to me to wonder if my
remaining guinea wouldn't be too big a piece for the server to
change. And how would I get back across the river?

When we'd finished the pie and were sipping the brandy and water I asked to see the suit. She fished it out of her folds and held a slightly opaque, rolled-up device across the table for my inspection. She had pretty hands; her under-wrists were scarred.

'How does it work?'

'When your work's got a stand, he sticks it on the tip and rolls it down. That's only with these fine ones, though. These are the best sort. Cost the most. Otherwise there's any old bit of sheep's insides. Look.' She took the kitchen knife, the same one that had damaged my coat, and held it up so that the handle was clear. Then she started to roll the suit down the handle. 'See?' she said. 'Then he gets on with it the blither, thinking at least he's not going to get fired out this time. And the better he feels the more generous he's likely to be. Hard to roll back up.' Completing her efforts, she stowed it carefully away.

'Does it protect you from him?'

'Supposed to. I've been caught though.'

'You have? That's terrible.'

'Terrible. I should bloody say so.' She went for a pair of pipes from the server. 'You?'

I shook my head. Two men stood up from in front of the fire, the one steadying the other to the door. We moved to sit side by side on their settle. Our talk was broken while the ritual of filling and lighting took place. I watched in amazement as she hurled the glowing knob of charcoal from the tongs back into the burn with practised ease, and spat after it.

'This stuff's supposed to help; but I don't believe it makes much of a toss. If you get it, you get it.'

'Does the suit stop the . . . child?'

'It might do. And if you get the work out of you soon as he's come off. That's what most of the girls try to do. And stand up so that the whatd'you call it, the homunculus, can't crawl up you. Maybe jump up and down a bit,' she laughed. 'That's what my Mum said, anyway. Didn't do me no good. I was fourteen. But the child died.' She drew on the pipe, pulled herself nearer the fire and pulled her skirt up like a peasant woman. 'Let me get some of that heat on my William and Mary,' she said, and lolled her head back. 'And two others didn't last the course, thank God. Mostly I try to block myself up before I go out. That's our favourite foible. Plenty of girls still fall, though.' She sucked on her pipe. 'When I bloody fall next time, I don't know what I'll do. Mrs Clog for me, I guess. Nobody loves you when you're stuffed.'

'Mrs Clog?'

'Trade secret.'

I looked at her as she stared into the fire, sipping her brandy. Something in me was ravished by the tragic freedom of her statements, her demeanour, and her history. It was freedom in the wrong sense, but she was my Sarah Stout, perhaps, ten times multiplied in ruin. She was another gap, one of those breaks in the smooth tale folk told themselves. Her naked knees were spread, the soiled ruffles of her hems rested, turned back, on her pale thighs; she'd pulled off the coarse handkerchiefs and eased her stays so that her breasts were loose under the bodice. She was in the act of taking her hair down now, black edging the tired paint of her profile. I wanted to keep her; to put her in a jar; keep her from her tomorrow. And the next day.

'Your wrists?'

'When I was nine. Next time I'll go in the river. That's favourite with girls round here.'

'Where shall I find you again?' My heart ached. For her, and for myself perhaps. It wasn't like me to respond so strongly to another creature. I felt strange; overpowered; as if we'd sat here for ever.

'Why?'

Then tears pressed at the back of my eyes and I turned away in my fool's clothes; clothes that were a travesty of gender, of identity.

'You want to sleep with me tonight? Cuddle up?'

'No,' I said. My eyes started to overflow. 'All the world is so wretched. All that might be beautiful is defiled. And no one cares. No one cares.'

Two women came in for brandy. An old man emerged from the upstairs, stretched, looked very hard at me in the half-light and spat into the fire before he turned away.

She took my hand and cradled it in hers. 'You're in a poor way, aren't you, Mr Puss? Plenty of money it seems and no merrier than the rest of us. Has this rich work of yours got you poked up?'

It took me a moment to grasp what she must be meaning. 'No.'

Then my emotion overcame me. She pulled me over so that my head rested in her lap, and put the wig to one side on the seat. Her fingers smoothed my own hair, smoothed my brow, and my bump.

'Where shall I find you again?' I moaned. 'By that wall? By the park?'

'I'll come to your bloody door for a guinea,' she said. 'No questions asked. But I don't see what you want out of it. And maybe you're some lure. I don't follow tonight.'

'Neither do I,' I said.

'What's he like?'

'My rich work?'

'The very one,' she laughed. 'Is he clean?'

'Clean? I suppose so. I haven't exactly seen him wash his hands.'

'No, Henrietta. Has he the pox?'

'I don't know,' I said. 'That guinea. How long will it keep you?'

'Depends if I hand it over or keep it.'

'Hand it over?'

'Nothing's for free, dear.'

'If you kept it. How long?'

'I donno.'

'How long would it keep you from . . . working?'

'Where I live I'd have to work.'

'You could get somewhere else.'

'What're you trying to do?'

'I want it to stop. I want you to be free of it. I'll give you more.'

'It doesn't stop, dear. It never stops. One half of the world fucks the other half, and that's the way it goes on.'

She knocked her pipe out. I sat up and put my arms round her. She pulled away at first, then allowed her head cautiously on to my shoulder. 'This is a bloody mad night,' she said.

'Say the guinea kept you out of it for a week. I could get you some more.'

'What do you get out of it, sister? What's your pay? Are you trying to place me up for someone? Or are you . . . Oh I don't bloody know. I can't think. Perhaps there was something in that bacca. Perhaps when I wake up you'll turn into an ordinary work.'

'Try me,' I said. There was a shouting outside, matched by a shouting upstairs. Shortly a man and a woman came down. The man was drunk. He sat briefly next to Ruth and started some sort of a conversation; I say briefly because the server and the woman pulled him up and walked him out into the air. Yet that was enough to alert me to the danger of the place and the unstable hour.

'Help me get home,' I said. 'How can I get back across the river?'

I remember her body against me as she adjusted my wig back on. I recall waiting on the quay in the dark.

'Will you give me the suit?'

'Oh, so that's what you want?'

'No, that was an afterthought. It'd be a help.'

She took it out from her pocket again and looked at it affectionately. 'They're like gold-dust, these. Quality ones. Look at the bloody stitching on it. Well, if it was light you could see. I got this one off a sleeper. Banker, he was.'

'Sleeper?'

'He went straight to sleep after he'd come off. It was at an inn, all fine. You can dine out for a month if a well-off work drops off on you. This was part of my score.'

'Can you get me one?'

'You're serious, ain't you?'

'Serious.'

'They cost.'

'I'd pay your trouble. When shall I see you again? To give you the . . . I will get . . . I can get money. What we talked about.'

'Yes, dear.'

'Well; where, then? When?'

'You bloody mean it, don't you? You really think . . . '

'Two weeks,' I said. 'Same place. By the park. Same time.'

'I don't know what the bloody time was, Henrietta. You were sticking your hand up me if you remember, and trying to bite my head off.' She put a hand up to her neck. I kissed the faint mark left by my teeth.

'Ten at night. By the Abbey clock.'

'Alright.'

'You won't be there, will you?'

'I might.'

'I don't want you to have to . . . do it . . . any more.'

'Are you in love?'

'If you don't come, I'll wait the next week . . . fortnight . . . I don't know. You must come.'

I remember the high tide, the warm night breeze sweeping down the river against the race, making the crossing rocky and turning the boat

110

against the city skyline. The dark, unconversational figure of the boatman, working at the sculls, splashed me from time to time with a fine spray.

Light, Sound and Heat

One morning not long after, when I felt better, I made an attempt on the convex mirror. I decided in justice to my suspicions that I should carry out a thorough survey, despite its mounting on the chimney-breast.

It was positioned slightly above where it would be most use, and was set firmly into the plaster. I couldn't budge it. I decided I must look behind it, though. I took a candle and got a light for it, and knelt in the fireplace, sweeping my skirts about in the traces of cinder dust, and poking my face up into the black void above. The candle set light to my hair – just a curl or two – so that I caught the smell and beat it out in time. But not before I banged my head on the stone. Pet came in at that moment to hear my curse, with her brushes and duster, and her linnet. This linnet was a present from Graveling, one of my amorous under-employed coachmen. It was cramped into a tiny wooden cage which she took with her everywhere.

'Oh! Miss Kit!' she said, and put her things down so that she could dab the smuts off my face and do something about the rest of me. Then she saw my hair. 'Lord!'

When she'd gone, I resorted to one of my shell-backed hand-mirrors. I angled this under the chimney space and held the candle next to it. But the glare from the flame spoiled the observation. Finally, I solved the problem by tying the mirror with thread to the fire-iron shovel, and holding this in the right place; I steadied the candle behind and under it so that the flange of the shovel protected the shell from the heat.

There was something. Truly. A blackened tube connected the front of the chimney to its back at about the height of the convex mirror. My mouth felt dry. I sensed my prison.

Behind this chimney was a guest chamber. I investigated that for a connexion, but found nothing. My uncle's bedchamber was skewed off further round the landing. Impossible. Nevertheless I knew I must research it.

He was very fidgety about his room; it was always kept locked, and he took the key with him to the Mint in the fob pocket of his waistcoat. He said he had delicate things set up there, which was entirely likely. I could think of no way to get in.

But I determined to be bold and forceful. I went down to the kitchen and demanded my official housekeeper's bunch of keys from Mary. Then I applied each of them energetically to the door in turn. Although none actually fitted my uncle's lock, I was lucky to find one that would just force it. Here my boldness paid off.

Having checked that I was unobserved, I slipped inside. It was like stepping back ten years – to Cambridge days. In here there was no extravagant redness, no grotesque attempt at style. Plain chairs, his plain desk, his plain bed and the wonderful clutter of all his enterprises. Books lined the walls, instruments lay about on every surface, and, in a corner, there was even a partly dismantled alchemical furnace. But I had no time now to remind myself of all that; no matter how the old images flooded into my brain, triggered by this set of tools, that great clay crucible. I even made out, under a mountain of open books and miscellaneous note-sheets, the old horsehair couch I'd lain on after the change. No. I had work to do.

And, yes, I found what I was seeking. The desk stood next to his fireplace, which looked as though it was served by an entirely different chimney from mine. But over the desk, a species of thin boxed duct, decoratively carved to look like a regular fitting, ran horizontally along the wall towards the corner one way and the fireplace the other. At the latter end there was a little cupboard that seemed to grow up out of it and share the woodwork of the fire surround. I opened the doors to this; and found inside the prism, eyepiece and mount which were the true evidences of my uncle's art. A little notebook lay beside. I put my eye to the eyepiece, and saw – my bedroom, sharp and clear.

My heart raced, and my stomach turned over, so that I felt sick for a moment. I had to admire the wondrous craftsmanship and concealment of the device. Somehow the light from the half-silvered mirror in my room had been led undimmed through a series of, I supposed, exquisitely contrived prisms, and offered up to whatever magnification the gazer chose to fit into the mount. It was brilliant, and unnerving.

I wondered, though, why it might be that he'd taken so much

trouble to bring the image this far into the room. Surely it would have been easier to place the desk in the corner, nearer to the source of the rays, and catch them as they emerged from the aperture in the wall there. I put my eye back to the lens and saw Pet come into my room with her little birdcage. She started making my bed. Then, as if it were right next to me in the room, I heard the linnet chirruping. I even looked round in case it was. Sweet sounds of chatter song filled my ears. And now I understood the siting of the desk; the sound was coming out of the fireplace itself. Once more I was amazed at his skill: some sort of cross-piping between the two chimneys, so organized that the sound retained most of its quality in the journey. I watched and listened, fascinated, to Pet's activities in my room. I even saw the corners she cut, and wondered whether I should reprimand her for them later. I watched her pick her nose to the sound of the linnet, and scrape her finger on the back of my dressing-table. I watched her peer into my chamber-pot, then heard her use it, and park the receptacle by my door once she'd finished, ready to be taken out. I watched her scratch herself and clean herself, then make my bed. I was enraged, but I kept looking. I knew that by this act I'd changed my relationship with her for ever.

When she'd gone out and my anger had drained a little away, I speculated on the meaning of this. Why, I had become as a God, seeing into the secrecies of others' hearts by their actions. I had in some sense encountered truth. Indeed, I had in some sense created a new Pet. I had disturbed the surface and gone, frighteningly, beneath. But now what power I possessed over her whom I'd observed.

Still stirred by all these feelings and implications, I looked at the notebook. He was not so skilled a draughtsman as he was artificer. The indices of my gender were crudely marked but neatly labelled; my headless body was captured and dated on page after page. At least, I assumed it was mine. I left, and, having secured the room, felt myself in some degree of shock.

Charles was visiting us again.

He'd been to the races at Winchenden in Bucks, near Wharton's country seat, and spoke confidently and pleasantly to me about it all, as if there had been no hitch; as if we were nothing but old friends. We were never alone together.

My uncle gave a rallying 'Whig dinner', and invited also some of his scientific acolytes. Twenty places or more. We couldn't seat so many. It would have to be a stand-up buffet occasion, with the great table pushed to one side; and we should have to hire in chairs and little tables for people to sit around for cards and so on. I can't remember exactly who they were – I know Wharton was invited, and Russell – they'd been warned by Charles to behave themselves because of my uncle's sensitive primness – and Halley and Gregory must have been there. I believe I remember the levelling radical Lord Charles Spencer, who said he was on the point of renouncing his peerage and prospects of becoming Earl of Sunderland when his father died. I gathered Charles and the other Junto lords were working very closely with Spencer, whether because of his republican views or his marriage to Marlborough's daughter Anne, I couldn't make out. It was all shrouded in political secrecy. I did grasp that Spencer was very close politically with his mother-in-law, Sarah Churchill, who was the Princess of Denmark's intimate, they said. And there was somebody called John Smith. But I was the only woman; wives and mistresses were to have been left at home.

I should have liked the reassurance of my own slowly widening circle; I should have liked Betty Germain or Anne Long, not to speak of Etta. These London ladies seemed to know how to do everything, and to run their entertainment and liaisons with some casual deftness. However, at our soirée the likelihood of subtle conversation and quiet cards was minimal. I made it my business to buy in the best food, served by the best caterers, so that our reputation with these grandees shouldn't be compromised by my uncle's innocence about how much people actually ate and what they liked to drink.

When it came off, I tried to work out who was pulling whose strings, who was backing whom. And where the Master of the Mint fitted in. They all took over the house and were a roaring, but not actually offensive, company. Nevertheless I found myself uneasy in this scrum of confident, noisy men. Charles, I sensed, was preparing to renew his assault, on power and on me. This evening he made sure he was well wined; and the others, I noticed, left me alone, as if it was an accepted thing that I was his property. Although I put a good face on it, I felt truly crushed by the certain knowledge of my imprisonment, and the inevitability of my service in the cause of sex and science.

After the meal, Charles forsook the dispute that was being carried on about the vilification the Party was suffering in the press, and the consequent tactics that were required, to play Piquet with me. He said he'd had enough of the vilification business.

'But I've not had enough of you, Kit, though you put me about,' he whispered. 'Do you use the coach?'

'Not much.'

'You will use it, though?'

'Where should I go?'

'Go where you wish. There are sights enough to see.'

'Why have you given me the coach, Charles?'

'To show you I'm in earnest, Kit. I can't put your image out of my mind. It has continued for months. I tried to forget you, but I've had no success. You know I'm a wealthy man. I don't just trifle with you. I give you securities; pledges. If the time isn't as ripe as I thought it was between us; if you're not ready – if we're not ready; then I make some means to show you that my affections haven't cooled by our differences and our . . . difficulties. I know I'm impulsive, difficult myself. I don't like being crossed. I'm not used to it. I've sulked in my tent. And meanwhile in the House, the Junto – all hell let loose, sometimes. I work hard, Kit.'

It occurred to me in a sudden flash that if Charles was in a sense one of my jailers, he might also be the instrument of my escape. I could turn him to advantage if I really had some emotional hold over him. I opened the game.

'I shall be Elder. You're feeling worn out, so you shall be Younger.'

He dealt. Piquet is a mathematical game of constant ritual verbalisation, and so it was apt for us: I was becoming, like him, a politician of the new economics.

'Point of four,' I said.

'Making?'

'Thirty-nine,'

'Not good.'

'Queens and tens – six.'

I led an ace. It was the Ace of Spades. 'Seven.'

He capitalised on the symbolism because he was slightly tipsy, and given – he rated himself a poet – to this kind of figurative courtship. He whispered. 'When shall I die in your arms, my dearest, I wonder?' He counted his hand. 'Point of four – forty. And tierce to the jack – seven.'

'In?'

'Hearts. My hand on my heart; or yours it could be.'

I laughed. I felt suddenly safe enough in the company, even normal, since there might be a way out. I was challenged – there was a chink. 'How much have you had to drink?'

'Enough, Kit.' He played the Queen of Spades on to my Ace. 'Kit, you must have me. I'm burning still. Seven. There's an honour.'

'A quean rather. The Politician's quean. I lay to your Knave. That's how it seems to me, Charles. And that's how it'll seem to the papers.'

'What? The papers!' His face went stormy. 'By God, are you threatening me?'

'No. Of course I'm not. Be calm. There must be talk is what I'm saying. I shall be a target. I want to know what I'm expected to do. You don't intend marriage, I take it.'

'Kit. Be fair.'

'One hand, one night?'

'What do you think of me?'

'What, then, Charles?' My loud whisper. 'What? Why won't you tell me?'

'I'm to think of the progress of my passion for you like a dry old notary, am I? I have to spell out in advance what should be a matter of the heart, my feelings, my spontaneous emotions. You want me to court you as old Somers would?'

'I want to know who I shall be.'

Charles regarded the strewn cards. 'You want to cut a deal,' he said.

'You want a mistress,' I said. 'Yes? For how long?'

'I love you, Kit.'

'Love. No one can love me. Which part of me do you love?'

'Your heart. Do you love me?'

'I have no heart, Charles. It's one of my charms.'

He didn't know what to reply to this, I think. I smiled at him. We played out the hand. My last card, the ten of Clubs, leading, took his King of Diamonds. 'Sixteen. And the cards twenty-six. My hand. Your deal.'

'Why don't you tell my fortune?'

'The Tory news-sheets say you've made so much that no one can tell *your* fortune.'

'Rascals.'

I laid out the cards in a random manner, pretending to be very significant, as if I were a gypsy. He laughed again. I picked one and turned it over. It was a seven. 'Seven is my number,' I said. 'This card stands for the lady in the case.'

'Go on.'

I turned over another. It was a ten. 'And that's my card?' he said.

'No,' I said. 'Ten is the length . . . '

'You flatter me, Kit. I shall think of myself as a greater man.'

' . . . of time. It could be ten weeks; it could be ten months; it could be ten years. Or it could be ten minutes.' He laughed again. 'And the next card,' I said mysteriously, 'stands for the man in the case, and is the number of your coming.'

'It's what?'

'It's the number of your coming.' I turned up a deuce.

'What does it mean, Madame Kit?'

'It means you'll come once, you'll come twice, and you won't come again.' He roared with laughter and I joined him, so that the company turned round briefly to look at us. I remember Russell's eyebrows and the interruption of Wren's attempts, as always, to leave early.

'I am a virgin, Sir, as I am a woman,' I whispered, when it was safe to continue.

'You assure me of that?'

'As I am a woman. I want a contract. And you shall not have me in this house.'

'My God. A Pallas Athene.'

'Just a wise virgin. We shall be seen out together, but you must show the utmost formality. We shall not touch in public. We shall live separately. This would be obvious, but I spell it out. You shall not invite my family to town, nor do I want to see yours. You must give me money for my project.'

'Your project?'

'I have a project.'

'Your uncle's niece, I see. He has an academy full of projectors, half of whom are here tonight. What could a virgin's project be? Probability?'

'I have a project. A serious one. A secret one, for the moment, which you shall take seriously. And you must promise me one other thing. No – two.'

'Which are?'

'That when I ask you for information about mathematical or economic matters you'll answer my questions without trying to fondle me or see me as merely a woman. And that you'll help me kill a man.'

He gasped. 'Is that all?'

'In return I shall make over to your use those parts of my person that you're in love with.'

'Is that all now?'

'No. When you do it, you must wear a suit.'

'By God . . . Where did you . . . ? Damnation! How is it you . . . ? It's intolerable.' He got up and drank off his glass. 'I'll think about it,' he said, 'when my blood is cooler.' And, bending to kiss my hand, joined his friends. I went to look for Pet.

Emotional Research

The discovery of the mirror system proved that beneath the face of things there lay some other, unspoken text. On the surface there was family, housekeeping and polite society. But for some reason it was important for my uncle that I should be under surveillance. Well, surveillance gave a sense of power – I'd seen that for myself. Beyond that it conferred actual power, since I now knew things about Pet that I could, if I wished to, use against her. It followed that my uncle felt the need for power over me. It followed also that he must figure me as dangerous to him.

I checked that through again in my mind – I didn't dare commit it to my notebook, knowing now what I knew. Yes, it made a degree of sense; though it ran completely contrary to how I actually felt. I felt power*less*.

I formulated two hypotheses. The first was that my transformation from male to female during the production of the Stone threatened his reason and his status. That it had finished his career as a chemical projector, mathematician and experimental physicist I knew in a vague, childish sort of way. I'd known it all along – he'd told me himself. But being young we don't *understand* what we know. We don't see it in the context of another person's life, or from another point of view. Perhaps I began to understand it now; that it was as big an explosion for him as it had been for me.

I thought back. What had gone up in that moment? The bid for love – that was something I'd left out of the count absolutely. Yet he must have had that somehow invested in the experiment.

In addition, the permanence of gender. I wondered who it was had found me in the wreckage. I wondered whether the change had been instantaneous before their eyes, or subtle – for I'd little idea how long I'd lain unconscious. Who had noticed first? What had that person been doing, to notice? Who had wrapped me in all that frothy linen?

Leaving aside these details, the shift of sex must have frightened him immensely. That gender was mutable suggested Mercurius, which was all very well for the metal, but pretty disturbing in a real body. He'd been trying to kill off those pictures – to demythologise them; and their sexual connotations, I suspected. And had nearly succeeded. It could be that he was making this demonstration to Nick. I wondered just what advantage he'd been hoping for. An all-male world? A scientific world?

But then the whole thing had bitten back, in the shape of me. Yes, horrifying for him.

That brought me to my second hypothesis: that I was a prime opportunity to study the great enemy, the Whore – which was to say, thinking about it in his terms, woman in general. In this view, *I* was irrelevant except as a specimen. Yet as a specimen I was All. I was the Universe. I was a scintilla, a spark, a fragment which was not a piece broken off but itself mysteriously contained the whole in microcosm.

As such I was the climax of his whole Oeuvre, and he had not moved here to London in defeat, but for the realisation of his life's work – the detoxification of the Whore, Feeling Nature.

This was terrible. He *needed* to render me harmless to him.

I wondered if those little drawings he'd made had done the trick, as the focus for some ritual activity, like a little bargain with the Devil. Poor him. Poor me!

On the first fortnight after the meeting with Ruth I took Charles's carriage round to the edge of the park and waited. Tom and Graveling were edgy about the night call: 'What's this all concerning, Miss Kit?'

I made a joke about it and passed them up the smokes I'd brought them. They lit them from the householder's lantern that, public-spiritedly, lighted the wall as before. The Abbey bell sounded and we waited another half-hour. People passed, and the occasional coach. One or two dogs made their preoccupied way into the pool of light, sniffing into the base of the wall; but no Ruth came.

It was the same the next week. I had no one to whom I could pour out my feelings for her. The time I'd spent with her kept replaying itself in my recollection; while I helped Mary sort linen, while I checked over the ordering of provisions, while I sat reading in my bedroom under the eye; while I walked, while I made ready for sleep, while I attended the service on Sunday; while I longed for release. My heart, such as it was, yearned for her. For what of her? For her safety, perhaps. For her person? Perhaps. For her company, her condition and her suffering. She made me feel. I suffered the pangs of a lover for someone I might have hurt and might have relieved.

Do you notice how I seek to gloss over the fact of my assault on her? I notice it myself now that I'm further from it in my narrative: how I covered the deeds of that night with an account of chimney research under the formula 'when I felt better'. Even in the describing of it I sought to make it her fault – for trying to run away. I was ashamed. Am ashamed. And aware? Aware that what moved me to behave so was to look down on her exposure. Looking down – as if from ceiling height? The truth is very difficult. Easier far to occupy oneself with scientific investigation.

On the third time of waiting, when I was despairing of the agreement, and we were on the point of leaving, a skirted figure flitted out of the wake of a group of night folk into the edge of the lantern light. It stayed as they moved on. I opened the glass and called. She came over to the carriage. It was Ruth. She wore no paint. She saw me framed in the window and therefore, as I'd planned, she recognised me from my face rather than my attire. Breathing a sigh, I opened the door and got her in.

We sat opposite each other in the dark carriage, dressed this time both as women. She peered at me as if I were a curious portrait she was trying to make out.

'Christ. You *are* the bloody goods.' She felt the material of my dress, and leant forward to lift the hem, so that she could get an idea of the petticoats. 'Bloody hell,' she said, and sat back in the murk of dimness. 'Suits you.'

'I'm so glad to see you. I've thought of you . . . very much.'

'Why?'

I couldn't answer. Instead I reached for her hands and tried to look into her face. Without the paint I thought it showed its pain.

'I've brought more . . . money for you.'

'Why? What do I have to do?'

'You don't have to do anything. Look. Here.' I passed across a net of some of the new-minted silver coins my uncle was responsible for. 'And this.' It was a gold chain my uncle had given me. It had a gloam of a shine you could just see. She looked at the items with a degree of caution – as if she were reluctant to touch them.

'No,' she said. 'I can't take 'em. I don't see this. You don't get something for nothing. *I* bloody don't, anyway. There must be some hook. Something you want me to do.'

'There is,' I said. 'I want you to be free. I want you free of having to . . . work.'

'Work work, you mean.'

'Work work.'

'Why? What's it to you?' She looked at me hard. 'Are you trying to buy me? For yourself?'

'I want you to be free. I can't be free, myself. *You* must be.'

'Bloody hell,' she said. 'You can do what you bloody like with all this chinks.'

'I can't,' I said simply. 'I can't. But if you got a place, I thought, maybe this side, away from . . . where you are, you could set yourself up without having to . . . do it. And you could be whoever you wanted. You could be who you really are.' I was surprised to find the words coming out that explained what it was I hoped for.

'But this is who I bloody am.'

'With or without paint?' I asked.

'That doesn't make no difference. Except that getting here without it on was a bloody risky matter. When you've got your face up they leave you alone unless they want a go. Then they know they've got to pay for it – mostly. You go out at night without it you're fair game. So maybe I'm more at home with it on. I'm a whore, that's who I am.'

'And do you like whoring so much? Does it pleasure you?'

'Get me to come off, you mean? Fat chance.'

'Does it make you glad? Full of joy and freedom? Does it make you stand in the liberty wherewith Christ hath made us free, and not be entangled again with the yoke of bondage?'

'No it fucking doesn't. And don't give me none of that Christ palaver. I see what you're at now. My God, you're a bloody bent one. You want to save me, don't you? After you tried to get your hand up; and Christ knows what. Don't think I've forgotten, dear. You want to put it all right and bring a penitent whore back to God. You'll feel better then, dear, won't you? What's God ever done for me? I've had a parson or two I can tell you. Yoke of bloody bondage. I'm bloody off. I knew there was a hook.'

I knocked on the wood of the coach. Graveling flicked up the horses and we lurched forward. 'Don't go,' I said. I held her wrist. 'It's not what I mean. Not like that. I don't like churches. My father was a parson. My uncle thinks he's ... Listen, that's the only way I've heard it. About escaping. I am bound down. One of us must be free!'

'You're bloody Bedlam, darling,' she said softly, sensing I might be weeping, I believe. 'It's me that should look after you.'

'Now go, then,' I was crying. 'Take the coins; and the chain. Come again in two weeks. You must. I just want it to stop. Do you understand? I just want it to stop.' My tears overcame me again in her presence. 'I prayed to Christ. The man in the wig. And he didn't make it stop. He had a stick.'

She moved next to me in the little jolting space.

'Go. Go, now, and be safe,' I sobbed into her neck while she held me in her arms. 'Go. Go.'

The coach rattled on towards the river, while her brown calico soaked up my tears. 'I got a suit for you,' she said. 'A good one.'

All the way on my drive back I peered out after her, after the direction into which she'd disappeared. I saw by the light of flares the beggars and the filthy starving people flickering into side-streets – sights I had trained myself so far to miss. I saw the not-seen.

I didn't tell Pawnee about Ruth. Pawnee and I maintained a strained acquaintance for some time, meeting as we'd done before, at Etta's, or at Mrs Gregory's, or at picnics. My uncle asked: 'Why don't I see your savage round the house these days, Kit?'

'She's training to become a slave,' I answered, but I don't think he registered my bitter incoherence, being preoccupied with something else at the time, and not seriously waiting for an answer.

One high Summer's day in the park, Pawnee boarded me directly.

'Do you hate me now, Kit?'

'I avoid you. That's all,' I replied.

'Do you detest what I did?'

'I try not to think about it.'

'It's not the custom in my country. Don't think it's my . . . primitive lack of scruple.'

'I didn't have any such thoughts,' I said. 'And don't think I avoid you because I'm shocked.'

'You're *not* shocked?' She looked hard at me.

'I am not shocked,' I said. 'I am hurt.'

'I didn't hurt you? Kit, I . . . '

'You didn't hurt me. I am in the condition of hurt.'

'I'm sorry, Kit.'

'Don't be sorry. I'm also in the condition of being, for much of the time, numb.'

'Kit. Will you walk with me?'

We followed one of the paths. She had some bread for the birds. We stopped out of earshot of any of the others, and threw the bread out for the starlings and pigeons and sparrows and wagtails. A bell rang out from the Abbey tower.

'Kit. Who is going to love me? Who'd marry me? I'm a curiosity. Oh everyone's very polite – everyone *we* know, anyway. But you must see that I'm utterly untouchable in this world, on this side of the ocean. By man or . . . anybody. If it's to be honourable.'

'I hadn't thought about it; but I suppose, yes.'

'I'm a talking-point. But with you . . . '

'I see myself as a talking-point.'

'You?'

'Yes. But people don't know.'

'But you're launched, Kit; or about to be. I believe he really cares for you. And so you've got Halifax' – she aspirated Charles's new title in awe – 'on your string! You'll have a place in the world and a man to touch your body. As I once had in my own place. Before it was all broken.'

'I'm a prisoner in my accursed body, Pawnee. Of my body's arousal.' I turned to her. I touched her. 'I'm glad we can speak. If I hadn't wanted what happened I'd have put a stop to it. No, that's not true. I couldn't decide. I felt myself paralysed. And couldn't respond or deny. And that is what tormented me. And torments me now, when I let it.'

'May I be your friend?'

'Yes. I'd like a friend.'

We walked back to Etta's and played with the baby until Etta took her to put her to the breast. Then we helped Etta's maid change the child and fussed around with the water and ointment and the clean and dirty cloths and talked as though we knew what we were doing. Etta sat listlessly.

'What am I?' she said. 'I thought he'd love the child, and me, and that we'd be so happy. Nothing is as it was.'

'It'll pass,' said Pawnee. 'You'll both adjust.'

'Adjust?' said Etta. 'My body's ruined, I believe. Who'll love that?'

'He doesn't just love your body,' said Pawnee.

'I loved it,' said Etta.

I wrote in my notebook, under the heading concerning the discharge of passion in women:

Ruth ⊗   Me ⊗
Etta ?   Pawnee ⊙

Then I listened, as I'd grown accustomed to doing by way of continuing my investigations, at my own fireplace, to see whether there was any transmission of sound from my uncle's chamber. But as always there was none.

Pet and I were playing some card game. My uncle sat in his great chair with his wineglass to one side, a sheaf of accounts on the floor, a letter from his half-brother Benjamin Smith on his one knee, and a scientific pamphlet from a German court on the other. 'Monstrous!' he claimed. The saloon clock ticked. Pet won.

'I have to learn to dance, Uncle,' I announced.

'What? I thought young women were born able to dance.'

'But not all of us young women were born . . . '

'Kit.' He cut in quickly, pre-empting the finish of a sentence that could have proved unsettling. 'Of course you shall learn. Have someone come in to teach you next week.'

'It takes more than an hour, Uncle. And there must be music.'

'I've seen these people,' he replied. 'They come with a fiddle thing of their own. Why do you mention it?'

'Somers's masquerade. Which is some joke I don't understand. Yet. Is he still Mr or Lord? I get overwhelmed with these great Juntos. Outside if fine – he's become a gardener – which is also supposed to be part of the joke. We shall be invited. I shall be asked to dance, but I don't know the steps.' I'd decided that if Charles was renewing his attention, I couldn't gain anything by being unprepared. I'd need to be more confident, to step forward; to attack as a kind of defence.

'I thought you'd driven my friend from my house. When was this mentioned?'

'He hasn't mentioned the part about us being invited, but I expect it daily.'

'I heard he nearly challenged a man, he was so exasperated. You expect him to pay any more attention to you?'

'Charles spoke to me about our lives before I was ill. Time had brought us together, he said. I believe he . . . has invested heavily in me.'

My uncle turned in his chair and sent Pet off to make a drink.

'Charles has a profound regard for you, as have I,' he said.

'What is the purpose of this regard?' I asked.

'Kit. Why do you keep assaulting the sensibilities of your hearers?'

'I beg your pardon.'

'Charles is furious.'

'Am I responsible for that?'

'I should think you are. He's a very good friend, Kit.' He pulled at his cup of wine. 'Perhaps my only true friend. I'm much indebted to him. And so are you. Think of it.'

'I do think of it; now that I know it,' I replied.

'Do you dislike him? Have you an aversion to his . . . person?'

'I like him, Uncle. As a man. But what am I obliged to do, I enquire. Shouldn't I enquire?'

'Some things are obvious. Doesn't your . . . inclination teach you?'

'Does it teach you?'

I counted ten strokes of the clock's pendulum.

'Do you seek, by the manner of your speaking on these subjects, to intimidate me, Kit?' His voice was icy, slow. I hung on to my sense of myself, and could have opened up all his wounds with a few choice memories. But although I had no physical fear of him, I didn't necessarily want him to know it, in case he sent me home. Although I felt as vexed as ever by my uncle's secret trespass, I no longer wanted him to know I knew about the eye.

'No, Uncle. But like you I wish to determine the causes of things. I'm not content with ignorance. This is the same stuff you're made of, surely. It's become our business, you and I, to enquire. To want to know. Now, he won't marry me, because of his rank. How long, then, have I got?'

'How long? What do you mean? Kit, he loves you. You've got as long,' he said, 'as love.'

'In your mouth, Uncle, the precise becomes poetical and the poetical precise.'

'Don't confuse me with one of your poets, Kit. Those liars are the very damned source of the problem. Which I've devoted my life to untangling.'

I refused to be diverted. 'So I have a month? A year? A day? A moment? It's not like Sir Isaac's Law of Cooling. Love, as you call it, is likely just to . . . disappear. What then? A child?'

'Charles is, I'm sure, Kit, an experienced man; a skilful man.' The second time I'd heard that phrase, whatever it meant. 'And if the worst came to the worst, everything would be provided for. Charles is honourable. You may depend upon it.'

'And I should become somebody's leftovers. Left holding the other leftover. What about my life? My . . . business?'

'Your business? What business have you? You presume, Kit!'

I realised I'd made an error of tactics. I played my only card. 'But you brought me here, Uncle. You educated me. You chose me. You rescued me from the obscurity of a provincial marriage. To be with you here in London. Why? Surely not to become a dishonoured mother – unmarriageable in London. At least out in the stalks I'd have had my credit. Why, Uncle, did you send for me?'

'Family love and loyalty. You're my flesh and blood. I did something of my duty.'

'Why me and not my sister? Why not my brother?' I saw that he sought to distance himself from the memory of earlier days and causes. He looked wildly at me; his mouth set in a thin line.

'I sent for you because you . . . because I . . . I . . . Time has softened perhaps the intensity of those reasons. I taught you some things. You were apt. I saw we were . . . alike, you and I. There was an . . . identity between us. You admit this?'

'Perhaps. And Charles?'

'Charles is my friend. Has been my friend for a long time – since before your birth.'

'But I put it to you that I represent a dangerous secret, which you seek at all cost to preserve. And Charles . . . '

'How dare you, Madam,' he thundered. 'It's high time you were elsewhere!'

'You men!' My anger surged up into my voice. 'You think time just ticks along. You think things go on. In smooth curves. Don't you look? Don't you see? Me? It's not the same for me, for us.' I identified myself with the gender of my body. 'Our experience is more like discontinuity.'

'Discontinuity? What do you know of discontinuity?'

'What little I know, you taught me. Our time comes in small bundles. In pain. Our time ebbs and flows. We leak blood, Uncle. Do you understand? Did you know? Every month. Every moon. Not, I hasten to add, as a result of gravity.'

'Kit! How dare you! Go to your room! At once! I keep a decent house here! These matters are not to be mentioned!'

I stood up, not to obey but to storm out. I came close to blowing my position away. 'Decent! You whoremongers! Don't think I don't know what goes on!'

'Kit! This isn't the time. Or the place.' Pet stood, having just come in, holding a tray in the doorway. Her mouth was wide open over the steaming chocolate.

'Time! Don't tell me about time. Mine's running away with me. Its parcels are becoming tighter, smaller. You know nothing of women. Our lovers come in little squirts, uncle. And it doesn't take a moment. One fuck and we're in a whole new story.' The tray crashed down; I stepped over the chaos and slammed the door on my way out. Between us we'd sketched out the bones of a quantum theory of time; but I was in no mood to want to take the credit for it.

Localised Interference

I was granted the dancing lessons on the grounds of political and scientific need. You might call it a research grant. A man came in to teach me. But my uncle and I made up. We didn't kiss and make up; we agreed to say no more of the matter. We treated it as if it hadn't happened. Maybe he filed my violent statements away as evidence: the irrational moodiness of females, or the threat of Kit getting out of hand. He did give me a peace offering. It was a little clavichord and some books of music. When it arrived I was ashamed of my thoughts about him, the instrument was so lovely. I hadn't played since my organ lessons back in Bridgstock. I couldn't be dragged away from it for days, seeking to recapture and build upon my skills. I think it was a genuine gesture of care, for he still had no real pleasure out of music. I filled the drawing-room with its pretty tinkling as I did my scales and tried over my new pieces as a kind of harmonic bandage for my uncertain involvement with Ruth. Quieter than a harpsichord it was more than a harpsichord, because the delicate jacks remained in contact with the wires to create the sound, and by the merest shake of your finger you might make the thing speak like a living voice.

Four weeks passed, during which I learned to dance the Almand and the Corranto and a couple of country dances, and wondered whether my heart might be broken. No Ruth had appeared, though I'd waited in the coach as before. Charles sent me an extravagant gold locket. It rested in my jewellery box. I took it out and weighed it in my left hand. Then I picked up the suit, which looked to be made of the filmiest snakeskin; I compressed the one carefully in the other.

The joke about the Somers Masquerade was that Somers wasn't giving it, and Somers wasn't going to be there. Despite his incredible influence on the House and the Government, despite his wealth and power, despite the fact that he held everything together for the Party, he was modest and temperate. He was also poorly a lot of the time, and escaped from the city to Tunbridge Wells whenever he could, to take the waters and be nursed by his modest and only mistress. The Junto's roaring boys, Wharton and Russell, who'd always needed his brains and restraint to channel the energy of their political lives, still couldn't resist these jokes behind his back. I say still, since they were pushing on in age. But Tommy Wharton was as devilishly anarchic, as corrupt, and, curiously, as obsessively loyal to the Party at fifty-odd as he'd been at thirty.

It was at his London address (a mansion by most people's standards, acquired, they said, through his skill at farming – farming bribes) that the Somers Masquerade was to take place. Or the Not-Somers Summer Ball, as I heard Charles calling it.

I wasn't surprised to receive our invitations.

The occasion was a massive one. It was London in excelsis. Half London – not the Tory half. Under the long, mild, evening light, coaches and chariots were stacked almost back to the Strand as we queued to get in. When we did we were stunned by the spectacle. The great hall was aflame from old-fashioned torches inside, while sunset streamed in through the huge western windows. All this lavishness of illumination fell on gods and goddesses, fauns, pirates, shepherds, stags, birds, savages, Romans, apes, bishops, ghosts, martyrs, lions, a Pope, and a fiend or two. They walked, or at times floated, rather, in a kind of artificial forest contrived out of intricate and stylised trees, hung from the high, painted ceiling so as to appear free-standing, or mounted against the plastered pillars. A band of top musicians wafted elegant strains from a cave in one corner. From another, the bright mouth of a vast cornucopia, filled with delicacies, seemed to stretch appetite out of the space, and off down its interior towards some secret and enticing promise of the forest. Servants of both sexes, in provocative woodland uniforms, minced their attendance to our every need.

My uncle suffered it for my sake – or perhaps it was Charles's. He'd refused to wear anything hinting at costume or mask, and, having been accosted by him, sat outside with the only other philosopher present as long as the light lasted.

The dancing was continual. It was enlivened at intervals by professionals in short knee-length skirts who danced gauzy French extravagances and revealed as much of their bosoms as they dared. I limited my activities to the dances I could do, and when not doing so, sat among glittering people wearing my Florentine wolf's face. It was an incredible, coy, feminine wolf, of exquisite manufacture, and with suggestive velvet ears. It covered my nose and eyes and most of my hair, but left my mouth exposed beneath it. I wore a shimmering, silky, shot damask with trimmings in a dangerous soft-grey fur.

Wharton himself found me out, though. He must have enquired about me. He wore no mask but had got himself up as a Roman Emperor, in purple and bronze, with sashes, and ornate, studded belts, from one of which hung a short sword. He looked the part. He took me on to the floor as if he intended us to form up for the next set, but instead we remained near the edge while he talked.

'Montagu wouldn't let me near you at Newton's. I only wanted to have a look at you.' He spoke as I imagined he might about a race-horse. 'Still, afterwards we went on somewhere. Martin's I think it was. Do you know Martin's? No. Of course you don't. So Charles has thrown his heart to the wolves. It's known about town as a serious case, Mrs Barton. Would you take that thing off for me?' He pulled gently at the edge of my mask, as if to act out his request, and then let his fingers trace the outline of my bare shoulder. Through my mask, I smelt his breath. He kept his face close to my ear. 'I suppose you're not going to tell me whether you've let him fuck you yet, or not. Whether his intoxication is ante or post coitum. My money'd say ante. Am I right? Clever girl if you can pull it off. Get it from your mad uncle, I shouldn't be surprised.' Then he let me go.

When the night was advanced, and the fireworks were over, Charles, in the patched shape of Arlecchino, manoeuvred me through the knot gardens into what he said was planned to be a continental grotto – when it was finished and covered over. He made me hold the wineglasses, and himself brought two plates of cold meats and country salads. A few other couples had also taken the opportunity to dine in the cool of the garden. We could make them out by the light of the flares; they were like mythical beasts in a dream.

Around us also there were cries and roars, and laughs from the party; while from the other end of the gardens additional music drifted on the air. It interfered, I knew enough to give the scientific term, with the jigs from the hall.

'Have we forgiven each other, Kit?' he asked, balancing his plate on his knees.

'There was nothing on my part to forgive,' I replied.

'I confess I'm still desperate for you. You've caused me a deal of anguish. And anger, you dubiously divine wolfess. By God, you and I could found Rome. Or should I nominate you the delicious vixen? You've led me a long enough chase. What are we to do, Kit?'

I picked at my food. 'I'm sorry, Sir, to have put you out.'

'Kit. Don't be reserved and formal. We're good friends, you and I. Aren't we, after all?'

I thought of my position with him, and I thought of Ruth; I thought of Wharton, and I remembered my project.

'There are so many folk throughout the city who can't guess where the next meal's coming from, Charles. I know this. I've seen it with my own eyes. Yet we sit down to this splendour. Can we just court in our finery, when not far away there's such suffering? Such uncertainty?'

'Well. You're a ranter, and I love you for it. Or in spite of it.'

'It doesn't make me a ranter, Charles, just because I can't close my eyes to what I see when I go out in the coach you gave me.'

'Well again. These are serious matters. I'm not impervious to them, dearest. Nor is the Party. Have they been disturbing you much?'

'Very much. But I am not a child, thank you.'

'Half the empty-headed women in there,' he finished his mouthful and gestured with his head at the great house, 'don't know. The other half don't care. You're worth much more than the lot of them. You have the grace of discernment.'

'They're empty-headed because they're required to be. If they weren't, things couldn't go on as they are, Charles. I read a fiction by a woman. It was about a black slave. A man.'

'Oh. Mrs Behn. You've been reading Mrs Behn. I also am a poet. Was a poet. Perhaps you judge me only by the company I keep in the Party. Not all rich men are like Tommy.'

'You could do so much.'

'It may be you're right. What do you want me to do?'

'It's certain I'm right. *We* could do so much.'

'We?'

'We could, I think.' I stood up and turned away from him. There was a sudden noise of extra shouting and laughter. A crowd of revellers swept by us holding their own torches. They'd got one of the violinists.

'You have your own plans for us?'

'You don't know all my history. It allows me to see my sex from a curious vantage. And so I also see the empty-headed men.' He came to stand behind me, putting a hand on my waist. I threw it off immediately. 'But you'd not want to know my history, Charles.

You'd not pay attention to me like this if you did.' A great splash was heard, followed by screams, and then another. There were volleys of cheers and laughter. We listened, then returned to our sparring.

'Why is it, Kit, that you tie my sensibilities in knots within minutes of our conversation starting? By God you make me mad. But this time . . . This time, by God you shall taste me, woman. I'll not be diddled and fiddled about.' I didn't entirely understand what he meant by this. He went back to his plate, but put it aside again, and, holding his glass hard in his left hand, stared out over the dark wall of the experimental, part-finished grotto. 'Damn me!' Then he grew calmer. 'Tommy didn't get this . . . creation finished before the event, I see. Should have got Wren. He'd have seen to it. Before he left.'

I laughed. 'A smile,' he said. 'Shall I ever learn how to manage you, Kit?'

'Manage me, Charles? Manage me in hell! Horses are managed!'

'And wolves?' He turned back to me with anger again. 'Wolves are kissed.' He threw his glass away and made a move at me I wasn't prepared for. I found myself embraced, and backed into a private nook out of the angle of the flares' light. I tore my mouth away while he continued to hold me. 'Forgive me, darling Kit,' he said, not letting me go. 'I'm not used to being denied what I want. It makes me behave badly.'

'I can't kiss, Charles,' I said, quoting Ruth approximately. Kissing touched the nerve most strained of all. What could I do? Scream? Here? In Wharton's garden? Amid all this? They'd just laugh all the more. Another roar went up at that moment. It wasn't the bargaining position I'd planned. Things were suddenly out of control again.

'I can, Kit.' His mouth was against my throat. 'And you will.'

I tried to argue for delay. 'Yes. Alright. I'll try, Charles. But not now. Not here. Not this time.' But he held me all the tighter, and pressed himself rhythmically against me. I pointed my beautiful, expensive half-mask over his shoulder and fixed my eyes on the silhouette of the great house roof with its new-style chimneys against the intense night sky. Then the mask got pushed out of position and I couldn't see anything except blurred, dark leather. I felt myself swung over and scattered on to the grass floor of the place. Flickerings of torchlight worked at my brain from the displaced eyeholes. My skirts were pulled up; planted knees held mine apart for thirty seconds. Then there was his weight on me, and the pressure of his raw flesh on to mine. He manoeuvred matters with his hand. Then I felt my body conspire against me; the resistance gave way, and I was entered.

He was breathing fiercely and calling very quietly in an under-voice: 'Oh, Kit, my darling, at last.' It hurt somewhat, and I could think of nothing to say, except 'I can't see,' which sounded inappropriate. So I didn't say it.

But he didn't get straight on with matters. He seemed as it were to want to meditate on me with his body and his hands. 'Why it's only a *young* vixen, Master,' he said, as if these words gave him power over me. 'I dare say she's not been out.' Then: 'I must see you, Kit, before I let the hounds loose. But I shall be careful, my darling. I shall. Don't worry, Kit. Darling Kit.' He struggled at my clothes, I assumed he must be resting on his elbows, seeking to force my breasts out from the top of my stays. Then I managed to get one hand free. The mask wouldn't come off because it was pinned so to my hair. I prised its lower edge away from my nose and at last got a view out. Charles's hands had stopped for a moment. I could see them holding the locket he'd found tucked on its chain between my breasts – my locket – his locket. 'Oh, Kit,' he breathed from some-where above me. It seemed he wanted to open everything about me. He had it in both hands. The locket was undone, and the suit sprang out into the torchlight with a life of its own.

My lover shrank within seconds, and, shortly, I was my own woman again.

Bonfire Night

'Why don't I want to murder Charles?' I wrote in my notebook. 'I'm not in love with him. But I don't detest him. I don't wish, in Pawnee's phrase, to sew his balls to his tongue. I even quite like him.' And then I wrote: 'I know why. It's because I won. He didn't have time to put his mark on me. We came broadside on, but I got off clean without a shot being fired. Perhaps I've got the worst bit over with. Victory was mine, saith the wolf. And he knows it.'

And I still had the coach.

And I would have Nick. One day. Weak, cruel, insignificant, irrel-evant Nick. How he loomed in my thoughts still, blotting out, sometimes in a way I almost grasped, the claims of the last of my Questions; subsuming the nag of what I meant to address, but couldn't bear to. I mean the iceberg of which he was the tip – my forgotten self. I meant to. But it wouldn't come. And if I couldn't hang the burden of my revenge on him, surely I should have to visit it upon myself. Certainly not on Charles.

After the event Charles was horribly apologetic. His discomfiture knew no bounds. To be so much in love and to fail at the consummation of rape in quite such a way was almost insupportable. If ever we were alone together at my uncle's even for the merest instant he insisted on abasing himself and castigating his appalling lapse in the most penitent tones. He said his only excuse was that he had drunk too freely of my beauty and Wharton's Whig-funded wine. I insisted that he continue to call on us as normal. For the sake of both our honours, I said. Otherwise people would talk all the more – more than they talk already, Charles.

I had gained time again, but my own was racing away. I felt it more every day.

Someone else's time evaporated: our deposed King James died in France. His son, the Pretender James the Third, was proclaimed in Paris as the rightful heir. King Billy was in Germany on vacation. We were exposed. Everything the Whig Junto, and my uncle, come to that, had worked for since the Revolution was in jeopardy; the establishment of Protestant semi-democracy, a rational basis for social growth and financial administration, a liberal policy towards offenders, a measure of freedom from the arbitrariness of Kings, the chance to speak one's mind, and the opportunity for self and friends to make enormous profits both over and under the counter. The very system in which I had the ungratefulness to wish to find out the gaps. Well, I didn't like the French regime either; but *that* was open oppression, and its *gaps* were blindingly obvious. It didn't have the peculiar brand of benevolent commercial hypocrisy which interested me so much and touched me so nearly.

Jacobite agitators poured out of the political woodwork and on to the streets, offering their sugared pills, which, as far as *our* people were concerned, concealed no more than a return to the poison of absolutism, torture, maiming and superstition. Could the country be trusted?

On November the fourth of that year, 1701, King Billy, hastening back, landed at Margate. To the enormous relief of everyone of my acquaintance, the people of London set about making the most dazzling November the Fifth in living memory, by way of celebration: of his return to deliver us, of his birthday, and of the anniversary of his previous entry at the Glorious Revolution.

We drove out in the evening at about five, in hope of seeing the royal arrival as well as the other celebrations. Pet sat up with Graveling in the driving seat, while my uncle, quite out of character, insisted on riding up with Tom at the back, and waving his wig.

A great procession was winding itself towards our park, which is to say St James's. They carried a great number of things that were on fire, and so made an incredible spectacle. At the heart of the procession what I can only describe as a giant tray was being supported at shoulder height on wooden poles. On the tray itself stood a huge stuffed Pope, wrapped round in a sheet and tied off with a purple sash. Actually it reminded me of Wharton as Tiberius, except for the pasteboard triple crown on the head. To the accompaniment of cheers, jeers and other ribaldry, this figure lurched along in the centre of the thoroughfare, horridly illuminated. Despite the biting damp chill of the air I got my window open, and heard my uncle's voice joining in. 'Antichrist! Antichrist!' Then came another swaying effigy, this time wearing a mock-up of French fashion with a sun on its chest and a huge pair of horns on its straw head. Between its legs it had a rude baton sticking up. Fixed between the horns was a placard saying 'JE FROG LE POPE'. It wobbled past to more jeers and I saw that its baton continued out behind in the form of a great forked tail. Then the first of the gunpowder shells went off in the park. From my seat I could just see the streaks in the night sky.

Thus began an evening of detonation. The Pope and the Prince of Darkness went on towards their destined bonfires, but our coach got jammed up in the press of vehicles so that even a walking pace defied us. My uncle, Pet and Graveling got down to follow the crowds. Mary and Tony, who were in with me, decided to chance their arm as well, leaving me alone inside under the protection of Tom, who took his gun in one hand and the reins in the other. I'd have liked to have gone but felt I should have no personal protector – my uncle having lost all thought for me in his enthusiasm. Tom would have to stay with the coach. I resigned myself to my female situation, pushed up the glass and made all fast.

The horses had to stand for a full ten minutes. Then we inched forward again. Then we stopped again. Then started. Tom tried an outflanking, overtaking sort of manoeuvre and the coach lay across the traffic to the accompaniment of shouts and roars. I was frightened. Faces, some without teeth, appeared against the window. Some just peered in. One made driving observations; one shouted obscenities. I gathered, when I heard Tom's voice from the front, that he was waving the gun about over the crowd. Then the coach began to rock from side to side. I saw hats and faces horribly close up all around the little box I was locked in. I realised they were trying to turn us over.

'Off!' came Tom's voice with a note of panic. 'Fucking get off or I'll shoot the lot of you! Get off it! Get off the bloody coach!'

'Shoot, then you bastard! And see what you get!' came a voice from the crowd amid the general vocal mayhem. Tom's gun went off; but there were by this time bangs and explosions from all quarters by reason of the Celebrations. It was hardly noticed. The terrible rocking continued. A hideous nose set in a hideous face seemed to have taken it on itself to become one substance with my window. I clung on to the seat. Beyond that I was quite paralysed with fear. With the next dreadful heave of the cabin the flimsy glass gave way. I put up my hands against the drunken, idiot head that smashed into my space.

Suddenly a different, louder voice shouted. Mercifully, the rocking stopped.

'Get off that coach you bloody dogsmeat. By God I'll hang every man I don't kill now. Do you know who I am, you fucking scum! You damned stinking offal! Do you see . . . ' The face at my window gave a shriek of agony and fell away. ' . . . whose badge is on this door!' I dared fractionally to peer out. A figure sprawled on the road writhing and screaming. Charles's horse snorted smoky breath. His sword's end had a dark smear on it. 'It's my badge, you whore's dogs! Halifax's badge!' There was a local lull. Even the screaming stopped. The mobsters considered their position. All around, the unheeding dark carnival surged on with its torches and explosions. Charles seized his moment of initiative, and pressed home his advantage. 'Take that trash up!' He reared his horse, and pointed down at the wounded man. 'Get him a surgeon, or get him to hell! I care not which, but take him away!'

They took him up, screaming again. I felt the coach jolt forward as Tom found room to turn. We were away. I was very, very grateful.

It was when I looked down that I saw my dress covered in blood, and my hand jagged across in the palm and the fingers. What could I do but press the material of my skirt against it to stanch the flow? As I sat dumbly, immobilised, I could just make out the murky stain spreading through the fabric all the halting, jammed way home.

He rode beside us to Jermyn Street, and would have seen me in, but there was no one at home and my uncle had the key, I remembered. He peered more closely in at me through the shattered glass.

'My God!' he said. 'You're hurt! Why didn't you tell me? Kit! Kit!' He got in with me.

'It's alright,' I said stupidly. He made me show him the wounds. Then he looked round wildly as if deciding what to do. He declared I must not be moved until help could be summoned. He ordered Tom off to find a doctor or a neighbour; I, for some shocked, irrational reason, wouldn't let him go. I said: 'Tell him to find my uncle instead, Charles. It's not far on foot. He's in the park. He'll know what to do.' I insisted. Anyway the bleeding had stopped – more or less. Charles was beside himself with me.

'Kit! Be serious.'

'I can't see someone I don't know.'

'Kit. You've lost blood. It may be serious.' But I was adamant.

'It doesn't matter,' I said. 'Just stay here with me till he comes.' We sent Tom off at a run to find my uncle – an almost impossible task, if I'd really thought about it.

He held my hand back against the cloth. So we sat in the blood-stained coach together in the deserted street, and prepared to freeze until someone from the household should come home.

It wasn't long before we both started to shake, and not just from the cold. I shook from sheer terror; he shook from the aftermath of having acted entirely on impulse and at the risk of both our lives.

'By God, Kit. I've never skewered anyone before.' His teeth chattered. His sword lay on the floor of the car between us, its end independently marked with its own black stain. 'I should clean the thing, but I can't bring myself to touch it. We carry them about, but when it comes to it . . . Tommy Wharton's always at sword's length

137

with someone but he has a knack of bedazzling them and getting the weapon out of the issue somehow, so that he needn't shed the poor devil's blood. He's quite incredible. I feel sick.'

'That horrible face at the window,' I shivered. 'I really hope you killed him, Charles. I was so frightened.' I caught my breath. 'You won't . . . The law . . . ? It wouldn't be murder, I suppose?'

'In defending a lady's person and honour from a gang of violent criminals? It shouldn't. It would depend on who gets hold of the story. If anyone.'

'And whether the man should happen to die,' I added.

'Whatever,' he said, 'I claim it as a point for love. I scorn the consequences.'

Had I been an authentic heroine I should really have swooned into his arms at this point. Perhaps I was expected to. Perhaps I should have liked to. It would have been so much easier to have had no other identity or history than my female body's.

We remained, however, sitting opposite one another in the cold. But the point had been taken. The rape had, to some degree, been atoned for, and the balance of power, the famous balance of power, had shifted slightly in his favour. My cuts started to hurt.

'You speak of the face at the window,' he said shortly. 'It reminds me, I was going to tell you. Last week I was in my coach by White-hall – or what's left of it. They're still clearing away the charred rubble. Should I say at last rather than still. I wanted to see the progress. Anyway, a poor woman thrust in her head in the most extraordinary way. She said: "Oh! I was looking for 'Enrietta!" And vanished. It was only afterwards that I thought how familiar; and how very strange a mistake to have made. A funny thing, Kit, don't you think?' I nodded and turned away, working out that it was the coat of arms on his coach. I started to shiver over again. He went on: 'I believe Billy will have to dissolve Parliament. There'll have to be an election. I have great hopes, Kit. Great hopes once again.' My mind raced on its thoughts of Ruth. I let him hold my damaged hand there in the dark, while all around us the distant night exploded; until, sooner than seemed reasonable or likely, my uncle was found, and brought the key, and got me inside to be seen to.

Bracegirdle

It was a miracle that I had been delivered from the mob, still more of a miracle that within four days the evidence of my wounds had disappeared. There were no scabs – no scars even. 'That strikes me profoundly,' said my uncle. In my notebook I wondered whether it was at last hard evidence of the speeding up of my time.

But our medical speculations were soon overtaken by a political condition: election fever.

It was a vigorous, vibrant and vitriolic campaign. Our people threw themselves into it with all energy and funds. My uncle put up as Member for Cambridge, which he hadn't done since he'd taken on the Mint, I think. Everyone was scared of the chance of regression and spurred by the prospect that the tide had turned for us again. The Tories ran a disgusting campaign, full of lies and bribes and appeals to ancient Civil War anxieties, about Presbyterian killjoys, crypto-Roundheads, or horrific taxes imposed by corrupt, overspending ideologue ministries. Smear-sheets about Charles and Tommy and the rest of them flew like confetti.

Perhaps our greatest difficulty came from the formation of a new Party, who came to be called, when they could sort their name out at all, the Country Whigs. Among their big guns the glozing Harley was our greatest threat. We became the City Whigs and were pasted as speculators and entrepreneurs, who cared for neither King nor Country, nor Church for that matter, but only for amassing fortunes out of the Recoinage, the Exchange, the Bank, and Charles's other inventions, which only we understood. And despite the vote-splitting label of Whig in his self-manifesto, Harley seemed to be running with the Tories. His every cunning utterance was inked out in Grub Street and printed up to our disadvantage. 'Devil roast his liver,' said Wharton. But our campaign was equally and deliciously squalid, and profited from the fact that all the great Junto lords had been so roundly insulted during the last three years that they'd become inoculated, and the gibes failed to bite. Whereas we had magnificent anti-Tory material, not just regarding the Jacobite connexion with the hated French and the hated Pope, nor the state of the economy, but solid evidence against Tredenham, Hammond and Davenant, together with a wealth of fabrication, innuendo and squalor on the rest.

Every householder in London was leafleted by both sides. Every spare wall was daubed. Political slogans loomed out of the accursed smog at the traveller, wary and unwary alike.

Twice in that hectic month I accompanied my uncle down to Cambridge. I saw again the place of my one piece of evidence. It brought my tears up, and I struggled to turn them into my just anger. But there was the campaigning. Hammond, who stood against him, circulated some nasty documents, personal attacks. By these, as you might guess – as *I* might *guess* because I didn't know exactly and in precise detail what they might be hinting at – my uncle felt very threatened. His secret unorthodoxies were his Achilles' heel; I had only begun to uncover them. What people knew about, what they might dare to print, what terms they might dress it all up in, threatened to bring his mind down again. He didn't like it at all; it was all too public.

But the election result was a great success. Isaac Newton came off without noticeable taint, and the Party recouped its losses, so that the balance of influence was much more even; and for a short while after December we all lived buoyed up with the business of what might be called scramble-dog-fight government. My uncle sat in the House like a mascot.

Charles threw a Winter party at his lodgings in Hampton Court. I say lodgings, but he had sumptuous quarters there which I saw for the first time, and was much impressed. For my uncle and I went; but nothing like the event at Wharton's was allowed to occur, Charles and I each treading very cautiously around the other's sensibilities. In fact we circled so for many more months, like planets careful of their gravitational field. It seemed that we never should touch again, but should only continue in a more than casual mutual regard. He took up with other women. I knew this.

And I? I saw my first of the *other* shadowy backers (I mean as opposed to the political and educational beings who'd advantaged Isaac's career), those *unseen* suppliers of alchemical books and materials who had accompanied all my uncle's academic achievement. It wasn't at Cambridge; it was in London. I drew up home in the coach having hoped to meet Ruth again at the old place. At our steps a man turned and stared into my eyes. He held a set of volumes by a string in one hand, in the other a glass retort. He had very regular features; striking, beautiful, not entirely masculine, nor particularly feminine. Long fair hair, which wasn't a wig, splashed in curls down on to his coat, which wasn't quite of English cut. Leaving his burdens by our door, he drew near and helped me from the coach, then kissed my hand. He said: 'We've been waiting for you. You'll see Mr Newton receives the message.' Then he mounted his horse and rode off down the street, leaving me altered somehow. Yes, somehow; I knew this somehow also related to the business of time. It was as if my sense of things were subtly changed so that I could see now what I could never have seen in the ordinary way before.

It was after Christmas that I found, or was found, by Ruth – in daylight, what was left of it. I was driving out to see the progress of our order at a furnisher's workshop; which was a pretext, because really I just wished to drive somewhere out of the house. We were stopped behind a heavy dray at a turn.

'I could do with some more,' she said, climbing in.

I wanted to put my arms round her, to know that she was real, and that her cheeks weren't at risk. Why her cheeks? It seemed to me that her essence was concentrated in that vulnerable skin which she had used to paint, and which now was laid open, transparent, to the world's dangers. It was a foolish thought. She wasn't receptive to my demonstration. She just sat down in her cheap mantle – more like a blanket.

'Are you . . . ?' I held her hands.

'Working? No. I got a place this side in a fence woman's house. More respectable like.' She laughed. 'I keep it up with a grafter as well.'

'A grafter?'

'Yeh.'

'I don't know what a grafter is.'

'It's a man. It's a man with a steady occupation. I do for him; he does for me.'

'What's his occupation?'

'Nicking.'

I wanted to get back what it was that I had felt before with her. Or *for* her. But she was far off from me this time. Closed.

Still, she needed the money. I gave her all I had on me, which was

141

quite a considerable amount. She took it and kissed me; and made to go.

'I still don't see where you get it in this. I really don't see it.'

'What's your man's name?'

'Charlie. Why? What's yours?'

'Are you . . . pleased?'

'I donno. Are you?'

'Ruth. I want you to . . . ' but it was lost.

'I'll be back,' she said. 'Why don't you tell me where you live? I'd be careful.'

'Perhaps.'

'Alright,' she said. 'This should last a while, anyway.' She kissed me again, on the cheek, and left. I felt for a moment the old wolf feeling again, with my lip lifting uncontrollably away from my teeth. But my heart also contracted with sadness.

I serviced her at intervals over the months. She found me when she needed me and I knew I was being foolish. I'd got it out of Party funds so that my uncle shouldn't raise a query about the household accounts. Our house was awash with money in transit. At least it was until King Billy died in March – from having fallen off his horse. Well, they said that having a broken collar-bone reminded him of his broken heart, so that he decided to take himself off to join his wife in a better place. But for all his soldiering he was never well.

Then there was a new dissolution and my uncle wouldn't be cajoled into the political kitchen so readily again. Charles, however, and his four mighty partners – the Junto, which now included Charles Spencer – set about salvaging their position with the new monarch; formerly Princess of Denmark, now Queen Anne – that debilitated dumpling, as he called her. Cruelly. The Tories were crowing because they reckoned she was one of their own, and very soon a bloc of three great men was seen to be controlling her: Marlborough, Godolphin and Harley, a triumvirate of the centre, what we should call the centre-right. It was no secret that Charles and the Junto were politically unattractive at court; indeed they soon found themselves removed from the Privy Council, and hence from a voice of power in government. The triumvirs talked to other, less articulate and committed Whigs when they wanted an opinion. But I gathered there was great pressure exerted on our behalf by Spencer's mother-in-law, Sarah Churchill, who was fiercely for us compared with her husband, Marlborough, and could speak directly to the Queen's sensibilities.

I wrote. I read. I kept up my notebook. I spent some months devising a fiction about Ruth in which a male Virginian savage fell in love with her having met her once in St James's Park. I became very involved with this until I found that the plot required both of my characters to have lives and relationships apart, which were full of suffering or betrayal. Nothing would bend them back towards each other. In fact they seemed to take a perverse pleasure in spiralling grossly away from the great chaste fulfilment I planned to end with. The more they followed their daily concerns the more they became victims to the carnality of others or themselves. I left this part of my project.

But I began to move in literary circles, thanks to Charles's new vision of himself as a great patron of the Arts. It may be he cultivated alternative routes to power, while biding his time. It may be he simply had more leisure, and pleased himself with the thought of employing the wealth he'd accumulated to become the Maecenas of his age. In this he showed himself very different from his Junto partners, who cared not a fig for the Arts, unless it were the Arts of Indulgence. I met his smooth protégé Joseph Addison for the first time, and began to make my uncle take me more to the theatre. Anne Bracegirdle, the actress, became *my* backer: on stage, when I watched her, in some scene alongside Elizabeth Barry, she altered me, my sense of time and space, my emotion; off stage, I discovered, she was proposing to supply the needs of my life.

'Kit, my dearest.' She saw me as a daughter, or younger sister. She was the first person who correctly identified my mood. I think she was moved by my air of sadness, an air which she penetrated with ease, but which I hardly knew about. I'd felt no other way of being. How should I *know* that I appeared as sad? It seemed it was, despite my flashes of wit, my conspicuously dominant mode. So she took me under her wing, and I pressed myself into her soft, feathery breast. I was beautiful, she said. She too was beautiful, I said.

She was – tall, and hauntingly beautiful, a brunette with black eyes, and nobody's mistress. At least, this was the public perception of her. She was the theatre's answer to the Blessed Virgin; her chastity both on stage and off was a matter of continuing amazement and fascination in London. And, of course, it was a point of publicity which it was necessary for her to maintain at all costs – her whole career, her stardom you might say, depended upon this persona. She *was* a star. They called her 'Cara', the stage's darling; plays were written to exhibit the wonderful chemistry of playing between her and Barry, rather than for any poetical statement their author might intend. A few years ago at the height of their fame, they'd both been painted alongside the King, Anne lovely, delicate, as Flora; and Barry, fuller and more senior, in profile from her more flattering left side, as Ceres. The King was on his horse.

'And what about the matter of Charles?' she said.

'What matter of Charles?' I said.

'Heavens, girl, the whole of London knows the two of you are in love. It's worn-out gossip and has become an established thing in town, so that foreign visitors include it on their list.'

I begged her pardon.

'They admire St Paul's a-building and the other glories of Wren, they soak up the horrors of the Tower and the Bridge, they dine and titillate their senses at Covent Garden or by Leicester Fields, they browse among the bookshops near your house, and they enquire where they may view the lovers. And by that, Kit, they mean that great Minister and the pretty daughter of science, whose joint air of connected disconnexion has fascinated everyone for the last couple of seasons.'

We were all, it seemed, actors on a stage. I had no idea I'd taken on such significance. Besides he had other lovers.

'I shall take you in hand, Catherine, and shall lead you to the jumps. You must either leap over cheerfully, or scratch!' We exited together, arm in arm, stage left, with a flourish.

So: 'Why is it, Sir,' I said coolly to Charles, and in the public pit, 'that you need to be in love with two Countesses, a Maid-in-Waiting and a Lady of the Bedchamber at the same time?' We were all at the theatre – the old Duke's. The play was a pitiful thing, quite coincidentally Colley Cibber's *She Would and She Would Not*, my uncle attending any such nonsense with great reluctance, and sitting through it with a bad grace. He was unable to see the purpose, he said, of people who had been designated at birth by one perfectly serviceable set of names getting up on a board and informing the company they were somebody else. Two people in one body! Our 'all' now included two poets and an actress: Addison, Mr Congreve and Anne. She'd been as good as her word. She'd schooled me. Tonight, when she'd bought me the large brandies, she'd dared me to confront Charles.

Charles took in the pair of us with a cool look in his turn. 'In love, Kit? Me? In love?'

'I'm reliably informed that at your latest gentlemen's cabal – what is it, Anne, you were telling me?'

'The Pussy Club, Charles?' she said, with a straight face. 'Out at Barn Elms.'

'I think I heard Pussy came into it somewhere,' I went on, lubricated by the alcohol. 'Anyway, I'm reliably informed that glasses were engraved, healths were drunk, and verses offered up. Then these same glasses were dutifully and passionately smashed by the lovers present.'

'Your sources, Madam?'

'I shall never reveal my sources, Charles. Are you denying the list?'

'The Kit-Cat Club, *Kit*, as you well know, is devoted to pie and poetry. Perhaps I need more inspiration than the average man of letters. Perhaps I struggle more against the dullness of my wits and so need these *stimuli*. But *in love* . . . ? These courtesies are literary conventions.' He turned to Congreve, as if to invite his approval or to find some male route of escape.

'But another name was celebrated in addition to these aforementioned beauties, we hear, by Baron Halifax,' said Anne, slipping an arm though mine and Congreve's at once so as to suggest a wall against which he was cornered. 'Also for the sake of literary convention, no doubt.'

'Entirely, my dear,' said Charles.

I record the fact that Charles actually if briefly blushed. And that I was pleased. It was of course my name she was referring to.

'Then, Charles, aren't you a monstrous hypocrite and a traducer of reputations; unless all these ladies have been informed of the conventional use to which their names are being put, and have agreed to it?' She smiled her gorgeous Millamant smile, and fanned and fluttered at him as if the attack she'd just delivered had been no more barbed than a buttercake. And in front of his *clients*, too. If she'd been a man, he'd have had to meet her outside and try at running her through. Addison's jaw dropped. Congreve's leg appeared to pain him. I thought of Charles shivering with the bloodstain on his sword.

But his reply was equally extraordinary.

'You're right, Anne. In fact I love Kit, and the others are diversions, genuine diversions, by which I attempt to convince myself that one woman is as good as the next. Unsuccessfully; which accounts for the brevity of the liaisons, no matter for their rank.'

My turn to blush. Violently. Despite my attempt to retain some sense of my purpose. Despite my attempt not to feel for him.

There was a hiatus both in our dialogue and that on the stage, since just then by miraculous chance the hapless lover forgot his lines. Poor Susannah Mountfort fluttered her eyelids and her fan in an attempt to cover for him.

Anne said: 'I think, if you'll excuse us, William, Mr Addison, I must take these people off in serious . . . conclave. Sit down, William, why don't you.' She shepherded Charles and me out of the auditorium. 'I take it you won't miss the comedy if we find a private place to talk.'

Being intimate with the theatre she led us to a little cubicle near the actors' dressing-rooms; it looked out over a great wooden capstan, where pulleys hung and ropes flew up. Littered about were furniture and properties, stripped, I noticed, of all theatrical power, by the lack of light and lack of context. Stage hands – they were known then as undertakers – prowled about in rope-soled shoes.

'You claim serious feelings towards my friend, Charles. I've drawn you on that at least.'

'Drawn me, Anne? What *is* this? Kit and I know the state of play well enough.'

'Heaven knows I'm no prude, but the girl has no mother.'

'She's in the care of an excellent guardian. A man of unimpeachable morals.'

'Newton? The man who became world-famous because he wrote a book no one could read? On that reasoning you might as well leave her in Colley's care.' Charles laughed. Anne went on: 'The man's a social disaster. What does he know of young women? He's obviously thoroughly . . . How shall I put the best light on this, Socratic?'

'Isaac? The man's immaculate, I'd swear to it.'

'You mean he's never made advances to you. Anyway, practising or not, we in the theatre can tell these things at a glance. And the point is he has no idea of women. Has he, Kit?'

'Well . . . ' I said.

'Is your mother living, Kit?'

'She's alive, yes. But she doesn't come to London. And I shouldn't want her to.'

'So you have no one to speak for you in this negotiation. Charles, you must know that being so young she has everything to lose from an . . . association with a man like you. I tremble to hope that she's come thus far unscathed.'

'Kit's made all the scores quite clear, Anne. She seems to know very well what the dangers might be.'

'Well perhaps she lacks a counsel. I've spoken to her. She and I have talked. What exactly is it you offer her?'

Charles looked down, as near to sulky as I'd ever seen him.

'Charles, what is it prevents you from putting something definite on the . . . ' she looked around in case there was one, 'table?'

Up to now I'd thought that if there were problems between us they came from my insistence on playing for my scheme of release, and from my distorted self, my sexual confusion. Now I began to see that there was an oddness on his part. I allowed myself to feel for him – just a bit.

'Let Kit just trust me. If she loves me.'

'If she loves you? Does it matter if she loves you? Do you love him, Kit?'

'In as much as I'm capable of loving a man, I've assured him that I love no other.'

'My God!' said Charles. 'You hear that? How should that make me feel?'

'Is it necessary that the lady in the case should declare her heart,' said Anne, 'provided she's willing to come to terms? How can she love a man without substance?'

'Without substance! Who's more substantial, Anne, in the damned kingdom? What do you mean? And if, being who I am, if I declare I love her, in public, by Christ, and before witnesses, why isn't that good enough for her? I *shan't* be dictated to by a . . . '

'Yes, Charles?' said Anne. 'By a . . . ?' He continued silent. 'Shall we fill in the blank for him, Kit? A woman? A mistress?'

'A whore?' I said, my tears and anger rising, my thoughts on conspiracy and the Newtonian mirror in my bedroom. 'A drab? A country jade? A cheap young slut?' I stood up to storm out, but Anne yanked hold of my skirt and sat me down again. There was a blare of patriotic music from the band in the gallery. That year; what was it? '03 by then, and there was the new war on.

'As to the matter of substance, I meant that in her eyes you must have no more substance than your masculine person. For heaven's sake Charles, assuming you don't intend marrying someone else, and you can't socially speaking marry Kit, at least offer her a house, an allowance, a position – some stable platform from which she can think about falling in love.'

'And if I lay out all this money for the gratification of my finest feeling what does it make *her*, with your list? And what does it do to that feeling?' Now he stood up in the little cabin space. It made him look tall.

'Sit down, Charles,' said Anne. 'You're both my friends. I see the pair of you caught up in some web of feeling, and I would like to help you.'

I tried in some emotional confusion to hold on to what I was trying to do. I wondered if Anne knew what she was getting into, but then again I felt for her as well.

'I have a set of terms,' I said. 'They're not essentially financial – not about me, anyway. Charles knows.'

'Do you know of them, Charles?'

'I do,' he answered moodily. 'I tell you I'll not be dictated to by . . . cold contracts in the matter of my heart.'

'Is that why you've never remarried?' she said.

'Is that why you could only bring yourself to marry for money?' I said.

'This is intolerable!' He got up again, and Anne imperiously motioned him down again. 'The lady in the case is willing, in her own way. The gentleman is willing. But they cannot agree. What if *I* put her provisos to you, Charles? Provisos seem to be my stock in trade.' She joked about the marital stipulations she'd made so often on the stage, and lately in William's *Way of the World*.

'They're unrepeatable,' he said.

'Are they indeed?' she said. 'Kit?'

'They're . . . secret,' I said.

'I see.' She hesitated a moment. The music, thankfully, stopped.

148

'Could you bring yourself to accept these secret conditions, Charles, in the spirit of a lover?'

He wrestled with himself. At last: 'Since you chain me to the point, Anne, perhaps I could.'

'Well, Kit?'

Eventually I nodded, knowing that the letter of them would give me at least some achievement, and some time. 'It must be written down, though. We must meet to write it all down. I must have that security. It must be signed. I am kept prisoner, otherwise, to the designs of lust,' I said.

'Rubbish!' he exploded. 'Do you hear this?'

'It's true!' I replied angrily. 'You must know as well as I do what I'm talking about!'

'You're hysterical!'

'I am not hysterical!'

'It's obvious! This is insufferable!'

'Insufferable for me! At my house!'

'What on earth do you mean?!'

'Children! Children!' said Anne. 'Collect yourselves.' Then: 'Will you meet her to sign, Charles? I shall be witness . . . '

'But shall not see the contract,' I said anxiously.

' . . . to the signatures alone.'

'It's intolerable,' he said.

'Very well. I shall advise her to admit no more of this suit, in any degree. I shall take her entirely under my care, and endeavour to find her a suitable match, so that she shall be happy and secure. Secure from . . . speculative and thoughtless male interest.'

Perhaps it was my sharp intake of breath.

'Very well,' he said. 'I'll call tomorrow. And now I shall leave.'

When he'd gone Anne pulled me up and embraced me. I wondered if this was what it felt like to be normal.

Conjunction

'I've spoken to her. She and I have talked.' So Anne had informed Charles, and indeed we'd combed the matter through minutely – both his intentions and my doubts. Our most significant conversation had taken place at her house on the river, just off the Strand. It had been on the evening before the theatre visit.

'You must understand, Anne. I don't love him. I cannot love him.'

She had been trying clothes on me, and on herself. She had an excellent wardrobe. It was her theatrical wardrobe to some extent. We sat on the floor in our stays, lace and stockings, amidst a confusion of silks and lawns and taffetas and hats and ribbons.

'A girl needs love, Kit.'

'*You* say that? Who've given your life to your profession, your Art. You tell me a girl needs love.'

'Yes, indeed I do. For how could there be Art without love? It'd be quite a wretched poor thing.'

'But everyone knows . . . You let it be known . . . '

'Yes, I let it be known. And I'm not a common lover. But I do love, Kit. It's a quiet, unspoken thing, and we're not familiar in public, but it is mine and it is obvious, really. It's the secret under people's noses which may be the best kept.'

'I don't understand,' I said. 'It's not at all obvious to me.'

'I shall let you into my secret. I think you'll come to mean a good deal to me, and I trust you not to reveal it.'

'I shall not, I promise.'

'Well, then. You know this street has often had a number of theatre people and poets living on it.' I didn't know anything about Howard Street, but I didn't say so, for fear of seeming gauche and still countrified. She went on: 'William . . . Mr Congreve . . . lives through there.' She pointed to the door opposite the one out to the stairs. I realised it must lead to the house next door. 'In public we appear good friends. In private we're better friends, and did once catch the public notice. Despite the stories we were obliged to put about we have been very constant. There. That's my heart. It's a small thing.'

'But your own. I'm glad. I'm very glad. And touched by your confidence. It's obvious, you're right, that someone couldn't play as you've done and look as you do unless the heart . . . were alive.'

'So you agree with me. You're in need of love.'

'Ah, that's as may be. We all need to be loved, I daresay, and Charles is all very fine. But I can't love him back. No matter how you seek to encourage me.' I looked into her dark eyes to let her know that I wasn't speaking ungratefully.

She pushed her knees away from her, stretching her legs out

straight and stuffing her hands into the petticoats between her thighs.

'I speak from what I see; what all the town sees. I should say you love him. Because you watch him earnestly, Kit. Perhaps you don't know you do it. Perhaps you don't yet entirely know your own mind. It will come.'

'Perhaps I've the habit of watching where there may be danger. It's the habit of wolves.' I began to root around for my original dress.

'You have a curious turn of phrase. You trouble me, Kit, some-times. Has he given you cause to fear him? No, no. Put that one on. The last one you were trying. Keep it on. Keep it. The orange colour with the slashes. It suits you.'

'Are you sure?'

'Quite sure. Well? Has he?'

I hesitated. 'No,' I said.

'And is he respectful?'

'He is.'

'Well then.'

'Anne, I'm truly grateful to you and I like you so much. You're easy with me – I don't feel so alone. I do feel you want to help me. But you must believe me. I can't love him. You can't make me happy like this.'

'There's someone else?'

'I have no other suitors. They don't dare! I don't flirt. I don't encourage anyone. There's no man I pine for.'

'Nor no woman neither,' she quoted.

I hesitated again. 'Nor no woman,' I said. 'I can't love in that way. It's because . . . It's because . . . There, I can't tell. And I can't tell you, but I know I'm not like other people. My uncle and I, both; we're different.'

'The blessed Isaac? Kit, you're nothing like him. I won't hear of it.'

'How can I make you understand, Anne, when I don't understand myself?'

She hugged her knees back up and thought for a moment. 'If I had a daughter of my own I should love her as I have begun to love you. I should want her to find a good man who would also love her. Charles is a good man, Kit. A brilliant, sensitive, rich one to boot. You're young. Young girls often have these . . . humours. Very well,

151

he's full of himself sometimes and has an eye for pretty women, but these are the faults of bachelors with money. Admit you like him.'

'I like him. We're friends when we're with friends.'

'Love will come. He's besotted with you. It's obvious.'

'Oh, he's besotted with everything in a skirt.'

'There. You're jealous.'

'I'm jealous of anyone who can go among the opposite sex naturally and not feel their heart wrenched out of their body with pain and sorrow and murder.'

I felt the all too ready tears prickle behind my eyes and turned away, half in the orange dress.

'Kit! You amaze me sometimes. You hit these notes of agony as if from nowhere.' She got up and laid her arm on mine. 'Is it the act that frightens you? Is all this about the matter of the bed?'

I fixed my eyes on my nails, and fought for what to say. 'I could consent to the act,' I said, 'but I should hold myself aloof. In fact, I resigned myself to it long ago, but things between us have been at an impasse for many months, so it hasn't been an issue for me. What I'm telling you, my dearest Anne,' I turned back to her and took her hand, 'is that you can't create my happiness out of this, even if I were to take him on.'

'Let me try, Kit. Let me try, poor child. Perhaps to make me happy by making you happy. That's my Art, after all. My trade, Kit. I make others enjoy. "I say I am a magician. Therefore put you in your best array; bid your friends; for if you will be married tomorrow, you › shall." '

'Well, Rosalind,' for we'd dug out the old, unfashionable Shakespearean folio she had to divert ourselves earlier, 'you may try. I have my own axe to grind in the matter.' I thought there was nothing for it but forward.

She lifted her eyebrow, but made no comment. She mixed us a Gineva cordial jug with orange slices in it. We toasted ourselves and became merry mistresses.

And so the following night I was put to Charles at the theatre, willingly and brandily as you've heard, and found myself contracted to secure my contract and pledge myself for the next morning. And my uncle knew nothing about it. At least I fervently hoped that in this I might have slipped his espionage, whatever forms it took which I hadn't yet discovered. I fervently hoped, as I say, that his interest was purely anatomical, and didn't extend by some tyrannous magic to the whole of my thoughts and activities.

But in the night a shadowy backer appeared in my bedroom. Though part of me knew the hour was well past midnight, I saw him in an unaccountable light. Or her? It wasn't the same figure as the first I'd seen all those months ago. It had dark hair and was altogether sterner, though very beautiful. The clothes were likewise more extravagant than the English cut, and very rich. He, if I attend to the dress only, held a Testament. He read: 'Though I speak with the tongues of men and of angels, and have not charity, I am become as sounding brass, or a tinkling cymbal.' My room filled with strange musical noises. I said: 'Is it charity that you bring? Are these the notes of charity? Do you seek to bring me consolation? What was it you brought to my uncle?'

He answered: 'I obey instructions.'

'Whose instructions?' I said. 'My uncle's? Are you his servants? Or he yours? With your talk of charity. Do you inform on me?'

'There are misleadings,' he said. 'It is Amor.' Then he left.

I came to myself in the dark. I lit a candle to work over the details of my contract, and pulled a cover off my bed to keep myself warm.

I began to scratch down my demands in my notebook. Then I put my ear to the fireplace – but as always I heard nothing. I continued:

Not in this house
Money for project
Information
Nicholas
Separate lives
Private individuals
Suit

Then I put out the light and went back to bed.

I dreamed that I lay on my front and that the shadowy backer lay on top of me and took me in an indistinct way. And then I was half asleep, and felt the rainy dawn light creep round the curtains of my bed. I slept again. Briefly; tossing and turning, until another, horrible dream woke me up sharp. There had been scenes of filth. There was a small piece of shit in my throat. I must find the chamber-pot to get rid of it in. It was larger now. It lay as a turd against the roof of my mouth. I must not move my teeth or tongue until I could void it out. I found the pot. There, it was out.

Such a relief to wake, and yet once I'd come to myself the freight of this foul dream lay on my mind so that I felt a gross sickness throughout my body, which remained with me while I washed and dressed enough to go down for some change of place. In the warmth of the kitchen I made myself a hot drink and talked with Mary of normal things. Then I went back up to my room and wrote to my night-time notes the element of the contract that I'd forgotten: Not to kiss on the mouth.

Later Pet came in and helped me finish getting ready for the day. Later still I felt firmer in myself and took some breakfast. I drafted my contract out neatly on a sheet of good paper, and wondered at the difference between day and night.

Pawnee came. Anne came. My uncle went out to the Mint. Charles came with his servant at about eleven.

So Charles and I were regularised at the hands of Anne Brace-girdle. It was in our saloon. Pawnee was a sort of bridesmaid.

Charles had his own piece of paper bearing his seal already. Sitting at my uncle's writing table with me looking over his shoulder, he began to adapt the sheet of my demands that I placed for him to read:

I, Charles Montagu, Baron Halifax, etc etc agree to . . .

Anne and Pawnee turned their backs.

    1) refrain from demanding the kiss;
    2) assist in the . . .

He stood up, holding the pen. 'Kit, this is ridiculous. If I give you this and you put it about you could ruin me entirely and absolutely. You must be content with my word of mouth on your paper. That's as far as I shall go or can go. Marriage itself requires less.'

'Very well,' I said. 'Give it then.'

'I'll abide by your terms, Kit, and your two witnesses may hold me to account for it.'

'Good,' I said.

'And *my* terms are . . . '

'Obvious,' said Anne. And everybody laughed. I handed him the

154

locket containing the suit as if it were some prearranged token of my heart. He gave me diamond earrings.

To my surprise, we were all swept out by Anne as the mistress of ceremonies. She'd bespoken a meal at an inn. There we met Congreve and dined, and Charles and I looked at one another, while the others kept up a conversation. Afterwards they discreetly left us alone by the fire in a corner of the coffee room. He sat next to me and, when we'd finished our coffee, he held my hand.

'What now, Kit? Will you have me tonight?'

'Where?' I said.

'Come out to my own house.'

It was a squally April afternoon. We drove down to his place on the river by the old Chertsey Road. It took three hours or more, and ended in impenetrable swirling darkness. We made a transit of the river. His house emerged as no more than an outline. We found inside no more than a skeleton staff. The strange place flickered from the single candelabrum he held in his haste up the broad stairs. Then he took me straight to his bed.

The Collection

I was an incongruous sort of a woman. But in this it strikes me that my experience wasn't unlike the lot of many who found themselves then, or find themselves now, married to suit someone else's requirements; part of a sophisticated entertainment industry, and in bed with a person they don't love.

He wore the suit. He kissed, if not my mouth, then everywhere else. He played with my breasts and sucked on the nipples. I couldn't but become aroused, and my body engineered a sort of response, which occurred together with a certain amount of pain. When he slept I didn't. I spent some hours of wakefulness during which the thought of tearing the skin from his back until the bones were exposed ran again and again through my mind. It wasn't a personal thing against him – just repeated images of violence. And when they'd subsided and I felt the frightful state give blessed way to sleep, I nestled against his body and dozed off as well as I could in the big, foreign, aristocratic bed. In the morning he was clearly reassured to note there were a few bloodstains on the sheet, and asked to be further reassured that he hadn't hurt me. Then he employed the suit again and told me he loved me. This time I didn't let myself become involved.

There. It was done. And that was that.

If I'd had my notebook with me I should have enjoyed the chance to spend a little time alone to digest my experience in it. How un-idyllic of me! But I craved a few moments of privacy, and my brain would run on, as if thought upon thought could spin a cocoon all round my mental being and protect it from my body. I was unaccountably elated. I thought, yes, that my uncle's experiment with me had passed a crucial stage, but I believed I'd escaped observation. Ha! Surely the experiment was void! The chemist had missed the conjunction. It had evaporated and was beyond him. He could only stare at his empty glass, unable to be sure that anything at all had occurred, and hope to catch hold of any distillate. In hazarding myself I'd eluded his eye.

But as for me there would be tonight, and the next night, and the night after that. Press that away. Think of the present hour. Think that if my time did indeed come in little discrete parcels, then between them there might be gaps, through which I might wriggle. And think of the contract – that the fulfilment of *my* designs was now brought that much closer. Surely we were all transformed. Charles was obliged, my uncle was to a degree dis-enabled, and I was not quite what I had been.

He showed me his little riverside house. Little! In all the years of our courtship I hadn't seen this house. It wasn't as big as a palace, of which there were several along the Surrey bank, but it was substantial. A substantial old manor house, with an imposing, modern, classical façade. It was called Abbs Court. At that stage, having arrived in the dark, I wasn't sure where exactly we were. We'd come over a ferry, coach and all. That was all I knew. He'd mentioned Sunbury and Walton and Hampton, so I assumed these in some way located us.

He was a collector. He showed me his collection of coins. I saw the Roman ones he had – they'd been handled by the dead so long ago, in and near the London of their day. I turned them over in my hands, adding my essence to the accumulation of theirs.

'The recoinage; you and my uncle working on it all these years – it makes me feel strange, Charles, that all that sort of thing which was so important and new, and *charged*, for *us*, must have been gone through before. By another Charles who designed it, and another Isaac, who inspired and implemented it; and possibly another sorry Kit, who troubled everyone.'

'You don't trouble people, my darling,' he said. 'You lighten their hearts though you say you have none yourself. It will be alright in the end.'

Also in the room were some little Italian bronzes. There were horsemen and a bound slave, wrestlers, a soldier, a young man, a madonna, a courtship and a copulation. 'Don't flatter me, Charles. Don't pacify me. These pieces; why do you collect them?'

'For their beauty.'

'You're a connoisseur of beauty? But why *these* things, coins and lovely metal dolls. I call them dolls because my uncle always refers to statues as dolls. He can't understand why they should be made in stone or metal. But your answer's insufficient.'

'The people who made these, I understand them. I understand their labour and their desire for value, and for things to work out. Casting one of these, for example,' he held up the lovers, 'is a risky, sparky business. It may not work; it might cause a terrible injury, or simply all go wrong. You will not know while the process is happening whether you'll succeed or be fooled by your materials. But if you succeed . . . ! Government, for me, Kit, isn't just administration and profit-taking; it isn't just the use of power; it's the chance to forge something new.'

'But it isn't new,' I said, pointing to the coins. 'It's all been done before.' And I took the lovers which he still held and said again: 'It's all been done before.'

'There's always a virginity in things,' he said and kissed my cheek.

I said: 'That is *your* project, then?' We moved on to the great stairs. At their top were his pictures, hung all round in the light of the high windows that served the landing gallery. There was a conspicuous gap on the wall of the stairhead, as if a painting had been removed for attention, or was not yet ready for hanging. 'What is it you're trying to create? Are you for a republic, like the Protector? Or for an empire? Do you see a new Jerusalem? What do you make in your fire?' We'd never spoken before of these serious matters that touched him. By the look on his face I wondered who had ever asked him these questions. Whether men in their clubs, their meetings at coffee or wine, sat and asked each other: where do you wish to go? What do you want to build? Or whether, under the umbrella of Party, they each scrambled away at an unspoken, unacknowledged, personal goal which concurred vaguely with Protestant wealth and Protestant sex.

'You speak to my heart, and perhaps I shouldn't open it to you.'

'Why not?'

'Have you told me your project? Will you tell me?'

'Well. I'm a woman. We have the right to reserve ourselves.'

'Unfair, Kit. But I shall tell you something of myself; perhaps these are things I keep too close. My project, dearest, if you could call it that, is to create a nation that can live in peace and brotherhood with its neighbours and within itself. I should call it a post-military State. But it would probably have to become a post-military empire. In such a structure men might practise the simple arts of agriculture, husbandry, fabrication and trade without the constant angry dislocation of factional dispute or religious violence. Without the superstitious fear that makes fools of the best of us.'

'You're seeking an end of Party and of Religion?'

'No, indeed, my dear. An end of Party bickering and religious disagreement; the business that makes bonfires under heretics in Spain; the acrimony and backbiting that threaten the simplest and most rational reform here at home. Sometimes it seems a mirage, to hope for stability, when everything riots and goes against what is its obvious good. But we do hope. And we strive.'

'We, Charles?'

'I'm not alone in this, Kit.'

'You make it sound admirable. I haven't seen you like this.'

Pleased, he conducted me along the row of pictures: a prized Cranach figure of a woman with a strange child, old Flemish scenes of ritual activities, tortured Italian saints in dark depthless backgrounds. He had a Holbein which the King had sold him, and there were some women from his family. He also had a Van Dyck. There were a number of Venuses, and some society women posing as Venuses in various states of undress. His own picture by Godfrey Kneller, the portraitist member of the Kit-Cat Club, was modestly displayed in a corner. It resembled the one in my bedroom, but was better, and struck you inescapably as you moved along the landing. A few pictures were of dogs.

'I have a room full of prints as well,' he said. And then he said: 'I should like a portrait of you, dearest. You've never sat yet, have you?'

I said, reflecting on what he'd told me of his aims: 'Your vision is Saturnian; you want the Golden Age. It's a myth, I believe.'

'I see an active future. It's the product of the rational mind of man.'

'My uncle?' I said. He showed me into a small room off the landing. On a table in the centre there was a curious machine. Or should I say the round table in the centre was in itself a curious machine. Set into the table's circularity was a great round brass dial, marked not with clock figures but with letters in divisions. Within this set of outer rings was a complex system of gears and chain-driven bands of both letters and numbers, which rose up around a central spindle, supported at its top by engraved brass stays leading back to the level of the table. There were also movable grids and combinations of lines which looked like the evidence of analytical geometry, engraved with little Greek characters. Elsewhere were marks and scripts in other languages I didn't recognise at all. From the side of the table a pretty handle protruded.

'Turn the handle,' he said. Gingerly, I did. It was a most wonderful toy of motion – the whole thing moved round in its train of wheels and contrarieties while the belts with their hinged, enamelled squares clicked into one combination of symbols after another. It was a model of change. He said it was a Lullist machine which had been made in Switzerland.

'What is it for?' I asked.

'It's supposed to generate knowledge,' he said. 'I'm waiting for a German to come and tell me how it works.'

I laughed. He said: 'So there I am. And you? What's your project, Kit? About which you're so secret, but which you'd have me fund.'

'It's the opposite of my uncle's,' I said.

'That's a cryptic reply. I might ask my machine.' He twiddled another handle so that the little plates and wheels clicked and fell past each other with their tiny intriguing sounds. With his spare hand he embraced me.

'I'll tell you this,' I said. 'My uncle's project is to control; mine is to escape.' And I turned out of his arm. 'And you have contracted not to toy with me during philosophy.'

'What do you want to escape from? You're free,' he said. 'You negotiated your own contract with me. A mark of freedom. You're with me by choice, Kit, we both know that.'

'I'm free and I'm bound, Charles. So it seems to me. It's a commercial position.'

'Perhaps that *is* our condition,' he said softly.

'I wish to kill a man. I told you this. You agreed to it. You've had your side.'

His face suddenly registered how disconcerted he was by the seriousness in my voice. 'But I've done that. I ran that villain through. For you.'

'That isn't the man.'

'But . . . Is this your freedom? Your escape?'

'It's my . . . release.'

'What has he done that so offended you?'

'You don't have to know. It's my wish.'

'And is this the sum of your project?'

'It's the start. It's an element.'

'It's . . . unfeminine.'

'If you had doubts, why did you agree?'

'I . . . don't know. I thought somehow it was a symbolic request. A test. Which I reasoned I had already passed.'

'No, Charles. I wrote it down. It was explicit.'

'Who is he?'

'I'll point him out. When I find him.'

'And I'm to run him through as well?'

'I shall kill him. You shall merely help me.'

'How help you?'

'I can't act without a man. I can't go about and attend to my business. Could you carry out any of your . . . work, with your body in a cage?' I jiggled my skirt, and knocked against my stays with my knuckles.

'What is it in you that I love? Where did you come from? How is all this . . . nightmare in a woman's heart? How, Kit? Women aren't capable of feelings such as these.'

'What?'

'I said women aren't capable of such feelings as these. This is madness. This might have been called . . . witchery.'

'You're going back on your word?'

'I didn't think . . . '

'What didn't you think?'

'I didn't think you could possibly be serious. Beyond what had already been done. Kit, I *have* killed a man for you. I didn't attribute it . . . '

'But I made it absolutely plain. You've had your part. Are you telling me you're not a man of your word?'

'Kit! It's a mistake. Sometimes we wilfully misread. I know this.'

'You couldn't have misread.'

'Kit, I did, I say!'

'I should call you out. If I were a man. Charles, you must. You must help me.'

'Kit, darling. It's impossible. I'm a man of honour. How can I, in my position, aid and abet a murder? Don't you realise the consequences? It's hanging for both of us.'

'Aren't you and I clever enough to do it without detection? Between us?'

'But . . . The principle. Kit. My darling.'

'Don't call me your darling, Charles. You gave your word. Before witnesses. How can you humiliate me like this? You've had my body. Damn you. You raped my body, at Wharton's house, and you talk of honour?'

'Kit!'

'Take me back to my uncle, Charles. Take me home to your friend. He only draws pictures of my naked body. At least he doesn't penetrate me and then betray me. Why, you're such a gentleman, Charles, with your schemes of brotherhood. But you're an utter hypocrite.'

'He what . . . ? Draws pictures . . . ? Isaac?'

'He does. Now take me back there. It's less of a prison than your house.'

'I don't understand . . . You let him? He comes to your room?'

'If he came I couldn't stop him. What should I say? The great Isaac Newton comes to see me naked. Who would believe me? Or who would be seen to believe me, shouldn't I say. Plenty would believe me in private. But in public I should be a prime case of *hysterica passio*, and they'd take steps to confine me the more closely. But no.

161

He doesn't come to my room. He has a most miraculous and optical scheme of mirrors by which my intimate secrets may be covertly observed.'

'I'm amazed.'

'If you were a woman, Charles, you'd be amazed by so many things. He doesn't know that I know. Now take me home.'

'Kit. Look. Let me think.'

'Take me home. To Uncle.'

'I can't let you go back. To that! On my honour!'

'You have none. I insist. Why, we're at war. When campaigning starts again men will slaughter each other in droves. Do you stand in the House against the war? You don't. The government pays for the war, and profits from it. From killings of thousands. And you deny me *one*?'

'But it's so . . . cold-blooded. It's against Nature.'

'Then take me home.'

'I will not.'

'Then I shall not stay here.'

'You'll stay where I tell you, woman.'

'Ha! So you think I'm your wife, Mister! You don't love me at all.'

'Kit! Very well. We shall talk about how it may be done. Come.'

As we left the room of the machine I saw my shadowy backer standing in the corner. He put his finger to his lips.

A View

It became clear soon enough why this matter was more than a moral problem to him. We were in bed.

'Forgive me, Kit. I'm not myself.'

He got up and walked around. He tried again. I tried – for his sake. It was no use.

He was much put about.

'If I were to take you home, as indeed I must, Kit, would you be safe?'

'Safe from my uncle, you mean?'

'Yes.'

'Of course.'

'You're sure?'

'I change my clothes behind my bedcurtains. Otherwise I'm grown used to it. I believe it goes no further.'

'I apologise to you profoundly, my dearest. It will pass, I'm sure. I mean, my difficulty. I trust it hasn't altered our regard for one another?'

'Not in the slightest, Charles,' I said. 'Our contract is intact if you'll keep it.'

I was returned to Jermyn Street.

He took to his London *pied à terre*. I noted that what actually happens can turn out very unexpected. I began to see myself more genuinely as an experimenter in my own right. My attitude was grossly unscientific by Newtonian standards. Where was the demonstrability in the notion that the gamble of one's nominal *virtue* under properly drawn up conditions could leave Cupid unstrung after only two arrows? It certainly wasn't repeatable. I thought of Ruth. But I felt cool and in command.

Perhaps to show me that my body hadn't maintained such detachment my period came on with such violent, wrenching cramps that it kept me in my room for two days. I made sure, though, that this distress was all quite patent to my uncle's secret eye, in hopes to confuse the message he might read from my absence.

Thereafter Charles took me out. I mean in the modern sense. My uncle must have gathered that we were now established in some way. It would have been an inference after the fact, but a blurred one. We appeared in public as man and woman; I went to theatres and gatherings with Charles, rather than my uncle. We were very formal, and the town approved once they had grown used to it. But when we got alone his eyes took on a glassy quality, and there was the awkwardness of testing – he held me in his arms to try his own experiment. My arms were round his neck and my head pointed over his shoulder. And he would seek in movement and touch to find the key to unlocking his embarrassment. But, of course, the more he tried, the worse it got, and the more pained and dislocated from his confidence he became.

Eventually he gave up the struggle. I believe every time he saw me now he saw an Amazon who conflicted with every preconception he had of woman's place and function in the scheme of things. So that although he was a modern and enlightened man who had engineered a modern and enlightened age, I awoke for him a witch terror he couldn't put aside. It came from some dark irrational awareness there was no controlling. And I wouldn't give up my purpose.

With another man I might have run the risk of violence, but I knew that for the moment he'd not admit he wanted to burn me out of existence – it would have meant he was no better than the superstitious inquisitors he so loathed in our country's enemies.

I heard by a French refugee from the war who was at our house once, that on a time there'd been an Arabian princess – Sharazad, she was called – whose husband would kill her once he'd had her, so she kept him at bay with stories for a thousand and one nights. It reminded me of my long gamble with Charles. Now his impotence had made me potent. I felt so strangely powerful for the moment I suggested to Joseph Addison that he write an opera book of it – of Sharazad, I mean, not me and Charles. London was beginning to be caught up at that time with the opera craze. The idea nearly took off. Yes, I felt my power, and it sustained me. Charles remained very angry with me and himself – his work suffered – but he continued to suppress his feelings.

One night he said: 'Kit, I cannot go on with you as before. You must understand this. I suppose it's nobody's fault.'

This was a thunderbolt. 'But my contract,' I said, horrified.

'Yes, yes. Your contract. Well, Kit, I shall honour it. You'll see I am a man of my word after all. Devil knows where it will end. And I don't mean to drop you – if we're not seen out together now, the world will point the finger with a vengeance. I know this. What I mean to say is that we shall not . . . try. We shall be as strange in private as we are in public.'

'I understand, Charles.' I was greatly relieved.

'I'm damned sure you do understand, Kit. I wish you would find this . . . victim. Perhaps when it's done we shall all be the better off.'

'So you'll help me look?' I said.

'Tell me who he is. I'll have him found.'

'No. No. *I* shall find him. *You* shall take me about. I shall begin to make enquiries as to whether he's in London.'

One night my shadowy backer appeared and sat on my bed in the uncanny light I'd seen before.

'Who will deliver me from this body of death?' I found myself asking.

'Sleepest thou? Couldst thou not watch one hour?' he read from his Testament. 'Have I not told you? It is Amor.'

'Amor is love,' I said. And I felt overcome with drowsy lust that this ambiguous figure should take me in his arms. 'Give me release,' I said. But he said again:

'Couldst thou not watch one hour?'

'My time is speeding up,' I said. Then he drew back the curtains of my bed. There, in my chamber, a man and a woman stood on either side of a vessel. She stirred what it contained, an open egg, while he tended the fire beneath it.

'My uncle. He will see you. He sees everything in this room.'

'He would not see. He suffers like you. From the same history as you. The time does hasten on.' He drew a circle with his finger on the space where the egg stood in my line of vision. It was as though I looked again into the shimmering shuddering process – as I had under the influence of Nick's smoking drug in the laboratory at Trinity, the moment before it all exploded. The circle that lay between them, Charles and the woman, was that snake. As before, I observed its obscene tail rammed into its own mouth, the jaws bound tight shut. 'If it could speak,' I said.

'But it was beaten, and bound, poor creature, by this injunction: that if it should speak of what had been done, then its mother would surely die.'

'That's a wicked injunction,' I replied.

'But we may read,' he said.

The little scales of the creature's body became frighteningly active, whirring and revolving and clicking into place. As they did so they made words, it seemed, for some had tiny letters glowing on them. I read before they changed – they were always changing into nonsense – *Grandfather Barnabas*, then once more *Uncle Benjamin*. A new figure stepped up between the couple and behind the snake, which appeared on the instant cast in bright metal, fixed.

Mindful of the pictures in the old Chemistry books, I said: 'It is Volcanus the Smith.' And then I went back to sleep.

I dreamed Anne was in a sung version of *The Tempest*, but everybody forgot their lines.

I stirred just at dawn and, still between the worlds, laughed to myself at the curiosity of dreams and visions, for I cracked the puzzle. Smith was, of course, the family name of the two, my uncle's stepfather and his half-brother, my mother's brother. But by daylight I felt that if only I could find Nick I could activate the next phase of my Project, revenge, now that Charles had given his assent to the detail of the matter. It was a matter of economics: a payment was due to me.

Time flicked on – so fast for me. Charles went, or was summoned, or was ordered to go quite often to see Sarah Churchill at St Albans. She'd left the court, distracted at the death of her son from smallpox while at Cambridge. Perhaps he went to comfort her. Anne was my comfort and point of reference. I mean Bracegirdle, not the Queen, although I'd become quite close with another Anne I've mentioned: Anne Long, a spinster of good family! Charles and I became an outward form, like so many of the marriages around us, I gathered, somewhat to my surprise. I say surprise, but you must remember I had no experience of the town when I came and it had taken me a good while to build up my circle of acquaintances. When I was new, everyone had seemed to suck their fulfilment out of each other in an easy way before moving on, like bees on summer flowers. It had left me feeling I was the only soul who was ill at ease. Lately, I'd begun to realise, from Betty Germain, chiefly (the ultimate gossip – a woman who had the entrée to every salon), and the other society ladies I was increasingly moving among, that London people also had their toils. It was a toilsome world.

I also found out though that Charles was keeping a carefully clos-eted whore of good family and documented health. He could do it with her but not with me. Maybe money shaped desire? I couldn't say what I felt about that.

What of the rest of my research? I'd drifted out of touch with Ruth. I wrote and thought, but I was much occupied with day-to-day matters as my uncle ran into various indispositions soon after he was knighted in Cambridge by the Queen – possibly against her better judgement. She didn't really take to our Party. She remembered the fate of her grandfather, and imagined we were the axe-grinder's babies.

Babies. Babies. Babies were happening all around. Mothers and nurses took them to the park. Pet was pregnant. Graveling and she, a respectable married couple, lived out, in a little place near our stables. Etta had had two nasty miscarriages, and was unwell.

Pawnee nursed her. I nursed her when I was there. I didn't make any theories about the mysteries of generation. The frightful, wonderful appearance of a bloodstained being from nowhere seemed to me beyond theory. They said that woman was the vessel, like the soil, and that each sperm contained a tiny huddled person waiting to implant him, or herself, in the furrow that was his mother; but the thought of my uncle going about with a regiment of coiled soldiers in his scrotum was too ludicrous to give the beginning of credence to.

What could I do in my stays? I did what all the women I knew did all the time. I waited and hoped.

Months was it we went on? Years? I can't tell in my memory how it worked out, because my time raced increasingly differently from those around me. I remember the celebrations for the victory at Blenheim. That obscure name suddenly became the most powerful word in the language. Sarah's husband, Marlborough, on his own initiative it seemed – for who could give the order for an adventure like that? – had marched in secret down the Rhine to support the collapsing Emperor Leopold against the French and Bavarians. Had he not won a most audacious and famous victory, the precarious equilibrium of power against power, Catholic against Protestant, Tory against Whig, under which we lived in those years could have toppled into chaos and threatened everything we'd worked for – even to devastating invasion.

The success at Blenheim, coming as it did out of nowhere, suddenly gave us the keys of Europe. We became secure overnight. Secure to operate our new system of the world. I remember the return – a winter parade through the freezing streets of the capital. It seemed the whole army had turned out in its full harness. It was dazzling and frightening. It was the power of men – our boys. It was Roman: our *new* New Model Army. It was a Roman Triumph: twenty-eight captured standards of the French legions were marched past, followed by cartloads of confiscated armour and wealth. In the park throughout the ceremonial they fired off forty heavy guns in unison, until everybody's windows rattled. That was when the Marlboroughs were given a huge fortune to build a national monument in Woodstock, and go and live in it. The battle, far off, out there in another land – another world even from mine – brought our Party once more into the ascendant. Charles, back in some degree of power, became more cheerful in spite of our problem.

Eventually I had the word I'd been waiting for: Nicholas Fatio de Duillier. He'd been a tutor to the Duke of Bedford's family. There'd been some scandal. It came out of nowhere in a conversation – I can't even remember who with.

At the same time it went about that Isaac had the Stone. At that point he was stumped – he could make no way, least of all with me. He contented himself with being vile to the Astronomer Royal. But the story broke over him. It was one of those inexplicable leaks that get into currency nobody knows how. Soon everyone had heard of it; while no one knew who had told it to whom, nor who had the story first. Pawnee, when I tackled her, absolutely denied having said a word about the packet and the crazed letter my uncle had sent to her in Woodstock.

'What do you think I am, Kit? How would it serve me to put it about?'

'I believe you, my dear. But where is the packet?'

'I don't remember what I did with it, Kit. Perhaps I left it in Woodstock. I don't know.'

Nevertheless the story seeped into the press:

It has come to our notice that there is a certain Vir Doctissimus *residing in this City who is in possession of that wondrous* Stone *of the Ancients. Alas these are credulous Times and many are those who seek to abuse the Public Ear with idleness, and tales of this or that Marvel. And are there not in every Age dupes and fools enough to swallow down these spurious Baits, and so fall prey to wily Cozeners; of which there exist in corresponding plenty. Yet truly few there are among us of so Stoical a cast that in their bones they do not fear the stalking on of Age, or the* agonies *attendant on the fleshly ills; so that the very breath upon the Forum or ἀγορα that such and such a person has the Universal Cure, will send us all a-running up and down to find the truth of it or no. For if liars and practicers abound, yet so does Truth; and there are Honourable Men who have attested throughout History, and with Integrity, that the Stone exists, and might indeed bring Remedy to a tormented,* Pestilence-afflicted Nation. And *certainly, we would not, in these pages, lend credit to such a Report as this did we not find it laid at the door of a Scholar of great Note and Consequence, renowned for unattainted Temperance. Therefore we wait upon the outcome with an equal mind: if this be true, then we live indeed in extra-*

ordinary Times and may hope Great Things; if false, then we shall all of us wake up the wiser on the Morrow.

And:

Turn back, O man. O thou sinful man that seekest to set aside God's blessed instruments. How shall the sinner be apprized of the vileness of his error? Who shall teach the harlot her evil and corruption? And how shall the righteous man uncover the sinner or guard himself from Satan if an overweening wizard shall set himself up to seek to remove the very signs of their iniquity? Let the learned doctor return to the way, and think on his own terrible end. Let not the world delude itself with mumblings of this Stone, with rumours of ease and idle deliverance. If these be indeed the Last Days, look not for cures, look rather for His harbingers, famine, war, plague, the great and small Pox. Verily the city sweats in its own corruption; noble and mean houses rot with sin. Victories abroad are delusions. Avaunt, thou whoremonger mathematician. Beware the thunder of His wrath. Guard indeed that there comes not a great clap into thine own house. Let thee cure first the stink that is under thine own nose, if thou canst. And if thou hast this Stone in truth, hide it thou presumptuous politician, lest the vicious prosper and the House of the Lord become an ordinary house of lewd entertainment. As for this generation of vipers, let them sting one another with their noxiousness; let them blast one another with great blains until they can dress it no longer but that their inner defilement burst forth from their gross impostumes like so many shitholes of Hell. Let the face grow flat, let the babe die and the old whore run mad. Or let this city turn from its Romish ways, as thou Dr N —— should turn from thine. Amen.

And:

They anoint his scratch with pus taken from the infected person. This dire recourse they claim will armour him against the like scourge of infection. It were a bold or desperate fellow to try it. Some there are who claim this is the Stone of the Philosophers, discovered newly by some Royal Society doctors, to make the small Pox a thing no more, and all human suffering to end. A fond dream, we think.

And this one, slightly incoherent and probably publicly punishable, was put about anonymously:

Is Art about to vanquish Nature? We believe the Philosophers' Stone to have been made at last by a distinguished Master of Arts, resident in

London. This claim, if true, (and have we not good reason to expect it?)
shapes to be something More than All Previous Claims to which the rumour
of the famous Elixir has often lent spurious credit. If the great Dr Newton of
Jermyn St. let it be known that he has made this Stone then the world should
bestir itself. We well remember that this Doctor stood up against tyranny at
the Glorious Revolution; how many modern great ones have done so much?
How many now that trim their course and line their pockets have forgotten
the tyrannical corruptions we are newly delivered from? In small part.
There are other tyrants than those in fleshly form; let all rational and
inspired men know this still, and put their sinew into the continual
struggle. It is fallen nature the Stone comes to cure; our parents in paradise,
if the fable is true, had no need of cures. Their nakedness knew no sin, no
leprosy to blight the fruition of their unmarried state of love; no murrain of
dukes and lords to infect the body politic with social and corporal ills. No
bloated bishops. Wit, vision and invention, not superstitious fears of fabu-
lous punishment, should be our watchword. We defy your Church. Let him
come forth if he has it. We see the vision of a new city. Let Albion restore the
fall, let new Adam consort with his New Eve without fear. What you are
pleased to call Eternity is at hand. Take up your wits and your weapons,
Brothers and Sisters.

And:

Can we not stir about these recent weeks without some sudden-made Philosopher *accosts us with his provoking Hypothesis of the Stone? My young*
Lord Quickmode assures me it is found at last, and has the power to
Vorticise Nature. At White's, honest Mr Oaktimber, in most weathers a
skeptical gentleman, boards me with Trismegistus, Ancient Memory, and,
for all I know it, the Pyramides in tow. 'The Stone!' says he. 'Its compo-
sition is all uncertain; its Essence is its own contradiction. Whoever
thinks he hath it, hath it not!' *And makes a face of profound significance,*
as if he has uncovered some Principle. *At Mrs Pengallant's salon I partake*
of tea and ratafia, and find the entire company professed Hermeticks; the
fashionable talk all of ἱεϱος γαμος, *the Sacred Marriage – a* Conjunction
of Opposites *indeed! Are we all laid under an Enchantment from this*
flim-flummery? In St James's, even Spring Garden grows new-season's
Chemists; for, walking out in search of clear air and clear Sense, I overhear
one speak earnestly of 'Light that may not be disclosed to Common
Sight'; *another replies with the* 'Grain of Ecstasy'; *and yet a third pipes in*

with 'Symbol of Truth, the Sophic Child'. *Aye, a symbol, Gentlemen, and a great one; but of little else, I fear, than giddy and childish Folly!*

And further:

Dr Newton's Stone or Elixir of Life may be had for 40 shil. at the house of Mr Littleton in Cheapside. It will cure all illness, restore the hair of a bald person, and give great extension and vigour to life. Cures barrenness in women. It may also be efficacious for the bite of a mad dog.

And, deliciously misconceived:

Dr Newton, of Jermyn St, was cut for the stone last week. It is believed he may recover.

Marlborough did it again at Ramillies. That must make the year '06. More triumphal celebrations, I recall. Charles was sent as Special Envoy to Hanover. To carry the Garter to the Elector was all he could say. He told me that he mustn't talk to me about State business. He was bound by secrecy. It made me feel my status all the more.

When he came back, he sent his man to arrange to see me, and then called for me. I could tell he was intrigued by the reports of the Stone.

He said to me, as we left our house amid the pack of interested parties who'd taken to hanging around outside, 'So your uncle has become a special cynosure, the focus of everyone's attention and invention.'

'Yes, Charles,' I said. 'He's quite distracted by it. We must keep our drapes closed and see no unidentified visitors. He doesn't go to the Mint on his horse now, he takes my carriage – your carriage – and drives with the shutters up. Even so there's a camp outside our house. Well, you see for yourself.'

We ignored the shouts and questions. We sat in his new chariot.

'Is it true he has the Stone? I never knew it. He told me nothing after . . . Cambridge. There was an experiment, you see. Some days before you came – and were ill. When I first saw you. Well, I say, there had been an experiment. You would not have known. I assisted him. But I believe there was no outcome; except that a serving boy was knocked unconscious in the process. Ugly fellow – I helped pull him out. But I've been assured he recovered. So is it true, Kit? Has he been at the metals again?'

171

'To my knowledge,' I said, 'he hasn't. As to the Stone . . . ' I looked at him carefully, 'I can't say.'

'Have you not asked him?'

'To ask him any such thing at the moment would be an act of gross folly, Charles!'

He laughed, but uneasily. He was wondering about the chance of a cure, no doubt. 'I still love you, Kit, damn it all to blood,' he said.

'Ah, love,' I said. 'What is that?'

'What indeed?' he replied moodily.

Having dined out at the Terentius, Charles and I came walking back to his chariot along Floral Street in Covent Garden. It was a hot Summer evening. Food smells and sweat and alcohol were on the air. People milled out of the doors of both Aston's where there was dicing going on, and The Chequers, on opposite sides of the narrow route. I looked up; a star or two in the deepening purple; lights in upper windows. We hurried past the sound of raised voices and turned into the larger thoroughfare. There were chairs and torches, and the rattle of horse traffic. In front of us we came upon a stir on the raised sidewalk. A small crowd had gathered round a shape lying by the kennel-edge. Their movement was to bend down, rise, look round and turn back, as if uncertain whether to tend to the victim or give chase to the assailant – for I caught the mention of a loaded stick and heard the words 'stone dead' as we approached the buzz of consternation. We halted on the edge of the ring. I knew Charles well enough to feel that he was worried he might be recognised. But we did peer down to see if anything helpful was being done. A man in a dark coat knelt at the head of the corpse, his knee and one black shoe carefully positioned to avoid the pool of blood that had run from the shocked head to gather into a dark mirror. In it floated a hat and a star.

I looked up across the agitated group. 'A body,' I thought to myself, 'continuing in its state of rest. According to his laws. Lord now lettest thou thy servant depart in peace, according to thy word.' I remembered the night of my delivery from the gunpowder mob. As I lifted my gaze, I found myself staring into the foxy eyes I had so often dreamed of seeing. It was Nicholas. I registered. He registered. He immediately looked away.

Could he have recognised me? Impossible. Impossible that he

172

should with his conscious mind make any connexion between the fashionable woman and the wolfish boy. But his eyes had known something.

Charles pulled at my arm to move on. We skirted the group. 'Do something for me,' I said.

'Terrible. Terrible. Commonplace. What can be done? Cheap spirits coming in. It's going to get worse,' he muttered.

'That man over there.' I was already searching with my eyes the place where I'd seen him.

'Where?'

'He was there. The hell.' My heartbeat was fierce. 'I can't lose him now.' I made my way round the scene of the tragedy. 'Is that him?' to myself almost. Charles allowed himself to be yanked along.

'What're you doing?'

'Yes. There he is.'

Nicholas's back appeared twenty yards away illuminated dully by the shaft of light from an open doorway. The lining to his expensive cape glowed scarlet where the edge was flicked back – like an underwing.

I couldn't just snatch Charles's short sword from its interior pocket in his coat, where I knew he carried it. I couldn't just do this and run after my enemy to impale him there and then, through the back of the neck, and then through the mouth. Through the mouth; while the rest of the street bothered about the man with the hat and the blood. We cannot and do not do these things, no matter how much they've preoccupied us. I dithered, lost for words, like anyone else, and furious with myself. And a gap had opened. And closed?

'What is it, Kit?'

'He mustn't get away. We must go after him,' I managed to say.

'Why?'

'It's him. Charles, please. This is him. Help me now.' I pulled him along.

The man in the cape looked back once. It *was* Nicholas, I was sure of it, and I danced myself in a great swirl in front of Charles so that he might think I was merely some courtesan drunk and showing off to her client; it was all I could think of to do, and it matched my rush of elation. Then I pulled Charles into a doorway from which we both peered cautiously round like conspirators in a play. Nick crossed into St Martin's Lane behind a pair of coaches. And then Charles screamed involuntarily because he discovered that our doorway was already occupied by someone trying to sleep rough.

Our chariot was back past the bludgeoned man – Charles had given instructions for his driver to meet us. We were caught between the need to follow our quarry – my quarry – and the danger and difficulty of proceeding on foot. I didn't know these streets. I didn't know at the time that this would be the area of my future home when my uncle removed here much later.

But we had luck. I saw Nicholas get into a chair that was waiting on a narrow corner. The chairmen hoisted it up and set off at a good pace, turning Southward in our direction.

We shrank ourselves into a new, unoccupied doorway until they were past, and then hurried back. I hoped desperately that there would be no trouble at the scene of the accident and that Boyle, Charles's driver, was as good as his instructions.

He was. Once inside we were completely incognito, and could follow the chair without hindrance.

That was how I found out where Nicholas lived, although we had to wait at a club, and wait again while he called at another house, so that it was the small hours before we got home.

Chocolate with my Enemy

The house was at the end of Millbank. At the first opportunity I made Charles take me to reconnoitre. It was a muggy Sunday afternoon. We joined the couples and families out strolling, taking care not to be too fine. Charles brought his spaniel Jeff, so we should look the part all the more. We followed the river past the Westminster Mill and out into the flat waste to which the Mill gave its name. Charles threw sticks for Jeff. I leant on his arm. Eventually we came up to the house, which looked out over the river and was made, like ours, in what they referred to as the Dutch style, only it was more idiosyncratic and slightly countrified. At the rear there was a walled garden, behind which ran the road, or path. Then on the right-hand side of the road there were outbuildings and farm sheds which led the eye out to the first hedges of the fields. Clearly it was a house of some consequence. Charles knew it.

'This belongs to a Royal Society member,' he said. 'I forget the

174

man's name. It's some time since I attended. It's on the tip of my tongue. I haven't kept track of the new members, they're aristocratic sops and well-off makeweights many of them, but I remember being told about this place; someone had had it built.' He raised his eyes, and shook his head. Then he snapped his fingers: 'I've got it. Morland. That was the man.'

Jeff pulled us conveniently close to the wall, so that we could snoop with some legitimacy. The wall had in it, to my great satisfaction, not a close-fitting door, but one of the new style of ironwork gates, so that we could stare in with ease at the back elevation of the house, while pretending to hustle the dog along. Within was an unremarkable sight, the rear of the building rising from a functional kitchen garden. We could hear a snorking sound close up against the other side of our wall which was most likely to be a pig. I say the view was unremarkable, except for one thing there was a little summer-house, over to our left amongst a few shrubbed fruit trees, which seemed very pretty; round, and glazed above a waisting of brickwork. Glazed, in a manner I had never seen before and which most caught Charles's attention, such that there was no thatch nor tiling for a roof, but a contrivance of curving glass, which continued the frames and leadwork of the sides until it knotted at the top. It was what we should now call a conservatory, but I describe it as it seemed to us then, a new phenomenon. I bore it strongly in mind.

We walked on. A few drops of rain dashed down out of the sultry sky, which all afternoon had threatened more than it actually delivered. I didn't know what to do – how to proceed from here. I got Charles to stop. Jeff ran round, panting.

'Well, Kit,' Charles said.

But before I could answer the skies opened. It solved the immediate problem. We called at the house.

Even so we were pretty wet when, the 'Master' being absent, we were shown into the drawing-room by a young servant dressed in a long black robe; 'to wait until we could continue our recreation'. I took the opportunity to look around the room, but once again it was nothing remarkable – a comfortably furnished new place belonging to a comfortably-off man. There was no fire lit, because it was Summer, so we had to stay in our wet things looking at the downpour outside.

The servant came back. It seemed he was some sort of trainee of

175

the Church, since he showed strict white throat-grabbing bands at the top like a regular hard-school clergyman. But the extra lace that protruded from the long gown at every opportunity reminded me of caricatured images of Catholic priests I'd seen. And perhaps there was a trace of faint perfume in the air.

I took a chance.

'If the Master is out I suppose Monsieur is with him?'

There was a raised eyebrow of surprise – no more – before the reply came back. Was Madam acquainted with the Master's friends? He had no idea. Thought we were passing persons of quality, who happened to be caught in the rain. Of course if they knew the Master personally . . . He would go and see if Monsieur was at home to visitors or whether he was indisposed at the present. Whom should he say . . . ?

I launched in: 'Lord and Lady Barton. We left the coach some yards away.'

The young man wafted out.

Charles and I stood looking at each other. His features were pinched and tense. I suppose otherwise, however, we appeared nondescript enough – his lesser style of wig still held a considerable curling frame around his face, and his neckcloth went up under his chin, so that he might have been any personable man; while my lace cap and hat had taken so much rain on board that I felt as though I was presented from under a shapeless tunnel.

It wasn't long before the 'servant' reappeared. Behind him, dressed in a similar long dark robe with the sprouting white, was the man I'd been waiting for.

More than ten years had passed since I'd had a clear view of him. He looked smaller, weaker, and of course older, beneath his flowing wig, than I remembered. But the foxy face, the insinuating look – now over a pair of spectacles – was still there, pointed at me across the room. I caught my breath in spite of my resolve to remain in control. It brought it all back, the smoky chamber in Cambridge, the charged frenetic atmosphere of the two men and his horrible deed. Three men! Of course, Charles had come – a fact which this impulsive probe had driven from my mind, possibly because I couldn't actually recall having seen them together. I prayed that his present mode would be disguise enough.

My enemy spoke. 'Lord and Lady Barton,' in that instantly recognisable accent. 'Nicholas Fatio de Duillier. Allow me to present my compliments,' and he stretched out to us a black arm with a white-rushed hand on the end of it.

Charles muttered: 'So sorry to intrude. Caught in the rain. Dog. Morland's house. Royal Society connexion. Hope you don't mind.'

'Think no more of it,' Nicholas said. 'Enchanted, Sir and Madam. So sorry not to have greeted you properly – and dear Morland has ridden into town. Will you take something? Chocolate? Gabriel, could you manage that?' The gowned servant lifted his eyebrows again.

We looked out at the continuing rain.

'Please,' I said, before Charles could refuse.

So I supped chocolate with my enemy before preparing to send him down. We learnt that the house was given over to the prep-aration of Prophetic Ordinands, and that Nicholas and Morland pre-pared them. The two others, besides the simpering Gabriel, were out in Preaching and Works. At least that was the story.

I wondered if we might see where the candidates studied. Charles looked fiercely at me, desperate to leave the falsehood, clearly recol-lecting the acquaintance and protective as always of his public per-sona, not to mention his career. But, thankfully, I saw no evidence that he was recognised, nor indeed any indication that Nick had the remotest idea who *I* might be. The flash of recognition which had bound us for a night-time second in the London street where an incidental victim lay in the pool of his own blood – that knowledge wasn't operating now. I had the chance to observe him from the genuine protection of my incognito.

Nick was pleased to show us the back room. It had little sign of being used as a study, beyond the fact of the writing desk and some incongruous male martyrdoms on the wall; but there were a few scientific instruments: a Newtonian telescope, and a Galilean. And an orrery occupied a corner. In here the faint unpleasant religious perfume lay heavier on the air.

'I see,' said Charles, altering his voice 'that your ordinands con-template the heavens in more than one way.'

Nick smiled. 'We calculate the date of the last days, Sir. It is a mathematical and, to some degree, an astronomical task, besides the fact that we toil to understand what is the secret language of the Holy

Prophets of both Testaments. Though naturally our study is always and chiefly upon Revelations.'

As I stood at the window looking out, I recollected that this was material that he'd 'borrowed' from my uncle. I said: 'What a delightful summer-house, Sir. A little bower. Such an original.' A shaft of sun broke through the cloud and illuminated the garden.

'Indeed, Madam. It is our little observatory. The Master of the house, he has a consuming astronomical passion. It is, as I believe you say, his Hobby-Horse.'

We all laughed. Charles made the appropriate meteorological remarks to get us out, but I had fixed the interior of the glass summer-house, with its little couch, its chair and table, in my mind, with a kind of intuitive awareness that that was the place.

'Anne, I must go into disguise.'

'Why, Kit. Have you turned common thief, or strolling player?'

'It's a secret matter, connected with Charles's government work. Beyond that, my dear, I'm not permitted to say; but it's a matter of great urgency. I need your help.'

'Are the French coming? The Austrians? Oh, Kit, not the Austrians! He wouldn't hand you over. He loves you, Kit.'

'Just be serious a moment. I'm to become a personable young man. As personable as possible.'

'Well,' she said. 'A breeches role. Try my get-up for the *Adventures in Madrid*. I never liked doing it. Crowd-pleasing. I'm reduced to this to hold my career together.'

We made our way to a theatre, possibly the new Haymarket, but I can't be entirely sure, where Anne took me backstage. It reminded me of the eve of my contract with Charles. Here she bustled about to find me a suitable costume. 'Look, these are Laura's legs.' I started to climb into the garment she held out. 'The only consolation is that one's calves are still shapely enough for Mr Citizen to want to see them and take the memory home with him after the show; that's a boost to morale if not to Art. We do it for the money. I suppose I can't complain, Kit. You say you don't want a coat?' I told her no and that I could secure a good wig through Charles, although she insisted on trying out various designs which she found, and showing me the result in the actors' mirror. In everything I looked distressingly like a girl in men's clothing. Very promising for the stage, titillating even, but not what I was trying for. My spirits drooped.

But then she brought out her make-up box, and in this lay the key to the matter: false hair. She showed me how to make very delicate adjustments to the eyebrows and the upper lip.

'Well,' she said. 'But you are still too beautiful, too sweet. We shall have to paint a little, perhaps.' So between us we contrived a slight darkening of the skin, and the hint of razorableness. It wasn't the unhealthy face of the wolf-boy, but it made me feel curiously possessed by my old self again, the longer I walked and talked in my painted shape – which she made me do, taking a professional interest in her creation. She re-educated my movement, inducing a swagger and a stride which I'd lost the art of entirely. Then we searched for a cane to create some sense of male authority.

'You must practise for a week,' she said. She would allow me no less.

So during this week I had Charles make discreet enquiries concerning Morland. His house was indeed a house of curious religious intent. The sect was an extreme one, obsessed with the last days, and the entry into alternative states of mind. There was chanting and ecstatic speaking, but also a predilection for fine lace. They were, at least ostensibly, a quaking fraternity of the fringe, deeply confusing, and perhaps themselves confused, as to their theological position. Charles said his sources gave Morland as a simple figurehead with an interest in science. There was, however, a frequent resort to the house by all kinds and conditions of men, who attended meetings and chantings there, but left afterwards; whereas the ordinands lived in. I had my own dark suspicions about Nicholas's infiltration into the group.

I was most pleased, out of all this information, to hear of the services for non-residents. As my last requirement from Charles before the event, I asked him to have a man research the times and days of attendance. I should have liked to have a companion for my visit, but this would have run the risk of finding myself somehow incriminated. So I went alone in my male attire and my old restraint coat made up to look more of the fashion.

Abel Slaughter

Dressed as a man, and with my usually slow oddity of a heart knocking against my ribs, I attended the Tuesday evening meeting, loosed down the Millbank path by a deeply troubled Charles. I was welcomed warmly into the community – chairs were placed in the main room, the one Charles and I had first waited in – and here we sat to listen to the address by Mr Morland. I was acutely aware before proceedings started that I was wearing the wrong sort of hat; either I'd missed this curiosity during our arrival, through my nervousness and animation, or they'd all come hither under their regular covering, and had whipped these roll-rim specimens out of bags to put them on as soon as they'd entered. Whichever, they all except me had a unique kind of headgear, which, astonishingly, no one removed during the worship.

Mr Morland was a tall, cadaverous man, who talked above the assembly; literally above their curl-brim hats. He seemed not to like to catch the eye of anyone present, but fixed his gaze on the wall beyond the sea of brims, while he preached of the last days and the seals and the beast. He was so unconvincing, in the religious sense, that I wondered what any of the company came for. I looked around me: I supposed they were mainly people of a middle sort of rank – householders probably, or skilled professionals. I say mainly, for there were also a sprinkling who might be the ones I was seeking to join.

When the address was finished the humming started. It came out of nowhere; suddenly the room was filled with a species of human vibration, a deep welling up of someone's being. One in the group must suddenly have felt moved to begin. Gradually others joined in, and soon I thought I could detect the gaunt tone of Morland himself. People would pump themselves up after the great run of their humming, so that I saw men's chests heaving in a random pattern of renewed breaths all around the room. There was something haunting about this randomness set against the strange harmony all about. I hummed myself, and then suddenly stopped because my voice came out in the female register. Thereafter I pretended to hum.

Mr Morland started his preaching again. This time he was different, charged. He talked about sin. The young man next to me suddenly began to oscillate – I can think of no other word for it – he oscillated about the fulcrum of his sitting-bones, backwards and forwards in a see-saw motion, while still continuing to hum. Soon, others were moved to follow his example, until the room became a harmonic wash of hats and waistcoats. Mr Morland's eyes went even more distant as he preached, until I distinctly saw them cross, as if he were losing himself in contemplation of his nose even as he jerked out his meditations on the carnalities of the world. He was particularly concerned with the evil possibilities of women, a matter in which he resembled my uncle at his most paranoid. I felt the affront, being there as a representative of both genders.

Suddenly Nick was with Morland, as hatted as the rest; I don't know where he entered from, he just appeared there. Morland left off the struggle for coherence in his argument and launched into a strong new tone in the humming, to which a number of people in the company gave spontaneous reply. Then he gave himself up to what sounded like haphazard denunciations of particular sins. These were eagerly responded to by those seated, so that they stood up to give back the sentiment, before subsiding to chair level. Another dimension was added to the heaving space:

'If he sin with a beast, let him be stoned!'
'Let the beast be also put to death!'
'If he be taken in adultery!'
'Whoredom! Whoredom!'
'Let the adulterer hang next to the adulteress!'
'Let them both be stoned!'
'It is the last days. Prepare ye, brethren!'
'We are prepared!'
'It is the time of the Lord's coming!'
'Leave your fornication!'
'Fornication!'
'Jerusalem! Jerusalem!'
'I have coveted her mightily!'
'Turn ye from her. Turn ye!'
'I have spilled my seed!'
'Sin no more, brother!'
'Yea!'
'For the Lord He is coming!'
'Famine!'

'Fire!'

'Earthquake!'

'Yea! Brethren!'

Some of the calls lost their relation to language altogether, becoming simply syllabic concatenations. I tried to give the impression of full and active participation, while keeping Nick as closely in my sights as I could. He appeared artistically rapt: in full view and profound trance, with his spectacles balanced on the bridge of his nose.

This ecstasy then was what the people came for; I saw that now.

It lasted about an hour, then died away, leaving the men changed, glowing, purged, prepared for the dreadful hour and the coming week. Morland left without speaking to anyone. A youth in the corner sobbed audibly. Nick was with him.

'Bear witness, brethren, that the Lord, the most high Seigneur, the Pantocrator, the Architect, has given token of mercy upon our brother's soul.' His accent was hypnotic, his English much improved. 'He weeps in repentance for his sins. He is prepared. His soul is washed whiter than the snow by this weeping. Whiter than new wool. Bear witness to his contrition. His act has been accepted. I feel this. I feel it. Can you also not feel this, brethren?'

A mutter of 'Aye, we feel it' from those around. Another was moved to weep – a fat man at the front. He called out: 'I am bereft of hope of eternal life. I am no more than a worm!'

'See to him, brothers,' said Nick, his arm still draped round the youth. He kissed him openly on the cheek. 'Thou art accepted, child.'

'I cannot be received,' said the fat man. 'I am heavily oppressed.' While earnest attempts were made by his peers to wrestle with the fat man's despair, I saw Nick lead the stricken youth out of the chamber, with his arm about his shoulder.

'Where should I acquire my headgear, Sir?' I asked of a fellow aspirant who was just coming out of his state of rapture. I hoped to have to say the minimum in case my voice should give me away.

'Of Mr Kettle, here. They are his manufacture.'

Mr Kettle promised to have the proper thing for me at the following Tuesday's meeting. Cheerfully, I gave my name as Abel Slaughter.

'Well?' said Charles, meeting me at the mill.

'Well enough, indeed,' I said. I felt keyed up and thrilled, even a little faint now it was over.

Nevertheless, I became a properly head-dressed adept, and went back three times on the next three Tuesdays. On one of them, I saw again Nicholas's skilful harvesting of a pretty weeper. Then I cunningly left out a week. By the time I was ready for my attempt there was a hint of Autumn in the air.

And if any mischief follow, then thou shalt give life for life, eye for eye, tooth for tooth, hand for hand, foot for foot, burning for burning, wound for wound, stripe for stripe.

Payment in kind: the old market-place. I remarked the personal nature of the trade I was about to embark on. A query had been buzzing in my mind during the month leading up to this my attempt. It was partly the question of memory. I suppose it was the sighting of Nick and all that brought up. I saw myself pushing away the recollection of that night in Cambridge even as I was intensely motivated by it. I recalled it and I didn't recall it. That very focus reminded me I had no memory of what went before. Here, now, I sought payment. But no money would do. Anonymous money would diffuse and disturb the overriding importance of 'It was him. That one. He did it. I remember. I witnessed it myself. I saw it all.' Only the direct, Biblical payment would do.

And here it was. It was the connexion between the bargain and the memory. For without the explicit memory I might collect my revenge from anyone – for money. Like a whore, and like a whore's client. No. I sought justice, and to end the thing, not perpetuate it. I wanted the original offender. And Nick was the only one I had. I wanted him. No one should make me, see me, call me whore. Please God I was not a whore.

Athene

Pet gave birth to her third. 'Shelling peas? Not quite,' she said. 'Can a body stop, or does it go on for ever?'

I was appointed to sit for my portrait to Mr Kneller at Whitton. Charles took me to the studio – we should call it so now – in his unfinished country house; I was got up in my finery, though it was still comparatively early morning when we arrived. Posed in the soft, equal, northern light from his casements, I attempted to hold my excited self still, while the ponderous German prepared his sketches and starts. A small fire struggled on the far wall to warm the considerable space.

The painter peered closely at the chromatic texture of my face from a variety of angles. He humphed. He wandered further off. He returned, placed a hand on my brow to adjust me, and then grunted as he encountered my bump. But he did not, I was thankful, betray it to Charles; who, for all his love, had never probed my hairline during our years.

The artist placed his apparatus. Then he moved it. Then he moved it back nearly to where it was before, closer to the fire. He approached me again and studied the revelation of my bosom. Suddenly and delicately he pinched the flesh – not so as to hurt, but to assess, so I supposed, its nature. I was too taken aback to speak. Kneller turned to Charles.

'She would make an excellent Athene.' His German origin still coloured his intonation. 'Strip off all this.' He jerked at my bodice, still looking at Charles. 'It could be done if you wished. A pastoral background.' The 'R's bubbled at the back of his throat. 'The helmet and so on I could put in later. It would be no trouble. It would be an interesting challenge, this face.'

'Just as she is, Gottfried,' Charles said hastily. 'Eh, Kit dearest?'

'Well . . . ' I thought about the change of plan. It aroused me; I was all stirred up anyway. 'I'd love to be an Athene, Charles.'

'You have to take off all these – to be draped, uncorseted, free. You do understand?' said Kneller. 'I don't usually employ the classical mode; but you are so striking, I make an exception.' He took hold of my jaw and moved my face thus and thus, studying the bones beneath my skin against the dark remission of space behind me. Then he peered down at my neck again. 'Ah,' he held up his hand. 'I have no lewd designs, just in case this worries you. I've had my fill of women just now. To me you are merely the still-life. Ha ha.'

'I'm not in the slightest worried about that,' I replied. 'I have Charles to see me safe. But I'm deeply flattered that you view me so, Sir. Athene and a lobster fruit bowl in the same breath.'

Kneller roared; Charles looked furious.

'Come then. Off with it all. Go behind the screen. Or shall I?'

'Yes,' I said. 'Here will do for me. Help me, Charles.'

I knew he was fiercely against the whole idea, so I struck for it. I could sense the heat of his rage. Soon I was naked in my chair and the equal northern light, except for my little silver satin shoes with the low heel. Kneller, with only a casual discretion as to my modesty, came out with some filmy sheets, and I tucked them round me. Then he arranged me, exposing this, concealing that. Charles sulked horribly as another man tweaked my charms into the image of his fancy.

So Kneller got to work. He painted and humphed and grunted for two hours. Then he left us alone in order to walk in his garden and smoke, promising to return shortly with some refreshment. 'And, by the by,' he added, 'the chamber-pot also is behind the screen.'

I got up and stretched provocatively, then huddled the classical sheets round me.

'What do you think you're doing?' Charles hissed.

'Doing, dearest?' I replied with my eyelids, mostly.

He pulled suddenly at my gauzy cover. It came away. I stood nude.

'Come, Kit. I believe I'm enabled at last. Come. Look, the sophy in the corner,' He was urgent at me and struggling out of his coat.

'What do you think *you're* doing?' I threw back at him, furiously, stamping my little shoe.

'Kit, my love, I'm restored. Look! Feel! We must seal the matter before Gottfried comes back. I'm all aflame for you,' and he caught me up against him, swept me along and pushed me towards the sophy, so that my shoe slipped under me and I bumped painfully down on the edge of the upholstery with half a raw buttock.

'Charles!' I cried, but he took no notice because he was fiddling with his buttons.

'Kit!' he breathed, lowering himself over me, one hand still wrestling with his breeches, the other between my knees. I clamped them shut, then rolled off the seat, crawled and slithered to the fireplace and took up the poker. I suppose I was more like the warrior maiden Athene at that moment than at any other. My legs were planted astride and the poker was raised above my shoulder, ready to do battle: I didn't see why I should be instantly available just because he'd been triggered by the Classics, contract or no contract. Charles came over at me, holding up his breeches with his left hand.

'Kit!'

I couldn't strike him, but I stood there quivering with energy until he changed hands at his breeches and grabbed my wrist. Then, abandoning them to their fall, he disarmed me of the poker and struck me with his open hand hard across the face.

'You damned whore!' he said, and struck me twice more, once in the face and once across my back as I turned away from the pain. Then he got dressed, pulling up the worsted past his forgotten manhood. I caught up my draperies again and retreated to the chair of portraiture with them pulled all about me. I fixed him with my furious eye, and sat it out there, absolutely still until the painter returned.

Long minutes passed.

Kneller came in with some Chinese tea, the big man with the exquisitely small cups and teapot before him on a lacquered tray. He looked at Charles, and then at me. He placed the tray down on a small footstool in the middle of the frozen space between us. He poured.

'Tea?' he said.

It was an uncomfortable second sitting. Athene's noble face had a great red mark across it. Her eye blazed Greek fire. The artist was much challenged regarding the preliminary tones of her cheek.

Later, in the coach home, I broke the electric air between us.

'When you hit me, Charles, you called me a damned whore.'

'God forgive me, Kit.'

'But will I forgive you?'

'I entreat you. Forgive the unforgivable.'

'You may entreat me. I've been thinking, about the whore you called me, by the by.'

'Kit! I meant nothing. It was the heat of the moment. As you might call a man a dog. And regret it when you was cool.'

I would play with him. 'And yet, Charles, there's a kind of truth, the more I think of it. I have a whore's mind, I believe.'

'Dearest!'

'No. Listen. I put up the terms to your desire. That you should teach me and finance me and help me and so on.'

'Then marriage itself is a whoredom. Kit, we've been here before. It is the condition of man. Commerce, agreement, trade.'

'Of man? It is the condition of woman, my dear. Commerce. Doesn't the word itself have that very meaning: you've had commerce with me – so some would say.'

'Well, well. You've the advantage of me just now. As always, it seems.'

'I wish it could be otherwise, do you know. I do, Charles.'

'Well indeed, I say. And so do I. What can I do to make up for my . . . treatment of you?'

'But you must pay me. According to our bond, you know. You must. And so I want to know, Charles. This recoinage of yours. Where does the money come from? I must understand these things. Do you see that?'

'No I don't. What damned use are they to you?'

'Well, no matter. Just tell me.'

'What? You want to know about all this now? You really do, don't you?'

'Indeed I do. Where does the money come from? That is what I want to know.'

He heaved a great sigh. 'It comes from what the land produces.'

My mind was racing. 'Stones, alligators, mists and blackberries, Charles. I can see how a blackberry is a form of wealth to a hungry person, but not an alligator or a mist. And why is one stone worthless and another priceless?' I flicked at the diamond earring he'd given me.

'You're right. The other factor is need. There can be no wealth without need.'

'Wealth. I have what you need. So trade. I understand this. Yes. We know these things, but somehow we don't know them until we tease them out, as in our mobile academy of two here, Charles. Platonically. Human needs, what are they?'

'Food. Shelter. Clothing. Without these we die.'

'Love,' I said. 'So he who corners the market in such commodities grows rich. Is that what you've done, Charles?' Before he could answer, I ran on with my questions. 'And toil? Labour? Work?' I made him tell me his conception of it all – the production of value. So that I could demolish it. He built it all up patiently, using the folk at

187

work in the fields of Middlesex beside us as his exemplum. He justified beautifully, brilliantly, logically the primacy of property.

'By what right does the owner own the land?' I cut in.

'By hereditary right. Or by purchase. This is the foundation of the State.'

'Ownership?'

'Property. Since from property springs wealth.'

'But how does the owner get it?'

'How did you get your beauty, Kit? By birth.'

'I think not, Charles. I think by Art, but we'll say no more of that. The father of the landowner, how did he come by the birthright?'

'As you say, Kit. It's a birthright.'

'But Adam was cast out from his land to labour in the sweat of his brow. Who then took the garden? Whence came the wealth? That Abraham passed to Isaac, for example. I said once to you that the Golden Age was a myth, but Pawnee tells me that in America there was a paradise where all needs were supplied by Nature without husbandry and the savages dined off gold without regarding it.'

'Kit.' He held up a hand but my thoughts tumbled on. It was the prospect of my revenge. I couldn't stop it. It was like a sort of hunt. I said:

'The Spanish and Portuguese took away the gold and set light to the savages. And we sent ships to pirate a little of this wealth from *them*. Why not? asked all England. This money, I say, came from nowhere. A miracle. It was gold that just appeared. Your family is very rich, Charles, up in Northampton where we both, by chance, have our roots. How did that come about, your family estate?'

Again, painfully, logically, he justified his noble family's stewardship.

Then he gestured out over the flat fields by Hammersmith. 'London's full of wealthy men – well, has there ever been such harvest of wheat, such abundance of all other crops, such availability of beef, so many herds of sheep? No there hasn't. And certainly not before '88. These are the fruits of wealth creation.'

'Then why, when I drive about the city, do I see so many filthy beggars a-waiting on corners, or harbouring down alleys? Why is my coach accosted by the swarms of ragged children when I go beyond Leicester Fields? Little animals of dirt requiring only a few more years of thieving and starvation until they may be ready to whore themselves to survive. Why do I hear of so many abortions and infanticides? Yes, I read what I read. Why do so many day-labourers, as I hear, have to toil hours into the night so they can feed their families? Why are these things, Charles?'

'Do you think I don't care? Do you think I too am not horrified? But it takes time. In the establishment of the future there must be an organisational policy for labour. Hands must be put to honest work.'

I gazed through the glass, unsatisfied. In my excitement and anger, I saw myself on the very brink of connecting what had happened to me with the general expression of the system. We trotted smoothly here on the well-made highway. Far off I counted four great windmills strung out along a faint ridge.

'Charles, I understand these affairs of land and labour. It's clear enough, we said, didn't we? What preoccupies me is your market. Trade, dealing, exchange. How is it that the rich scramble to buy these stocks of your creation?'

'Not of my creation, dearest. I'm not responsible for *every* financial institution.'

'Aren't you, Charles? I sometimes wonder. Well, how do great profits come from the Exchange?'

'I risk,' he said, 'therefore I may gain.'

'So we escape the curse of Adam by hazard? As you would at cards or dice?'

'How should a great enterprise be begun if not by the subscription and choice?'

'How is it that with all this choice they never choose to relieve the suffering of the wretched houseless rabble? They are human beings, and they have no hope of property. The whores and their choking babes?'

'You are concerned. Well and good. But consider your own situation. You owe your own health, your very security to what we've done, your uncle and I and the rest of us.'

'I'm conscious of it. I feel it.'

'Then feel that an assault on property would be an assault upon your own prosperity, my dear, as well as that of the State. On your security, on your freedom. Blow down those walls and what do you have? You remember that night when they tried to overturn your car. That fellow I skewered; would you want him sharing your table? Your bedroom?'

I put my hand to the still-stinging welt on my cheek. He went on: 'Thank God *you're* not poor, Kit. Just thank whatever God it is you acknowledge that you're not poor.'

'To what do I owe it that I'm not? To the God who gave me my beauty? This, it seems, is my stock in trade.'

'You will have it so. It's always flung in my face.'

'Fists are flung in mine.'

'I've told you I'm sorry. I am human. I've done what I could. I do what I can. Athens was a democracy, by God. And I am a man. I have needs. I believe Pericles himself may have felt that after his labours he had a right to the comforts of the love of another human soul when he turned to his Aspa . . . ' he halted halfway through the word, aware that he'd caught himself out.

I leapt on his discomfiture. 'Yes! Exactly! Aspasia! An elegant whore. My original point exactly, I believe. Pericles, it seems, was one of the few privileged and elegant Athenians who preferred, while balancing above a social pyramid of slaves, fornication to sodomy. It won't do, Sir. It all sounds very familiar, seen from my side.'

'Can't you just be grateful? For what is well in your life? Without dumping everything that damned well offends you at my door. You bite the hand that feeds you, Madam. Will you be satisfied with nothing?'

'Am I to be satisfied with blows? Just tell me; I'd like to know. I'll tell you what I suspect, my dear. I suspect that at the root of it all there's nothing more than piracy. I'm not satisfied that I should look back on Adam's disobedience, nor Eve's concupiscence, nor leaves of shame, nor apples of guilt. More likely I think the Eden business was the same case of expulsion as for the American savages who dined on their innocent gold: more powerful, greedier folk turned up. Me? I look back upon an original violation. In the beginning was the rape!' I turned my flaring cheek into his line of vision. 'Saving your reverence, my Lord.'

He took out his enamel snuffbox, and pushed, between the sway-ings of the cabin, some traces of the mixture into his nostrils. 'It's a world in which the strong survive,' he said.

I got my window open and spat contemptuously out at the speed-ing hedgerow.

We made the rest of our journey in silence, but my brain was a ferment. I wanted to have Nicholas at my mercy.

Moth

I'd grown quite accustomed by now to putting on the tiny traces of false hair, glued without hint of artifice, and the male clothes; I regarded myself as approaching the professional. For the final meeting, though, I took some extra items concealed in the inside pockets of my old coat of restraint.

On the assigned night I was so exaggerated in spirits that even as I was dressed to kill, so to speak, and Charles and I were making our way down Millbank to the place where we would hide my female clothes (in case Abel Slaughter should need suddenly to vanish into the night), I couldn't desist from engaging him still further about the financial question. Forgive me. Charles hardly could. It mattered so much to me. It was as though *everything* were immediately within my grasp.

'Money, coin, is an index of value, yes? An *idea* of worth?'

'Yes,' he replied wearily – weary of my insistence on what he regarded as an irrelevancy, at a time when our lives possibly were at stake. Certainly his career.

'Gold is in itself a nonsense. This you realised, in the Exchequer bills. It has no value in itself?'

'As little as the diamonds in your ears, my darling,' he said. I put my hand up to my ears with a start. In my haste and overconfidence, I'd forgotten to take them out. My hand shook. He took them out for me and pocketed them safe.

I continued. 'So what coins do is to make the matter of trade – the market-place of goods for goods – into . . . ' I groped for the concept. 'Money makes the market-place, the Agora, into a thing of infinite extension and duration.'

'How so?'

'If I pay a tradesman in Smithfield with coin for a pig, and he buys a coat in Cheapside a month later with the same coin, then what might have been an instantaneous exchange of coat and pig has been opened up by the gold coin; expanded in time and space.'

'Ingenious,' he grudged. We stooped in the dark under the low bough of a great elm by the river bank, and scrambled down to hide my bundle. We covered it over with vegetation.

'I say this is a gap, Charles.'

'Whatever you wish.'

'No, more though. It's a gap peopled with the man who sold me the pig, and his wife and troubles. A whole new universe. What do you think? One that wouldn't have existed before. Why, the pigman might never have been born. Unless it were the tailor. Or me!'

'Oh Kit! We're nearly there.'

'Now your paper money. What sort of world would that create? Do you think fictional money would create fictional time and space? And then we could cash it in at your Bank!'

'Kit!'

Charles's instructions were to wait for me outside the little wrought-iron gate to the garden.

The meeting worked up to its usual excitement. This time I was bold enough to surrender myself a little to the emotion. I knew I should have to secure my place with Nick by breaking out in tears before anyone else, so I thought hard about the suffering I'd had at his hands, while we all rocked and swayed and hummed. It was a powerful recipe; I found myself caught up despite myself. At the end I judged the moment for my tears, and called out, in as deep a voice as I could construct: 'I was lost, but now I am saved. My heart is unbound!'

I wasn't a moment too soon with my sobs, because a rival took up from the other side of the room almost immediately. Nevertheless Nick's arm was soon around me and his lips were brushing my cheek.

'Ah, dear brother Abel,' he said, 'I have seen the contrition in your heart waiting to burst forth.' Then he turned to the company. 'Brethren, the Lord has moved our new brother Abel to walk in His ways at the last. Have you not seen in him, as I have, the heaviness of vile sin which he now throws off, thank the Lord? Did you not perceive with me that he was ripe for God? Truly he shall receive. Praise be!'

There came the replies of 'Praise be,' and so on. I tried as hard as I could to persevere with my sobs of deliverance. Nick escorted me from that room into the study.

It was dark outside now. The study was hardly illuminated; merely the glow from a little fire in the grate and the throw from a single candle. In the study sat the black-gowned Gabriel, smoking a short pipe. The air was heavy with that religious fume I'd noticed lingering on our first visit.

Nicholas wanted to sit me down in the study, but I laid my head against him weakly.

'Sir, I'm most grateful to you for your tender care, but I feel as though I shall faint. Could you bear to support me a turn in the garden? It is the air I need. How should I have fallen upon such human love, that has brought me to His grace? Indeed I was a broken sinner.'

Gabriel laughed.

I felt Nick's fury at him. 'He laughs for joy at one sheep who returns to the fold before the terrible days. Open the door for me, Monsieur.' There was a French door which gave on to the garden. Nick manoeuvred me towards it.

'Must I, dear?' said Gabriel, drifting unhelpfully over and undoing the bolt.

'A thousand thanks,' Nick gasped as he pulled me out of the room. I laid much of my weight about his neck as if I had in fact almost fainted. Thus, lolling my head, I saw out of one eye Gabriel's tall, robed figure watching us ironically from the doorframe. I hoped to God that Charles was by now in place.

Pretending to come round a little, I said, whispering in the dark of the garden: 'But I fear I am still confined by my sin, Sir.'

'What sin possesses you Abel?' Nick replied. 'Do you not accept the sign of weeping?' He held his arm tight about my waist.

'My tears, Sir. They will not flow as they ought. I am still stricken, I fear. God sees all. He knows my heart is not yet washed free.'

'All in time, Abel. All in time. You have set yourself on His narrow course today. It is a great step.'

'Alas I am confined. I cannot breathe for fear. Even here. These walls. They menace me, Sir. I see the fiend. He would have me here in the garden. He sees my knotted and ingrained soul. Ah! Ah! He clutches at my throat. Sir, I cannot breathe.' I clung to him. 'Stay with me, Sir. Please, good Sir, stay. Don't let me fall again into his evil ways.'

'What evil ways, Abel? What is your state of ungodliness?'

'Pray, Sir. Can I truly put my trust in you? I am a deep and benighted sinner, I know it.'

'Indeed, Abel, you can trust me implicitly. I am a man sanctified by the Word. You can tell me all. What are these evil ways? Tell. You must tell.' He held me hard against him. I made as if to faint again. 'No, boy. No. What is it? I can help you in your search for righteousness. He has given me power.'

'Ah,' I whispered. 'The Fiend has ears about me. He listens. Surely there's one concealed within the garden. I cannot speak. He will rend me. Oh!'

'Listen, dear Abel. You are safe in my arms. Unburden yourself to me now. I command the evil one to depart. You may give yourself up to me, his Minister.'

'All these weeks I have looked to you, Sir, as one whose countenance bespeaks the Lord, whose very touch I am not worthy to accept. I have marvelled at you, Sir, but I have not heard even your name.'

'My name is Nicholas, Abel. Nicholas is here with you and touches you now thus. I know you are worthy, Abel. I know it. Loose yourself from your trembling and give in to the Lord.'

'But not here, Sir. Nicholas. I cannot do it here. He sees me. He sees me. Take me beyond the house, and I shall tell you all my sin.' I had 'walked' him as far as the end of the garden, playing on the extremity of my wits. 'There!' I said, pointing at the iron gate. 'There is the strait gate. There is my salvation. If I could but pass through, I should be His and His alone.' I broke free of him and ran to the gate. 'Ah, Sir. Nicholas, my true guide and rescuer, but it is locked and I am lost.' I threw myself upon him pretending once more to weep. I felt him wrestling with himself as to what to do.

'Nay, my dear,' he said. 'Here will do. We are far removed.' His hand reached for the flesh of my thighs and my stomach heaved inside me.

'I cannot, Nicholas. We are overlooked. It is too near.' I ran to the gate again and stood like a convict looking out of his gaol. 'My salvation lies beyond. There is my satisfaction.'

He made up his mind then. 'Stay, boy, and I shall fetch the key. But you must not move. You understand. Not one inch. Your very soul is in peril if you move. Stay!'

'Oh pray do not leave me, Nicholas. I fear the Fiend.'

'How shall I find the key, if I do not leave you for a moment? Courage, Abel. Have you the courage?'

'Perhaps I have,' I returned, snivelling. 'I shall try, Nicholas.'

'Then I shall be back again immediately,' he said.

When he had gone, I called to Charles. His head appeared cautiously round the wall on the other side of the gate.

'Kit! What in the name of all hell are you doing?'

'I'm getting the gate open. Now keep out of sight if you love me.'

'My God,' he said. 'This is intolerable.'

I heard soft footsteps behind me. 'Leave me, Fiend!' I called. 'Leave me, I say!'

'There, Abel,' said Nick, putting his one hand on my waist again, and making for the lock with his other. 'Let us make your passage through the narrow gate together.' I waited till he'd turned the key before breaking away again and running back into the garden. At about ten paces away from him I let myself drop to the ground. He was soon beside me.

'Ah, Sir. I am truly not worthy. Even as you opened the lock I saw the fields of paradise all lit up, but the Devil barred my way and stole my nerve. I cannot walk, Nicholas. It's all up with me. I am lost. I'm lost.'

He was becoming exasperated. I could see that even in the gloom of the shrubs and trees that stood over us. His hands began to reach for my belt as if to have me there and then on the ground. I pretended to come round and sit up, and then to notice the summerhouse. 'In there, Nicholas. Oh, it is an oasis, a rest-house for weary sinners. There, perhaps I shall draw the breath of peace, and suck the milk of paradise.' It was enough. He lifted me up and we made our way into the summer-house.

Once there, and with the little door shut, Nick said: 'Now, *mon cher*, we need no longer pretend. If I do not mistake, Abel, you are an adept at another mystery altogether, come here among the prophetic brethren to solicit custom.'

I grew very frightened at the change in his tone.

'Sir? Kind father, Nicholas. What can you mean to say indeed?'

'To say? Come, Abel, you are a whore. Admit! You are a Ganymedes.'

'Oh save my soul, it is the Fiend! He calls out thus on me. The voices slander me thus.'

'*Non, ce n'est pas le diable*. You come to abuse the grace of our house, Abel. Why should I not here and now hand you over to the Master, as an impostor, indeed?' He held me hard by the wrist. I played on.

'My sin is the sin of . . . Nay I cannot confess.' He held me tighter so that I cried out.

'Why should I not hand you over directly? Eh? *Chéri?*'

'Sir Nicholas. I don't know what you mean.'

'I think you do, *mon poulet*. Come, I shall expose you.'

'No, Sir. Pray! What must I do?'

'To be saved?' he said, maliciously.

'To taste of paradise,' I ventured, desperately eyeing him in the dark; although it was less dark now – the sky, which had been overcast, had cleared. We saw each other in the starlight.

'What is this sin you suffer from? That you lust after your own kind, Abel? Confess. You lust after men. This is your abominable sin, is it not?'

'I cannot say, Sir.'

'Cannot say? Cannot say? But can do perhaps. Then I must purge this vile abominable lust from you. It shall be done to you so that you never wish this filthy sin again. It is my religious duty, Abel, to wrestle with your gross impulses, your villainous soul. Oh yes, Abel. There is nothing we would not undertake, no matter how much it revolts us. Such is the love I bear you, Abel, that I would do anything, yes, anything to win back your soul. You shall verily be purged, my dear.' He wrestled me down to the floor of the little house so that one wrist was immobilised. I was terrified; the daring and simplicity of my plan had evaporated in the twist of power that he had worked on me. He should have been easy and soft in my hands, but he'd turned into a perverse tyrant, unbuttoning his coat and breeches with his free hand, advancing his naked self towards me, while I grovelled helplessly below him. It was a horrid re-run of the very origin of my grievance against him – so easily this configuration seemed to reappear in my experience. And here in my terror I sensed the root of the absolute hatred I had for him. For his pleasure was not in the act but in the brutal humiliation of another. What could I do? What could I say?

'Sir Nicholas, I am a woman.' In my proper voice.

He stopped for a moment and eyed me very closely through his spectacles. I completely changed my bearing to him, dropping totally the abject Abel, and addressing him woman to man. It set him back just long enough for me to wriggle free. 'I shall prove this to you, Nick – *mon cher*,' I said standing with some pain and difficulty. At last I had him where I wanted him: kneeling and exposed – while I stood. As if to expose myself, I reached into the restraint coat's inner pocket. I took the Batavian thorn dart which the Royal Society bequeathed to my uncle's care. It fitted inside a gourd which protected the supply of nerve poison around its tip, keeping it moist and active. 'Or am I a beautiful boy? *Chéri*? Or am I an avenging angel?'

As I said these words, I took the thorn from the gourd, so that it lay in my right hand, and offered to enflame his lust. There I ran my hand along his stiff yard, and then pressed the thorn tip as hard as I could into his groin. He half-screamed some muffled obscenity in French, then lunged at me. But even as his hands caught me about the neck in a throttle, the poison started to take effect: his knees gave way and he toppled forward, grasping now at my ankle. I kicked at him violently until he let go, and got myself out of the summer-house. He went limp. Then he got up again, right on to his feet. Would the wretched stuff not work?

I shut the door and held on to the handle, watching him through the windows. His eyeglasses still clung all awry to his face. A bespectacled horror, he moved his arms, but it was as if he had been tied to the air. He tried to maintain his standing, then fell forward on to his knees again with a thud, so that his head, shoulders and wildly spread arms pressed against the glass above the level of the waisting and the ledge. In fact his cheek and nose moulded themselves ridiculously in the grey dark to the little leaded pane they occupied. I moved round to look directly into his eyes through the window, peering, I hoped, into his still-active soul. He gazed back in anguish.

Then I went back to the door, opened it and entered. From the interior I could see that he had fallen beside the end arm of the finely upholstered miniature couch, so that he was propped up by one armpit. His muscles twitched in tiny movements but couldn't lift him. I knew he was exerting every effort to mobilise his body, but that it was a thing he was trapped in, and that it would never respond again. Besides this, I was infinitely relieved that his fall hadn't broken the glazing, for my full revenge called for a sealed chamber.

From the other inside pockets of my coat of restraint I took a net of crystals and a large horn of powder. Then I realised I needed water. I looked round, and miraculously found it in an ornate starlit pewter jug where some cut flowers stood on a ledge. I threw out the flowers and judged the water quantity left in the jug. Then I opened the net, emptied the crystals in, and grabbed back a flower stem to stir them with. They took an inordinate time to dissolve in the cold water. Fatio flapped feebly. For the second time I grew panicky that all would not go according to plan, or that somebody might come.

At last the solution seemed ready. I placed the jug as near to him as I dared and poured in the horn full of the powder. It started to bubble and foam immediately, and the choking stuff came straight to my nostrils as I hovered over my experiment. That was enough – I knew I'd done all I could. I left, shut the door and retreated to observe the result.

Inertia

After I'd done with Nick, I expected the world to become a different place, but it was ashes. Limitless, slakeless ashes. All my charge had voided itself.

There'd been a chase. And a last drench of desperate adrenalin. Morland had appeared: a dark, rapt, telescope-bearing shape which brushed past me on silent shoes as I studied the fate of my enemy. He'd leapt in fright – we both had. We stared at one another for a moment. His telescope dropped and smashed its glass; I heard it. Then I ran for the gate, and the security of Charles's company. There were shouts behind us. 'Job! Phil! We are robbed!' We both hurried off along the path to the place by the Thames where my women's clothes were hidden. Two or three minutes must have passed before booted figures lurched out of the night at us while I was half-naked and pulling up my gown. I expected – I think we both expected – some terrible attack. In desperation I threw myself at Charles in a passionate kiss, moaning and shivering and writhing against him. The pursuers were taken aback at the sight of my moonlit female flesh. They stopped at us and then veered off. Then one called: 'Have you seen thieves? A thief. A young man; not so tall.'

I shrieked and clutched my gown to me. 'Are you murderers?

Help! Save me my dearest! It is my husband's man! We're found out! I knew we should be!' Charles drew his sword.

'Keep off, you whatever you are! Leave us! It's alright my love. We've seen no one! Begone! Or I'll use my sword!'

In this confusion of meaning the voices from the dark retreated, muttering.

And so we got off, and picked our way home to Charles's Westminster rooms. And there I collapsed.

There was no murder charge, for there was no corpse. Charles told me.

'He's not dead, Kit.'

'What? But I saw him.'

'He is alive. I made enquiries. But he's paralysed. It's given out that the Swiss gentleman at Mr Morland's suffered a terrible stroke. He cannot speak, and is confined to a chair.'

'Well,' I said, 'I'm amazed. But perhaps . . .'

'He may recover.'

'Then I shall try again.'

'Kit! Isn't this enough? And if he recovers the power of speech? What then?'

'Do you think we shall be touched, Charles?' I said. 'Do you think he knows who did for him? And even if he does, will he come out and say Catherine Barton dressed as a boy and that well-known assassin Halifax gassed and poisoned me as I sought to have obscene congress? I don't see it. Do you?'

But even so I had no release from myself. Indeed I suffered a continuing fall into a kind of lethargy. I became as I had seen my uncle become: motionless in the saloon, withdrawn and collapsed, not moving the whole day sometimes, yet preoccupied and intensely active in my head with irrational terrors, and visions of wolves and children in the forest. The shadow of a great evil one seemed to come over me, so that I genuinely believed myself possessed. Around the place where I sat I felt as if a Cartesian vortex had opened up which threatened to curve the world and me into an unspeakable black otherness.

It went on for days until, unable to treat me, Charles and my uncle sent me back to Oxfordshire to stay at the Gyres' farmhouse.

All the way there, alone in Charles's coach and four, and with his servants to guard me, I wondered why it should be that after the crown of my desires I found myself so ill. Why had it not worked? Why wasn't I cleared of it? It was an illness I'd never known before. When I looked·out from the windows of the coach and saw walking tradesmen on the road or peasants working in the field, I became oppressed with thoughts of anal penetration and the copulation of men. I would be out of it. Sudden noises were the announcements of the Devil's presence; of his evil desires upon my soul. I cringed and my stomach churned. I believed my coachmen had stolen me, but I couldn't move. I could hardly breathe. Nor could I bear my own thoughts, for the age was suddenly not modern; it was dark with superstition, with the terrors of the night, the tortures of hell. If I could die.

It was a journey that took an age yet left hardly a trace on my mind, so little did it fit into anything previously known. I say it was the world made strange. When we stopped at an inn, for example, people went about their tasks, but I couldn't understand them, why they did it.

But at the farmhouse all was much as it had been before, and though I shook and wobbled my way in, I felt safer, and was put sitting in the sun in the walled garden, amidst the Autumn flowers which I knew were beautiful, yet couldn't quite bear to see. And I saw no shadowy backer until a week later, when I'd calmed down.

It was in daylight – well, afternoon. The field I walked across was laced in the low sun with a million shining webs. My damp shoes left a trail of footprints right across it. There at the corner by the elms the backer sat on the stile; the one with darker hair, it was. His unusual coat was washed and illuminated by the special light of the afternoon. He rested by him what it was he carried – what he presumably had been carrying: an object I knew had great value but of which I couldn't grasp the shape or design. It changed like a thing in a dream, not obviously but subtly, so that it was of gold and was electric with jewels which were not jewels but intricate gears of glass which were not again what they were.

He said: 'It is the machinery of love.'

And I said: 'I am not such a fool. What have I to do with it? I am a monster; who could love me? A creature from the moon. From behind the moon. Do I not destroy what I touch or come near? It were better I had not been born.'

He said: 'Your heart is abnormally slow. Can you read?'

'I can read, but I have only read my Daddy's Church books, and what I could occasionally steal from Grandad Smith's shelves.'

'Do you think Isaac was safe with that family?'

'I have no family,' I said. 'They are all dead. Grandad Smith was an old man when Isaac was a boy. He died before I was born.'

'There are all kinds of legacy. Many mansions. Many rooms. The boy is in hell while you delay above. Do you feel what he feels?'

'That is why I am here. It is so hard.'

'Why, you would fly to the moon.'

'There is a man at the Royal Society who believes that can be done. His name is Wilkins.' The backer had disappeared and the day returned to normal.

It was so hard; wrestling day after day with the impulse to die. Stasis. Which only yielded by infinitesimal degrees and the support of those kind ones about me.

I enquired at the farm, where Lucy'lizabeth was. To reach her on horseback – at a walk, I hasten to add – I was led across the Royal Park and saw Blenheim Palace a-building, in a huge wilderness of men and machines. The very mud was coloured all about with the dust of the yellow stone they were using. Lucy'lizabeth, in a village several miles beyond the confines of this special territory, sat in her untidy, smelly cottage, next to a dying child. She was exhausted and in despair over where she would live when the child was gone and her money ran out, since her husband had died recently of infected blood. She was too numb to have her mourning feelings either for the man or his son.

I kept up my visits until the child died, which was a terrible thing to see. Then I asked her to be my maid. She came to live with me at the farmhouse once the funeral was over. When she lost her fear of me, she spent most of her time weeping, which nobody minded. And then, when she felt better, I gave her some of my clothes to wear. People said how alike we looked, but that Lucy'lizabeth appeared the older twin now.

I spent six weeks with the Gyres in what I referred to as the oasis. I had never expected to come back there, so that was sufficient miracle and brought me back to the world of health enough to contemplate return to London and my old life. The shadowy backer sat in the coach with me and Lucy'lizabeth going back, but she didn't see him. He said, from his corner: 'So it is that we rest among friends, and then come back.'

For the first time Lucy'lizabeth asked me about the life she was to enter.

'Are you married, Miss?'

'No, I'm not, Lucy'lizabeth. In London we don't always marry the man who provides for us.'

'Then you have a man, Miss?'

'Yes. I have a man.'

'That Charles you spoke of, when you was here last?'

'You remember? Yes indeed. The same man.'

'Are you in a state of sin, Miss?'

'I believe I must be, dear. Does it trouble you to be my maid? On that account?'

'No, Miss. I'm very grateful.'

Later on, as we jogged and jolted, she asked: 'What's he like?'

'He's a great politician of the State. That's why he can't marry me.'

'Lord. Is he very tall?'

'No. He's not so tall.'

My backer leaned over and said: 'The world is full of miracles, but it is not always easy to be quick enough to catch them.'

Later in the journey I read over again the latest of Charles's letters to me:

It is so long, my dearest Kit, since we have been together. Time for those who love and are apart creeps hampered by. Yet my duties have been manifold; what with administration and business, and speechifying to their Lordships. And I have been travelling for my family – to see to Northamptonshire matters. Travelling also on Her Majesty's behalf, further afield. And as I return I look for your letters but find none. Why do you not write, my darling? It is so many months.

I looked up at where the backer sat and said out loud the words which had puzzled my mind since the letter arrived.

'So many months?'

The backer said nothing, but Lucy'lizabeth looked hard at me.

'Mistress?'

'I'm sorry.' I went back to my letter. On my reckoning I was sure it was six weeks at the most. I tried to make sense of the weather outside the coach window as if it might give some clue to the season, but it was typically English grey all-purpose climate, not much different from when I came up. Had I somehow slipped a year from being at Woodstock? We got held up at the turning of an inn. Someone with a guitar was singing a crude popular song:

> When as Queen Anne of great renown
> Great Britain's sceptre swayed,
> Besides the Church she dearly loved
> A dirty chamber maid.
>
> O Abigail that was her name,
> She stitched and starched full well,
> But how she pierced this royal heart
> No mortal man can tell.
>
> However for sweet service done
> And causes of great weight
> Her royal mistress made her, Oh!
> A minister of State.
>
> Her secretary she was not
> Because she could not write,
> But had the conduct and the care
> Of some dark deeds at night.

There was a roar of laughter from the inn yard. We moved off. I felt frightened by the violence of the satire, and was glad to get away. It reminded me of how I'd felt on the way up. I returned to his letter:

Your uncle tells me you are soon to return and are restored. I rejoice. Can I believe it to be true? I would hear it from your own hand. My dearest, I do most sincerely believe that the indisposition of mine that came so uncomfortably between us, to the detriment of all the loving society we had hoped for and worked towards, will no longer hamper our prosperity. I confess your single-mindedness towards your end troubled me as no one has troubled me before. It seemed indeed an upsetting of all that is natural; and proved itself so upon my own body. However, there is a matter à propos which I have so far refrained from telling you of, on account of my uncertainty as to your state of mind. It concerns your victim, and strengthens my own vigour in as much as the State appears to see matters your way, and so restores a degree of conformity to the world as I perceive it. In short Fatio has been pilloried at Tyburn. Yes, he did make a recovery. This business relates to the extremist French Prophets, coming as refugees and causing much of a stir in town. I regret to tell you that your uncle was drawn in – I cannot imagine how. These Camisards, so they were called, would rant and prophesy that the Revelations were fulfilled and that the time was now. Fanatical and extravagant, they wound the population up until the government was forced to move against them.

I smiled to myself at his detachment from the matter. Who was it who was in the thick of government?

Your man became one of their leading lights: in the last days you may do what you wish – so he was taken as instructing the people, who came to hear in droves. So he was arrested for saying, not to mention a good deal of other treason, delivered in 'inspired tongues' he claimed. I believe you would have admired to see him pelted.

I put the letter down. Charles restoring his manhood.

At home I said nothing about that matter to my uncle. I slipped into my world again, and requested quiet and a suspension of information. In addition, I had my bedroom redecorated. Not in red.

But one evening he needed my ear to his troubles.

'All's lost, Kit. The Book of Daniel, Kit. I've been made a fool of, Kit. This is the work of the most accursed! Kit! Kit!'

'What, Uncle? What is it?'

'The Book of Daniel. Daniel, Kit. The more I look in it the more I'm distressed. It is all slipping away, further into the unspeakable future. I must talk with someone about these things, Kit, or I fear I shall be mad again.'

'Tell me, Uncle. What's the matter in all this?' I went to get the brandy bottle and made him some with only the merest drain of water. He took it, drank a little, and sat staring into the glass with its sluice of transparent brown.

'It's the problem of time, Kit. And who we are.'

'I want to know, Uncle.'

'It's the task set by God to certain of us – who live not as other men – to seek to grasp His Mind, and know His Will. Prophecy, Kit, is the highest calling. This is not generally known, even to the Brethren of the Order of Salomon's House, which is an uncommon name, Kit, for the Royal Society, though not for all those within it. Prophecy has been my life.' I didn't interrupt him; I was interested in his unaccustomed flow. 'We must grasp the language, Kit,' he went on, 'in which the world is written. Nay, the universe itself. To which I have devoted my time,' he said, slowly. 'God speaks to us. God is absolute. God is extended utterly throughout all space, and throughout all time. It was I and none other who read His holy words of movement.' He brought his fist thoughtfully down on to his thigh. 'It was I and none other who read His original Light, His divine Gravity. Who then am I? He showed me the tools by which the future might be predicted: this moving body, in this system of other moving bodies, is now here. Tomorrow it will be there. This I have known.' He drank.

He'd grown calmer now. The agitation of his features had given way to a certain composure in sadness. 'It would be reversible – that is, to know what must have been – except that He chooses not; as a watch is so contrived as to escape always in one direction, although we could in theory have it run itself backwards to what it has told before. Time, then, my dear Kit,' he looked penetratingly at me. 'Where is its language? It's written in His Book. He who would understand time must learn the language of His Scriptures. The world is made in six days. What is a day? What is the horn on a beast? A thousand years? It is a metaphoric measure. He speaks thus of time. In symbols. Who is the Whore of Babylon? Well, that last is obvious. The rest I have sought to decode, Kit. All my life. By this we may know who we are. And what we must do next. Otherwise we are lost, I fear.' He lapsed into silence, drifting off on his thoughts. My thoughts ran on my own time, of which he seemed to take no heed.

'My researches years ago, Kit, pointed only in one direction; I could not bring myself to write down my conclusion even in my most private manuscripts, for fear they should be searched and read. And that I should be . . . that they might . . . before my time. I cloaked all behind some gentle cunning miscalculations, putting off the dreadful date which I had found by two hundred years. Armageddon. But I knew what I knew in my head. And who I might well be. And what I might be called upon to do, in this New Age. Why,

Charles – look how *he* rose; as if placed there in power by some Godlike hand. And then the war against the Whore, with its attendant victories – despite the man himself and his wife – I mean Marlborough and Co. Well, well, Kit. But it's all as nothing. Get me some more brandy, would you, child?'

I did so.

'But the Book of Daniel,' he went on. 'I hadn't reckoned with Daniel. Not enough, Kit. The time cannot be as I thought. Everything is thrown out.' He shook his head wearily. 'It is my worst fear. And I am so tired.' The first tear I had ever seen him weep rolled down his cheek.

'The Book of Daniel is unquestionable, Uncle?'

'I take it to be so. It is in Hebrew. I take it to be so. Kit, I cannot go through all that again. I'm an old man now. I believe my powers are failing. Descartes. The pack of relativists. I thought I'd done for them. And now this German impostor Leibniz.'

Double Vision

No more than a short while after this conversation, my Uncle Isaac suffered an attack, not of the madness he'd predicted, but of a bodily illness which put the household in a condition of solemnity. Never had such a thing occurred before – his was an exceedingly robust frame. His diet was spare, his exercise moderate, his indulgence minimal. Neither did he smoke. The human substance in him was distilled and rarefied by years at the refiner's fire. With hindsight, though, and mindful of the excessive silver of his natural hair, which lay out on the pillow like a corona, I assume it was heavy metal poisoning – mercury mostly – that had begun to take its effect. When I was a child I'd seen him dip his fingers into so many odd concoctions; plenty of it must have made its way in at his mouth or his skin. He always tried things out on himself.

We were the same in so many ways, he and I, both finding our methods of dealing with the universe; which were opposite. I would say equal and opposite, did I not find his way negative. It negated. I hoped it wouldn't prevail in the long run. *Magis amica veritas*.

It was natural then in my nursing of him that I should reflect on my own recent indisposition, and on the nature of illness. I came to no very good conclusions. Who has? I wasn't cured. Cured of being me? Here lay my uncle, full of a poisonous metal. His being was attempting to flush it out of him. He felt awful. But it was a positive impulse from his nature, and reassuring if he should live. I had lain in Woodstock for a period either of six weeks or more than a year, depending on whose scale you used to measure it. My being had flushed something through. During that I'd felt awful, physically and mentally. I believed it might be a great sluice of the emotion I'd missed having before, and so formed a tentative theory that being out of the body at extreme moments, though necessary at the time, left one disabled of proper response. It could be that the emotion remained below, locked in raw narrative form and somehow sealed into the very structure of the body, waiting to pounce on one's awareness. I'd given it dramatic cause, and it had certainly pounced. But now I knew I could feel more – perhaps even good things. I was more alive.

Nick had served his purpose then. I might even remember who I was in truth. Or was there a mathematics of it? A space for new life whose quantity was directly proportional to the quantity of emotion I'd flushed through. How much more was there to go? I felt, yes, better, but vulnerable, and very emotional indeed sometimes. It could change from one thing to another in a moment. I suppose I was *more* mercurial! I hoped my poor uncle would become *less* so. There, I could feel for him. That must be good. For the present, that was all I could say to it.

At the beginning of the illness, Mary and I had to entreat him to unlock his door so that we could attend to him. Otherwise he would have lain alone, griping, unwashed, and virtually disabled. He tolerated only me to nurse him, so that I found myself with proper right of access to that holy chamber I'd stolen into before. I longed to reassure myself that my discovery of the mirror system had not been just a dream. It is very hard to believe, when everyone acts as if all is polished and normal on the surface, that there is an unimaginably strange secret in the house. He was always much agitated when I was in the room, watching where I went, and what I touched, and so forth.

But one mid-morning as he lay at last fully comatose, I did go to the apparatus. The little crafted cupboard opened as it had done those years ago, its doors cleverly forming shutters for the viewer, or blinkers against the daylight in the room; and the eyepiece was mounted, adjusted, and in place. My bedroom offered itself once more to the observer. Lucy'lizabeth was there, tidying my clothes from the chair. This time, however, there was no sound coming from the fireplace as had been the case before. I remembered how every vibration had leaped then to my ear – now, there must be some shutter adjusted, to block out the sound; which would explain why I'd never heard him from my own fireplace.

She picked up my gown from last night and held it against herself to the mirror on my dressing-table. Then she took off her cap, which was a full one and made her appear very subdued. She pushed up her hair from behind so that it looked more like mine when it was done for the day. I watched, amused and fascinated to a degree. It seemed her fantasy began to overtake her. She glanced towards the door, then turned back to the mirror; then, as if some resolution had formed itself fully in her mind, she went to the door and turned the key in it.

Now it was that by a most strange reversal I became the replacement of my uncle's eye, watching, it seemed, myself undress. For Lucy'lizabeth took off her own clothes, looking round at the door all the time as if she suspected the lock would give way suddenly and she would be discovered, and put on mine. She did it with a kind of social and sexual awe, lacing herself in; forming with the ruffles the exact presentation of my, or should I say her, décolletage; using my own ivory combs and headpieces to lift up her hair; and then powdering herself off with my own cosmetics. I looked on with a mixture of amazement, suppressed laughter and annoyance.

Finally I wondered whether I should go round and interfere. But I think she'd just decided that she'd done enough, and had better undo, when I saw her head jerk sideways as if at a sound. It was clear to me that for a whole minute almost she was panic-stricken. Perhaps the knock at the door came again. She fidgeted with the laces but seemed unable to decide whether to dress or undress, there were so many. Then she moved to the door. There may have been some kind of a conversation. I longed to have the answer to the shutter mechanism which would allow the sound out through the fireplace. Did she disguise her voice to seem like mine? I out-thought her here, for whoever called and waited would expect me to come out and not her, so that she would be caught. But if she'd not disguised it then she must open the door at once, since my maid could have no pretext for privacy in my room. Then again she must have known it wasn't me at the door, for I believed she wasn't afraid of me and would have known that I should in all probability merely have laughed to find her so.

She turned the key. All her movements displayed her uncertainty. In walked Charles. They fell into each other's arms. I observed his good clothes – he must be en route to some government meeting and had called to see me. But the kiss was ecstatic, mouth to mouth, and seemed to go on and on, while his hands roved all down her back and up again to smooth the soft skin at the nape of her neck. I found myself paralysed, and riveted to the scene in the eyepiece. Soon it was he who fumbled at the laces of her bodice that she had so carefully secured not five minutes before. She backed away to sit on my bed, thrusting my drapes aside. He sat beside her, and for each undoing, bent forward to kiss the exposed flesh of her bosom.

It wasn't long before she was in her stays with her arms out of the top half of my gown. They seemed to be talking softly to each other while he, and she, concentrated on the unfastening and removal of the stays themselves and the chemisette underneath. His hands toyed with her exposed breasts – they were fuller than mine – as he nibbled her ear; I saw her chin lifted in pleasure, and her cheek laid on his shoulder. What were my feelings? I couldn't receive them for the moment; I felt the detachment of the scientist.

It was her hands that pushed my dress away from under her, until it was no more than a collapse of costly folds around her feet; her fingers that searched blindly but deftly to untie the tapes of her petticoat. But Charles stood up away from her, threw off his coat in the flush of excitement, and unbreeched himself. His problem in relating to me was clearly quite over; he didn't wait for Lucy'lizabeth's success with the petticoats but scooped her feet out of the pile of my gown and rushed the lacy things up round her waist. Horrified, fascinated, I watched her knees spread and lift as she lay back for him to come into her. My observation of the love of others, which I took somehow to be the love of me, concentrated on the silent raising and lowering of his part-exposed behind, and the appearance of genuine enthusiasm on her part; until there seemed to be, after several minutes of fervour, a genuine climax and resolution in both lovers. I saw them, deep in the pulled drapes of my bed, kissing and showing each other an after-the-event tenderness which should have been beautiful, if I could have appreciated it. My view of them was absurdly angled as in a perspective chamber, so that most of what was available to my eye was their bared foreshortened nether parts still half over the end of my bed as it faced the eye.

At last I broke away from the sight, and looked back at my dormant uncle, snoring in his silver mane, also foreshortened by the angle so that his strong nose stood up, offering his nostrils to the air. I shut the cupboard doors.

There was a stink in the room. His sheets would have to be changed again. It was a small beginning of the slight incontinence problem which was to bother his later years. I went to the door and looked out, expecting to see Charles or Lucy'lizabeth come out from my chamber. But instead Mary came along from the back stairs.

'Oh Miss Kit! I told Lucy'lizabeth you'd gone out to Miss Etta's.'

'Mr Isaac has fallen into a coma, Mary, and the sheets are dirty.'

'Dirty, Miss?'

'Dirty, Mary. Will you help me see to him?'

'If you say so, Miss.'

It took us the best, or worst, part of an hour to sort him out. We washed and changed him and put a new feather bed under him, protected by an old oiled canvas until we could get something more effective sent round. He came to partially from his swound, and grew very agitated about locks and bolts for his cupboards; he insisted that we get the Royal Society demonstrator and technical steward round to fix all this. Hawksbee, his name was. My uncle said anyone else would ruin everything.

When I got to my room it was empty, and there was no sign of either of the lovers. I said my feelings were volatile. I felt very distressed over the empty bed. I went to Anne's.

'She did what? My dear!' Anne put her arms around me and sat me down and went to organise chocolate and came back and sighed and put her arms round me again. 'I was so sad you had to go away. I wanted to be with you then. And now this.'

'Anne – my friend. Who will comfort me? Because I can't tell anyone what is the truth of myself.'

'Wait till I have a word with Charles. This is scurvy treatment, Kit. He's a villain, and I shall tell him so.'

'But perhaps he thought it was me. Perhaps he was happy with me at last, because at last I was normal to him. She was normal to him. She loved him back.'

'How do you know this? Is that what the hussy said?'

'I do know it, Anne. I can't say how. It destroys me that I cannot speak about myself – everything about me is odd, mysterious, forbidden; I know this.' I was extreme.

'You look so . . . I don't know. Beautiful as ever, but not quite here. Do you know what I mean?' The chocolate came. With great tenderness, she held her hand over mine as I sipped it from the little bowl. It was a bitter blend.

'I know what I feel, Anne, and it is as you describe me. I believe sometimes I am not of this world. I see things.'

'What things do you see, Kit?'

'I call them shadowy backers. No one else does. See them, that is. I think. Am I going mad, do you believe? Anne?' She was looking abstractedly in front of her as we sat together on her settee.

'You don't seem mad to me, dearest,' she said after a while, and laid her head on my shoulder.

'If there were release,' I said.

I went to Etta's house and sat with her, Pawnee and the children, who bounced and fought and hurt themselves.

'I won't be parted from them,' said Etta. 'Some people say I should let the nurse do everything, and become much more of my old social self, but I say they're my children and I shan't be parted from them. But they do exhaust one. No, Tansy, don't touch. No! We call her Tansy. Since last Thursday when she fell into the patch. It seems to suit her. Come to Mummy then. Teddy, she can sit with me if she likes.'

'Did she plan this?' said Pawnee.

'How would I know, Pawnee?' I lowered my voice so that Etta couldn't hear. 'I saw them through the eye.'

'How else, Kit?' said Pawnee.

'No, you inscrutable American. The *eye*. The magic mirror in my bedchamber.'

'Ah,' she said. 'The mirror of memories.' She put her hand high up on my thigh. I quivered.

'Shh!' I said.

'Do that climbing thing, Auntie Kit,' said Tansy. I did the climbing thing. Then little Edmund – Teddy – wanted it. Then I had to do horses.

'Oh, he's so *sweet*,' said Etta. 'I could eat him. He keeps waking up at night, though. And the nurse won't get up. Kit, I'm exhausted. Come here then, Edmund. Come on Teddy, then. There's a clever boy. No! Not swords! No! Edmund!'

'So who actually knows what?' said Pawnee, getting Tansy in her lap and jigging her, while Tansy tried to poke her breadstick in her mouth.

'Lucy'lizabeth knows that she and Charles . . .'

'You know that she and Charles,' Pawnee said. 'And what does Charles know?'

'Charles knows nothing, I assume,' I answered.

'That he can make love with her and think it's you.'

'Well, he would love to believe it. He doesn't wear spectacles. Perhaps he needs to. I don't know. I've been away. She looks exactly like me. Everyone says so. You saw it yourself. She was wearing my clothes. She was in my room. How shall I know, Pawnee? What would the difference be? To a man? With what exactly is he so much in love, as he keeps telling me? Would she do?'

'She did do. Come on then Edmund. But . . .'

'Tansy, not in there,' called Etta. 'Tansy, come back!'

Pawnee carried on, ' . . . but can you be sure they didn't both know?'

'The girl was caught unawares,' I said.

'How do you know that?'

'Well, it was obvious she was panicking. You could see that . . .' It dawned on me that my reading of Lucy'lizabeth's movements and gestures was capable of another interpretation than the one I'd given it. They could have arranged it between them. Lucy'lizabeth had been told I would be out. My mind went into a spin as the various possibilities and combinations of possibilities began to click one with another, like the letters and numbers on the Lullist machine at Charles's house. He might have known, but she might have had no prior agreement with him. She might have played on him. He might have seduced her. He might love her for herself. He might love her for me. He might . . . She might . . . And as for me . . . 'Pawnee,' I said. 'What shall I do?'

'Perhaps between the two women in the case . . . ' she said softly.

'As for the man. Let him be. Who knows what they think? And does it matter? But between you two, might there not be a profitable arrangement? Everyone could become happy. No one need ask too much of another.' Tansy shot by with Edmund crawling fiercely after her.

'Lucy'lizabeth. You may leave off that. Come in here, dear. Sit down. We shall talk, you and I.' We sat down in the drawing-room.

'Yes Miss Kit?' There was a hint of fear in her eyes.

'Lucy'lizabeth, I shall speak to you very indirectly.'

'Pardon me, Miss Kit?'

'Just listen. You and I look very much alike. Very, very much. So that there might be times when no one could tell us apart. If we were dressed alike. And if you spoke more London-like, which I have noticed that you do lately. Perhaps undressed your figure would be the more fuller. It may be so. But dressed and corseted in, there is hardly anything between us.'

'As you say, Miss.'

'I do say it, Lucy'lizabeth, and we both know it.' I paused, and sighed. 'There may be an advantage in this, to both of us.' She looked up sharply. 'I'm not like other women. Entirely. You may know this.'

'No, Miss.'

'Well, it's true. I can't ... You must promise me never to repeat this, Lucy'lizabeth. Now. On your honour.'

'Yes, Miss.'

'Say so, then.'

'I promise.'

'You promise on your honour never to repeat what I am going to tell you.'

'I promise on my honour never to repeat what you're going to tell me.'

'Good. Well. I can't love Charles ... in a womanly way. We have only ... twice. Ever. I can't do it willingly. There, I've told you. And I am horribly ashamed.'

'Don't be ashamed, Miss. Plenty of women don't enjoy it.' Her voice reassured, yet her eyes widened.

'But I can't give him *love*, Lucy'lizabeth. Nor to myself. I cannot receive it. He says he loves me after all our difficulties. He comes to me for love. He thinks it's all solved now, and that soon we shall ...

But I ca . . . ca . . .' My voice broke down. I felt the terrible tears welling up in spite of all my intentions to make this a scene which I controlled and she was intimidated by. It was not so. 'I can't do it, Lucy'lizabeth. I can't. I don't feel.'

'There, Miss.' She was at my side, kneeling, her arms around my shoulders. I wept and shuddered against her shoulder – into the very place where Charles had so recently imprinted his kisses. My kisses. I couldn't stop crying.

'Tell anyone, Lucy'lizabeth,' I hissed, 'and I shall kill you.'

'There, Miss,' she said. 'It's alright.'

I told Anne the disaster of my interview with Lucy'lizabeth, but not the details of Pawnee's intimate scheme of double-dealing.

'Kit,' she said. 'I have plans for you. You are made for the stage. Tomorrow afternoon you will come with me to call on La Colomba. She is heavenly, divine. Before she returns to Italy she shall teach you to sing. By the way do you know Swift? He's in town again.'

I had visions of swallows making a summer, fleeting appearances, temporary visitation. 'No, my dear. Who or what is Swift?'

'And for dinner tomorrow there will be you, and me, and my dear William, and Joseph and Swift.' She pronounced it with a run, showing off her famous delivery.

'Does he have a Christian name?'

'Possibly he does. I believe it begins with a Jay, but everyone calls him Swift.'

Later that night I received Charles coolly. I told him I was indisposed. He went into my uncle's bedroom to be shown the new locks and bolts.

Indeed I was indisposed. Lucy'lizabeth came in to see to my hair and get me ready for bed. 'Sleep in here with me tonight,' I said to her. 'I need someone with me.'

We lay on our backs. I linked with her arm. I said. 'We shall become interchangeable.'

'Miss?'

'You shall be me. And I shall be you. In some things, Lucy'lizabeth. In some things.' I felt she must have turned her head and be looking at me intensely in the dark. 'And sometimes I shall be in two places at once. That is when we are both me. I can't see the advantage in both being you. But there may turn out to be a need for this at one stage or other.'

'You're mad, dear Miss Kit, if I ask your pardon.' She attempted the familiarity. 'I don't understand you.'

'I think you might, my dear. For we're very similar in one other thing.'

'What's that?'

'We've both been had by a Great Parliamentarian.'

Her breath hissed into her mouth with the shock of it.

'How do you know?'

'I know; and not by Charles. And that's all you need know.'

'Have you brought me here to kill me? Are you a witch?'

'I've brought you here to strike a bargain. You shall continue to do it. Because I can't. I told you so. Will you?'

'You mean you know and you don't mind?'

'I am relieved.'

'Oh, Madam. Then so am I.'

'But I am still very sad, Lucy'lizabeth. For who'll love me, and whom can I love?' I slept in her arms. Like a baby.

Swift

I took my first singing lesson. It was at La Colomba's lodgings. I stood next to the harpsichord, which was played by her limp compatriot, while she boozily *formed my breathing* by shouting at me and hammering at my stays with her fist. I ignored her and was a great success. Anne, it seemed, could fix anything.

'Partridge!' said Swift.

'I believe it's a pigeon pie,' said Joseph, 'Anne?'

'You told me grouse, my dear,' said William.

'There were none to be had,' said Anne. 'It's quails.'

'A Parliament of Fowls,' I said.

'Excellent!' said Swift. 'I love this. Excellent!' He laughed at me. 'But I meant Partridge the almanac-maker. The preposterous astrologer Partridge. The town's full of monsters, and Partridge is the most monstrous of the monsters. What could be more monstrous than a humming, quaking cobbler who gets the whole town by the stars?

What could be more monstrous than that, dear Mrs Barton? I may call you dear, I believe, because I feel I know you are with me. You'll not take offence. She'll not be offended, Anne, because anyone can see that I'm a harmless old bachelor cleric.'

'I'm not offended, Sir,' I smiled. I felt at home. 'I see indeed that you're quite harmless.'

'Utterly,' he went on. 'Of course you may fall in love with me, and I with you, when Anne and I have concluded our business, but there shall be no harm at all.'

'Don't mind him, Kit. Swift's impossible,' said Anne.

'She's forgotten our vows so soon,' said Swift. 'And I not long away.'

'I too am quite harmless,' I said.

'Beauty such as repairs within these four walls cannot be spoken of as harmless. Lesser men,' he looked at Joseph, 'and fellow students,' he looked at William, 'would be bound to – have succumbed, I think. It is I who am old and ill and shuffling and inky – I who am, I assure you, harmless.'

'You don't suggest I need to repair my beauty yet, I hope?' Anne raised a hand to the diamond-dusted patch that set off her left cheek.

'I'd have to call him out, if he did,' William said, 'and I'm reluctant to leave off my dinner.' He poked and peered at it uncomfortably because of his poor eyes. 'Of whatever flying creature it should be.'

'I don't think you're in the least old, Sir,' I said.

'I assure you I'm monstrously old, Mrs Barton. Too old. Too old and too late. Had I met you twenty years ago . . . '

'Yes, Sir?'

'Oh call me Swift. Everyone does. And then I may have the pleasure of calling you Kit.'

'You're an Irish flirt, Swift,' I said.

'A failing fart, merely, Kit. I pollute as I go. There's nothing in me but Irish air. And I offend Addison here on every account.' I looked at the smiling, imperturbable Joseph, so neat and smooth and English patrician that his elegance was almost palpable next to the hastiness and disorder which seemed to surround Swift.

'Nonsense, my dear man,' Joseph replied. 'You delight me.'

'Look at him, Kit,' Swift bustled on, chewing at his meat, and pausing for a great gulp of wine. 'Purely medicinal. I'm serious. But,' he pointed his fork rudely at Addison, 'I hate the fellow. He's done it

216

all, been everywhere, the friend of the great – and he can write, beautifully, in four languages, two of them dead. I would assassinate him. But my pen is blunt. And as coarse as my wit. It's too coarse for *him*. Whom have you assassinated, Kit? With your beauty, Kitty? You make me want to stroke you.'

'Swift!' said Anne.

'Harmless, dear Madam. And I suppose I'd have to reckon with Halifax, then. Or is no one supposed to mention him and dear Kit in the same breath, and talk of stroking, stoking or other rhymes?'

'Swift!' said William and Joseph together.

'I assassinated one man,' I said, 'but he recovered, and then lived paralysed. Now I believe he's recovered altogether.'

'You paralysed him? I can believe it. It's been my own constant affliction. Paralysis. Giddiness. Divine paralysis. Were I not a very good churchman I'd say that God had no hope for me at all. He afflicts me like Job for my sins.'

'What sins are these, Swift?' said William. 'You've never been taken up and prosecuted by the Philistines for the indecency of being a poet. Of making folk laugh. By telling truth. Some of us have. I wear my scars with pride.'

'Of the mind, I suppose. My baser self tries to commit those of the flesh, but they never get beyond the censorship of my cloth. These collar bands, Kit, are a band*age* against the descent of wickedness from the corrupt mind. Nevertheless I'm sorely punished one way or another.'

'There is truth here, Kit. He does get very ill,' said Anne. 'That's why we make allowances for him.'

'And pretty women rally round, with soup and consolation. Which is the only compensation. But they don't love me for long once they see into my grossness.'

'This is not true,' said Anne. 'You're morbid.'

'There are clerics enough whose bandage is ineffectual,' said Addison.

'Regrettably,' said Swift. 'It's a world of sin, in which a few lights shine. I mean present company, not myself.' He looked rather sadly round at his friends. 'The Church at risk from all sides.'

Joseph Addison put down his knife and held his glass up to look at the colour of the wine. 'You were in Dublin during the latest ecstatics. You'd have relished the Camisards, Swift. They were so wildly transcendental that the courts had the rare and pleasant opportunity of taking action.'

'Of what kind?'

'The pillory.'

'Excellent!' cried Swift. 'I wonder sometimes how it should balance so quaintly that our Church is menaced by two equally noxious European imports: on the one hand extreme anarchical dissent, and on the other extreme Inquisitorial orthodoxy.'

'As one curve tends asymptotically to the axis at infinity, yet seems to reappear from the opposite extreme in the twisted reflection of itself.'

Did I somehow blurt this out? I blushed.

'Is this a woman speaking?' Swift looked astonished.

Anne was used to me. 'I've been besieging Joseph's defences in the matter of another English opera,' she said. 'Had I had my Kit tuned up in time for fair Rosamund, the piece would have run for thirty days instead of three, and dear Joseph wouldn't be in such a dump about all things musical.'

'Ah. The opera,' Swift smiled again. 'I overheard one wracked old dowager the other day asking,' and he mimicked a quavering tone, 'What is it about the town? These young gels are always out at some Uproar or other. What can they be, pray?' There was general laughter. 'And you're having success?'

'Not in the slightest. But at our magnificent Haymarket we shall take London with William's *Semele*.'

'*Semele*,' said Swift. 'Who's doing the music?'

'Eccles,' said William. 'He's a good way with a tune. They're more native. Addison's piece was ruined by that Clayton, though he won't say so himself. It's the very hard way we've all learnt how an English audience won't stand to hear their own language puffed and stuffed into Italian pantaloons. That music's all against us.'

Swift said: 'Now I declare myself. I can't abide the Italian opera. I'm sorry but there it is. Three things of Italy are unacceptable in a decent commonwealth: opera, knifings and sodomy. Oh; four things. Popery, which sums up all the others.'

Anne said: 'Poor William's new work will finish off his eyes, I'm sure. It's a tragedy in itself and I love him so.' She got up and laid her palms over his eyes to warm them; and he left off the pie and laid his head back. 'And I am out.'

Swift said: 'Out?'

'Out,' she replied.

Swift with a glass in his hand. 'Out, Anne?'

'If there's one here who's truly too old, I am she, Swift, you fool of a man. Younger than you and still too old. That's a woman's life, Sir. Except for Kit who changes nothing and never, beyond that she grows more ethereal every day, damn her eyes. But I cannot hold it up any more against the new young Oldfield, damn her eyes as well.' She cradled Congreve's head still with her hands, warming his incipient glaucoma. 'But Kit will be Semele. She'll do for your opera, William, what Anne Bracegirdle did for your plays. Who'd have thought that she's an instinctual native prima donna? La Colomba said as much.'

'The woman's a fat impostor.'

'She's not. My intuition was infallible. Kit, I'm determined, shall sing your Semele, William. We shall take London by storm.'

'Well enough, if you say so my dear,' said Congreve. 'Then it must be finished. And very soon.' He sighed. I loved her too.

After the meal Swift sat with me. We played some word game. He seemed to like these quibbles excessively. Then he said:

'On the subject of assassination: I've resolved, after hearing you speak so deliciously about it, to assassinate this Partridge. He really is something of a pox upon the body of the polis. It's a thing I should dearly love to do and would consider to be the Lord's work. Partridge will have to go. Will you join me at it, Kit, being so to speak an old hand at the murder game? I warn you I shall love you for it.'

'It's not an easy game,' I said, somewhat warily.

'What entertainment would there be in it if it were easy? Come along, how shall we do it?'

'We should lure him into a poison jar, and there prick his parts with the most delicate and supernatural unction, so that his wings would beat once, beat twice, and never beat again.'

'I'm in love with you more quickly than even I could have dreamed. Beware, Halifax. Swift is quicker. Let no one trust an Irish vicar.'

'I could in all matters accommodate you, Sir,' I laughed.

'Avaunt, Jezebel. Put your pussy away, Kitty. Tuck down your petticoats. Let's return to murder. Didn't I tell you how *harmless* I am? So you want to inoculate his posteriors. This is very crude and impossible. Which is to say it's low and difficult and lacks subtlety; and thus appeals to me immensely. Let me try you with another; a time-honoured remedy for astronomers – saving your revered uncle, whom I should strive to save and deliver at all costs – which would be to observe where this lunatic Partridge is accustomed to walk while gazing up at the stars, humming and muttering to himself; and have ready a great pit of marl and sluice beneath a false path. You and I, Kit, would hide ourselves behind the hedge, indulging in minor amatory pursuits and holding the string to this wattle construction which we had scientifically made up with clay to resemble the accustomed path. I shall not call it straight or narrow, for it's a fanatic's path and must be presumed unutterably mazy. When the fool came by we should leave our toying for an instant and pull the string. Whereupon he should plunge headlong into the shit and drown to the sound of love's quick pants.'

'It sounds a consummation devoutly to be wished,' I said.

He held up his hand in mock blessing. 'Harmless, Kit. Your turn.'

'It'd be fitting for a prophet to predict his own end. Whereinto he might disappear,' I said. 'We could, perhaps, steal by night, hand in hand, in at the casement of his printer, and substitute a page of predictions in his proofs.'

'Oh Halifax, you've found a jewel among women. If I were only a great lord and not an inky, poverty-stricken parson who must tend his flock. Why then you should see the old devil in me, Kit.'

'Put your inky devil away, Swift. So you like my plan?'

'A wrinkly stinkly inkly devil. He likes her plan. Though he's small and old and poor he likes her little little plan. Faith, I like it. It's beyond a joke. I believe it shall be done in earnest.'

So was hatched the Bickerstaff plot, which ran and ran.

People on Paper

The Bickerstaff name arose of course from some minor obscenity, which I don't recall beyond that it was probably Biggerstaff, or worse, but rapidly developed a wonderful momentum of its own, managing to career hopelessly and fictionally in its right line for some years. My world at this time was a world of fictions too miraculous to be remotely credible. In the first place, I was who I was.

Which was an original impossibility. In the second I was Lucy'lizab-eth and she was me. In the third, after a wild course of training I was pronounced stunning, stupendosa, prodigiosa, by La Colomba, who, pulling heavily at her little flask of theatrical brandy and saying *non posso insegnarle di più*, there was nothing more she could teach me, promptly returned to Italy. Thus I entered the fictional realm of the opera under an alias for reasons of propriety. At the Opera House in the Haymarket they kept, as does our modern film industry for directors who wish to work incognito, a spare name, acquired when a promising soprano had eloped with a flautist after the dress rehearsal of *Astolfo*. They kept it for revenge; and it appeared in subsequent programme notes, as and when some need arose. On my début, therefore, I would be listed as Isabella Girardeau – the flautist was French. In short I became more unreal than real. There. I said at the start you wouldn't believe me.

But I shall disentangle all these separate strands.

I threw myself into rehearsal as if I'd found a new life, which indeed I had. We met at Mr Eccles's house in Chelsea. He sat at the harpsi-chord, and there was a cellist who added breadth and sonorous depth. I learned my words and my tunes and my English recitativos, which weren't like the Italian ones. Opera was finding its feet wobbly in London now that the craze had run more than a couple of years. The novelty of Italian *donne* and *castrati* jangling passionately, thrillingly, incomprehensibly to lesser parts who sang back rather poorly in English had begun to wear off. Opera needed to put down roots. That is what we were doing.

What was all this? What was going on? It was part of Charles's dream, I realised gradually – Charles seemed to be behind every-thing – to create England on an imperial scale. So, subtly, without any direct prompting or order, it came about that Congreve and Addison and Vanbrugh and Rich were promoting high culture to absorb and then to rival (theoretically) Europe. Wren must have been behind it all somewhere as well – another bird, always here or there. These were a different kind of shadowy backer.

But singing was me. It thrilled me. My voice flew up as if I were not in my body at all, but were become a column of sound, and then a dragon of sound, and then a soft dew of vibration which breathed down from the ceiling. So it seemed to me. I wasn't the least nervous or intimidated. And when we rehearsed in the theatre I knew by instinct what I should do, where stand, or how turn and gesture so that I should appear from the audience to be at one with the lofty perspective of the scene. It was, I say, as if I were watching myself from out there. The theatre was my world. *And* no one dared to insult me to my face, because of Charles; despite my alias they all knew very well who I was.

As for my character, I studied deeply the presentation of it. Since I'd started and abandoned my fiction of the slave, I'd thought of the possibility that someone could make a new version of Aphra Behn's *Oroonoko* – what better than an opera? But no one had. Aphra the Amazon, Swift called her. Instead, my conception of Semele was charged with that haunted inspiration of the primitive which had gripped me soon after I first came to London. And as for the present, I saw a curious appropriateness in the two operas that surrounded my tiny, but powerfully patronised career. Addison's failed *Rosamund* at the Theatre Royal, Drury Lane, was set in my beloved Woodstock – had I discovered my métier in time, I should have been cast as the romantic mistress in her bower or oasis, just like the Gyres' farm, while that old King Henry's marriage collapsed elsewhere. Instead, though, I was rehearsing to play a woman who was visited by a divine thunderbolt, which was closer to the truth than anybody else involved with the production ever knew.

Alas, Vanbrugh and Congreve pulled the English *Semele* in late November 1707, three weeks before we were to go on at the Haymarket. I believe my uncle, who had recovered from *his* illness, expected me to be laid low again with disappointment. But I was not. I took it professionally in my stride, having found my vocation; and I awaited pastures new. Nothing would stop me singing.

The reason for the decision after so many weeks of William's work was a commercial one. I was never told whose money beyond Charles's was chiefly behind the venture, but I do know that the appearance of Nicolini in London gave these backers, we called them subscribers, the shakes. In vain did Vanbrugh canvass and Congreve cajole: why not come and hear for yourselves at rehearsal – she may be unknown but she is a nightingale, and the rest of the cast are all strong, Sirs. Strong as oak. And the book is a masterwork. And the airs are divine . . . But the possibility of being caught with another

Rosamund, because all the town was talking about Nicolini, weighed too much against us, and we were dismantled. However, I had seen myself in my perspective, albeit briefly, and it was enough.

By the by, we lost no time in meeting the cause of the upset. Nicolò Grimaldi, who sang under the sobriquet of Nicolini, was a castrato. Because of this I was doubly keen to see him, since we both had a peculiar secret status with regard to gender. Indeed, part of his appeal to the whole town was his curiosity, beside his wonderful voice. It was always so with these exotic pruned shoots of a southern vocal vine. I recognised that he, as well as I, occupied some sort of middle ground between the real and the fabulous – in fact it was here that I understood my own ease at last in the theatre. For what else is the theatre than just such a meeting ground?

In the papers Nicolini was both raved about and scorned. The worst taunts were the usual English reactions to any implied or imported threats to beef and balls. He was jeered as another foreign *semivir*, a vocal unspecificate, or a squeaking shadow of a man. These comments were of course from the very same sheets that frequently inveighed against the improprieties surrounding actresses; while delighting to report them, laced with lies and embellishments. But I found him interesting, and not just because anyone with the name of Nicholas caught my special attention. He was tall and strong-featured, and very very large, with a great composure of manner. His every gesture was compelling, so that when he was on stage a great quiet would fall upon the company and the house, into which he would pour his unearthly stream of tone, like a disturbing angel. He had very little English – I had almost no Italian. We sat with one another without speaking. And I waited until we should sing together. If my fleeting time allowed.

Bickerstaff, however, was designed for April Fool's Day the following year. Swift became an habitué of Jermyn Street, where he and I sat in our saloon, planning the fall of Partridge and other schemes. My uncle felt himself haunted by the Devil, but I was uncaring of this, and pleased with my earlier thesis that the invention of banknotes had created fiction, which with Swift I was about to put to the test.

Isaac Bickerstaff was an Adam, a created person, a plastic and inflatable man into whom we breathed. It was my idea to make him 'a true astrologer'. I hoped, bearing in mind the effect of the earlier Stone rumours that had attached to my uncle some years before, to suggest, ever so faintly and without disclosing any real identities, the possibility that this voice was none other than that of the great astronomer Newton himself. This dream was to float hazily at the back of the enterprise. Bickerstaff was to redeem the art of prophecy for true Protestant science, by revealing the 'nonsense, lies and folly' of the raving poseur Partridge.

We had great sport with Bickerstaff's calculations, for which we called up my rusty mathematics. Bickerstaff's calculations showed that Partridge himself was doomed to expire on 29th March 1708. More: he demonstrated in our wonderful document that the crowned heads of Catholic Europe would follow Partridge in quick succession, with precise dates, culminating in the loss of the Pope on the 11th September that year. Thus, at a stroke, we disposed of extreme dissenters on the one hand and Papists on the other. At the beauty of the scheme Swift grew delirious with a delight that transcended his illness. He released our pamphlet in early February at the street price of one penny. I remember seeing a man reading it in the street. I thought, I wrote that. I remember the snow all about; how he stamped his boots. I can feel the cold under my own shoes as I watched him. His mouth opened to laugh, and his breath turned to misty vapour as it hit the Winter air.

The pamphlet's effect was magical; it immediately sold out. Soon all sorts of anonymous pamphleteers caught on to the main chance., There were Bickerstaffs and pseudo-Bickerstaffs, answers to Bickerstaff, denials and endorsements of Bickerstaff flying about all through March. London held its smoky breath to see whether Partridge would in fact die as foretold.

But the master stroke was Swift's own, and possessed of a vision, cunning and malice which left me swooning in turn. It was to confound the obvious probability that he wouldn't. Die, that is. First he wrote a brilliant anonymous suggestion that a person of discernment who sounded remarkably like Swift himself had seen through the hoax for what it was, and that the last laugh would be on the Town. This was to make a hiatus, a lull, a false falsehood. Then, assuming the literary disguise of a retired taxman – a figure he felt least likely to be credited with too much imagination – he published with joy on the 30th March a graphic account of Partridge's last hours and humiliating demise on the dreadful 29th, as from one who was there present. This dry tax inspector was made to report that the dying Partridge recanted all his phoney dabblings and predictions in the presence of a bespectacled fanatical preacher whom I supplied from life, taking Fatio and Morland as my joint inspirations. Swift surpassed himself by having the narrator note, with a kind of clammy precision, that Bickerstaff was actually seven hours out in his forecast of the time of death.

Now it seemed every journalist and scribbler who had a room in the tatty whoring quarter known as Grub Street caught on to the idea; and every writer of 'quality' got some delicious snigger into print. William himself composed an account, by 'Partridge', of coming downstairs on the morning of his death to confront the undertakers, who assumed he was his own brother and took no notice of him, no matter how much he howled his fleshly existence, danced on the table and laid about him with his stick. But the wonder of it was that plenty of good people now *knew* that Partridge was dead, and nothing could shake their belief; indeed his own publishers, the Stationers' Company, crossed him off their payroll. And when his next almanac came out with fierce denunciations of the airman Bickerstaff, there had by then been so many pseudo-Partridges rising like phoenixes from the ink and soot, that he was lost among them, and the proceeds bypassed their author's bank account.

I thus accomplished my second murder; and saw how it might be that one could escape the flesh, which was one of the aims I had outlined in the original statement of my project. Which brings me to Lucy'lizabeth.

I caught Charles as soon as I could after my bedtime discussion with her.

'Charles, my dear,' I said. 'You see that I'm better now after my time at Woodstock.'

'My darling Kit,' he said, 'I do see and I do rejoice at it. And I too am better, I think.'

'I hope so indeed,' I said carefully. 'Then I should like to propose to you an alteration in our contract, that will be to the benefit of us both.'

'Shall we have to have witnesses again?'

'I don't believe so; if we can just strike up an accord on these sensitive intimate matters, then that should be between us and no one else.'

'Well, Kit?'

'Originally, I stipulated that you should not have me in this house. You remember?'

'It's painfully tattooed on my awareness, Kit. I don't like to think of it. For we've not been a success abroad, as far as to that. Neither of us can deny it.'

'We shan't try to deny it, dearest. But the alteration is for that item to its opposite: that you shall *only* have me here.'

'Oh, Kit,' he said, and began to embrace me there in our drawing-room, seeking for the full kiss he'd given Lucy'lizabeth, and stroking at my legs through the skirt of my gown with his right hand. I pulled myself away. 'I don't deny you my dear, but here isn't fitting, and I can't relax. People are coming round to see me this minute and then I am out to Anne's and on to rehearsals. Come tonight, Charles. Come to my bed here. Tonight.'

I made him leave and found Lucy'lizabeth.

'Tonight you're me,' I said. 'To be safe we shall spend the rest of the day in *our* rehearsals. I shall be you.' My bedroom became all the more theatrical. I got Tony to bring up a bath and some ewers of hot water. Then I locked the door. We stripped and bathed her. I dried her back and powdered her off. We anointed her with my French perfume. We exchanged clothes. She was excited like a bride. I was excited myself. I put on the authority of the subordinate creator – in that a lady's maid is like the sculptor of expensive clay. I was going to do it properly. I boxed her into my best underwear so that her shape took on a powerfully aristocratic line. Then I adjusted the placing of the roll on her hips and began to arrange her, my, gown for the simple evening at home which secretly was to be a special evening of consummation, my gift to Charles and my line of escape. The gown was green – one of those silk creations designed to open like stage curtains at the front below the waist to show off the petticoat, and to offer the breasts, neck and face like a complex orchid in a wineglass. It was mightily erotic. Like everything to do with playing it extracted me from myself, so that in my comparatively low-key maid's dress, with my head somehow suppressed under Lucy'lizabeth's cap, I began to see how Charles felt perhaps; how the figure of me that sat at the dressing-table before me might be a very distracting one. Lucy'lizabeth's eyes flicked back at mine from the mirrors on it. Her cheeks were flushed with a kind of wild permission.

When I finished her hair I went for my silk garter ribbons and got her swung round towards me holding her skirts above her knee while I tied them on. My fingers traced the exotic softness on the inside of her thighs. I covered her up again and attended to the new black kid-leather heeled shoes which only just fitted because her feet were slightly wider than mine. Rings and jewels and two little patches for her face. I brushed a hint of colour on to her cheekbones. Then I lined her eyes. I craved her.

'Will I have another child, Miss Kit?'

'Don't call me Miss Kit now. Speak to me as I speak to you. Try now.'

'I'm scared. Lucy'lizabeth.' But she didn't look so scared. She looked as though she could cope with everything. I thought, if I've found my place in the theatre, she's found hers in the bedroom.

'Sure you're not nervous at all, Miss Kit,' I said.

'Perhaps I am not after all,' she breathed, softly hugging her sides and then lifting her gesture so that she stroked and re-stroked her upper arms, herself her own lover. 'Perhaps after all I am not nervous in the slightest.' She let her eyes close.

'There Miss Kit,' I said, finishing her neckline. 'And between you and me I wonder whether Mr Charles can get babies indeed. He'd have had something by now, I'd have thought, if he was able. Would you mind, Miss?'

'I can't say Miss . . . Lucy'lizabeth. My head's so full of . . . I don't know what.'

'Do you love him, Miss?'

'I think I may do, Lucy'lizabeth.'

Special Licence

Charles arrived late. He brought cut flowers tied in a basket, which he said a woman was selling by Leicester Fields and he hadn't been able to resist for me. Lucy'lizabeth received him and the flowers in the drawing-room. Somehow the requirement of conversation didn't trouble her or seem to matter between them. There were several reasons I could imagine for this, but I pressed them from my mind. I brought in a tray with two of our best glasses and a decanter of my uncle's most expensive sweet French white wine. He, Charles, was already on his knee beside the silk fall of her dress, holding her hand with one of his, while resting the other arm behind her neck and tracing the lines of her collar-bone with his fingers. They only broke the lock of their eyes when I was actually setting down my goods.

'Why don't you bring the wine upstairs, Lucy'lizabeth,' she said drinking of hers and looking back at Charles past the glass.

'Very well, Miss Kit,' I said. They got up very tenderly. Charles held the door for me and my tray, and so I led the lovers up the stairs into the warmth of my prepared bedchamber.

'Help me, won't you, Lucy'lizabeth,' she said, distantly, once I'd put the tray down and was making to leave.

'Help you, Miss?'

'Help me undress.'

'I thought you'd have help enough tonight, Miss.'

'Charles will need to attend to himself, Lucy'lizabeth.' Of course this was nonsense, and Charles showed no sign of attending to himself, beyond shedding the maximum number of outer layers in the minimum time – he was much more concerned with his attendance on her, repeating the kneeling pattern and unbuckling her, my, shoes. It seemed that sculpturally, my standing presence beside her as she sat by my table in the firelight released the lower space for him to work upwards. I felt he had his mind fixed on the garters. So it was that I set to undoing my earlier work until she was quite dishevellée. Charles's hands were under her skirt but his face hovered near her bosom.

Lucy'lizabeth took my hands around her neck and pressed them into the loosened bodice, saying: 'Charles may drink another wine if you'd serve him.' Surprised, to a degree horrified, but compelled by the drama, I caught what she must mean, and, cautiously easing her lovely breasts from her clothes, held them for him to choose which he would suck on first. He chose, and looked up at me. There was an exchange of meaning, but I couldn't read its message.

Yes, I found myself locked into a sexuality which I was beyond. Lucy'lizabeth laid her head back against me to enjoy the ministrations of Charles's hands and lips in a way I'd never been able to. Her legs lolled apart; her hips rocked languorously under her heaped-up

skirts, and her breasts in my hands heaved with a tangible deliciousness, as she breathed and hummed to herself.

'I've a good helpful maid, Charles,' she said, lifting her head
slowly. 'It's lucky she knows her place.' She laid her hands over his
face and burrowed in his shirt. 'How shall we ever go on to tell the
peasants from their masters and mistresses?' Charles, his mouth full
of beauty, made no reply. I didn't know how it was she'd acquired
such verbal assurance in so short a space of time – but she had and I
was angry. I squeezed my fingers into the root of her breasts, enough
to let her know my feelings. She jumped, and her pleasure-humming
concentrated itself into a yelp.

'Dearest Kit!' Charles broke off his activities. 'Forgive me. I'd
never intentionally hurt you. Come, sweetheart, let's go to bed.' He
stood up.

'Then finish my clothes, Lucy'lizabeth.'

'Indeed, Miss Kit.'

I set about getting her out of her remaining things as quickly as I
could. I wanted to hit her. Had she been drinking? Before the event?
Charles fiddled and fondled about as if he were helping, but my
sharp fingers worked more quickly and dextrously than his. Lucy
'lizabeth, becoming by the layer progressively more naked, draped
her arms round us both.

'She's my absolute intimate, Charles. There are positively no secrets between us; how could there be? We're so alike. I'm overjoyed to
have found her. A simple country girl – so perfect for my needs.' She
stepped out of her petticoat and hung about my neck, in such a way
that if Charles wanted to continue his embraces and stroking of her
naked hip he had to come in contact with me closely enough as well.

'Send away your maid, my love. Let's go to bed together.' I could
see he was beginning to be disconcerted.

'Why, Charles? Do you notice her? Do you fancy her? I'll have her
whipped if she plays the whore in my house.'

'No, Kit.'

'Don't you prefer kind Amaryllis, the wanton country maid,' she
quoted from the old song, slipping her arm down to my waist to
press me against him. I could smell the perfumed sex of her body.

'Come, Madam. You try me beyond my limits.' He grew rough
with her and took her away from me to the bed. His violence excited

him, clearly. Her eyes flashed at me over his shoulder with a kind of triumph.

'You may leave us now, Lucy'lizabeth.' It was his voice. Hers added:

'Iron my lace Lucy'lizabeth. Don't forget I shall need it for tomorrow.'

Outside the door I stopped. They were loud at it. I was excluded. I'd been included and then excluded again. I was aroused and angry like Charles; I was aroused and passive like Lucy'lizabeth. And I had only myself to a blame; a substitute was exactly what I had desired in order to escape my intolerable situation. I was furious. And then I remembered that the pressing of my lace for the gown I needed to wear in the morning – to attend some function, I forget what – was more than a taunt. It was a real necessity. For Lucy'lizabeth would not be reporting for duty yet awhile. And Tony and Mary were out at Pet's. The kitchen fire and the sizzling pressing irons, which I struggled with in my unaccustomed way, were fine images of my pent-up rage.

Charles left reluctantly after midnight; I heard his extended farewell. Exhausted from my seemingly never-ending chore of ironing, I crawled into bed half an hour later beside my sated rival. She was utterly asleep. She moaned with a drowsy pleasure as I heaved my head on to the bolster next to her. I felt like braining her. And bits of my bed were wet. It was too horrible. I couldn't bear it. I went to sleep in her bed and spent an uncomfortable night.

In the morning I went in, pulled back the covers and pinched her awake.

'What, Miss, do you think you're up to?'

She blinked and stretched, naked, mildly discomfited, and made to pull the clothes back over her. I wanted to do unspeakable things to her beautiful body. In practice I slapped her,

'Mistress Slug Bed!' And slapped her again. She woke up soon enough then. She sat up and tried to get the covers to her neck, but I wouldn't let her, so she had to account for herself with her hands folded across her breasts and the rest of her unprotected.

'Well!' I said.

'Well?' she said.

'Well, Miss Kit, to you.'

'Well, Miss Kit,' she said sulkily.

'Yes?' I said.

'What? Miss Kit.'

'What was all that performance last night?'

'I did what you wanted.'

'With a vengeance!' I said. 'You had me holding your tits and doing your ironing!'

'Your ironing,' she muttered. 'You're going to wear it. And your tits as well, in a manner of speaking.'

'Having me whipped? How shall we tell the peasants from the masters? How dare you speak to me like that! Is that how I behave to you?'

She was silent for a moment, sullen.

'Well?' I thundered.

'Well, it is in a manner of speaking if not in so many words. Miss Kit. And can I have something to cover me up, please? Miss Kit.'

'Not till I get to the heart of this. Do I treat you badly? Do I?'

'You don't mean it, I suppose. It's just you don't know no better.'

'Any better.'

'Any better. You don't know any better.'

'What on earth do you mean, Lucy'lizabeth? Aren't you now better dressed, better fed, better housed than you've ever been in your life or could ever have dreamed of being? Well?'

'Yes.'

'And because of whom?'

'You.'

'You, Miss Kit.'

'You, Miss Kit.'

'And haven't you just had the opportunity of being pleasured by one of the greatest men in England, with minimal risk to yourself? Is it not all gain for you? Hasn't wealth just been poured into your lap? Don't tell me, woman, that you didn't have a night to remember. Because I was there for a good part of it. And after that you had your little churn well creamed and have licked the butter of it I do not doubt, Lucy'lizabeth.'

'Yes.'

'Then why did you have to mock me? Good God, it's torture enough to me that I'm excluded from such pleasures as you obviously can take – which I am by my nature, Lucy'lizabeth – I say it's

231

torture enough, without having my nose rubbed in my abnormalities.'

'Yes, Miss.'

'Then why, Lucy'lizabeth? Why? It's you I could've had whipped or sent out when I discovered your first . . . fornication with my lover.'

'But I was being you, Miss Kit.'

'You insolent slut. Do I behave like that to you?'

'Yes.'

'What?'

'In a manner of speaking.'

'What?'

'Not in so many words; but in your attitude. Miss Kit.'

'How dare you!' I said, and slapped her legs. She pulled them up under her. In a rage, I threw the bedclothes at her and stalked out of my room.

But there was really nowhere I could go, seeing I was half-dressed after a difficult night in a strange bed and my sanctuary was occupied by a naked woman. So I stormed up and down on the landing for about a quarter of an hour. Then I went back.

'Am I really?' I said. 'Oh for God's sake stop crying, girl. Here.' I gave her something to wipe her eyes. 'Am I really so? I had a different image of myself.'

'He didn't pass no comment, Miss. It seemed to suit his reckoning of how you act. I thought I done good.'

'Did well. At least get my speech into your head. You managed last night, I noticed, not to be so . . . regional. Why not now?'

'I'm not being you now. I'm being me.'

A thought occurred to me. 'Tell me, Lucy'lizabeth. When you were married to . . . what was his name?'

'Ralphy, Miss.'

'Ralphy. When you were married to him. In this bedroom matter. Did you . . . ? Did he bring you to . . . ? How shall I put this? Did you . . .'

'Come off, Miss?'

'Exactly. May I ask?'

'No, Miss.'

'I may not?'

'I mean no I didn't.'

'But last night?'

'Yes, Miss.'

'You did?'

'Yes, Miss.'

'Lucy'lizabeth. Is there a great deal of difference in . . . skill, between Charles and . . . Ralphy?'

'No, Miss.'

'But Charles is . . . was . . . the more subtly pleasing, it seems.'

'I don't think so, Miss. No. Not so as to mention as it was anything to do with him, I think.'

'Not? Then . . . ?'

'It's when I'm you, Miss Kit. Then I can do it.'

'This is all very tangled, Lucy'lizabeth. I can't think of it no more.'

'Any more, Miss.'

'It's a great mystery, indeed.'

Charles lost no time in telling me of his new will. He'd had it prepared for some time against the fruition of our mutual happiness. It seemed that he'd placed inordinate faith in the effects of Woodstock on my recovery from my illness – a faith which, as it turned out, was justified; although not exactly in an orthodox way. Where should this extraordinary confidence have come from? I didn't like to ask. Perhaps he'd been to a wise woman, or someone such; even though as far as I knew this was opposite to his character. Still, I was constantly amazed by what really happened, as against what anyone expected to happen.

The will left £3,000 and all his jewels to me, 'as a small Token of the great Love and Affection I have long had for her'. In addition, I found he'd provided an annuity of £200 per annum for me, to be administered by my uncle.

But 'our' love life took wings. He called whenever he could. He was very busy trying to get into the Cabinet – he remained the only Junto lord in the time of their apogee not to have secured this distinction. But he was excessively tender during the day, or when we went abroad together in the town. We spoke of all the things I wished to speak about; and besides that, he sought my advice about the lesser issues of government or the schemes he was concerned in – things we were allowed to discuss. So that we could become free and natural together, drained of that anxiety and tension which had characterised our relations before. As to the bedroom, I told him to expect me to seem a different person at night in the candlelight or in bed, because I'd been taught by Mrs Gyre at Woodstock, whom we both regarded as a strangely magical person (by what means he knew of her in the first place I never enquired), how to metamorphose myself into a sexual being. I said I could only do it at night because I was still beset with 'female problems' as a result of my peculiar upbringing, and that he must leave before dawn. The daylight restraint, against the promise of nocturnal indulgence, excited him profoundly. I dramatised the uncanny element of it in my narration, to the extent that he was stirred up almost to the point of an ongoing intoxication with me.

Thus I explained my employment of Lucy'lizabeth. I must be sweet for him, and needed the skills and ministrations of a personal maid.

'You no longer feel you must kill that man, Kit?'

I answered him prettily, and in a way he couldn't possibly have understood. 'I blame you Charles, you and the Bank of England. It's your fault indeed. I've already achieved my second murder, but it was only on paper. Now I have my Art.'

He smiled uncertainly at my loaded nonsenses, and was relieved.

I was not free, though. My night-time body was not yet entirely my own. This was because of the way Lucy'lizabeth had started matters up – with me demanded in intimate attendance. The lovers needed me. They were reluctant to do without me; while I was reluctant to leave the deception to run beyond my control. So instead of effecting the changeover between my night and day selves in order to rush off to *Semele* and the theatre in my alias, I was often with them, and they sought by all means to delay me into their ecstasy. I was usually required to undress her to some extent, as before; then sometimes to help him. But my attentions were always protected by Lucy'lizabeth's jealousy; that if he dallied or responded with me at all, no matter what touches or provocations I was induced to render him, she'd have me whipped.

Of course there came the night when they grew bolder in my presence: she, with her shift up round her waist and her breasts revealed, sat astride his nakedness on the chair by the fire.

'But Lucy'lizabeth . . . ?' said Charles before committing himself fully to this adventure.

'She doesn't mind us, my dearest Charles,' replied Lucy'lizabeth. 'Do you, Lucy'lizabeth?'

'No, Miss Kit.'

'She is the perfect maid-servant. She is a Biblical personage, Charles; for don't we read of great intimacy in these matters in the story of Jacob, his sweet love Rachel, and the maid Bilhah?'

'Do we?' said Charles.

Where she got hold of this idea I never enquired – I guessed it would sound powerfully convincing to one who wished to be convinced, and I suspected Charles wouldn't look up the reference too closely in case he found out its casuistry. As I did as soon as I could get to my Bible. Nevertheless I was deeply impressed with her inventiveness.

Of course the idea was more applicable to her. I was the Rachel, if anyone was.

Charles, if he had any sense, would leave the surface of his happiness unscratched. And he would refrain, if he had any sense, from discovering during the daytime the little bump concealed in the forehead just inside his darling's hairline, and from probing for it during his passion at night.

But I digress. Her perfunctory and ingenious Biblical reference was quite sufficient to soothe his doubts and procure all the engagement she could have wished. This was the first time they abandoned themselves to the complete act in my presence. I hadn't expected it could be done in a chair. They began my *éducation sentimentale* so to speak. Once again amidst all the puffing and lubrication his eyes for a moment caught mine over her shoulder, before he gave himself absolutely to her. They arrived in a duet of grunts, moans and little cries: to the onlooker, by turns intriguing, incomprehensible, infuriating; to the participants, a species of paradise. When they'd stopped, I wanted to kill them both. She kept him inside her and collapsed on his chest. That lasted a minute or so. Then they slipped down to the blanket in front of the fire as if by unspoken agreement, billing and nibbling at each other; oblivious of my presence it seemed, but at the same time requiring my . . . what? Approval, agreement, permission, observation?

Yes, beyond the tutorial benefits which were my dubious profit, I speculated on my function for them. Why did they need me there? Why should my presence have so excited them, released them, you might say? Would it have been the same if I'd been a man watching them? Did my social rank matter?

I believe Swift fell in love with me. It was in the Summer when we'd heard the news of another victory by the prodigious Marlborough; this time at Oudenarde. Swift became very awkward in my presence. Poor man. He lost his delight, his innuendo, and became sorry and disturbed. Soon he stopped calling. I heard that he became for a while as twisted and puritanical as the dissenters he so hated. If he had the management of the commonwealth, he said, there'd be no lewd actresses permitted, indeed no theatres at all, for they were temptations to lust; no swearing, no disorderly intoxicated fornication, no access to the monarch by godless intemperate men. Was he jealous of Charles? Is this how he saw us? Did he think I was so charged with insatiable lust? How suddenly he changed who had been my friend.

Another night Lucy'lizabeth set it up cleverly that I should find myself in bed with them. And when I made to leave she commanded me to remain. To provoke a crisis of authority would have been to risk the whole masquerade being exposed, so I had to stay. But she had me on *her* side, so that she could monitor any stray attempts on his part to enjoy the same woman twice at the same time. This was almost more than I could bear. I longed for my shadowy backer to come and lie with me and love me to my own fatal climax, but he did not. I suffered the extreme of jealousy and exclusion. I was in hell. I was of the Devil's mind in *Paradise Lost*, whose most acute perception of his suffering is in contemplation of Adam and Eve embracing:

Oh Hell, what doe mine eyes with grief behold

and:

Sight hateful, sight tormenting! thus these two
Imparadis't in one another's arms
The happier Eden, shall enjoy their fill
Of bliss on bliss, while I to Hell am thrust,
Where neither joy nor love, but fierce desire,
Among our other torments not the least,
Still unfulfilled with pain of longing pines;

Except that my hell was a tactile one – I was closer than that fallen peeping Tom, and lay not within sight but within the very motion of their love.

Nicolini

My uncle was all on fire because he'd seen a demonstration of a working steam engine, made by a gentleman to pump out the Derbyshire mines, so that the families could go deeper and dryer. I wondered if Marlborough too were not some terrible engine, some created being of fire, a thing of victory and the sword. At Malplaquet they'd lost twenty-five thousand, we twenty thousand, so despatches informed us, and thus we were victorious. But the newspapers said Louis couldn't go on, having been nearly ruined by the terrible '08–'09 winter. Was it *necessary* to go on, I wanted to know. Charles said he would like to talk to me about it all but he was bound by his position. The war must be prosecuted if we're to maintain security, was the most he would say. But the tide in the country was turning towards the Tories, who capitalised on the calls for peace and the exhaustions and taxations of the war. They managed to get riots up, in the March I think it was. Pro-Jacobite riots. Unthinkable two years ago.

By the powerful agency of my lover I secured the chance, following the loss of my first opera, to sing for Nicolini. It was actually on the stage at the Queen's in the Haymarket. But Anne wasn't available to come with me. Nor was Charles, and my activities were in theory at least a secret from the rest of my acquaintance. I felt frightened and exposed, since I was used to having some protector or other, an attention which I took for granted then, but see now as the concomitant of beauty, which served to keep me . . . I was going to say childish, but this wasn't quite it. You will understand, perhaps, that I was neither adult nor child, but something experienced and in-between. But I had that in common with a great number of society women, because of the way things were.

There was a solitary keyboard player in the converted orchestra pit. The chairs and music stands of the band were all vacant. Loose in the auditorium sat the great man, together with Aaron Hill, the energetic, beautiful poet, John Heidegger and an interpreter. Heidegger was an impresario, whom cruel report cast in Aaron's shadow as the ugliest man in Europe. Which was a nonsense. He was no more than moderately ugly. Still, when they were seen together Rumour nicknamed them Grace and the Gargoyle.

Half a chandelier was burning, and there was some minimal illumination on the stage. I ran through a few airs from the Eccles/ Congreve *Semele*, and then felt bold enough to try him with one of the first act soprano arias from Bononcini's *Camilla*. He was, through the interpreter, polite but unimpressed. And it was over.

It wasn't that I stamped my foot and stormed out. I hadn't that facility. But I got up silently and let him know I was wounded. For I felt that the earlier tacit companionship we'd established was owed more than this.

What didn't he like, I asked. Was there any hope?

The voice was too English, he said, and he pulled no punches as he went on: breathy in the upper register, and weakened in the lower by tension in the diaphragm. He was utterly, coldly professional; his great bulk unmoved in his diagnosis by our previous contact or the thought of Charles's influence.

Mortified, I went to collect the copies of my music from the harpsichordist. I couldn't manage more than a half-thank you without giving way to the tears that threatened. The *panel* sat silently as I walked up the rake of the house towards the door to the entrance foyer where I determined to send a messenger immediately for Charles, no matter what he was engaged upon. At the door I turned to look back upon the scene of my humiliation. All four men stood looking at me. The interpreter called:

'But Nicolini offer to teach you!'

A new candle lit on the stage of my soul.

I spent the next two hours standing on the boards of the house having my technique overhauled and my laces loosened. He had by this time a few phrases of English – I soon acquired a few of Italian. And so we got on. He was all about relaxation of the *punti di costrizione*.

'The what?'

'*I punti di costrizione del corpo.*'

In answer to my bewildered expression he put one large paw on either side of my slender waist, raised them both up the sides to my floating ribs and pressed my solar plexus with his thumbs through my satin and whalebone.

'Ow!'

'*Un punto di costrizione!*'

'I see,' I said, doubtfully. '*Capisco, Maestro. Ma . . . como . . . quo modo . . . come . . .* ' I gave up in his language for the moment. 'How do I . . . ? What am I supposed to do about it?'

He opened his mouth, but it was beyond him to explain in English. He made wrenching movements with his arms and laughed. Then he made the gesture of soothing. Then stroking. Then snarling. I was pleased. Gradually we formulated a vocabulary of touch. He saw and felt I was strong enough in muscle to get out a good sound. An Englishman would not have done this to me. He wouldn't have dared, I think. It was to remove the impediment to the voice – this was so new to my technique, since La Colomba had always told me to pull in here, push out there, press this, hit that, until I was a bundle of twists, like a poor specimen of the knotting craze. Anne, who'd been taught by Eccles, had little technique at all – just a very pretty voice; for she'd really been instructed in music rather than singing *per se*.

Nicolini set about untying me; then, and for the next year, when-ever it could be managed. I had a sort of contract from Heidegger – I say a sort of contract, since it wasn't much more than an agreement to learn the whole art. Because of what? My looks? They didn't seem to think it was for my voice, I lamented to myself; or was I too lacking in self-esteem to see my qualities or my position realistically? Had Charles been pulling strings? Still, I was under contract to become florid, Italianate and excellent.

Yes, the management of it. I had to see to the running of my uncle's household; I had to be the witty self that Charles and our acquaint-ance expected, and keep up with my friends; I had to see to it that Lucy'lizabeth was primed and reasonably available according to Charles's inclinations; and I had in addition to attend my instruction and see to several hours of practice each day. My life became a series of watertight compartments, of chambers – like a heat engine. I put a great deal of puff into arranging them. But this was not so unusual to me because in our house we'd always, my uncle and I, lived compartmentalised, and from this separation it may be that the potential of our energy was drawn. My steam was cycled from one box to another, and put sometimes sweatily to labour. The really difficult region, the one where the pressure blow was most likely, was the deception involving Charles – of course he knew all about the singing and wasn't the man to be jealous of a castrato; though in fact some society ladies queued up for them. But I mean the deception of the bedroom. I wonder; perhaps it was his complicity, knowing or blind, which preserved me here. For I was preserved. Like Newcomen's engine, the system worked – just. While we were still on speaking terms Lucy'lizabeth and I developed a functional rhythm of illusion, which, with the exception of a few near moments, ran with success enough. We were the moving parts.

I had my experiences – I can hardly call them lessons, since they took the wonderful form of an endless opening of doors – in Maestro Nicolò Grimaldi's apartments off Suffolk Place, near the excellent Italian shop, where there was a top room with an instrument on which he could play. On hot days we opened the windows and let our music out to charm on the one side the throng and the traffic below, and, at the other extreme of the penthouse, the birds in the trees which bordered the deep ragged garden. The doves, the squirrels, the passers-by, the agitators of heavy goods vehicles, the pedlars, the idling gentry, the beggars, the *mutilés de guerre* must have wondered what sort of a creature was delayed in the upper storeys, when our two linked voices wandered down to them.

It was so hard. He had such awesome standards, it seemed to me. I loved Anne, and I loved the way she sang for our English theatre, pretty, charming, and, as I've said, as English as Eccles; I loved her for launching me – but the kind of singing she represented and which I'd been tried out in was, compared to this, idle vocalisation.

We began – no, to tell the truth we began with my wobble, which I didn't know I had; and converted it into a true vibrato of amplitude rather than pitch, establishing my vocal decency – but after that we began with my *messa di voce*, and practised for weeks it seemed until I could float my sound out into space from the softest of origins, locate it on the ceiling, and swell it to a great sail of sound in the room. Then I'd call it back, subtly folding it to myself again like a magical bird sent out and returned safe from an errand.

And while that was in train as homework, so to speak, we studied ornaments, shakes, runs and trills. I ran through my scales in so many combinations that if you'd imagine a housemaid dashing up and down stairs, called from above and below until she doesn't know which direction to give the priority, you'd have a good idea of my instruction. Sometimes he'd play over a passage, florid enough in itself, and have me sing it back to him straight – which was usually hard – once. Then it was *'Tocca a te!* Embellish, *Signorina*, decorate!', and I'd have to invent suitably interesting and extravagant ornamentation over and above what he played. My first attempts at this were laughable, but then he'd demonstrate, and produce musical rabbits out of hats. So that I began to see what was required; I gained a patent in dropping a succession of melting halftones down the cadence of a Scarlatti lament. This he approved at last.

Effortlessness. Lightness. And always relax, relax, untie, undo. That was the quintessence of the Nicolini technique. *'La gioia, Catherina!'* he'd shout. *'Coltiva la gioia. Sempre la gioia. E 'l centro del cantar'!'* And he'd rub his extensive stomach. 'So we charm *gli animi* . . . the souls, from . . . is it *from* you say? from the *Inferno.'*

Alas I had none. No joy. None of my own, properly. None of myself but in singing. And I saw sometimes a trace of the sadness in *his* eyes which accorded with my own.

But I began to sense joy's similitude, while we both acknowledged that my voice and personality lent themselves to wronged innocence and lyric heroine, rather than *un'appassionata*. This accorded quite satisfactorily with my looks, he said.

Range. High notes – my particular dread. He would turn them into my delight, he said. And he did. I learned to get out of the way of the sound. It was a curious sensation – like abandoning one's body to the wind. But it worked, after four months, as if by magic. My upper register, which had so disturbed me that I physically sweated with anticipation of failure in some pieces, and felt my throat lock up in despair of making a good sound when nearing those dreaded regions, took on a pair of wings. He was right – it did it by itself, if you stood back and let it. There were days when I knew my sound was glorious.

Low notes: how to locate them in the chest. How to secure my resonance from G downwards so that there'd be that eerie half-masculine availability, that bite in the tail end of the soprano voice.

Repertoire: he had me on everything. Monteverdi, Scarlatti, Purcell, Bononcini, Gasparini, Mancini and a host of other pieces from Continental bound-up octavos that he took from his leather travelling case. Everything, that is, except one key composer. Whose name I didn't know anyway, and so did not miss at the time.

So I didn't know what it was all for. Nobody mentioned performances, recitals. I was kept under wraps like a secret new cannon. It was all a mystery. I wondered if he'd take me to Venice. Sometimes Hill and Heidegger came to monitor my progress, but they never said anything more than pleasantries about my voice and my health, so I remained in the enchanted dark. But I did work at it; I went to his apartments every morning – I believe my household thought I was out calling, as if I'd suddenly grown ultra-sociable. The arrangement was that I might practise there, in the same place I took my lessons, whether he was available or not. I sat at the instrument learning *arie antiche e nuove*, or I wandered about the room with my scales and exercises, resting my hand on his suit thrown over a chair or his wigs on a special rack. Or I rehearsed to his make-up box whatever scene he'd set me.

And what was he doing when he wasn't with me? He was preparing and performing, sometimes in public and sometimes privately. In March I saw him theatrically naked strangling a lion in *Idaspe* in front of a short-notice heroine whose voice I didn't care for and who was undisguisably pregnant. It was at the Queen's, of course, and I sat with Mary Pierrepont and her formidable father. I took her backstage to meet Nicolini afterwards, since she was a devotee and knew him slightly from when he'd sung at Nottingham the Summer before. And she wanted to try out her Italian. I had to smuggle her there, since her father supposed her too well brought up to be seen in the tiring-rooms.

From the late Spring he went away for a month touring great houses and making money. Then back in London he was often on business at our Queen's Theatre in the Haymarket with Owen Swiney; some sort of business which wasn't discussed with me. You see how I call it *our* theatre. It was in a way. It was, I could see, in many ways a Whig theatre. I began to understand that political interest was clustered around it, and although I was a theatrical virgin, so to speak, I knew so much of what went on concerning its people that I thought of it as ours.

July. '*Buon giorno, Signorina Newton,*' which is what he called me for a joke. Then kissing me, '*E come va il cielo?* And how is *La Gravità?*' Which I think had some sort of pregnancy connotation he enjoyed the flavour of. Well, what of the man himself? Did I come to be in love with him? Or he with me? Yes, he was very large, if you will, and conformed to all the jokes about neutered Toms. Yes, I came to love . . . to admire his great robustness, which seemed like a vast warm male security from over the seas and mountains. Yes, he did embrace me, and kiss my neck and my bosom, but not my mouth. And I didn't mind. Perhaps because it could lead nowhere more than to mutual . . . warmth. So when I'd accomplished some virtuosity of *bel canto* to his satisfaction we'd share a little reward, which was a gentle arousal. Or perhaps he couldn't share it except upon the surface of the skin, somewhat generally distributed rather than localised. And I'd sit on his great, harmless lap at the harpsichord while he demonstrated the intricacies of his breathing technique. Thus he would sing with my hand on his stomach under his waistcoat, in order for me to feel the muscles of his diaphragm working. Then we would try a duet, and I left my hand there, while his found my equivalent secret vocal source through the fabric of my morning gown. And found that I'd cut away most of the lower part of my stays the better to conform with his theories on freedom of the bellows.

Each of us lingered our hands, and looked closely into the other's eyes.

So by our . . . love, we invented two great things. The first was the separate brassière – what I left was loosely laced and for form's sake, in both senses of the word; and the second was the erotic possibility of the human lungs. I allowed myself to be the girl child I'd never been, and kissed his cheek, and pulled off his wig, and stroked his hair. And perhaps he played at beginning the begetting he'd never achieve, fondling my breasts through my new invention with his palm and letting his fingers toy with the tops of them, naked under my handkerchief. But nothing below the waist. Ours was *una carezza* only of the North. We reserved ourselves from the scars of memory.

Then we'd go back to work. Half an hour's sight-reading, perhaps, or the expression of the face and its effect on the sound. And we'd act our love scenes and battle scenes, like the crazy moments he adored from *Tancredi e Clorinda*. He was a wonderful actor and made my heart melt – a little more than I was used to.

So we went on, all through the hot Summer of 1710, when the dust and the hazy blue were almost un-English, and I could believe that Italy herself had come up here to me and taken me over. Smoky London, Dutch, Gothic, Wrennish, already tarnished, suddenly scene-painted after the Venetian school. And twice we shared the cool groves and purling streams as if of a conventional second act – we went boating at Ham, and lay in a gondola until evening. There was even a guitarist. To join him I went broad daylight in my mask – and came back in it, using a two-horse hackney carriage. Even so, one or two scurrilous newpaper comments appeared, but at least my uncle didn't see them.

So I came to love the mystery that hung over my intensive preparation, not minding that no one would tell me what was afoot, even when I'd become good enough for my *maestro* himself to say so after a session in his rapidly improving English; rapidly improving for one reason at least, and that was from our lying together on his bed with the window open while I read the *Tatler* to him, and he stroked my hair.

The *Tatler*, by the way, bore my creation – well, mine and Swift's – at the head of its every edition, *and* my uncle's name, three times a week. *The Tatler, by Isaac Bickerstaff*. Mr Steele had taken up the name for the prolongation of the joke, and Mrs Manley, who was just about to enter my life in a significant way, had brought out last Summer a semi-scurrilous alternative, as you might infer from her sobriquet, called *The Female Tatler, by Mrs Crackenthorpe, the Woman who Knows Everything*. This had run for quite a few weeks. I had some copies and I sometimes read them to him, but got confused myself about my political drift. I lost touch in that special Summer with the immediate problems of our Party. The dismissal of Godolphin unsettled us. Parliament was prorogued. Thus John Smith lost the Chancellorship of the Exchequer, and Charles's brother James was dismissed as Attorney-General; but to me it all seemed far off suddenly, to be taking place somewhere else.

I was fascinated to recognise in Mrs Manley, who was clearly paid by the Tory propaganda machine, someone who did in her way what I was doing in mine. She was looking for gaps. For I'd previously learnt much that Charles wouldn't or couldn't tell me from reading her first novel, a scathing portrait of Sarah Churchill, as Queen Zarah of the Zaraziens, and her great husband the Captain-General. What if Harley and the Tories *were* fixing appointments until it was safe for them to call an election? I'd responded to a glittering ruthlessness belied by the sweet opening: 'Once upon a time . . . ' I sensed an image of myself, sweet, harmonious on the outside; dark, murderous within. I hadn't met her, well, only once: a curious, handsome, big woman of forty-odd, who had a little difficulty walking. She advertised, I felt, by the title of her recent satirical novel *The New Atalantis*, and by the vaunted Universal Knowledge of the old Bawd Crackenthorpe – alright she was Steele's cast-off mistress and had it in for him – but beyond this she advertised herself, to one who would heed the cryptic message of her publications, as a thinker female and dissatisfied with the very meaning of the Royal Society. The Royal Society was after all the incarnation of Bacon's New Atlantis. What did its hegemony over the thought of the future offer a woman? Nothing. My own problem.

My thoughts tumbled over each other in the flash of awareness. Mary De La Rivière Manley, no doubt as conscious of the femininity of her first names as the irony of her last, which Etta told me she'd acquired twice; once by birth and once by a nasty fraud of a marriage to her cousin, which amounted to a legal form of rape. I digress. Mary Manley, I fantasised, *might* have sensed that to whore her pen to the Tories *could* allow her to demonstrate an alternative to the pure masculine power. Power epitomised by our Party as it stood at the time. And the alternative she'd chosen was scandal, romance, intrigue, gossip. As if this *knowledge* was somehow as valid as that ideal matter the doctors occupied themselves with. And possibly as powerful; was she not arrested last year? I knew my hunch would turn out true. It came to me almost telepathically while I read to my wounded *cavaliere*.

Within a week, however, my hunch took a heavy body blow. My copy of her new book reached me: volumes three and four of *The New Atalantis*, published under the title *Memoirs of Europe, Towards the Close of the Eighth Century. Written by Eginardus*. It was biting towards our Party. I appeared in it as Bartica, mistress of Julius Sergius of Constantinople, which was a very thinly veiled portrait of Charles. It appeared I longed to marry him: 'Twas ever a proud Slut!' She must have been thinking of Lucy'lizabeth, I thought, hissing

through my teeth in fury. I left off the *Female Tatler* as source material
for his lessons, and twisted them up for Winter firelighters. Nicolini
was annoyed. He'd enjoyed them. I told myself I didn't have the
linguistic resources, or the inclination, to entertain the sensuous
Papist who kissed my ear the while, with the intricacies of my morti-
fication – or my project.

I turned my thoughts to the singer's preoccupation, the body. Yes,
we relaxed beautifully together, but I had regions which now I saw
might never relax; regions of me I'd never known about. Why? Perhaps the lion's probing touch had reached the sleeping wolf. But I
put the thought from my mind and let him and the warm wind of
Summer continue to breathe on my neck.

Lovers

To vanish as myself. To slide another, identical person into my life
and disappear into the arms of Art.

But the idyll of our Summer came to an end with the arrival of the
Boschi couple, and a number of other Italian singers. Nicolini was
too busy with them and his artistic life, and with the work on the
Theatre. Privately he was monopolised by Henrietta Churchill-
Godolphin, who swept down and snapped her fingers and had her
way over everything, of course. The air of expectation grew. I sensed
it. I continued going to his place whenever I could, and devoting
myself to practice. Charles, who sometimes came to Nicolini's empty
rooms to hear me, became also excited by it, and perhaps my voice,
so that I had to fend him off, reminding him of the strict terms of the
whole agreement, and that I was a professional woman in the best
sense of the word not the worst. He accepted this well enough and
seemed brimming with some delicious intelligence that he longed to
reveal to me. When I got home I had to brief Lucy'lizabeth on the
details of my day's vocalisations so that she could make the right
responses to Charles in bed, as well as understanding his cat grin at
the non-disclosure of the great secret. I found the strain of this,
and the fact that they still enforced me often into their lovemaking
when my mind and heart were full of music, very trying. I had now
no embraces of my own with Nicolini to look forward to. I longed for

it not to be Charles who held the secret to my training; I longed to be free of the pair of them. To leave.

I've written of leaving the body as a child, and of my one memory of actually doing so; now in my first adulthood I was seeking to recreate the escape more permanently by my Art. My participation in their amours nauseated me. Though I pushed the whole thing to the back of my mind, it was actually myself I blamed, myself who somehow bore the disgust. I tried to share it with Anne.

'You don't, my dearest Anne, have such a . . . *distorted* view of things as I do, I believe.'

'Meaning what, Kit? You're so ready to accuse yourself of abnormality. I've grown a little accustomed to your bombshells, at least.'

'Our ménage. It goes on. Even since the move. Shall you be shocked if I explain?'

'I expect I shall, but never mind.' She'd come out to visit me at the lodgings Charles still kept at Hampton Court, where I was living while my uncle relocated to central London again. I haven't mentioned that our domestic arrangements had been in turmoil for several Autumn months which had somewhat cramped my own schedule, though hardly daunted my pair of demanding doves. But the Chelsea house had proved too far out to be really us.

That afternoon, strolling arm in arm in Bushy Park, we hitched our skirts up and kicked outrageously the copper layer of new-fallen chestnut leaves that lay deep on the pathways. Though I dramatised myself to her, I suppose, I always felt better in her company.

'I would leave them to it,' I said. 'I would escape. I seek to, by this incredible device that's grown up around us. They are absorbed in their caresses, their intimacy.'

'Escape?' she said. 'You're intending to go away?'

'No, Anne. Merely to leave the trap of the physical obligations I've always, it seems, been heir or heiress to. I shall carry on just as before; I shall be myself. I shall develop into a brilliant vocal butterfly, I think, once the shackle of what happens in private is off from my ankles. As, Anne, it so nearly is. So very frustratingly nearly.'

'Because of your double.'

'Because of my double.'

'And Charles still suspects nothing?'

'He must; and yet he doesn't. And I can understand, indeed. It's a case of wilful blindness – who could blame him? He's a new man.

The truth of things is very, very monstrous. Very strange indeed. Charles too has a double, did you know?'

'This is madness. You mean someone else is involved in the deception?'

'No. No one else is involved with . . . us. But I mention it as an example of the overpowering strangeness of things. It's a detail, no more. A meaningless detail. He's not like Charles. Not at all. I don't even know him. But his name's the same. I believe they're related, but the other Charles Montagu has been abroad. The diplomatic staff. Our ambassador in Venice.'

'Everything becomes quite impossible, Kit, the way you put it.'

'I know. It *is* a madness. Of a kind. My odd uncle has explained the world, and that is why things seen from the outside go on as they do: sensibly, rationally, decently – at least in overt intention. I mean a table stays a table, buildings don't seem to move, manners are maintained in despite of scandalous exceptions, and the affairs of the government roll on. That is their rhetoric, these great men; that's the keynote of the new, the modern, the keynote of our so-called Revolution. They talk and talk in their Parliaments. They are all honourable, decent men. Or if they aren't then they're corrupt in an ordinary way, and anyone can understand that. And as for the intensity of politics – why, everyone knows there are two sides to an argument. So decent honourable *men* can argue *rationally* across the House. Yes, even Tories are explicable. And our lawmakers can quite decently, quite acceptably, become heated and blast off their anger at one another. A sword is occasionally drawn, a challenge issued. Thus it is quite logical that, by the same token, they can send our forces off to fight rational wars abroad, killing and maiming thousands, once they've talked it all out in the proper dialectical manner and taken a vote.

'It is all in the spirit of Pericles, Athens, Rome. Greatness.

'And after that? Why then they are sometimes friends across the divide even, and might go out whoring together to show that no harm's done. Or cross-marry a daughter or two for the sake of an entailment.

'And the poor? The beggars? The terrible poxy scabbed and limping monsters who lurk just beyond the broad thoroughfares of the city? All in good time. A scheme of work for idle hands – to be drawn up next session. These learned men understand each other.

They have a secret language – well, they have one literally: the Latin they learned at school, by which they may travel the world and pass understood. Cicero was scalded into the bare flesh of their buttocks on the flogging horse. Quintilian and furtive sodomy, poor boys. Rhetoric . . . '

'Kit!'

'But if that rhetoric once stops, if that story halts for a moment; then a gap opens up, Anne. And we peer transfixed into the unbelievable strangeness of things.'

'You frighten me, Kit. You really do.'

'I frighten myself. I look into the gaps I have exposed and sometimes I'm comforted, but at others I'm very disturbed by them. My uncle's notions are above all secure, and people have grown rich.' I picked up a beautiful dry leaf and crackled it in my fur-trimmed gloves. 'You know the Queen has given Charles the honour of Park Ranger. That house, the Lodge there, is being decorated from top to bottom. For me, he says. For both of me, as I say to myself.' We paused to take in the prospect of the fine new house at the end of an avenue.

'It's a great gift,' she said.

'He's a very fulfilled man, who has the pleasure of the one woman and the attendance of the other.'

'Attendance?'

'Attendance. At the very time. Do you see what I refer to?'

'No.'

'I'm to be *there*. When I'm Lucy'lizabeth. I have to *attend*.'

'You mean he requires you to . . . watch? Dressed as your maid? Kit, this is . . . well I don't know what it is. And to think I know the man!'

'But it doesn't originate strictly from him.'

'From you, then? Is this the distortion you wish to confess and shock me with? You're succeeding quite admirably, Kit,' and she dropped my arm from hers as if I were something a fraction contagious.

'It isn't *my* wish.' I caught her to me again, suddenly desperate that I might lose her. 'It is my *torment*!'

'Then how . . . ?'

'It's *her*.'

'Lucy'lizabeth?'

249

'Exactly.'

'She's a servant, Kit. Why don't you inform her of her place? Smartly, Kit. I'm surprised at you.'

'Don't you see the power she has, Anne?'

'Power?'

'Of course. She holds the key to everything. She knows she's in a position of absolute power over us both.'

'Yes. Well. But you have power over her. You could turn her out.'

'At the expense of Charles's entire happiness. And blackmail?'

'I see.'

'And of my escape. It's she who insists that I . . . attend them.'

'Why?'

'I don't know. She seems to require it. That she should become me, to the life as it were, seems to require my presence and, to some extent, my humiliation. I'm still not free.'

'You don't have to be . . . actually involved, do you?'

'Almost, and in a manner of speaking. Anne, I'm so ashamed in front of you. You won't cast me off for it will you?'

'I see,' she said for the second time. 'No, I shan't cast you off, my dear. You poor thing. As I go on in years, Kit, I come to view the world of *my* Art, despite popular opinion, as a good deal safer and many times more regular than real life. Frightful things go on, on our very doorsteps. I'll tell you . . . You know my friend was murdered outside my house?'

'Murdered? William? When?' I choked.

'Not William. Mountfort, his name was. Some . . . gentlemen of quality tried to abduct me. It was a long time ago. A friend and innocent protector. Susan's first husband.'

'Centlivre?'

'Verbruggen. Mountfort as was. He was lured. I tried to send warning, but . . . to no avail. It threw me off . . . Listen. Let us not talk about it; I'll tell you another time. I have something entrusted to me – a happier commission: Aaron Hill will see you in two weeks. At the theatre. And will enlighten you. I'm so happy for you, Kit. Nicolini will be there. This business with Charles . . . No. Sing for me. I haven't heard you lately. They say you're very good. You've exceeded my ambitions for you. By a mile!'

We turned. It was a bright November day; early November, almost warm now since the morning's sharp frost. I thought of Nicolini and the Summer. Of reading to him. I thought of Swift. I'd heard Swift was back from Ireland, but I hadn't seen him. A little herd of deer flitted across the vista of our return route. The low sun on the banked trees to the left of Hampton struck more than alchemy from their remaining leaves.

We were silent for a while, stood still. I opened my mouth and wondered whether I should sing. A few lights appeared in far distant windows. I fancied there was a trace of a mist coming off the Thames, trailing itself about at ground level.

Anne waited. Then disengaged, and turned to me.

'I'm going to say something you probably won't like me for, and may not forgive me for. Nevertheless, I shall say it, Kit, because I believe it will be for your good; it isn't meant otherwise, no matter what you think.'

'Well, Anne, I can't imagine what you could say that would put me about so. Except that I'm too bad a person for you to associate with.'

'Don't be foolishly self-indulgent. It's this. In the matter of the . . . attendance at the bedchamber. You've told me you're still not free.'

'Exactly. I wish with all my heart I were. You know how I've longed to be myself. To be free to be myself.' I rushed. 'It's been my dearest wish. And I've worked and thought and gambled and bargained about how it might be done. And now, just when it seemed that a stroke of fate had given me the means of deliverance, and I'm poised like a linnet by the opened cage, within sight of the Summer window, my very maid draws me back and ties my feet again by a subtle sexual thread, so that I'm more a part of this trade than I was before. I'm exposed. I'm made into a . . . I don't know what I'm made into, but this time it's not a man but a luxurious, pert, insubordinate young slut who makes me dance to her absolute tune.'

'Enough, Kit! If you won't sing for me, just hear what I have to say. I don't believe you're as powerless a victim in this as you claim to be.'

'Aren't I? Then just what do you think she'd do if I crossed her wishes?'

'Have you spoken to her about it?'

'A little. But it's . . . Anne, there aren't words for it. It's all too elusive to grasp hold of. Exactly what could I say to her?'

'Kit. I believe you feel so. But I don't believe it *is* so.'

'What do you mean?'

'That a woman of your undoubted intelligence could easily deal with Lucy'lizabeth if she really wanted to. After all you're a match for Charles, and he's a wit and then some.'

'What are you saying then? That I wish to be used in this way by them? That it's something I desire?'

'What else can I conclude, my dear?'

'My dear? I thought you were my friend.'

'I am your friend, Kit.'

'How is it the action of a friend to call me worse than whore? That I desire it? That I'm no better than my knighted uncle, who peeped on my nakedness through my mirror?'

'He did what?'

'Yes. You don't know the half of it. In the Jermyn Street house he peeped, half-silvered; before the move, no doubt at the three of us. When he was well enough. And you make me out to be no better than that?'

'Kit. I meant to speak only for your good. You poor child, I love you dearly. I want to see you free as much as you do. I merely draw the conclusion I must, and tell you as a friend.'

'You aren't my friend. I believe you're a serpent. I've been horribly deceived. Why have you all kept the . . . project from me, whatever it is. "Aaron Hill will see you in a fortnight." What is it about me that you all know and plot that I do not? And now this? Am I not fit to know? May I not be told? Am I too disgusting, untrustworthy? You name me whore. Do you understand? By this you kill me! Kill my affection! I have no friends now and that's the truth!'

I stamped off along the avenue, turning my back on the incipient sunset. Anne followed, but I was locked shut, sulky and furious. We parted at the gate of Hampton Court. I said only the curtest and meanest of goodbyes and left her with one of the palace servants to sort out her transport.

For days I remained furious and difficult. My break with Anne coincided with the onset of Lucy'lizabeth's menstruation, so we weren't called upon for the moment to play out our deception. Since it was the week before mine, I used hers as a pretext to be sullen and miserable with Charles. And as for anger, I let him feel the full weight of my passion over the smallest irrelevant detail – after all what was he? How should he know the subtle differences between the pre- and post-menstrual condition? He was a mere rapist. Anyway I hated him. He took himself off to some fatuous gentlemen's leisure pursuit in the country around. And as for her – I hated her more. I mean Lucy'lizabeth. Anne I was angry with; her I hated. For the two weeks Lucy'lizabeth found herself occupied with more pressing and ironing than she would normally have to see to in two months. I gave up trying to practise at the Hampton apartments and, not hearing my own sound, grew terrified that I'd lost it for ever. Which made everything worse. Then we left and I carted her over to stay temporarily at St Martin's Street where the new house was, and had her stitching, mending and sorting my extensive wardrobe; and just when she thought she might have finished on one task I'd change my mind and have her unpick, or rearrange, or completely reorganise. She ran specially designed humiliating errands; she stood for hours in shops while I sat sorting through fabric or furniture patterns that I didn't intend to buy anyway; she found herself closely involved with my uncle's incontinence and Pet's new baby's cloths. And she felt the edge of my tongue. At every opportunity.

I ignored Anne's notes. And on the day before my assignation with Hill and everybody, I ran into Nicolini at the theatre in the morning and rowed publicly with him for being away. There I picked a wrong'un, because once goaded he was a more calculating and maleficent prima donna than I was; and, although I didn't know it at the time, my chance actually to occupy the Girardeau alias came within an ace of evaporation.

As for my singing – for when Nicolini had finished roasting me in choicest Neapolitan street terms, I was called upon to stand up with the new Italians, the Boschi couple etc. whom I've already mentioned – *dramatic* would have been kind; *strident* probably more accurate; *shrieking* what was no doubt said behind my back. Heads were shaken. Did I hear giggles stifled?

While it lasted, though, I enjoyed the power my rage gave me. It didn't of course last. In spite of my sincere prayers Lucy'lizabeth couldn't menstruate for ever. Charles slunk back to his luxurious peasant that afternoon – well, to me really, bearing gifts of nebulous atonement, which he said he'd save specially for when my new bedroom was finished rather than handing them over now. That didn't help. But I began to see that everything I'd worked for, both in the home and in the theatre, was in jeopardy if I kept on with my mood. So in the disordered guest-room that night before my call, with Anne's accusations smarting at my fingers' ends, I resumed my ministrations on their laces and buttons, their all too sensuous déshabillé, and their damned exotic interpenetration.

But I *had* thought over what she'd said. I had. Had I not tried to get away from them, yet they'd think up some new service for me just as I was about to leave the room? Had I not sought to detach myself from the obvious rapture they found in each other's arms, until they'd refer some fond matter of sexual arbitration to me? Wilfully? Had I not asked straight out in the voice and character of Lucy'-lizabeth to be released from such duty as it offended my sense of what was right and proper, only to be told to forget my prudishness and do as I was told in such a tone as to make any retaliation a mortal stroke to the whole deception? Did I not suffer? I was sure I did. But if this was true, then why had Anne's simple words touched a nerve stretched and sore enough to catapult me into such open wrath as I'd never known?

Then I was monstrous. She was right. I must make it up with her. It all wouldn't stop going round in my mind as I lay awake in Lucy'lizabeth's bed, but in the occasional moments of relief I speculated on the 'announcement' of the following day. They would try me out in a private concert? The best I could hope for was a little scene with my maestro; the worst, some sleazy offer of a part in one of Heidegger's girly shows in that place in Covent Garden. The desperate, self-engorged quality of the small hours resolved me that this would most likely be my fate. Was I not depraved, after all? My best friend had hinted as much. They must all hate me. Perhaps, worst of all, the contract was being terminated. It was all over.

Orpheus

I arrived at the Haymarket at eleven in the morning, feeling small. But I'd expected somehow that the event, whatever it was, would be devoted exclusively to me; to my enlightenment. I would know my fate. That would be its function after all this time. That was what Anne had given me to suppose.

I entered the auditorium to find it bristling with people, many of whom I recognised, and none of whom took any notice of me. I entered as Kit Barton. Had I known my musical milieu would suddenly become conflated with my social one, I might have come under some cover, and possibly sneaked into the circle of the theatre to watch from a safer vantage. I dithered by the side door at the top of the rake, wondering whether to retreat. But then Mrs Barry caught my eye and waved me to a seat next to her in the pit. Awkward, sweaty and disturbed, I looked around at all the folk present and mentally listed some of them to judge the significance of the moment. Many were standing up, talking: Addison, Edward Wortley, Betty Germain, both Charles Montagus, that is to say my Charles and his relation – not forgetting that Wortley was also a cousin – Vanbrugh and his brother, Anne with her back to me luckily, and Aaron Hill arguing with Heidegger. Beyond them, I noted Clayton, Greber, Rossi, Mr and Mrs Steele, and the Italian contingent with Nicolini. Swiney stood by a table with a German called Roner. I also recognised Johann Pepusch, Nicola Haym, John Hughes, together with a variety of Kit-Cat Club members, and miscellaneous Whiggish nobility. Others were already seated; I could only guess at their backs. It was, truly, significant enough.

I directed my attention to the theatre itself, which in my fury yesterday I'd hardly noticed. It was remodelled and redecorated, subtly and distinctively, but quite lavishly. I turned to Elizabeth Barry and commented on it.

She replied: 'Nicolini's had it turned into an Italian opera house. Stunning, but I'd miss the old raw. I couldn't go on, my dear. I wouldn't know where to look. Lucky Anne and I've retired. Still, I'm assured this place is now nudging Venice. And as for backstage. That's where the fun starts. They can fly you to the moon. It's not what I call theatre. I played a hundred and forty roles, girl, and the best of them in the old Lisle's Tennis Court when we went out on our own. Had our own bloody revolution, eh, Bracey?' She leant across the aisle to where Anne was standing with her back to us, and rapped her smartly with her closed fan. My heart turned over, for we should have to speak. But before Anne could leave off her conversation to get involved in this raillery there was a general hush, and people started making for their places. I saw that the orchestra space was opened to reveal a large harpsichord of fine quality. Already seated at it was a striking-looking young man in a full-flowing fair wig. And as soon as the theatre was in silence he began to play.

I'd never heard an instrument do what he made it do. He was a phenomenon: such energy, such precision, such speed, such grace. What more can I say? I forgot my anxiety, my mood. The wooden box before the stage – for that's all it was when it came down to it – spoke, sang, danced almost. Everyone was astonished – and rapturous.

While there was still the din of clapping, I addressed myself to Barry's ear.

'Who is he?'

'Don't you know?' She poked at her top lip with a scented favour bottle, then offered me a sweet with her other hand – delicate little candies in a lined Turkish box.

'No. Should I?'

'The Saxon Orpheus. Having moved Italy, he comes to conquer us. His name is Mr Hendel.' As she finished speaking, one of the Italian singers, a dark woman with passionate eyes, got up and stood in the crook of the harpsichord. I'd met her yesterday and knew she didn't like me. Aaron stood up also, introduced and thanked Mr Hendel profusely, and went on to announce that Mrs Elizabetta Pilotti would favour us with an aria from Mr Hendel's opera *Agrippina*, much esteemed in Italy.

She sang to his accompaniment a haunting sarabande which began '*Lascia ch'io pianga*'. I forgot the woman herself. It was enchanting. That is my memory of first hearing Hendel's writing for the voice. Enchanting. I confess I was utterly ravished.

Our select gathering burst into wild applause as soon as the last note died; Charles's 'double', the Earl of Manchester, the ambassador who I learned later had played a central role in getting Hendel to come to us, shouted 'Bravo!' in the Italian manner, and one or two of the others joined in to show they'd been on the Grand Tour.

Aaron stood up for speechmaking, and raised Mr Hendel – whom I'd better start to call Handel, since that's how everyone now knows him – to bow with him. They both remained standing.

'Your Lordships and Ladyships, Herr Hendel, *Signori e Donne*, Ladies and Gentlemen, would that I too could sing, for words alone cannot express the delight I feel on hearing this exquisiteness, this more than music.' Everybody clapped. 'Ladies and Gentlemen, it has long been my private dream to see the best opera in Europe here in London, in its true lights. Already this theatre has enjoyed the credit for introducing last year the first opera entirely in Italian, and therefore the most true to its original conception yet seen in this country. A very great success it was, indeed, but yet still not ornamented and graced with such lavishness of scene and spectacle as is the proper native glory of the form, and which, at that date, we could not house.

'A private dream, I say. Almost a secret dream, for there are those who, had they known of our intentions, would undoubtedly have engineered plots against them; plots and schemes against the enchantment we have just heard. Scandalous but true, such is the malice of faction; such is the spite of petty jealousy among those who no doubt wish they had more influence at court and more fingers in the pies of the town, and would stop at nothing to gain ends or to line pockets. A number of us, therefore, have bred up this dream close within our bosoms; and it is its fruition that we christen here today. The great, nay the inspired, Mr Hendel, is, by our invitation, newly arrived in London only yesterday. Against his coming, I have made up a design in the Italian style of an heroic encounter from chivalry, and engaged the finest vocal musicians of Europe and the best bandsmen of our capital. To my immense, to my boundless, gratification, I am able to announce that Mr Hendel has kindly overlooked my proposal, and has pronounced it . . . may I so express it: consonant with his muse's fancy.' Applause broke out. 'Ladies and gentlemen – subscribers all – I can assure you we have a composer,' delighted applause for Handel, who bows moderately, half smiling, preserving the decorum of his wig; 'we have a librettist,' Hill pulls out Rossi from the front row, and the assembly, who aren't quite sure who he is, clap enthusiastically; 'we have a company.'

Up stands Nicolini to a rapturous ovation. He has Boschi join him, and then his wife, Francesca, and the woman who has just sung for us. They each make their curtsy to the audience. And then Nicolini peers about in front of us as if studying our faces. He lights on mine. His great suit and wig loom up the aisle towards me, his eyes pierce mine, he smiles and extends his arm in invitation. I feel my astonishment write itself on my face, but he nods and insists by his gesture that I make my way along the row to join him. My hand shakes on my brocade as I manoeuvre my gown towards him past the compressed legs of others. And then I am standing with the Italians and receiving acclaim from hands and voices as surprised to see me there as I am to discover myself. 'Mrs Girardeau,' says Aaron, 'who demonstrates by her presence that England contributes a single rose – that in her voice we have the beginnings of our own place in this the highest and rarest of the dramatic Arts.' Continuing applause, with, I sensed and shared, an uncertainty as to who I really was.

Few there were aware of my try-out in *Semele*, since it had never got beyond intimate rehearsal stage. I was and was not me. My heart was thumping, and yet the trace ran through my mind, quite coolly and clearly for a moment, of a mirror toy that I'd seen at a Northampton country fair, too expensive and rare for my possessing; and today I seemed to have as many selves as the multiple world there revealed. I stared out over the faces I knew. There was the bereaved Mrs Betterton, the Shakespearean, in her special wheelchair. Some instinct told me to put up my fan as soon as possible lest I should be too exposed.

Aaron, slender, expressive, a little like the wondrous German himself in face, went on: 'And, Ladies and Gentlemen, we have an opera house.' His hands went up to invite them to savour the new fitments, and, as he did so, the curtain lifted to display a magnificent perspective, of a quality and size not previously achieved. A great swell in the applause. There was a rumbling in the back and the scene changed miraculously to a shady grove. Thunder, and we were transported to the rugged Alps. Handel, laughing, ducked himself back to the stool of his instrument and improvised the lightning and rain. A flash, and we were back in the imperial perspective. He made a scintillating run and closed on a cadence. The curtain fell. The gentlefolk stamped and clapped.

Aaron waved for a chance to speak. 'But best of all, friends, if I may take the liberty of such familiarity, we have a date – by the end of February!' To renewed applause and cries of 'Bravo!', Nicolini and the others hurried me out by the pit door.

'Why didn't you tell me?' I said to Charles afterwards. We were still in the theatre, sitting down backstage in the promise of refreshment. Anne hovered a few feet off.

'It was to be a surprise, my darling. And besides no one could be sure it'd come off. It was all in the balance until yesterday. It still hangs by a thread. This German fellow has to go to work mighty sharply if he's to have a piece for you all to rehearse in time. I still don't see how it can be done. I would have hated to see you disappointed, especially after *Semele*. I believe your disposition is . . . fragile, my dearest.'

So that was how he saw me. An unstable female. How disturbing to catch yourself as others perceived you. I turned to Anne. We might as well speak.

'You knew all along.'

'Not so much, Kit. Charles swore everyone to secrecy. As far as you were concerned.' I didn't know what to think. Aaron came into the dressing-room without knocking. He handed me a sheet of his scheme.

'Almirena, in love with Rinaldo. Nicolini thinks you can do it. So do I.'

'What do I have to do?' I said, terrified of the international company and that Pilotti woman. 'It's a walk-on, yes?'

'Yes, indeed, Mrs Girardeau. But you walk on more than once.'

The sheet was headed 'Rinaldo'. Below that was entered:

> Rinaldo —— Nicolini
> Argante —— Boschi
> Goffredo —— Mrs Boschi
> Armida —— Pilotti
> Almirena —— Girardeau

'How much do I sing?' I said.

'Four or five, I should think.'

'Lines?'

'Arias, dear. What do you think we've been doing with you all this time?'

I felt my mouth fall open. Then I burst into tears and dived on to Anne's neck, but pulled back when I remembered we were at odds and that she'd played Charles's game with me all that time. I heard them all laughing, but hers died away when she saw the look in my eye. I hated myself; I couldn't control it.

Nevertheless, it was true. I was to play a major role opposite my lion. It took Handel an astonishing fortnight to put the music together. When mine arrived I was encamped at Etta's with Anne Long, whom I'd stayed with briefly in September, before she'd had to flit from her creditors and go down to King's Lynn under an alias. She'd sneaked back to London to see Swift. I snatched my score from its wrapping and found a closet where I could deal both with the pounding of my heart and the hand-written code of my music. It fell open at the divine '*Lascia ch'io pianga*'. For me, Almirena. Wonderful. My eyes were full of tears again. When they cleared, though, I understood how Handel could put the opera together in a fortnight: he'd already written most of it for other pieces. Now his box of treasures was being reshaken for London. I smiled. A fox.

I soon discovered by the way that this was only partly true, and that my cynical assumption was a slight injustice; he wasn't offering Nicolini old standards, but had written him new material, as he had even done for me to some extent. It was this that had taken the fortnight, plus the various recitativos. That was indeed prodigious!

I couldn't wait to try my pieces. Hasty apologies to Etta, to Anne Long and Pawnee. I disappeared into my Art, and threw myself into work. They were wonderful arias, but fiendishly demanding. It would be touch and go on the edge of my nerves and my lungs with no more than about eight weeks to be absolutely ready in, blocked, costumed, and rehearsed. A good while for a professional, but for me the mere blinking of an eye!

Well, with all this private ecstasy of work, normal life went on as it had to. After Christmas I moved permanently to join my uncle in St Martin's Street overlooking Leicester Fields – where Leicester Square now is; and I still hadn't really apologised to Anne. We'd met only occasionally and were as icy as the new rooms which, for some reason, my uncle had been airing for four days. Doubtless he had a theory of some kind. Or perhaps had forgotten to close the windows.

He'd rented a handsome modern house on the end of a block – Queen Anne we'd call it now: obviously. I was pleased with its classic lines and four storeys, and my new bedroom was light-flooded from its enormous casements. Since we had the decorators in, and my uncle had done next to nothing about its appointment – a large number of our effects were still in Chelsea – my part in the move itself, though delayed, was a great undertaking. It put off any more *intimacies* at least until the world could settle down again. But it was owing to my exhaustion with rehearsing and several weeks of domestic organisation, that things were finally brought to a head;

Charles, frustrated by my excuses, was keen to resume his delights. So was Lucy'lizabeth.

'My' bed was a large new one that Charles had bought especially for me, or for us, so conjugal had he become, so wedded to home comforts.

Lucy'lizabeth, acting my role as mistress of the move, improvised an initiative. She claimed that she was too tired to receive his Lordship's ardour, but that she couldn't bear to send him away, loving him as she did with a consuming sensibility etc., so that he might, she said, stay with her and her maid so long as he kept himself to himself, and offered her only an amorous and beguiling closeness. She claimed she needed a piece of female insurance beside her to reassure her and see fair play. He must accommodate himself to a greater delicacy for tonight at least. It was a new departure for her, into chaste converse and the possibilities of intimate tenderness.

I *was* tired. Too tired to protest. It looked a safe enough situation. A pleasant change, even. In fact I was exhausted. So was she in truth, because I'd drawn up her day's schedule. We dropped all three of us into a heavy slumber in the big new bed, Lucy'lizabeth strategically in the middle.

My shadowy backer came to me in the small hours. While the other two slept, we sat together and looked at the illuminated pages of a beautiful book, full of delight and flesh-tones and the philosophy of love. He (was it a he?) spoke a great deal, but it was in a musical Latin (I use the term in the old sense of any forgotten mysterious language – it could have been birdsong) that I couldn't understand; which left me sad and frustrated. On one of the pages a lovely naked couple sat upright, front to front, she with her legs about him as they maintained a holy kiss. On the next there was a human back portrayed, and on it, marked up the spine from base to crown, were the seven stages of the alchemical work, each with a little delicate illustration and surrounded with red writing. I wanted to look longer, but felt that somehow Anne was peering over my shoulder, and so I turned over the other pages with him until he left. I had the knowledge that another of his books might tell how poor souls were restrained in hell, but I wouldn't look at it. I said: 'When and if I am stronger.'

He said: 'Do you want me to spell out the names?'

'But my mother will die.' I lay back down and went to sleep.

It must have been about dawn that I dreamt I was surrendered to a delicious eroticism, carefree, beloved, intoxicated. My whole body was alive with sensation, merged to the very nerve endings with my heart's angel.

The awakening was rude in the extreme. Charles was in the act of love with me and Lucy'lizabeth was standing beside the bed hammering on his back and screaming. 'Get off her! Get off her!' She tore at his hair, and at my face with her nails.

Charles got out and off. 'But my darling I thought . . . '

'Yes, and don't I know her tricks. The minute my back is turned. Even so much as to take the chamber out and call for breakfast to be sent up she has her wretched legs astride and hauls you into her oh so prudish little nest! Not that you wanted much asking I'll be bound, Sir!' She hit him again with her fists, then started screaming and battering at my face.

'My darling. Calm yourself,' said Charles. 'I assure you I thought we were alone.'

'You whore!' she hurled at me. 'Whore! Whore! Whore!'

'Darling, your voice!' Charles's misplaced anguish.

There was a knock. Tony's call. 'Everything alright, Madam?' But Lucy'lizabeth was beside herself. 'Come here, Tony! Charles, if you love me, do as I bid you!' I found myself speechless, paralysed by the absurdity, the enormity of the situation. And then there was small possibility of speech, for seizing her initiative she clamped a hand over my mouth and dug her nails in my cheek. With her other she grabbed the hem of my shift and, making a great meal of it, so that the two men could see as much of me as they might wish, she yanked the cloth down over me and made sure that the soft skin between my thighs was well scratched in the process. 'I'll teach this harlot some modesty. I want her whipped. Tony! I want her whipped. Cover her mouth! Take her down and show her who has given her everything she could ever desire. And this is how she repays me! Come, I'll do it myself!'

Vaguely I heard my uncle stirring in his room further off. But he didn't come out. I found myself hustled and bumped down the back stairs to the scullery. My mouth was held. The cloth on my back was ripped and a terrible stinging pain, like being branded, fell again and again across my spine.

Eventually it stopped. I was thrown, nearly naked, to the stone floor, to welter and shiver in my freezing tears. They all left. The door was locked.

I wondered at the number of ways a single scene could repeat itself; re-express itself like images in the fragments of a shattered mirror.

After

I believe I was locked in for some hours. I huddled in tablecloths, and had to relieve myself into a wooden bucket, which I covered over with a board. I did not cry out.

There was the sound of a key in the lock. Lucy'lizabeth, dressed in my morning clothes, came in, trembling visibly. I stood up. She shut the door behind her. With the back of my hand I hit her as hard as I could across the mouth. Something came out of her voice. Then, in silence, we changed clothes. There were some bits of blood on the torn back of my shift. Leaving the door open, I left.

I hardly need say that the outward marks and scars of my beating, as opposed to their inner pain, disappeared entirely from my body within a day or so. Not so with Lucy'lizabeth's mouth. She occupied now, as she must for a while, the position of a sexually offending female servant who must be on probation against dismissal. Which was a crude and cruel shame for womanhood in general; but, after all, I thought to myself, she in particular had set the whole incident up. She wore, for about a fortnight and to my immense satisfaction, the marks of my ring and nails across a disfiguring bruise and a horribly swollen lip. Her eyes, though, glittered with a kind of triumph. Charles found himself called upon to attend to pressing matters of State.

Swift had got back to London in September; but, having come out as a Tory, and therefore rendered himself unacceptable in our society, even though he lodged, I discovered, only a few doors away, had left it until now to sneak in to see me at St Martin's Street. And perhaps he was afraid that he'd be confused by his feelings again. Nevertheless he seemed determined to put his old face on it, when, that morning, newly dressed and let out of the scullery, I found myself very shakily receiving him. My coffee cup rattled. I perched on the edge of one of our expensive new chairs, not because of the infrastructure of my skirt, but because my back hurt too much for me to be able to lean. I refused to show it, however.

'Have you been keeping up with the Dubliners, Swift?' I would not mention opera. That must be my secret, and whom exactly could I trust? Let him guess what he liked from report.

'You mean MD? Yes in faith, Kit. I've told My Dears all about my beloved Mrs Barton and the new house, after her shipwreck in Addison land, which is to say darkest Chelsea. About how I'm no longer *persona grata* with her august lover since becoming responsible for this *Examiner*; but that *she* detains me vigorously behind the backs of the Whig. Shameless hussy. About the proposed *Rinaldo*, I might have written, but that it is not fitting for a man of the cloth to consort with these strutting whoring players, whatever their names are.' I winced; not just from my back. 'And about the continuing mystery of the lovely identical maid, Lucy'lizabeth, whom I suspect to be some dark secret (by the way where is she this morning?): an unacknowledged sister; or some sport of your family's. Perhaps Uncle Isaac's love child.' I hurt myself with the great laugh that escaped me. Swift pressed on: 'And all this spins a fine intrigue about you. I believe you've made Stella very jealous. And therefore we're cross with you, Kit.'

But my fascination with the Swift I remembered, which wore deliriously through the Bickerstaff affair, had frayed through his odd withdrawal from me before, to an underlay of irritation at his connexion with the compliant female correspondents in Ireland. Or correspondante, to be nearer the mark.

'You're all talk, Swift. Or as far as Stella's concerned mostly ink.'

'Precisely,' he agreed. 'Sadly. Or perhaps rightly. *For in the resurrexion they neither marry nor are given in marriage, but are as the angels of God in heaven.*'

'*Easier than air with air, if Spirits embrace,*' I replied,

> '*Total they mix, Union of Pure with Pure*
> *Desiring; nor restrained conveyance need*
> *As Flesh to mix with Flesh, or Soul with Soul.*

'And all this you carry on by letter!'

He looked disconcerted. It was happening again. I would lose him again. He was about the most *concerted* of all the men I'd met; *most* of the time. Provided he kept away from his heart.

'Exactly where . . . ?' he enquired.

'*Paradise Lost*,' I supplied the source.

'Of course. Yes. Unfallen Man's instruction by the affable Archangel.'

'How old is Miss Johnson, Swift?'

'Perhaps in the resurrexion there are no ages neither,' he whispered, into his dish of coffee.

'Come, when was she born?'

'1680, so it's said.'

'Then she's much of an age with me. Do you wilfully make mysteries about her? Why don't you marry her? I've heard she's in agony.'

'She is not. She tells me all is very well. You come near to hurting me, Madam.' I wished I didn't blurt things. My cruelty seemed to jump out these days. I tried to soften the angry muscles I could feel in my face.

He mastered himself, though. 'Do you make mysteries about yourself?'

'Who's told you so?'

'You are thirty then and look twenty-one? How is this, may I ask? And I shall say you give me a very dark reception this morning.'

'Have you talked with Anne?'

'I have not. I have come to you.' He paused, then tried to re-inject the wit and play by which, I knew by now, he controlled his emotional landscape. And those who strayed into it. 'Fallen Man comes for his instruction by his affable Angel, who won't be affable this morning. Poor fallen Swift. Hey, Presto. He shan't get up again now.'

'What work are you doing?' I gritted my teeth.

'You mean writing?'

'I do.'

'I'm doing Wharton. Wharton in Ireland. Wharton as a species of turd. Wharton as an example of fallen, fallen, fallen Man. Man? Of fallen Ape!'

I looked at the transformation that was visible in his face – or rather the sudden showing through of a kind of animal hatred, a snarling, chomping, sneering ape-faced hatred. Both of us. I thought myself of the touch of Wharton's breath upon my wolf mask at that great ball I'd attended.

I asked: 'Have you been to Mrs Van's?' I referred to our near neighbours, the Vanhomrighs, who'd been near us before as well when they rented a place in St James's Square, and now, through a dwindling away of the dead father's estate, were forced merely to take lodgings. But by fate, or Swift's advice, this was only a few doors away from our new home. I knew that he cultivated a much closer relationship with them than chance had ordered t) at I should. But I'd spent some time with the elder daughter, who was very brilliant and lively, though not well. Of this I shall tell you in a moment. He looked evasive.

'I stopped off briefly.'

'Did you speak to Hessy alone?' I asked.

'Hessy?'

'Will you walk with me to Anne's? Swift, I've given grievous offence to this dear friend of ours. Just pause a moment while I dash her off a note to say that we're on our way.' I had the note sent off by Graveling on horseback. I ordered him to find some rare import from the fruit and flower market at Covent Garden, and to take it with him to her as a peace offering.

It was a brilliant February day. Swift and I muffled up and linked arms to enjoy it. London at its purest, perhaps. But I hurt terribly from where I'd been caned. Perhaps that was why I still sought to provoke him along the way.

'And how is Hessy Van?'

'She is well, Kit. As well as can be expected.'

'You like women, Swift?'

'Like 'em?'

'You like pretty ones. Young ones. Clever ones.'

'Hessy Van pretty?' he pretended amazement. 'I suppose she's well enough, Kit, but I believe I hadn't noticed. Striking, perhaps, if you press me. To me she appeals for her mind. She needs bringing on, proper instruction.'

'Which you are qualified to give her?'

'I've read myself into a positive myopia, Kit, since Trinity.'

The word chilled me. But I recalled he meant Trinity College, Dublin.

'Ah! Your qualifications.'

'She is a Pallas Athene, Kit. One of those oddities of nature. A strong masculine intelligence in a weak female body. I mean no offence. I state merely what seems to be.'

'Well!' I said. 'But put that on one side. You respond to her. She is a woman.'

'Woman? A child, Kit.'

'A woman, I say. Yet you do nothing. You claim harmlessness and hide behind your cloth. Yet you are intimate. You touch us with your words. I wonder if you know how much we, women, can be touched, intimately, with words. What do you want from us, Swift? What is it that you want?'

'Ah, she's cross with us. I shall tell My Dears all your naughtiness, Kit Barton,' he retreated into play talk again. With the pain and humiliation of my morning still smarting so terribly in my body, I went after him, wolflike.

'And if the cloth were down, and you could have your way with me, or one of us, Swift; with Hessy, or Stella, or me, which of us would it be, and what would you do? At least two of us, I guarantee, wouldn't refuse you. Whatever byway your pleasure took.'

'This is greasy talk. It's almost man's talk. Why, Kit Barton, you stab me. You bite me. And I do hurt with it.'

'I'm a wolf am I not? I'm cruel, Swift. No, not Swift, that pretty bird of Ireland; but Shift, Stift, gross, fallen ape. I see into your soul.'

'Then you see how much *I* am in agony,' he said simply, with tears in his eyes. We stopped. I embraced him, and kissed away the tears, and so we walked on to Anne's. But I said one more thing on the way, in a kind of blaze of folly, which presaged the embroilment which was to follow.

'What if I told you I could cure Hessy, of whatever it is that she's sickly with? And Moll, too, who's worse?' I named her younger sister.

'Cure me too. Yes, that would be something, Kit.'

Anne bore no grudges. She embraced the prodigal with open arms, which loving comfort hurt excruciatingly because of my back. But I didn't mind. She embraced Swift too. She thanked me for the odd-looking cactus plant that Graveling had taken a freakish fancy to, and we all forgot ourselves and laughed at it. She had no fatted calf but a moderate luncheon for us.

'How can I apologise, Anne?' I said to her when we had a moment alone. 'I've been well whipped for my . . . whatever it is you showed me I was guilty of. My bordello complicity, shall we call it? I mean really whipped.' Her shocked face. 'I still don't know what on earth is going on with me, but I know I want you back. I'm so sorry I was impossible.' And once more I melted myself into her arms, wincing as she rode her affectionate fingers over my weals.

'Kit,' she sighed. 'What are we going to do with you?'

I soon had more need of her than ever. Incapacitated, there was no way I could attend my rehearsal. Swift and I went back to Mrs Van's and he stayed to dine there. Much later I returned to Anne's in a hired chariot, and once in the kitchen with her, out of William's hearing, I blurted out my breathless news; that I'd fallen in love with Hessy Van, who was in love with Swift, who was all of an absolute quiver.

Hessy

All this on the eve of *Rinaldo*! How can I render to you the immense complication of everything that happened around this momentous time?

At first the feelings I had for Hessy didn't trouble me overmuch. I believe they began when I saw her embrace Swift on the landing. No, perhaps it all began much earlier, and was simply set off by that nonsense of his about a male mind in a female body; which was his self-protective way of saying that she, as a young woman, had somehow escaped, been excluded from or fought her way out of the mind-numbing expectations laid on genteel females: that they should sew, simper and read sermons. Like so many men, I thought, his regard for gender accorded merely with a very primitive squint at the genitals of farm animals, and possibly with furtive glimpses of the human female's. As in the mirror or lens of prurience. From which the conclusion was drawn of passivity in the one sex and activity in the other. At the Royal Society a Mr Cowper had exhibited the penis of a possum which had died while under the organisation's protection. He'd been desired to write an account of it.

But of course for me, who genuinely remembered being a male creature and who now lived in a female body, Swift's description of Hessy as an oddity of Nature must have struck a chord. And when we went up the stairs at Mrs Van's, and were greeted on the landing, I was placed behind him, so that her face appeared over his shoulder. Her eye caught mine, and then she pressed her lips to his cheek with such utter delight at his return that I was moved and jealous; and wished it were me she was so glad to see that she must kiss my cheek thus. She did kiss me too, as I left, but not in that way. Yet there was something between us, I knew it. What could it be called? Soon, in my mind, I chose the word love.

Swift didn't know it but Hessy and I had shared an adventure. As I said before, chance didn't construct us as intimates at that time. I'd been caught up with Charles and my music and my researches since Hessy had grown beyond a schoolgirlish sort of condition. But it was in the course of my research that our adventure took place. Mother and older daughter had called on us one morning, during my first cluttered days in St Martin's Street, and they were received by uncle and niece. My uncle had just begun to suffer from Leibniz – an ailment like German measles only more mathematical. The cure was to dig up all the amazing breakthroughs he'd ever made but was too frightened to publish, and seek to prove that he'd thought of them first. It added to the disorder. It was one of those illnesses for which the remedy is worse than the complaint. He regaled the widow Van with it in what looked almost like an attempt at courtship – like the gambit of revealing the war wound or a not quite successful surgical scar.

Hessy meanwhile told me, as we took coffee together on the French settee, that it was on Swift's advice that they'd quit their former lodgings – I believe it was just before they made the final re-location to our street, but the details are smudged perhaps by the strong emotions that still surround her memory for me, even as I write. Anyway her eyes grew round as she told me that the reason for his intervention was that he suspected the house to be a false one.

'A false one?' I remember saying in astonishment. 'What's a false house, Hessy?'

She said that Swift wouldn't tell her – had made out that the landlady's eyebrows declared her to be untrustworthy, or some such nonsense. No, this is the truth. But that the family had been prevailed upon to move out on his advice. Hessy suggested that it would be an adventure to haunt the place on the next day to discover in what exactly its falseness could be constituted.

To cut a long story short, we'd done the risky surveillance and got our result, as well as feeling we'd been very advanced and assertive by successfully fending off offence from three loitering men. I referred to Pox! and Damnation! very freely. We were very effective.

One of these men had come from knocking at the house. Then a figure appeared at the other end of the street.

'That's her!' Hessy had said. 'That's the landlady. Let's pass her and scrutinise her eyebrows. You shall tell me your opinion, Kit, to see if it agrees with Cad's.'

'Cad's?'

'Oh, Swift and I have a joke name for him, as he calls me Vanessa. Cad is short for Cadenus. Which is an anagram for Dean – Decanus, do you see? He has hopes of an appointment.' Oh, Names! Disappearing people! Identity! Where is truth? Perhaps even then I started to envy them their intimacy.

We passed the landlady. I was thunderstruck. It was Ruth.

But I'm not cutting my story short. My feelings for Vanessa, Hessy, are leading me to expand where I hadn't intended. Briefly, then, the house was double in intention, and had a false face. It had apartments that could be let to genteel families in reduced circumstances, such as the Vans, in order to mark up its appearance. Honest guests could even be received in the sober lower parlour when need be – by Ruth and her three 'daughters'. Otherwise it had a red room and made its livelihood from gentlemen callers. This we got from one of them as we hung about outside. He took us for freelance rivals of the establishment and fancied his chances for a bargain. We were deliciously incensed and righteous. So he got short shrift once we'd relieved him of his information.

That Hessy and I had done something exciting together in a context which had overtones of sexuality, even though we rose loudly and firmly above them, must have bound us together in some preliminary way. We'd shared the discovery of a gap.

As I say, at first my feelings didn't trouble me, perhaps because they could lead, I thought, to nothing. So when I came back to Anne's to announce that I'd fallen in love, there was perhaps a touch of over-dramatisation about it. A kind of boast to myself that at last I might be experiencing some good thing, and a true good that would link me to the rest of the population.

'Oh you poor darling,' was Anne's immediate response. 'Sorrows in battalions.'

'What?' I said.

'Kit! Don't you leap from the frying-pan into the fire?'

'Because we're both women? But you see, Anne, I'm not a woman entirely.'

'Oh? Are you not?'

'No. Don't you wish for my happiness?'

'Oh, Kit,' she sighed.

Yes. My feelings, buoyant and signalling from far out as yet, did not trouble me. What lay under the dancing waves was still to manifest. Besides there was nothing carnal about it; no mental undressings nor intimate fancies of moist touch. I just felt a rush of excitement about the possibility of spending more time with Hester Vanhomrigh. In bed I rolled the curious name around my imaginative tongue. I played with the peculiarities that marked her out – and marked her out especially for me: her vibrant manner, her penetrating mind, her linking of my eyes with her own dark questing ones, her almost painfully communicative spine, her quirky, unconventional beauty, her infatuation with Swift. Perhaps also her sense of an entrapment from which she desired to be free.

So it was that I entered upon the last week or so of rehearsal for my first opera, which was to be, we all sensed, something out of the ordinary – the first real opera of quality in England. And I was entering upon it, had I but known, with two spurs to the forgotten part of myself: stripes on my back and an arrow in my heart. For these indeed were some of the markings of the wolf-boy I once was.

Gerusalemme Liberata, 1711

Time tumbled on in breathless haste. Backstage at the Haymarket, when I heard the rumble of the capstans, the pad, pad, pad, muffled puff of the undertakers as they worked them, and the whirring of the pulleys and machines, I thought of those lines of the Civil War poet:

271

But at my back I always hear
Time's wingèd chariot hurrying near.

Rehearsals ran out. The election? A Tory landslide. Confusion. Calls for an immediate end to the war. Calls for Marlborough's instant dismissal.

It was time for *Rinaldo*. This drama came to allegorise my life. A remarkable coincidence, surely a pregnant one; I had slipped into a musical night's dream.

On Saturday the 24th February 1711, wearing my costume for Almirena, I peered out of the pit door of the Queen's Theatre, and saw with horror the hundreds of people, dressed in their finery, who were attending the first night of Handel's first English opera; tickets and translations from White's Coffee House in St James's Street. Only just in time I found a cupboard with a chamber-pot in it, and was sick behind a screen. Then my guts turned to water for the twentieth time that day and I had to hoick up my skirts to use it for the other function. Finally I had to dispose of the ghastliness, and rushed along the corridors in my unbelievable costume and extravagant make-up like the goddess Cloaca holding my reeking trophy. I mention these revolting details because they are the stuff of my experience and stick powerfully in my mind. They were true. And besides, they made me feel a bit better once they'd occurred. I went to my table and threw drops of lavender water all over my bosom and my clothes, until everything smelled more bearable.

In the place that served us as a green room there was a decanter of brandy and some water in a jug. I made to pour myself some of the former, but Francesca Boschi stayed my hand.

'No! You mad! After. After.'

'But I've just been sick. *Sono malata!*'

'Let her drink it,' said Pilotti with saccharine intonation.

But Francesca put only enough brandy into a small tumbler to disinfect the water she added. I swilled out my awful mouth. Pilotti turned away huffily, while Boschi went back to her warm-ups and vocalises. I took myself gratefully off to try my own voice out. My table was littered with my paints and the billets-doux and quaint superstitious messages that Aaron & Co had sent. Staring into my mirror past three vases of flowers got from I don't know where at that time of year, I couldn't bring myself to make a sound. It was the constriction of dread. How could that bizarre, daubed phiz with the high waved front – to conceal my bump as ever – hope to survive the next three hours?

In the distance there was the sound of clapping, followed by the strains of the opening adagio. I'd heard it once at the dress rehearsal. The lovely woven notes of the oboes in the background only intensified my terror by their beauty. Then came the flighty allegro and the stringy scrubbing of the lead fiddle working his way down a progression of sixths and sevenths. When the little jig started I shook. Suddenly Nicolini appeared, got hold of me against his fake steel breastplate, and dragged me round to the wings – only just in time for his own entrance, for the clapping was ending and the curtain was going up to reveal Francesca's shapely legs in the breeches role of Goffredo the Christian Captain. Nicolini dumped me in my place, kissed me (by chance) on the bump, which hurt, and strode – out there! Into the brilliant illumination! Where shortly I must follow!

Francesca soared through her first number. Nicolini sang his brief reply. I don't know how I got on for my cue, '*Almirena ti fia bella mercede*'. Perhaps Aaron pushed me, perhaps it was my shadowy backer.

I just found myself on stage as the chord closed after '*mercede*'. There was an ominous pause as I opened my mouth: a hiatus. Handel looked up anxiously from the keyboard. Then something clicked in my throat and my voice came out with the recitative, seemingly of its own accord. The introduction to my opening aria was finished in the blinking of an eye. I thanked whatever gods I could that the tempo was so fast in this first test – it pulled me along. I made something of it anyway. It wasn't as good as I knew I could make it but I got through. I thought my sound was acceptable, and I covered up the stumble in the shaking decoration of the reprise.

I got off the stage to my applause and staggered to a chair. But I couldn't sit down. I stood, or rather hopped silently from one foot to the other, while the action raced on and Aaron's fingers flicked, at every second it seemed, one more page.

Someone pulled me roughly out of the way to make room for a great troupe of spear-carrying soldiers, who poured out of my half of the wing to flank the entry of Argante's chariot. Soon the stage was full of military. I could see Boschi's back. The piece was supposed to represent the struggle for the Holy Land at the end of the First

Crusade in 1099, but he was got up like a cross between Wharton as Tiberius and King Louis Quatorze. In the ensuing musical dialogue between Boschi as Argante, the Saracen King of Jerusalem, and Francesca as Goffredo, the Christian General, something of a Marlborough, I grasped what I'd not had time to think of before: that there was an overall design, a function to the piece. And here it struck me that we were *all* being used, even Aaron – or perhaps especially Aaron from the start: to personate our current war. I was increasingly discovering my own naïveté. I had just time to feel the soothing flush of anger. Well, no one outside government understood the true rights and wrongs of the war by now. I was a loyal Party adherent and I certainly didn't want to be tortured by the Inquisition – a thought which haunted me graphically, and which I believed would be automatically fulfilled should the Jacobites ever get back into power. Nevertheless this was the second feature of the opera which had been deliberately withheld from me, and I was annoyed. With Charles, specifically, and with everyone in general, suddenly, for sullying, as I felt it, what was mine.

Anger was better than brandy. There was the roar of an explosion and the crackle of fireworks as Armida the Saracen sorceress, the mistress of the King of Jerusalem, descended in her dragon chariot. The dragons spat real smoke. It was Pilotti. The violins went into agitation. Her first notes were an astonishing scream of female rage: '*Furie terribili!*' I'd not heard her full voice till now; she'd obviously saved it in rehearsal. As I received that unearthly sound a great chill went up and down my spine. She was magnificent. The audience visibly cowered. I hated her. We should have been like Bracegirdle and Barry, lyric and dramatic leads. But she had her grudge against me, I supposed over Nicolini's favour, though it could have been anything, religion, height – anything.

Nevertheless she was superb, and went on to polish off her second aria, featuring her stunning top C, with bravura. Her upper register was a phenomenon.

Her dragons went off upstairs and she brushed roughly past me as she came off. But not now to be daunted, I waited for the disappearance of Jerusalem, then strolled confidently on into a delectable semiformal garden with real fountains. Delectable from out front; from my angle, a mere disposition of painted flats which slid into place so that to the perceiver there should appear an effortless transition.

That was the aim; it didn't work if they stuck, or ran in the wrong series on one side.

Aaron had told me to dispose myself attractively in the bower while Handel and the orchestra did their bird imitations, with sweet twitterings and flutterings on the piccolo flutes and recorders. I wandered downstage, smelling a paper rose here and there, reached the wicker bower, then reclined, and languishingly showed off my legs by a twitch of the petticoat. Don't be surprised whatever happens, they'd said. Just stay absolutely pure and calm, rise, stand, and deliver. These instructions I'd almost forgotten as I enjoyed being angry, prettier than Pilotti and the centre of admiration. I could see the powdered people in front of me with a disturbing clarity, the jewels of the dames even. Sweet sounds filled the house; Handel's flutes charmed all London.

Leisurely, I raised myself slightly for my first phrase, uttered still seated. I sang. It poured out deliciously, swelled, sustained, and diminished. It was good. There was a whirr behind me. Suddenly the air was full of little live birds, and the music was cueing me. I held it. My eye caught the Duchess of Marlborough, Queen Zarah of the Zaraziens, in her box and her patches, covering her head with Aaron's bilingual courtesy libretto. There was a great temptation to laugh, but I held it, and warbled:

> *Augelletti che cantate,*
> *Zephiretti che spirate,*
> *Aure dolci intorno a me,*
> *Il mio ben, dite, dov'è?*
>
> *You pretty little birds who sing*
> *You zephyrs who breathe*
> *You sweet airs around me*
> *Tell me, where is my beloved?*

It is a divine piece for a lyric soprano. So beautiful.

Confident now, I delivered. If I didn't have Pilotti's range I had infinite legato control and beauty of tone. Some of them in the audience didn't even notice the twitchings and panics of the sparrows and finches netted in Hyde Park that morning; nor the white splashes that dropped now and then from the perches above. I became a bird. Charmed them too. And was encored. Twice. Which

I didn't know quite how to deal with. But Handel delivered too. I wasn't even put off by seeing out of the corner of my eye as we continued one of the hands dousing a little blaze with a stirrup-pump; pumping in time to my love duet with Nicolini so as not to clash with the band.

The first act climaxed with the Pilotti woman drawing a sword on my lover and sweeping me aloft in a dreadful black cloud full of monsters, worked by boys with gunpowder sticks and smoke bombs. We rose. The pit audience became an island of tiny folk, gazing up. We were a sensation!

No. I say climaxed, but there was yet to come Nicolini's meditation on chaos. The heart's desire is denied. Life is confusion; love is swept away, violated and sequestered by monstrous evil. He is informed that there is a man who can read the stars, and has intelligence of the plants and stones. Handel wrote specially for him his desperate appeal to the winds and turbines of the atmosphere for help in this, his solitary quest and crusade against falsehood. I meditated on my castrated Lion, on Hessy, my uncle and myself.

The curtain dropped. I can't remember what passed in the interval, except that Anne, Barry and Congreve, the two leading the one, came backstage with tears in their eyes. I rinsed and re-used my chamber-pot, then tried to tell myself that I could continue. I was buoyed up. It wasn't what I'd expected – being in an opera, as opposed to seeing one; it was a mixture of squalor, panic, drabness, irritability and music. But it was also triumphant. I braced myself for the second act, pleased to see that the others were nervous as well, Boschi in particular rolling little twists of tobacco which he smoked desperately behind a quiescent dragon.

Aaron's contrivance of the sea was the star of the second act. In parallel lines across the space behind the proscenium, the painted saw-tooth waves were activated by rollers and cams beneath the floor. Sound effects offstage opened the scene. A prospect of a distant island, with a galleon upon the flood, sailing thither. Where? The New Atlantis? There was a boat for one of the sirens to lure Rinaldo to the region of death and lost love, with the promise that I was waiting for him on the distant shore. Languorous dancing from the ballet girls while the sirens sang.

The poignancy of this curious parable, as far as I was concerned, lay in the fact that my beautiful 'Lascia ch'io pianga' introduced a bizarre melting-pot of sexual confusion. Pilotti pretends to be me, and I have to appear as her being me. She falls in love with my hero, while her paramour lays siege to me, being me, or was she still appearing as me – I was never quite sure myself. But it didn't matter. There was the music. I'm sure the audience was no wiser than we were. The emblem was of Eurydice, whom music sought to free from Plutonic promiscuous identity. 'Let me weep then, and let me sigh for liberty. Let sorrow break the bonds of my martyrdoms. Alone, yes, there's the pity of it.'

Rinaldo himself answers this desolate lament, without knowing within the drama that he is in fact doing so: 'Cara sposa, amante cara, dove sei? Dearest sharer of my life, my beloved darling, where can you be?' I render it like this not only because Rinaldo and Almirena aren't yet married, but because neither were so many of us: Nicolini, Charles, Pawnee, Lucy'lizabeth, Uncle Isaac, Anne, Handel, Swift, Stella, Hessy. Oboe and cor anglais. 'Ah crudel, il pianto mio deh ti mova, per pietà.'

My messa di voce must be in full employment now for another transcendent sorrow, whose middle section, for I was here supposed to be Pilotti pretending to be me, vowed revenge. Yes, even on the moth, her emblem for her victim, Rinaldo: 'forse qual farfalla ritornerà Rinaldo al suo bel foco.'

Then before the second interval Handel and Pilotti shared the final honours, he with an obbligato tour de force on the harpsichord, accompanying her florid aria, in which she declared holy war. I recognised only at this stage that Aaron, or his shadowy Whig backers, were using these subliminal cultural devices to shift blame for the war on to the Catholic powers. Possibly rightly, but how rich had the city warlords become during its course!

The star of the third was my uncle. If I speak flippantly, it's only in retrospect. In fact he wasn't there. He contrived an incontinence more risky than my nerves. Perhaps it was genuine. At any rate he had to stay at home. No, the opera solved its tangles of plot, not with a deus ex machina, but with a Protestant magus, whose rational solutions to the agonies of chaotic desire made all well. He gives Rinaldo, my stage lover, and Goffredo, my stage father, a symbolic rod. Aaron's rod, I couldn't help thinking; or was it Newton's ruler, exactly one measure long, which if spared might spoil the child? 'Il varco impossibile fora senza un poter prefisso, ch'i mostri suoi calà vuotò *l'abisso*. The chasm cannot be crossed without a preordained power which serves to eliminate the monsters of the abyss.' It came back to me, that morning in Cambridge when we, my mother and I, were about to leave for my new life. What had he said to me? That I, by my very existence, returned everything to the abyss.

Before the third act started I found my mind racing with these thoughts. I couldn't stop it. I stood in the other wing this time. It was a short last act. I didn't have to go on until near the end. It featured a wonderful phantasmagoria of shifting effects, with fire, thunder and enchantments of illumination. Essentially the stagecraft served to present life as illusion. The whore sorceress Armida has created by her magic a sort of alternative Jerusalem, a Babylon of the senses, high on a mountain. This is what Goffredo the Protestant general must pit his faith and his army against. He does. He rushes it with drawn sword, and then bangs on the city gates with the philosopher's rod. The whore's castle disappears to disclose a stormy sea. Excellent. And I remember Nicolini fighting the trees of the enchanted forest. As soon as he cut one down another popped up. A triumph. So the veils and illusions are stripped away by this patient endeavour until the truth of their mechanism lies open at last, and Armida is disclosed as herself holding a dagger to my beautiful throat.

Pilotti hustled me into position in plenty of time. With the point of the dagger at my larynx I waited for the final disclosure to fly up. Watching Aaron in the opposite wing with his master copy, in which every detail of the whole production was recorded, I perceived the opera itself as an intricate machine. How had it come into being? A man at the right place at the right time. War, Politics, Art, Life. It domed up like a bright bubble at the place where equal energies opposed their powers. The merest ripple on the interface and a whole cosmos appeared. Who was Aaron Hill? A child playing on the beach. If there were no errors, no anomalies, then we created from that washed figure in the sand an entire and self-consistent universe, whose being declared itself logically seamless. Yes, a glorious bubble alive with our colours and harmonies. Wonderfully, then, the occasional flat could stick, the occasional voice could dry, a dragon boy could be left in full view, holding his candle, a wrong note, a wrong entry – perhaps even the tiniest thing that we knew but the audience didn't notice. Gaps.

Pilotti and I were revealed, hostages to murder.

'Bleed to death!' she cried, on a high G.

'Oh Gods!' I yelled back on the same note.

My lover rushes forward with drawn sword, but her spirits protect her, and she drags me back by the hair. This really hurt. I felt the wooden dagger applied also. I don't know where the jugular is to be found, but I had the feeling Pilotti had studied the subject specially for tonight.

Yet Goffredo arrives in the nick of time, and at a touch of the wand all the painted female fripperies of Armida's garden disappear, and the Enlightenment has found Jerusalem to be a plain, ordinary city, just waiting to be conquered.

And I, enraptured to see my lover and my father again, am awarded by the one to the other, and sing my ornate *'Bel piacere è godere fido amor: questo fa contento il cor'*, which was very difficult to do well, but which I managed with some excellence if I say so myself. I suppose Charles had been moderately faithful; he was certainly contented at the heart these days.

There follows the battle, which entailed a good many of the military passing back and forth across the stage to the martial sound of trumpets and plenty of kettledrumming. I was very pleased to have Pilotti in chains at the end of it all, tight enough, I believe. She admitted defeat at the top of her voice and broke her enchantress's staff, ornate, superstitious; shaped like something the Pope might carry. Quite unlike our decent Rod!

And so the final ensemble brought my dream, my bubble, to an end. We bathed, we drenched in applause. We had taken the town by storm. I remember nothing of the feast after the event – as a bride forgets her reception. It was all a blur, except for Mrs Manley's comment, which lodged in the folds of my brain like a burr.

'Wonderful. But I've come to find it strange and a little annoying that it's always a woman who's supposed to be the worst kind of enemy.'

I hadn't known she was going to be there.

New Women

Charles told me I was wonderful. He showered me with presents, and with forced, hot-house flowers. The performances focused my absolute involvement; but at all other times I thought of Hessy, which was a fever, a delight, a torment. I remember that Spring as the ecstasy of singing, the ecstasy of passion, flowers everywhere and a chamber-pot that I had to carry about with me wherever I went, so agitated were my insides.

Between February and June of that year *Rinaldo* was played fifteen times. In those days a piece of theatre wouldn't go on night after night, because there weren't enough people to sustain the audience. London wasn't that big – more like the size of a provincial town now. So for purely commercial reasons runs were much shorter, and in our case, owing to the reloading of birds and fireworks, performances were spaced out. But fifteen showings was a runaway blockbuster, especially for something as highbrow as this. It wasn't even in English. In fact I was one of the few English things about it, and even then I was an enigma. For I had my stage name, which was French, and people seeing me in make-up and costume were never, it seemed, *absolutely* sure that it was me. Because I was a woman they *knew*, and therefore they *knew* that I was the same decorative house-keeper, gossip and bedwarmer that they were forced to be. How could Mrs Barton actually be that seriously professional about anything, and good at it? Was she not a society lady, like themselves?

Whatever was said, though, my bump-concealing front wave became the dominant note in hair fashion. I knew that I was famous for the moment under the name of Mistress Girardeau, and that Hessy had seen and admired me. This led her to become somewhat in awe of me I believe, and led me to become her intimate acquaintance by letter in the matter of Swift. I say by letter, for living so closely as neighbours we met almost always in company, often when Swift himself was present. In any case I was too busy to call as frequently as he did. The intricacies of her feelings could not be discussed openly between us. She took to me as a guide and adviser in the affairs of her heart. How could she do otherwise? When we met, there was the delight – I felt it was mutual – of a shared secret which wrote itself into our shared glances. We acknowledged her special inflammation, which blazed silently between us, binding us together. But as it began to root itself more powerfully in my heart, the enormity, the impossibility, the cross-purposes of it soon came to disturb me. What was I doing? In May, to my amazement and great discomfiture, Clayton got an opera on entitled *The Passion of Sappho.* It was a flop but I felt it as a personal wound.

I had to refer it all to Anne. I emerged at Howard Street, limp with the exhaustion of my triumphs and my passion.

'You were right again, I fear, Anne.'

'Was I, dearest? How's that?'

'I am certainly out of the frying-pan of Charles.'

'They no longer require you?'

'They don't. They could not after the master compromised the maid. Which is as well, since I'm a dishrag. While, because of the deception, Charles thinks I'm a vocal and sexual prodigy, and have the stamina of a mare. It's almost as if Lucy'lizabeth contrived the whole caning affair in order to clear the field for herself – God knows she could have had it without the need for all this. I do surmise though that she was prepared to pay the price of the injury to her face in order fully to vanquish me.'

'Didn't you realise you must have been her most deadly rival, Kit?'

'No, I didn't,' I replied. 'I didn't at all.' I felt my eyes widen. 'Is that it?'

'She loves him, Kit. It's clear – to me at least. Don't you see?'

'But she could have had him without.'

'Only on your terms, child. Yes, it was disgusting to sensibility. It's disgusting to mine at any rate. But I understand it. It was you he loved. How could she bear that without a fight? Now she has him. *She* has him, in *her* right. As herself. And whatever he knows or doesn't know, suspects or doesn't suspect, he's happy with her as he's never been happy with you. Does he call so much during the day, to enjoy your *conversation*?'

'He's very busy these days. As am I. He says he can't get away so much. He sent me this.' I showed her my latest sparklers, a brooch, a bracelet and two rings. 'And a lot of flowers. He's busy in the *House*, at *Court*, and in the *City*.'

'And you believe all that?'

I let the matter drop. She was, of course, quite right, and I knew in myself that I'd been forced actually to surrender him, without even knowing that I'd ever wanted him. It was to an extent mortifying; to find out about me again. But now I had Hessy, so that didn't matter.

'And are now in the fire,' said Anne.

She was right again, damn her eyes.

'Oh God! Delicious torment; joyful despair – everything they say.' I was near to tears, suddenly. 'Only worse.'

'Tell me, then.'

'If I tell you that the pain of my love isn't a normal pain you'll think I merely seek to plead for my own singularity. I know how it'll sound. Kit believing herself to be the only troubled soul. Kit, an arrivée in front of a true professional; Kit, once more shoving herself fretting centre stage rather than getting on with the whole purpose of playing. Kit indulging in self-hatred; a ragged passion. *Lascia ch'io pianga.*'

'Have I ever said any of those?'

'You think them.'

'Imagine not, dearest. Imagine that you can truly tell me of it all.'

'You'll hate me. You're known for your ... sensibility. I have nothing to tell but foulness. God knows I've already favoured you with enough.'

'Imagine not, Kit. Please. I have my opinions, my values. But I'm not shocked by,' she laughed, 'the true way of the world.'

I summoned my resolve. 'I don't want to lie with her, Anne. It isn't impure. It isn't. But then it isn't a passion that can ever be fulfilled. Because I just want to be with her utterly closely. And that can never happen. Because that will be preying on her, and keeping her close. And I could never bear to have hurt her or imprisoned her.'

'How could your love imprison her? How could love imprison anyone?'

The fears and self-disgust catalysed by my over-stirred emotions came out jumbled.

'Because my very presence near her must sully her, damage her. I'm a lie. Yes, on stage I am a glory. Everybody tells me so. But in myself ... I am not what I am. My very pretext for speech with her is a deceit. Why, she thinks of me as of a sister. She loves Swift. He's my rival, my friend. What can I offer her, more than my unnatural desires and my loathsome history? I shall kill her, Anne, I know it. I'm a damned thing. You don't know about me. I don't know it all myself – how I was before. It's lost from my memory. I believe because it's so evil, so disgusting. You don't know who I am. If you did you couldn't love me. You couldn't have me in your house. How can I think to place myself in Hessy's way? My love is a perversion and I'm a monster. I am, Anne. You must believe it. You don't know who I am.' I covered my face with my hands because I couldn't bear her to see me. The tears ran freely through my fingers. I stumbled on because she said nothing. 'You see, I can't permit myself to feel what I feel. It isn't right. It is so cruel. It's cruel. I was managing. I was coping. I was going to escape. I have to live away from other people. Away from . . . closeness. You were helping me – the theatre. Nicolini. He understood. He loves me – fellow monster. The opera. I had escaped. I would have dissolved into music and flown away. But that I should be struck *now*! A woman. No; a girl. Someone who's not strong. She trusts me. But I want to take her in my arms, for ever, Anne. For ever. She's shown me paradise and she doesn't even know it. And I can't ever go in. Anne, it's so cruel. Why does it have to happen like this? Why? *I* don't know who I am. Neither male nor female. Empty.' I kept my hands tightly over my face.

She said, at length: 'One minute you're one thing, Kit. This I see. The next you're something else. Yes. I do notice this. I ask myself how are we to comprehend you? Whence comes all this . . . chaos? This unutterable sorrow that flashes out from behind your beauty the more I know you?' She pulled my hands gently down from my face and held them. I couldn't look at her. 'What is this history that you speak of, yet dare not speak of?'

'I don't know.'

'You don't know. You don't know who you are.' She continued holding my hands, thinking.

'Am I mad, Anne?'

'I don't think so, Kit. I don't think so. As for loving another woman, it isn't so rare. It must be very painful. But what harm can it do? For goodness sake, I've lived among theatre people. But you feel yourself so bad, so monstrous.'

'I . . . was . . . I . . . I was a boy, a dog. I was . . . I felt as though a wolf . . . I was a wolf. That's . . . all I remember. My uncle changed me into a girl. I can show you the coat they had made for me.' There. I'd said it. I waited for the earth to swallow me.

'Indeed, Kit.' She spoke very softly and stroked my hands.

283

'And now,' I edged on over the precipitate moment, 'my hands that you hold may return to claws; and,' I felt my breath choke up and begin to pant, 'my legs become covered with a grey, pitiless hair, my pretty, harmless face peel back to show my teeth; and a vile, poking, animal maleness appear from . . . from . . . appear in a rush of blood from . . . I cannot say it. Aren't you afraid, Anne? Aren't you afraid yet that I shall leap upon you and ravish you? I am.' My voice was a whisper. 'My shadowy backer. My speeding up of time. These are my badges, my marks. I'm afraid that I shall destroy poor Hessy; that I shall bite her through to the bone even as . . . even as I . . . even as I . . . stab myself into her.' I dragged my hands back, and covered my face again as hard as I could – as if to prevent it assuming forbidden, muzzle-like features.

Once more she gripped on to my wrists. It was a struggle of kindness. I looked out from behind my fingers, and saw the fear in her eyes. We teetered thus on the brink of the abyss. On the one side reason, sense, progress; on the other a great drop into nightmare, fairy tale, a child's account, madness.

She spoke very slowly and a little shakily. 'Let me hear your story, Kit.'

'I can't tell you.'

'Come, you've hinted enough. You've whetted the appetite.'

'That is because I need to tell you. I must tell someone. But I don't dare.'

'Why not?'

'Because I'm not worthy of you,' I hazarded. 'Because I'm not worthy to lace up your shoe, to touch the hem of your dress.' I felt immediately stupid and humiliated by these Biblical references, but they were what came out.

'Kit. Listen to me. I shall not think the less of you for hearing your account of yourself.'

'Hessy will die!' I said, irrationally. 'And you'll send me away!'

'Kit!' She took hold of my shoulders. 'Kit! It's alright. You're safe.'

I held on to her and thus overcame my own shaking and panting. Without being able to look at her, I started to tell her what I remembered of my mother, who thought I had come from the moon, and who brought me to Cambridge to have me cured of my devil, among other purposes. Then when I got to Nick, my jaw literally wouldn't move. She had to help me by starting my last sentence once more. I cried again, hinted it out, and went on to relate the explosion and its effects, my coming to London and my wish to create a revenge, for which she'd actually helped me to prepare my part, believing my story about government work for Charles. I didn't tell her of my actual crime of attempted murder.

For a long time afterwards she sat completely silent. Then, 'To whose authority can we turn to explain all this?' She was shaking a bit too. 'You can remember nothing before you were fourteen, you say?'

'A blur.' Then one thing struck me like a flash. 'Except for a room. A man with a stick. I have to go in.' It left me. 'No more.'

'How does your uncle explain the *anomaly* of your present form?'

'I believe he cannot explain it at all. I believe it changed him as much as it changed me. Since I've existed in my present form, he's been unable to be the wizard, the artist, the scientist he was.'

'And Charles doesn't know, you say?'

'Charles doesn't know.'

'But how would he react if he did?' A look of preoccupation came into her eye. 'Isn't it a poor thing that there are no women about whom we could say, *Now what would she think of this?* Barring your mother, who gave her opinion early on and tied your arms behind your back. I felt earlier on the tip of my tongue the words of the commandment and the phrases of duty: the duty owed by a young person to her parents and protectors. But all you've told me makes these normalities ... vaporise, it seems. I seek authorities, but I'd have them female for once, I think, and I find none.'

'Pawnee knows. Authorities: the late Mrs Behn ... but they don't admit to her much. Mrs Astell; I don't know her. But Susannah Verbruggen. Mary Pix. Mrs Manley, my satirist, from whom I still smart, but must grudgingly admit. Well. You know them, Anne. They're your people, theatre people. *Our* people.'

'Some are. So you make our disreputable tribe philosophers, do you, Kit? It's fallen to this modern age to see women achieve something professional as never before – that I agree. It's a new thing indeed, Kit. We're its vanguard. The new women, if you will. You see I have thought of it myself too – quietly and in my own way – but more of its dangers. For I know we've already become a threat, and stand to lose. So we must educate our ... sisters. We must challenge to hold our property and estates in our own names – or not enter marriage. So we retain our right to vote. These are our only tools, Kit. Forgive me for riding my hobby-horse; but I'm powerfully conscious how many others of our sex have no voice,' she said angrily. 'I'm moved by your story, Kit. So many hurt at the hands of . . . Nothing said. So many. Women and children. Kit, we must retain our suffrage, I believe. Those women who meet the property qualifications are pitifully few enough. There'll be a fight, though. If they see us gaining ground. We're weak; they're strong. Parliament will take away our rights. We shall be thrown upon the devices of men – as usual.' She smiled. I tried to. It relieved the tension, and the pain. She went on. 'Charles should not be informed. You're right. Charles doesn't include the . . . anomalous in his scheme of things. These new men of the modern world. Though they have your uncle like a tame bear, for their mascot, he's not of this time at all. He's a figure from the past – even from the dark ages. I sometimes think, Kit, we come from very dark ages, we modern civilised folk. But that's by the by. Or maybe not. And Swift? Where does he stand? What counsel would the Church offer?'

'He's my friend. But I wouldn't tell him. He's a dangerous man. Dangerous at present – like me – to himself. The stabbing set his emotions into wreckage.' I referred to the assassination attempt on Harley, the former Country Party leader, now a Tory, during a select committee proceeding. The whole town was alive with it. Swift, whose faith in his prospective patron amounted almost to an obsession, had called at our house and declared himself heartbroken. I went on: 'Mrs Manley is at his right hand. They're beavering away about it for the Tories, writing their *Examiner*. Would he feel compelled to have me tortured and burnt as a witch? No, Swift doesn't burn. And as for her, I can't make her out. Perhaps he would bury me somewhere, Dublin perhaps, should I discover my filth to him.'

'Kit. No. He may be your rival, but this is from your view. He loves you in his way.'

'I love him in mine. But I mistrust his Church. Religion is founded on a miracle they all profess to believe. But they wouldn't find space for a compromising female one now.'

'We shall be a little careful in our freedoms, my dear.'

'Shall we, Anne?' I was suddenly ready to be overcome with anger, but controlled it as suddenly. 'I'm sorry. I hate myself.'

'You must not.'

'Discontinuity,' I said. 'They hate that. It's what I represent. I am revolutionary. I wish I weren't.'

'It's in the character of man to seek laws by which things can be governed, predicted.'

'Oh, Anne. Don't. You're talking like them. Law. Government. Prediction. You talk of the character of *man*. What about us? What about women? What about monsters like me? Don't we have a character? All these laws and predictions. Character? They come from husbandry. How to make your vines fruit; how to make your wheat grow; loose this cow to that bull; set up peeled sticks before your ewes while you watch your rams tupping them; compliance; gelding; improve; increase; market and marry; women used as currency. Calculation. It stands to reason. Government. Strategy. Dark, dark ages. But I exist. And these things do not apply to me.'

I found myself able to look at her. She looked back, earnestly, intently.

'No,' she said. 'They do not apply to you.'

Arcadia

'Very well, Lucy'lizabeth. You shall have it. You may take it. Take it all. The whole bloody estate. Most of it, at least. Leave me enough to live on as I'm used to. My wants are moderate. Moderately moderate. I honestly don't doubt of its being yours in due course. But just have patience, will you?'

'Very well. If you say so. Madam.' Her proprietorial eye took in the great chamber with its linenfold panelling, as if to say: 'I'm the one who's delivering. Where's *my* reward?'

We were in Abbs Court, Charles's huge manor house and farm on the Thames in Surrey, between Hampton and Walton. It was the place where he and I had consummated our contract. I spoke blindly, to shut her up. We continued our regular understated debate – which took the form of long stretches of wordless bitterness, punctuated by semi-polite insinuations. The catalyst of the present one was the fact that Charles had told her last week in bed, on discovering that I wanted to use the place, that he planned it to be hers . . . mine . . . after he was gone. She'd wept when she told me the following day. It was essential we informed each other of everything. Was she weeping at the thought of his death?

'I shan't hold you to it, Charles, my dear,' I'd said when I encountered him myself. 'You're in the prime of life. Let's not think of all this dying.'

'Nay, Kit. You shall be provided for. Depend on me, jewel. I shall see you well. Very well. It's my deepest wish.'

My uncle had come in. 'Charles, I shall demonstrate my primacy. I shall, Sir! Don't talk to me of notations. Why, I gave up the mathematics years ago after having gone further than any man alive. It was a thing of my youth. Just because a German follows a waymark or two I left as I went and finds himself at my heels after twenty years, does he seek to be applauded for it? The path was blazed. And he begs to write of notations.' Rapping a pamphlet he held in his hand. 'And *Impertinent Accusations!* A thief. A plagiarist. A peerer over the shoulders of others. An espial of Methods. A filcher . . . ' There was an awful hiatus in the room as we all realised that Isaac had inadvertently used for his vilifications of Leibniz the old nickname the hostile press had for Charles. But he recovered and continued, 'Of other men's constructions. Viz and per exemplum his claimed infinite series for the squaring of the circle – straight out of Pascal. A notable purloiner. There is a property issue at stake here, Sir. Does the gentleman who constructs an engine which brings benefit to all mankind have to rush out and publish his discovery? Lest another creep into his laboratory by darkest night to steal the design? I had not thought my fellow creatures were composed of that baseness, or I'd have shouted from the rooftops *I am Newton and I bring you Fluxions, Quadratures, Binomials, God rot you all for the little thanks you'll return me!* But that this . . . Monkey of Hanover should swing about Europe with his stolen fruits and his chatter of Differential Calculus, and his Derivatives. Ay! Derivative! That's the word! Mind me, Charles, if I don't have his eyes out for this! I am one who found . . . no, who forged a jewel, and must suffer to see another wear it!' And he went out.

'Do you plan to recreate yourself at Abbs Court?' Charles adjusted his wig in a hand-mirror. He was en route for the House of Lords. He took out the snuffbox I'd bought him the previous week, and stood poised with the pinch of powder at his nostril. 'So vile the smoke of London in this heat. I should like to join you if I can.'

'I want to spend a week with Hessy Vanhomrigh. She's not been well. Her brother died, not long since. Her mother wondered, since we've become friends, whether she could come to our house for a change. I said we might go further afield, for her health's sake. She's become my close friend and confidante. Or rather I am her confidante in a matter of the heart.'

The plan was that she might achieve a secret assignation with Swift, who was hanging about the court at Windsor in the hope of some advancement, some stay of banishment, lest he should have to return to obscurity: Dublin.

'She's bewildered by her feelings. And the man doesn't return her affection properly. He loves her mind but runs away from her body.'

'Who is this reversed male?'

'I shouldn't tell you. It's a confidence. And anyway you promised him everything and gave him nothing.'

'Ah. Your friend and fleeting neighbour Swift at a guess. The Mad Parson. Did I hear he's gone to live in Chelsea now? So convenient for the early morning dip. So health-conscious, and yet so . . . uncomfortable.'

'He says he must take exercise. He must walk into town each day. He says it drives the cursed old one out of his system. He keeps washing but remains scruffy.'

'Does he know you're a prodigy? Do you tell him? I think he must have heard your rehearsals when he perched for a full week in that little street behind the theatre. Did he know it was you?'

'He knows, but we have a tacit agreement never to mention it. He couldn't have it bandied about these days that he was intimate with an actress.'

'Ha! And you still consort with the man? As soon as real music, your music, permeates his walls he decamps to Chelsea.'

'He suffers from deafness sometimes.'

'I gave him a last chance to declare for the human race. When was it? January. I had him to dine at the town house. Impossible.'

'Why?'

'The man's obsessed with religion.'

'He's a cleric.'

'He doesn't have to shout about it. That and the back passage.'

'You must have got him drunk. One of his crotchets is the dissenters. Another's health. He's quite ill. We have very amusing times.'

'Well, he doesn't amuse me. Always uprooting, riding, doing it himself. The man's obsessive, I say. Like Wren. Flitting. Worse than Wren. Farting in ink. At least Wren gets things done. The larger things in London. Anyway I was proved right.'

'In what way, Charles?'

'In giving him nothing. Now he's in Harley's pocket. Or his wound.'

'That's disgusting.'

I left the matter. It was problematic.

It was our fourth afternoon at Abbs Court. Swift had made no response to her apparently artless invitations. Nor to those she had pressed me to send. Hessy was ill at ease. We'd walked in the dappled sun beside the Thames, and then diverted ourselves with the kids and lambs, talking of this and that. We saw the cows milked, and drank the sweet warm full-cream out of a little ladle the husbandman brought us. Then we sat on stones while he smoked and tried to make us think he had a rare way with fashionable women. The milkmaid mucked out the parlour. As we strolled on I tried to engage Hessy in female awareness – what we might now call solidarity. I loved speaking to her. She seemed to be the only person I'd ever met who knew what I meant. Even at Woodstock I'd been so ill that even on lovely Summer days like this I should have registered only the stink of the cowshed and the muck that trapped the buttercup's stem. Now with Hessy I was transported in a pastoral idyll, and smelled only ambrosia. I was already scheming that together we'd collect a group of thoughtful women together in London. We'd talk. About serious things, power, money, education, freedom. A female academy. Mary Pierrepont – consuming the hours of her youth in her father's library. Mary Astell, whom I'd begun to read. Had she not tried something of the sort? Why not? Now was the time. It was the age of the new Athens, so Charles said. Not just a male one, I said to myself. We'd meet at Anne's house. Hessy was interested, but preoccupied.

'There's nothing wrong with desiring someone, I think, Kit. It's not so unfeminine to initiate somewhat. And if he is a good deal older; well, what does it matter? It's known that men are slow to mature and must make their way. He is an oak. And I am . . . some other kind of plant, in need of . . . who has no time for the heaping up of Winters, anyway. Doesn't he like me? I know he does. Well then.'

'I've told you he's difficult.'

'Difficult. I shall go to Dublin to secure my estate, and in the meantime hire some ruthless Papist Teague to murder the Johnson woman. Stella! Bah!'

We dined late together across the narrow part of the great table. Charles's man and Lucy'lizabeth waited. Graveling, whom I'd borrowed for the week, on the promise of a holiday for Pet and his family, was in the mediaeval kitchen with the new coachman and Charles's staff. Hessy had drunk everything that was put in front of her. I didn't put it in front of her. Lucy'lizabeth saw to the drinks. Anyway, Hessy appeared to know what she was doing. She was twenty-one and socially assured. Heavens, I believe she wanted to live a bit. And no help from Swift.

She looked into my eyes. 'Kit,' she said. Nothing else. She took my hand, where it lay beside the candlestick. What was there between us? What name did it have?

We found another decanter in the great chamber, on a table beside the bed; a light white wine served chilled in an ice jacket. While I'd counted my last few days to *Rinaldo*, Charles had escaped down here and had them take a wagon to the frozen ponds at Molesey. They'd stocked up the ice cave he got dug out beside the large paddock. The result appeared here now beside a bowl of strawberries, a single burning candle, and a supply of amber tallows.

We undressed down to our linens, stuck our nightcaps on and, taking a glass each, climbed into the great Tudor bed. I got out again to open the casement window wide. Hot Summer air of animals and rose pollen drifted up so dense as to make me catch my breath. Sweet night air. Far off the flash lock in the river sounded. Two big moths came in and vied for the privilege of the flame.

Hessy had finished her glass by the time I got back. I was turning down the cover my side when she half-fell out of hers. She swashed about on the floor looking under the bed and giggling.

'It's here.' I got the Dutch pot from its cupboard. 'Take the candle in the light closet,' I said, thrusting the pot into her hand.

'Help,' she said. The pot trailed hopelessly down from her hand and she had trouble going straight. 'Kit. Help.'

So I steered her towards our closet, holding the light myself. Then wondered what was the point of privacy if I was helping, so sat her down on it on the floor at the foot of the bed. 'I need the Doctor,' she blurted. She meant Swift. She clung on to my leg, while I made sure her shift was clear of the pot's rim.

'Will you teach me Latin, Kit?' The sound of water in a pool in fine porcelain. I remembered that I'd told her in a letter that Edward Wortley first became enamoured of Mary Pierrepont on discovering that she'd taught herself Latin. 'It makes a woman mightily distinctive to a man of intellectual discernment.' She giggled, hugging my leg. 'Please.'

'If you like, Hessy.' My heart raced. I swung her up and back into the bed, laughing too. That was a relief.

The pot wafted up a faint winy acrid fume as I took it into the light closet. Intimacy. Through its window the starshine drifted on the drowsy meadows.

I drank off my own glass and lay down on my side, looking at her face. A moth at the candle flickered the light over her. She looked into my eyes.

'Where do you want to start?' I asked. '*Amo amas amat?* Like the boys at grammar schools?'

'I shall write to him,' she said, over-loudly, 'in broad Latin, like those books where passages unsuitable for women are left untranslated. Those places must be very broad, Kit, don't you think? He knows all those terms. He is a very ribald man, did you know? But of course you did. Come, what's bosom?' She said it with a pouting emphasis, as a child of a forbidden word.

'*Sinus,*' I said, suddenly very conscious of being desperately nervous. I spoke to quiet myself. 'The shape. In mathematics it gives its name to the sine. It's masculine.'

'Ha!' she cried. 'Mine isn't. My heart beats within my woman's breast.' She put her hand to her right breast, supporting herself on her elbow. 'Oh, where's the heart?' She changed hands and breasts and fell over, laughing. I reclined myself over the bolster and leant against the headboard.

'What's breast?' She raised her head and, holding up the tie of her top, peered inside.

'*Pectus*. That's neuter.'

'Neuter? Am I sure I want to go on with this language? It seems a very silly one. Had they no eyes, these imperialists?' She looked up at me. 'You are very lovely, Kit.' And she placed her fingers gently on my linen, where my own breast drooped over her.

'*Mamilla*,' I said, almost breathless, and starting the faintest of shudderings. The moths twitched the flame again, and the room danced.

'You're cold, Kit, dearest? Come down.' Her hand smoothed against me, reaching up for my shoulder, gently insisting. 'Be swift.'

For my mouth to move the twelve inches to hers seemed to take an hour. It was my first kiss – for love. I was very frightened.

Her mouth tasted of wine. I hoped mine tasted equally of something good. I was sure it wouldn't, sure that the closer she got to me the worse would be her experience. I waited for her to remove herself and kill me.

But she didn't. A great shuddering seized me again. She kissed me harder, more intimately, and wrapped her arms and legs around me to contain my shakings. Gradually they subsided. I melted against her – as much as I could melt.

'You're cold?'

'No,' I said. 'Terrified.'

'Don't be. And why? What of?'

'I don't know. That I shall hurt you?'

By way of answer she approached her lips to mine again. I lost myself. When we left off that fervid engagement and my cheek lay against hers, I whispered: 'I can't believe this can be right. You love Swift.'

'But he's not here, damn his eyes, and won't come. So I'm pretending.' My heart sank. It wasn't me she was kissing. Well, I'd known that, hadn't I? And who was I anyway, masculine or feminine? Or neuter? I didn't dare speak, in case the thread of our closeness snapped. But I became very still, and felt the swell of a tear under my eyelid.

'Why don't you pretend too? Imagine I'm Charles.' She was so confident. Or drunk. I gazed at her out of the restriction of my sorrow. *Ah crudel, il pianto mio deh ti mova, per pietà.* 'Nicolini,' I said.

Her eyes opened wide in amazement. 'But he's . . . '

'Indeed he is.'

'Well. Do you kiss me no more?'

'As myself?'

'Oh do get on with it, Kit.'

So I put my agonising aside and kissed her again. Gradually I lost my terror, which was a moral terror – not of hell or the wrath of God; I wasn't superstitious like my uncle – no, it was a terror of ... of I knew not what, that lived in the realm of who I was and what was the truth. Was she my true partner, my *cara sposa*? I supposed that if she were then whatever we did was alright. But what if she were a poor vulnerable inebriate whom I was doomed to destroy and then abandon ... But you see I was allowing my brain once again to whirr in defence of my emotional commitment: Latin, mathematics, optics, ethics. Such serious matters. Somehow our shifts were above our waists, and our thighs entangled.

'What is this?'

'*Latus.*'

'*Latus?*'

'A side.'

'But it's in front.'

'Poetic euphemism.'

'Neuter?'

'Neuter.'

'A very stupid language.'

'*Vagina*. A sheath for a sword.'

'Feminine?'

'Feminine.'

'Typical. We shall defer Latin to a less serious moment. Do you know any Greek?'

'Hardly a word,' I said.

'Reassuring,' she sighed.

The Bump

In the morning I got up in the first pale light, found the chamber-pot and added my fluids to Hessy's. Naked yet completely warm, I left her alone to sleep, and carried the vessel down through the kitchens out of the back door. I found myself in a perfect *hortus conclusus*, a walled garden in which were growing, separate, the herbs and flowers of the four continents. In the centre a pretty fountain played, and leaning against it, his back to me, naked also, was my shadowy backer. The dawn caught the curls of his golden hair. I remembered my face buried in Hessy's lovely long brown curls, let down and scented, in the candle's glow. I remembered her gasps, her sighs, and the final sweet cry before she'd softened to sleep in my arms. Leaving the Dutch pot on the ground, I went up to my backer. He turned. I kissed him passionately on the mouth, and felt the press of his hard penis against my belly, like a drawn sword. How passing sweet the touch of naked flesh on flesh. Arm in arm between the miniature box hedges, we strolled the walkways, whose sharpness I did not feel, and whose gravel was inlaid at intervals with thyme plants. Their fragrance filled the air when our bare feet crushed them.

Wherever the gaze fell, strange fruits hung, between exotic flowers, purple and yellow – from far-off rain forests in the South Seas, smelling of danger, meat, or Paradise. In the little lily pool around the central fountain, large curious fish disturbed the surface film. An asp coiled itself within the crimson lily cup.

Stems of over-arching trees: past their thickening gum, where the wasps were already at labour, we made our way. And three tiny green grubs swung on loose threads from above. We turned and kissed again, sinuous tangle of tongues while the faintest breeze exacted unaccustomed freedoms. I found myself looking down from a height as on a tapestry of unbelievable silks. A shifting weave, resolving and unfocusing certain words, which I couldn't read. One of us was being penetrated with hot-house fruits, possibly poisonous. A chamber-pot, now blurred, now sharp, stood on the gravel with a pale yellow pool inside its blue. Birds woke and sang. Perhaps it was him, perhaps me, receiving so slowly the entry of that long gourd. The world had slowed to an unreal dream alive with spines and strangeness.

In the morning I got up in the first pale light, found the chamber-pot and added my fluids to Hessy's; and realised that I'd been experiencing a false awakening. I hoped.

I left her alone to sleep, dressed and went down, full of possibilities and plans about the future of our life together. Crossing the gallery, where my Kneller portrait as Athene hung in the space that had always been reserved for it, I crept down the great oak staircase.

I wore my satin slippers. The servants were about. I gave good day to Isaiah and Joan, the knobbly husband and wife slaving at the black and white tiles on the floor of our atrium.

'Good morning, Madam. Another fine one.'

One of the lurcher dogs looked likely to foul a corner of the great hall. I ran at it with my day dress and managed to get rid of it.

'Don't let that bitch in here, Joan, please.' I couldn't understand the aristocratic love affair with the creatures. 'Dirty animal. Get it outside straight away.' Hessy missed her beloved spaniel puppy. I confess I was rather glad she'd left it in London. Moll, her sister, was looking after it.

The house was a mixture of styles. It had grown upon religious foundations that dated back to the Norman conquest. It wasn't a family home, ancestral. It was a rich man's great house, which Charles's father had acquired in passing, I think, and which Charles, a younger son of a younger son of a great family, now held. It fitted neatly into the riverside patchwork of palaces and mansions which lined the Thames on the Surrey side between Hampton and Windsor. If you were on this exclusive waterfront you had arrived. Charles's house was prime – not gaudy, but utter quality. Perfect for Court, separated from mucky Middlesex by the barge-frequented riverway, quick for Kensington and no more than a morning's drive from the city. The heart of the country a stone's throw from the town. Yes, I remembered: Charles's cousin Ralph had got it from the Northumberlands when he married one.

It had acquired heterogeneity, and consequently charm, as successive additions had been made. The great hall was original to Richard the Second's time, and probably ready to fall down. Its mood contrasted, perhaps, with Charles, a progressive and modern man. And was a niggle to us financially. I thought the Palladian frontage was more him. And was it more *us*? Charles and I had never been an us. Yet in another way we had, bound together by certain coincidences, struggles and beliefs. Now we were being prised apart. By me. By Lucy'lizabeth. By the crumbling of the triumvirate: Marlborough, Godolphin and Harley, and the possible ending of the war. By music and the recombinings of time. Hessy and I were suddenly 'us'.

I crossed the great hall under the massive, ticking, wooden roof, and went into the study to which you had to step down through an iron-studded door. I began my letter to Mary Pierrepont, about the future, about an emerging society in which we women were also the projectors of change. That was the logic of the Revolution – at least as I'd come to perceive it. I saw no serious problems. My pen scratched my thoughts on to Charles's fine notepaper. Dawn sketched incredible colours on to the visible rectangle of sky.

By day Hessy and I talked about Swift. I think the way she dealt with the affair – I mean ours – was to remove it from language. As far as daylight and English were concerned she continued, rapturous and frustrated, about her Doctor Cad.

'Do you think he'll write today, Kit? Send word that he's coming? Oh, he must answer. Why doesn't he reply? I might die with waiting.' We sat out on the terrace in the morning sun, taking our bread and wine. 'He's too old for me, of course. He thinks I'm a child. A mere girl. He sees himself as a friend of the family. He pays court to Moll, you know. Do you think he loves *her*?'

'Insurance,' I muttered.

'What?'

'He's difficult.'

'How I know that! Why has he never married, Kit?'

'Because he cannot place himself, Hessy.'

'Well, then let's hope Windsor is worth it. If he goes back to Ireland I shall die. Or go after him. For I know he loves me, Kit. I know it.'

'We could make a drive to Claremont and see Vanbrugh,' I suggested. The locality was thick with members of the Vanbrugh clan. His brother was our nearer neighbour but they were away.

'Another Van,' she laughed. 'But I'm uncomfortable with these great friends of yours, Kit. They think nothing of me.'

'Well, they shall learn to regard you,' I replied.

She looked at me, frightened. 'We could drive out, I suppose. Or perhaps not. In case a letter . . . Perhaps the boat.'

And we were at cross-purposes all the day. It was hot again. She was on edge; while I tried at various stages to initiate some discussion of what exactly we *would* do when we got back to London, and what we *could* do.

And the day passed. We didn't rush supper, but drank more judiciously perhaps. And played cards until quite late in the evening, for neither wished to be seen to make the first move. But her bright eyes watched me. And the midsummer daylight faded over the park, bringing the moths and the hot drift of roses into the Summer parlour.

I had an idea.

'Come,' I said. 'Bring the wine.' I led her to the room which Charles had shown me proudly on our . . . what shall I call it? Contract morning. I hadn't been in there for years – well, I wasn't the mistress of the house. I'd always felt there were certain places I had to be invited to enter when he was with me. Which had been always.

I turned the handle and pushed open the door. I took the tray and told her to collect a light from a sconce.

It was virtually unaltered. The Lullist machine still occupied its table in the centre of the room, polished and tended by somebody's hand. I put the drinks tray down on a spare space between the bands and letters. I don't know if the German had ever showed up, to tell Charles how it worked. The only German I could think of who might know would have to be Leibniz; and he was out of the question: my uncle would probably kill him if he so much as set foot on English soil.

Hessy was fascinated by it. There was a tactile satisfaction to turning the little handles and having the pretty pieces all click and tickle into place. It showed no sign of corrosion or damage. It worked sweetly, as it had done all those years ago. We faced each other across its workings, drinking our glasses; she turning the one handle, and I the other, smiling foolishly in the soft, soft flame.

She broke the spell that had lasted all day.

'What's Latin for chamber-pot? I need to use one. And you can't possibly know. Did the Romans have them?'

'By a miracle I do happen to know.' The miracle related to my uncle's incontinence problems and his conversations in Latin with Dr Sloane. 'It's *matella*.'

'How do I say, I need to use the *matella*?'

'*Mihi matella necesse est*, I suppose. Come along. It's in the bedroom.'

'Would you bring it here, Kit. I believe I've understood the secret of his machine. I believe it's yielding to my analytics.' She laughed. I thought she was so beautiful.

I went and got the pot, and left the room while she squatted on it. When I went in again she held it up.

'*Fortuna!* There, I know one word on my own. For luck!' She put it

298

on the deep window-sill, then came over to me, and held my two hands.

'Say something to me.'

'In Latin?'

'*Certe!*'

I thought for a moment, partly to construct my sentence. '*Utinam te pulcherrimam apertam contuear*. I think I've made it right.'

'What does it mean?'

'Nay, my dear. It's too broad for English.'

'Teach me. It sounds strange. And beautiful.'

'*Utinam.*'

'*Utinam.* How odd these words are. Is it something . . . private?'

'It means, Oh how I wish that.'

'All in that one little word?'

'*Certe!*'

'*Utinam.* What's Latin for Swift? No. I didn't ask that. It's dark now.'

'*Te pulcherrimam.*'

'*Te pulcherrimam.* Yes?'

'You, who're so very fair.'

'Well, I'm brunette, but let that pass, as they say. And?'

'*Apertam.*'

'*Apertam.* Mm?'

'No. I can't tell you that.'

'Can't tell me? You will, Kit. You will tell me.' She pulled my fingers back. 'This is what poor Ginkel used to do.'

'Ow! A spiteful brother you had, if that's his memorial. *Contuear.*'

'*Contuear.* Yes, *contuear.* What's that then? Printable?'

'Oh, the other's printable. It's just the context.'

'Well!'

'Ow! I could gaze upon.'

'It's a very economical language. That small sounds can say so much. So we have, I wish that you who're so very fair I could gaze upon. It doesn't make sense. And what was the middle one?'

'Ow! *Apertam.*' She was surprisingly strong for someone who was supposed to be not too well in general. Swift would have her riding, or running, or chopping wood if he ever got close enough. She twisted my arm up my back. It really did hurt. 'Naked!' I yelped. 'I want to see you naked! That's what it means. It's nothing. I am ashamed of it. It means nothing. Don't regard it.'

'Kit, my dear.' She released me and nursed my arm for me, kissing the inside of the elbow. 'Why didn't you say so?' She turned away and filled her glass; then drank, toying at the handle of the machine with her left hand. I hesitated, then stood close behind her and loosened her hair clasp from its pin.

Our single candle burned on an ecstasy of untying, and a world in the subtlest kisses, like an infinitely slow storm of butterflies. *Mille basiationes*. And when our clothes lay in separate heaps of colour, they still retained something of our whalebone shapes, almost as if the daytime creatures we pretended to be had only partially deflated to give us up. I felt awkward, inhibited. Hessy not so, it seemed. She moved easily about the room, throwing up her arms and spinning in freedom. She came to rest with her hand touching one of the Lullist machine's little wheels. I'd never been so naked. I looked down at myself, all foreshortened and lumpy seeming; and then at her, fluid, natural. A phrase came to me, which my lips blurted.

'*De motu corporum in gyrum.*'

'What's that?'

'It's the title of one of my uncle's treatises, all about the motion of bodies in their twists and turns.' I tried to get the machine between us, so that its gears and orbits should fragment my image to her, but she came round to me. I backed in a sudden confusion, turning away, but she caught up with me and held me to her.

'It was your idea.' I smelled the essences of her body, sweat, rose-water, the slight illness in her breath and the traces of pomade in her hair. 'Don't be ashamed. *Pulcherrima* yourself. I'm not ashamed. Why should I be?'

'You're right, of course. But we're told . . .'

'I don't care what we're told,' she said. 'Perhaps I shan't live long. I don't want to waste my time doing what I'm told.'

I pressed away the chill her words made in my blood. There was a deliciousness where breast pressed softly into breast. I smoothed the curve of her shoulder.

> 'Nor those mysterious parts were then concealed,
> Then was not guilty shame, dishonest shame
> Of Nature's works, honour dishonourable,

300

Sin-bred, how ye have troubled all mankind
With shows instead, mere shows of seeming pure,
And banish'd from Man's life his happiest life,
Simplicity and spotless innocence.
So they passed naked on, nor shunned the sight
Of God or Angel, for they thought no ill.'

'Exactly,' she said. 'Exactly. But you didn't just make that up.'

'It's from *Paradise Lost*. But he takes great care to distinguish the sexes.'

'I still don't care. So can I,' she said. 'How poetic you are.'

'The things I've read eke out my own bankruptcy of phrase. I'm speechless really. With joy.' I traced my hands down the shape of her and drew her skin with my mouth until I was kneeling on the tough boards and felt the little wiry hairs between my lips. '*De motu corporum nihil pudendum est*. Let's not be ashamed of the motions of our bodies.'

Later, in bed, lit only by the faintest starlight, I spoke to her about my conception of a society of women; that, protected from the mockery and insistent penetration of men, we might educate ouselves, and gather up strength, consolidate our property. So that we might be a match for the world.

'A cabal. And avoid marriage? Yet we seek to secure our property as an inducement to men to marry us.'

'Redefine marriage. Retain control of our estates as of our bodies.'

'And avoid fathers?'

I laughed. 'If you will.'

'I have avoided mine against my will – by his death.' She was silent for a moment. 'My property in Ireland's in dispute, you know. If I could get control of that, perhaps we should not be so reduced. Swift says . . . ' Her voice trailed off. 'But I shall think of him tomorrow. Do you wish for children?'

She caught me completely off guard. I'd thought almost nothing about whether I wished for children. I'd spent so much of my time, it seemed, plotting to avoid having them, and in a way distinguishing myself from those who had, that I found myself unprepared for the simple question.

'I . . . I don't know, Hessy.'

'I do,' she said. 'I love children. And perhaps I don't have long. We're all going. Father, Ginkel; Moll soon, I fear. I really do. It's up to someone.'

I'd thought it was my feeling – the rush of time. But I was still unaccountably young-looking, and unshakeably, uncannily, healthy. She felt the same urgency it seemed, but from the biological imperative of predicting her own approaching death. And she had the sense of family; I did not. I fished for the essence of what she was trying to tell me.

'I suppose we should be very careful, back in London.'

I sensed her gazing at me intently. I couldn't tell that well in the dark.

'I suppose we should, indeed,' she said.

'Secret, I regret, my dearest.'

'The secret women in Mrs Manley's book.'

'You've read her?'

'Everyone has, Kit. In private.'

'Yes, then. Secret. About which I'm not happy. But there it is. Until the world is educated. Which it will be. These are new times. They really are, Hessy. We're no longer in the old dark world. We are no longer required to be the spoils of warlords, we women. That and that alone. We're not Chinese to be buried along with our husbands. Or Indians, to be burnt.'

'Do they? How horrible.'

'I believe so. Nor like Hebrew women shall we be excluded from the centre of the Temple. But we are poised on the new age. Where it shall be different.'

She made no reply for a while. I heard a distant bell. How many hours had flown by in the profusion of our caresses. Presently she said:

'It'll soon be morning. Teach me. What's Latin for Love?'

'It is *Amor*,' I said. She lowered her head and took my nipple into her mouth, then more of my breast, sucking and toying with her tongue. I thought of a child. A child's needs. Blind, urgent. And I also thought that I didn't wish to be her teacher, and that she was avoiding thinking about *us* by this pose of the child, which she also used with Swift. Teach me. Teach me. And I didn't want that to be. For the marriage contract as it stood made women children again, and there was a certain safety even in its nightmare dangers; the safety of not having to think beyond the walls of the house. And so I was on the point of taking my breast from her, and making her kiss my mouth, but the honey of that unimaginable pleasure stayed me, and lost me, and so we made love again.

I think the dawn was just breaking.

'What's that bump on your forehead?' She poked it in my hair.

'I shall tell you, because I love you, my most involved and private secret.' And I summarised the Cambridge episode of my life as she lay in the crook of my arm and the room grew a little lighter.

'You were a boy? I can't believe you. You're making some . . . comedy, Kit. Don't tease me. Tell me the truth.'

'It's impossible. But it's the truth.'

She looked at me very dubiously. 'But what's the bump? I asked you what was the bump and you tell me this . . . I don't know what.'

'The bump's the scar of the explosion. Before, when I was a boy, it wasn't there. When I came to, and was a girl, there it was.'

She poked it again.

'Ow! It hurts!'

'I can feel sharp edges, just under your skin.'

'So can I. Ow!'

'And what was your uncle doing? This projection, you say?'

'The Projection for the Philosopher's Stone.'

'And did it succeed?'

'No. Well, yes. He's hinted that he did make it. Pawnee . . . Well, I've gathered, he has it. Or something.'

'But Kit. It's obvious. It's here. In your head.'

For the second time that night a simple thing, perhaps obvious to an outsider, made a stunning impression on me. For I had never connected the ideas together to make four. And always of ourselves we never see the most naked and apparent facts. I'd supposed the Stone to be entirely about healing and gold. And to be a superstitious nonsense anyway. I'd imagined, whenever I'd let the Cambridge incident surface to my mind, that the Change had had some monstrous connexion with Fatio and my former experiences. Even now I fought the whole context away from my imagination. Stupidly I'd never considered that my identity could be dependent on this one half-hidden detail where other women possessed a parting. I'd thought it was a fragment of broken bone.

But Hessy looked thrilled, excited.

'Get it taken out. Get a surgeon to cut it out. Then you'll turn back. And we can . . . ' She bit her lip. For she saw the tears pushing up behind my eyes. I turned my head away.

She flung herself on me and covered my cheeks and eyes with kisses. 'It's alright. Kit, dearest. I love you for what you are. I do. It's alright. Kit. It's alright.'

New Models

Waking at twelve, maybe. The room partially tidied. Something to eat and drink on the bedside table. Another burning hot day outside by the looks of things.

My body felt gross and uncomfortable. I went into the closet and squatted on the chamber-pot in fear; fear lest in my leaving her she would disappear; fear that the natural stinks of my human body, my ongoing functions, must inevitably disbar me from her love. I felt like the cat who must somehow immediately bury the evidence that it is alive, lest this betrays it to some lurking predator. I covered up the pot and put it in a drawer within the closet. I opened the window; then stood over the wash-bowl and began a freshening-up routine. In the little cupboard amid the various jars I found *The Delightful Chymical Liquor for the Breath, Teeth and Gums*. The advertisement had been cut from a newspaper and tied round the glass to identify the contents. It promised everything, including the securing of wobbly or blackened teeth, and had come from *Mr Payn's, a Toy Shop at the Angel and Crown in St Paul's Churchyard, nr Cheapside, at 2/6d a bottle, with Directions*. There were no directions with this bottle. I swilled some round my mouth.

I felt better, except for the tightness in my stomach, like the nag, the constriction, of continuing anxiety. The rest of the news-sheet had been used to line the shelf: *Mr William Moore, Print and Picture Seller, at the Blackamore's Head under the North Piazza of the Royal Exchange in Threadneedle Street; At the Upper end of Ax-Yard, the House fronting St James's Park are Two Ladies of Quality to be disposed of, which may indifferently pass as Mistress and Maid. If any Noble man or Elder Brother of Fortune . . . ;* it was torn off; *Spirit of Bohee Tea. The famous Chymical Quintessence of Bohee Tea and Choclate together – 5s the bottle at Mr*

*Lawrences Toy Shop, at the Griffin, the corner of Bucklers Berry Poultry;
Sum canna vocalis; Shameless Front MA, Fellow of Brazen College in
Newgate Street; Wash Balls without a grain of Lead or Mercur . . . ; Cure
for that dangerous disgraceful Distemper, by a foreign Physician . . . Sold by
Bernard Lintott, Bookseller at the Cross Keys between the two Temple
gates in Fleet Street. Pr 1s.* Shades of Crackenthorpe, and her motto:
Ridentem dicere verum quis vetat – who's going to stop me telling
the truth with a chuckle? In her sheet I never knew which of the
advertisements were genuine.

Throwing a robe around me I hastened to take the pot out of the
drawer, and remove it and its contents from the whole vicinity. I was
so sensitive to the possibilities of loss. Her love, I was convinced,
could never survive such evidence.

That done, I went back to lie next to her, waking her in my arms,
kissing her eyes and ears, and the corners of her shoulders, frightened still that my breath might contain some contamination which
would make her hate me and leave me on the instant.

'Oh, Kit.' She sighed, and stretched, and looked at me. 'Are we in
love?'

I nodded and smiled, unable to speak.

'Yes,' she said, and laid her cheek on the bolster, so that we could
gaze at each other in comfort. 'Let's not talk, because talking pulls
you along from word to word, and from subject to object, and might
make us get up.' She smiled at me. Her lips stretched out over the
matrix of her teeth, covering them with two strange pink tapes – how
can I describe this, the most common human expression, rendered
uncommon now by love? It wasn't beauty. All regularity was side-
waysed or stretched, as it were, by her lying on her side. It was
her . . . index. It was the sign that she was here, and that she . . . that
we . . . *knew* one another. It was her, but it wasn't *her*. That true *her*
was what I felt now next to me with no common sense. I felt it. No
examination of her skin, her eyes, her breathing, the morning smell
of her body, the salt-bitter interest of her collar-bone, her half-shuffle
in the bed to get more comfortable; none of these could possibly have
carried to me what it was I knew myself in touch with. She was
right: no language sufficed. This was beyond language: duration,
extension collapsed in on themselves, dived through a single point
and blossomed out on the other side like an unimaginable rose.
Her eyelids flicked to wash the surface of her eyes. Her attention,

complete, darted upon me as a soft sparking, as a silent shower of notice. I was bathed. I knew I too bathed her. I stroked her cheek, and the line of her upper arm. She took my hand, and brought it to her lips, and kissed the inside of my palm, then held it between us, stroking the back of my fingers again and again until I thought I should die or weep for being cared for. She touched my hair, and pressed her fingers to my eyelashes to make sure they were real; and our smiles came and went between us to show that we were mobile and intelligent of one another, renewing and relaxing, and again renewing whenever our gazes interlocked.

But even infinity passes its limit. The body's minor discomforts make even transcendence impossible to sustain too long beyond the world of speech. We lay back, both looking upward, our fingers interlinked.

She moved to scratch her ribs with her spare hand. I looked at the well-kept nails as they passed back across the bedcover, then caught the hand with my other one to kiss it.

'I can't see what we must do, Kit.'

I knew what she meant. I could almost touch her thoughts. I said: 'There aren't any models.'

'Models?'

'I don't say there are no precedents, but I don't find it recorded in literature or statute or sacred text, how it's done.'

'You don't mean because we're both women, I think. Do you?'

'No, my dearest. I mean because we're both equal.'

'But in Marriage . . . equality of rank and wealth.'

'But, as we both see quite clearly, great inequalities of permission, where the act of sex is expanded unimaginably to denote his and her entitlements; for he'll be ever puffing and swelling and probing to victory, while she'll be conquered and fertile and well-tilled.' Hessy laughed. I continued: 'For whatever they feel for each other before the day, as soon as it's done the form, the model, comes into operation. They'll cease to be the folk they were, and by law and custom and example, start to conform merely to the roles suggested by their own privy parts, which surely stand in no such proportion to their possessor.' She laughed again, cheekily. I went on: 'But it is strange, isn't it, that because an inch or two of a person goes in rather than out, she must spend her whole life in special wrappings – even as a slave, and in some matters entirely without rights?'

'It is strange, put like that. But I've always thought that the man has a different temperament. So I have read. They say he has different spirits, and more reason. More fire and hot. More hair!'

'I can't deny that. It's a different complexion. And they even wear wigs to show it all off the more. But then they say whatever suits them. It's the conclusions that are drawn from these things. When it suits them they're quick to pretend that women are the naturally overheated ones. Why else should we have to be so reined in?'

'Who are *they*, Kit? Who have ordained all this?'

'It's tempting to say rich men in government. They make the laws. But I'm confused about it all.'

'Because that means Charles . . . and your uncle?'

'I suppose it does.'

'And you love them.'

'It's not so much that. It's that I don't see them thinking all this out as we've just done. I don't see them give such matters a second thought, rationally. I don't imagine that anyone in the House of Lords ever says to himself scientifically or juridically that the possession of a prick must be supported by a wig; oh, and by the way, you can stride your legs, and serve on a jury.'

'Except perhaps the Queen might notice these things. In the House of Lords, which isn't the House of Ladies.' I laughed in turn, and squeezed her hand.

'And so, as to who *they* are, I'm at a loss,' I said. 'Men enforce these ways of doing things, but they don't seem to think rationally at all about the construction of these machines, these models. All comedies end in marriage. And for the rest, they say they're doing God's work. It's all taken for granted.'

'Perhaps they are, Kit; doing God's work. Perhaps we – you and I, though we're both accounted clever, unusual creatures – are very very wrong. For reasons we don't and can't understand. *Because* we're merely women.'

'Do you believe that?'

She turned her head to look at me. 'I hardly do,' she said.

I said: 'Putting aside that we're both women; let's assume that we were man and wife. I can't seriously imagine that God intends from this moment on that one of us should be so unequal in rights and restrictions to the other. I really cannot. Would you feel that as God's love? And which one of us would it be? How would He choose?'

307

'But the Bible says . . .'

'The Bible says a great deal, especially if you look at it closely. My uncle thought he'd grasped what it said. Then he found he hadn't.'

'I once asked Swift about the *Symposium*. My brother took me to *The Platonick Lady* at the theatre. It was by a woman.'

'Mary Pix. You saw Anne, then, before she retired. I'm glad.'

'I did ask Swift but he looked furtive, as if he shouldn't be discussing it with me. Do you think it might teach us? How to . . . go on from here? How to love? Is it a . . . a *decent* book? I read so many but rarely get hold of the ones that might matter. Oh Kit, what shall we do? How shall we do it? I know I love you and I know I'm frightened suddenly.'

I didn't see what I could say to comfort her, so I said nothing and held her in my arms, still worried that I should lose her.

We grew calmer, reassured perhaps by each other's closeness; making an unspoken agreement, it could be, to press aside considerations which had got too threatening, and to attempt to keep the moment.

Later, 'We should get up,' I said.

'I want to stay in bed.' She would delay me.

'I can't,' I said. 'Maybe I can't permit myself too much of the very freedom I've been seeking. I'm restless. It's for love of you. I can't explain.'

'Very well. We'll get up. We shall leave off our stays. It's too hot anyway. We shall be seen by the servants as bold sluts. We shall be on holiday and a disgrace.' I loved her.

We went down very casual, feeling like a couple of courtesans, who take the bedroom with them wherever they go, defying everyone and anyone.

Sunbathing

There was one day remaining to us of our week at Abbs Court. Why was it a week? Why couldn't we have stayed there for ever?

Because we'd said a week. Because we didn't dare disturb anything by altering plans and facing others; and facing the implications of having to talk it all through again. We both sensed, I think, that even our gentle conversation about relationship had threatened to put our intimacy at risk by running of its own momentum into impossible snares.

So we sought to regain and inhabit that ecstatic harmony of the morning when we'd lain on our sides. And we did, in a different but continuing form. How shall I describe it, that sense that to occupy the same few square feet of earth together was enough to justify anything else in the world?

'You love me more than Charles, then?' she said as we stood holding hands and looking into the sluggish, midsummer Thames, its surface just ruffled and at play with the brightness of the air. We were unhatted, unparasoled. We dared the sun on our faces and our wanton, undone hair.

'Poor Charles,' I said. 'I'd have loved him if I could. But he's alright.'

'How, alright? He must be the most unhappy man in the world if he misses you.'

I put her hand to my lips. 'He has my image in another world.'

'Indeed. Does he worship at your statue? Is he a Pygmalion?'

'I shall tell you a secret no one knows except Anne Bracegirdle.'

'Tell me.'

I told her about Lucy'lizabeth. She was amazed, and didn't believe me.

'I assure you it's true. It's very difficult but it's true.'

'You,' she said. 'Who are you? I'm in a dream, I think. You're here with me, quite real, yet you have the Philosopher's Stone implanted under your skin, and conduct your affairs with a great imposing Lord who isn't really so tall and frightful as he could be, by means of an understudy. And in the meantime you sing like an angel. Sure I'm in a dream, Kit.' She pinched my arm.

'I feel the same about you,' I said, laughing. We kissed, and I pinched her back.

'Let's run,' she said. We ran until we were tired, and threw ourselves down in the watermeadow. 'I think it rained in the night, but it's quite dry here now.' She lay back. The sunlight fell directly on to her fair face, her neck, much of her breast and her bare calves, where the hairs grew quite thickly. She straggled her hand out for a dandelion, and casually clubbed my face with its flower.

'And Nicolini? I must know, Kit.'

'We're very mild lovers, my darling. Besides I didn't know you

309

then. Not as I know you now. You must allow me some recreation of my soul.'

'Did you *do* anything? You don't have to tell me. Your privacy and your past are your own. I shall just be impossibly jealous and sulky if you don't.'

'We haven't kissed mouth to mouth.'

'What about – what was it – *mamillae*?'

'I confess.'

'Worse?'

'Nothing more. Nothing more than caresses. May I be allowed so much?'

'Perhaps. It'll have to stop, of course.'

'Of course.'

'The *mamillae* are not for just anyone.' With the back of her hand she touched my breasts loose beneath my day dress. Ah, that touch. They were full and sore and sensitive. She seemed to understand. Then I knew before she spoke what her next words would be. We seemed hardly to need speech at all, yet we loved to talk.

'You live so near to us, yet to your house come the famous and the very rich as if it were a special court and not just a house on a street. Of course your uncle . . . Do you like him? He terrifies me.'

'We have an identity. We don't get on in the common way; we don't share talk of this and that across our breakfast, but there's something that holds us together, some bond I think beyond the embarrassment in Cambridge which I told you about. Yes, I've given the matter much thought, as you would.'

'As *you* would, Kit.'

'Well yes, if that's my character. I've given the matter much thought, and I believe we are alike. And must somehow have gravitated together even if we'd not been related. It has nothing to do with the science. It's that we're joined by temperament, I think. By early experience, perhaps. We're both difficult.'

'Then am I fated to love difficult people?'

'You mean Swift.'

'Do you like living with your uncle?'

'I've never asked myself whether I liked it. No, dearest. No, I don't like living with my uncle. It's like the difficulty of living with myself. I'd rather live . . . some other way.' We both knew that the name of Swift hung perilously in the air. Neither of us dared provoke it again.

I wanted to ask *her* about *her* involvements and feelings, but since everything in her life and family was somehow so permeated by Swift, and had been for several years, I couldn't seek to gain the same sort of emotional security. It seemed unfair, yet I was scared to break anything.

'I can't wait for tonight,' she said, simply. She rejoiced my heart with her openness. 'But it's a rack. For it's our last. Before London again.'

Stroking each other's bodies in the absolute dark. A blue light plays around my hand on her; sometimes around hers on me. A light unobservable by any scientist. It is a participation, only present through love.

In the small hours, soon after we'd fallen asleep, my body awoke me with the most gut-wrenching cramps. At first I didn't waken Hessy. I tried to brave it out on my own. Then I slewed myself out of bed, and, nearly doubled over, got to where the loose robe was. With this round me I groped my way out and down the main stairs in the dark. It was a very eerie place, taken that way. Creaks and starts in the old woodwork made me wonder if the house was somehow busy with its own life. At the bottom of the stairs I had to sit and rest because of a great heave on my womb. Then onward, across the faintly starlit great hall, and down into the kitchens, where I found what I sought: hot water in the big black kettle which stood on the embers to be warm for the morning. Then I felt the blood start. I got a cloth for that, then poured some of the water into a stone jar from the rack, corked it up and, having wrapped it in a towel, retraced my limping steps to the bedroom, now doubly awkward from the cloth.

Hessy lay still asleep while I saw to myself and lay back down next to her with my hot water bottle. But the pains were strong and I cried out before biting my lip.

'Is it usually like this?' She raised herself dozily on one elbow and put a hand on my forehead.

'Not usually,' I said. 'It feels as if I'm giving birth.'

'You poor lamb.'

Another contraction. It felt as though a breadmaking housewife had her muscly grip in the bowl of my belly, both hands squeezing

311

for dear life and a family of sixteen. 'God!' I cried. 'And this is only delivering nothing!'

'My mother calls it Lady Sarah. After the Duchess of Marlborough.'

'The most powerful woman in the kingdom,' I said through my teeth.

Crackenthorpe

'It's Mrs Barton, isn't it? I suppose you want Swift. He's not arrived yet.'

It was raining in torrents. The street behind me was all puddles. I stood dripping from my hat in the doorway of the little printers' office from which they brought out *The Examiner*. It was Mrs Mary De La Rivière Manley, proofreading; and behind her a set of men and machines.

I'd swallowed the insult of *Bartica* before we came, though *Slut* still stuck in my throat. (You remember her novel? I did.) Nevertheless, I had new things to attempt. 'No in fact, Mrs Manley. We weren't in search of him at all. You, if you'll pardon me, will do very well, thank you. Good morning to you. Which it isn't so good. May we come in?'

She laughed. I signalled to Mary Pierrepont, who was waiting in the Hackney coach. She teetered in her functional galosh-pattens through the mud and muck in the gutter, and, skirts clutched high in the one hand, dainty useless little umbrella in the other, made it across the puddles to join me. I gave introductions; intrigued all the while by the chunk, whirr, thud, clunk of the two presses, as the men spun them up, inked the block, and ran them down again. An inky girl and a boy were unclamping a bed of type on a table by a tiny window, and sorting the letters into boxes held in a large tray.

'May we take a few minutes of your time?'

'You may. But I can't offer you anything. We have a rush on, or I'd ask Andy to make some firewater mint. That's what I call my mid-morning weakness. No doubt I shall pay for it. They've got some of that cheap black sugar spirits, but I don't recommend it.'

'Please don't trouble,' I said. 'We just hoped for a few words with you.'

'Smoke, either of you? I can spare you a pipe's worth of time, and you might join me if you wished. I have another.'

'If you please,' said Mary. 'That would be very agreeable.' I looked at her. To my certain knowledge she hadn't smoked in her life. There was a chair with wooden arms in what you might call the reception area, where we stood. Mrs Manley motioned Mary to it, and found a couple of stools from behind the counter. Then she occupied herself preparing the two small pipes.

'I don't have it in my house because it stinks the place out, and Barber has gone over to snuff, but I enjoy a light when I'm down here with the devil.'

'I admire your work greatly,' Mary launched in. 'It is so witty. And wickedly *outré*.'

'Thank you. If it's a compliment, which I believe it must be.' She smiled.

'My father considers it unsuitable, or at least he would if he came across it or bothered with it, but as I read it in my own chamber, I may do as I like there, I think.'

'Indeed, I hope so. I shouldn't like to offend Lord Dorchester's sensibilities.'

We were furthering my project, but I found it hard to concentrate properly. My thoughts were full of Hessy. This rain reminded me of the last morning at Abbs Court, the servants' boots on the wet front steps as they carried our luggage to the waiting coach. Hessy was coughing slightly.

And because of Lucy'lizabeth sitting beside us we couldn't speak freely during the return journey. There'd been some hold-up at Hanworth, a wagon broken down. I'd wanted to take her hands and talk, but we were constrained into platitudes all the long wait. And so it was throughout the drive onwards when the heavy horses had cleared the road. We'd not even said a proper goodbye.

Since then I'd not seen her at all. Overwhelmed by love, and by an imagination so profoundly and erotically stirred, I'd written a long letter in Latin, very explicit, tender and frank. Then I'd enclosed the dictionary I'd used, an expensive gift, bought specially and very prettily bound, and sent my letter round. I'd heard nothing. I sent Tony to enquire. He brought back no letter but the message from her mother that she was too ill to see me. I was agonised; very sick at heart. I blamed myself; sometimes I believed I could read pain and confusion in her mind and body through my own thoughts; sometimes I thought those were *my* feelings.

The pipes were ready. Mrs Manley took a taper to a little spirit flame that was under some vessel of the business. She lit, puffed, and then handed the pipe to Mary. Who drew, breathed in, and then exploded in a coughing fit.

'You may laugh,' she spluttered. 'But it must be possible.'

'Just puff. Don't inhale,' said Mrs Manley.

'I'm determined, Kit. I shall master this Art. At least once.'

'I'm sure you will,' I said, exchanging a glance with Mrs Manley, 'at last.'

'If you don't keep puffing, it'll go out.'

Mary tried again, then handed it back. 'Perhaps later, Mrs Manley. It's most kind of you to bother.'

'And a shame to waste it, I'm obliged to you.'

I decided we must press on. I said: 'Forgive me, but I heard there was once a scheme for an academy. A female academy. We, Lady Mary and I, have both acquired an education, a passable good one I believe, through our circumstances and our own efforts. As you must have done yourself, Mrs Manley.'

'I'm a scribbler of sorts,' she said.

I looked at Mary. 'We think you over-modest,' I said. 'But it's clear to us that we're all three the exceptions of our sex. This academy . . .'

The door swung open. It was drenched Patrick, Swift's man.

'He's on his way, Ma'am. A damned long way it is, excuse me. Chelsea! Pox on Chelsea!' He pulled his waterproof off. It hadn't been very proof.

'Here,' said Mrs Manley, handing him the unsmoked pipe she'd filled. 'Tabby!' to the girl at the type table. 'Take Mr Patrick to the back and feed him something. Let him sit by the fire.'

'Yes, Miss.'

'The academy was ready to take form. Astell did the touting for patronage. You know Mrs Astell?'

'I don't yet,' I said. 'It's my wish.'

'You should have said.' Mary looked surprised. 'She's an acquaintance of mine. But I never knew . . .'

'I suppose we acquired a habit of caution,' said Mrs Manley. 'We have to live in the world.'

'Go on,' I said.

'It all went too well. Her friend Lady Hastings – do you know Betty Hastings? – just went to the Princess.' She puffed her pipe. 'I mean the Queen, now. All too easy. Ten thousand pounds. A Kensington pledge. Straight on the table. "Talking of Royal Societies . . . " said her Highness. And left.'

I was amazed by the story. I thought of Charles. 'That dumpling,' he'd said.

'Then . . . ?' I began.

'We ran into such a fair-minded, decent, taking-the-points-on-the-one-hand and weighing them with prayer-humility-and-steadfast-ness against those-on-the-other-hand-my-dear-daughter-in-Christ, sort of Prince of the Church, that, in short, the whole project met with an axe.'

'Why?' Mary asked.

'Because, my dear daughter in Christ, the way we'd dressed it, thinking to soften the objections of the cloth – the way Astell dressed it in her Proposal – was as a free religious retreat for women, with the emphasis on education. Regular worship . . . well, you know Mary Astell. No, but you *don't* know, do you? Well, anyway, regular worship but *no Vows*. Free to come and go outside the walls. Safe within the walls from being molested. We even had an architect. Not Wren.

'But the Bishop gave his opinion at last. It had cost him much agony and wrestling with his soul in the small hours, but eventually God had revealed his wisdom. The whole idea smacked overly of Papism, nunneries, and the dangers of idle retirement. He pronounced, and that was that.'

'Who was this influential Bishop?' I asked.

'Burnet.'

'But he's my counsellor,' said Mary.

'Well, there we are,' said Mrs Manley. 'You're young and very well connected.'

'But he always encouraged me to learn Latin and so on.'

'And there we are again,' said Mrs Manley sourly. 'New Atalantis is a land of singular inconsistency in its practices. It is, like our academy, a curious island which doesn't exist.' She spat behind the counter.

'Would the Queen . . . If we were to approach her now, would she still be prepared to endow an institution? Even a more modest proposal?'

'With the war? And the taxes? Not a move she'd be able to sell to her politicos and generals, I think. Perhaps we could take a wing of Blenheim Palace. She's no longer her younger self. She walks a fine line. Why, I forget myself: she can hardly walk at all. And she is exhausted. I have no hopes.'

'Some other sponsor?' I said. I wondered whether Charles . . .

'You could try.'

'And if we were successful, would you consider . . . ?'

'I would. But I should perhaps be a bad advertisement. There are . . . forces who would do everything in their power to discredit the proposal. Astell is immaculate, but she's not well, I hear. I'm an old hack. Forced to ink my tongue for a living, and the mistress of a city man with only moderate means, Mrs Barton, for my housekeeping. Out of whose way I'm obliged to dodge down here, when he has taken a drop, as they say. I'm not as mobile as I was.'

Swift had appeared in the doorway and was creating a puddle on the boards from his wet things. 'Ah. The good doctor. I was speaking of a friend of yours, my dear.'

'Oh? Who's that?' He greeted me. 'Mistress Kit. What a good morning you make it.'

I introduced Mary, who was in awe a little, I think.

'Only my lover, Barber, Swift. Only my lover.'

'Barber. Yes. Excellent fellow, Kit. Alderman. How are we progressing, Mrs Manley? Did you tone it down as I said? Harley's advice. We can't be too careful, he said. But I can't be careful at all. We all know that. You, Mary Manley, are my Prudence and Temperance.' He threw his soaking mantle into the corner. 'Let me have a look at these proofs.'

'Would you lend your support to a women's academy, Swift?' I blurted. Manley looked fiercely at me.

'I didn't hear that, Kit,' he said. 'You must excuse us, ladies. There's work to be done. You beard me in my other habitat; here we can't stop for tea and . . . riddles.' He put his watch away and took Mrs Manley to monitor the work of the presses, scattering sheets of paper as he went.

'We were just leaving, my dearest Swift,' I said sadly.

Of course his arrival made me think of Hessy. I hadn't thought of her for at least a minute. Love! God, what had happened to me? I was like a taut string. More: some lute or guitar, that wilfully burst from its case at the slightest hint of her or her associations. Whose music was so exquisite as to be painful; a species of delicious tinnitus. And my bump – how she'd opened my eyes to the obvious. And the obvious surgical possibilities, about which I'd been unable to bear to think. Because *if . . . if* it was indeed a fragment of the Stone, and *if* the Stone could indeed have changed me so radically, and preserved me in the prime of life and health; then cutting it out might . . .

But truly I say I couldn't bear to think about the return of my wolf self, even if it gave me the one thing that would promote my interest with Hessy. She was so potent a vibration to me; I was overwhelmed and wished to be. But I couldn't remove that tiny plug on the nightmare of my childhood. For to do so might cause her to die. That was the bind, the force of the wicked injunction.

I thought instead of the strange dark intensity of the Lullist room, barely a fortnight ago now. Her under-petticoat, smelling of her who was my life, held up and then dropped in casual joy upon that futile, intricate machine. Its folds cascaded over the chains and belts and combinatory drives, half covering this design, those letters, threatening its whole operation with a pretty white fall. Plot that, Descartes! Newton! A three-dimensional, folded film. How could that coexist with London and this rain? Hot, strange, flickering; past all human belief lay that room in my mind; and now I stood on a foreign shore that was called normality.

Had I not been so fevered with my emotions just then, I might have pursued the petticoat folded on that rational structure to invent Catastrophe Theory, seeking mathematically to tame the successive flips and discontinuities that had been my experience. But I had more important things to do. And I would rather have had an hour with Hessy than that glory, I think.

I left Mary Pierrepont at her house. 'We can meet at Anne's. Anne Bracegirdle. I will ask her. You, me, Hessy Vanhomrigh . . . perhaps; Anne; Mrs Manley . . . also a perhaps; Susan Verbruggen; what about Wortley's sister, is she in town? Do you really know Mrs Astell? Mary Pix? Don't worry. We'll achieve something. I feel it. I'll write tomorrow.'

'Yes,' she said. 'We must keep at it.'

When I got back to St Martin's Street, I dashed through the down-pour to the front door in my little boots, and had Tony go out to pay off the driver. There was a letter waiting for me on the dresser. Nervously I unfolded it, to see if it was from Hessy.

Let her read her advertisement in this afternoon's Gazette, by which she will know if I am in earnest. She will need the best offices of his Lordship's purse, I think, if the case is to remain even as it is. But perchance she has forgotten the art of pleasing a man.

My ribs turned to spars of ice. Tony came in.

'Has the driver gone, Tony?'

We peered out. 'Not quite, Miss Kit.'

I gave him my purse. 'Catch him, Tony. Go in the Hackney coach and bring me a *Gazette*. Quickly, Tony. I must have today's edition.'

Indoors I shook uncontrollably. I could hear the voice of this brief-est of letters prying at my brain; its shameless blend of malice, greed and prurience.

Oscillation

A grubby little message at the back, next to Dr Pursey's Infallible Salve:

At the Opera *this year was given a Presentment of the* Passion of Sappho. *Unhappy of her reception at the Theatre, that* Creature *of Antiquity, we are reliably informed, has quitted the Stage, and now prosecutes her Ardours in our midst: a* Breech *in Nature, we think. Look to your own Breeches my Lord, your Whig and All, lest your Mistress should require them for a Cabal of Two.*

I felt sick. I went to my room and threw myself down. And Hessy would be named. Who had done this? Who? How? Why? I could answer the last, I thought. Cash. And Spite.

Had someone spied on us at Abbs Court? Some servant come in on us while we lay oblivious; entwined and naked in the morning? Lucy'lizabeth?

But what had she to gain? Revenge for her blow? Perhaps, although as I reckoned it, she'd had the better of me all along, counting up scores. Some other untraceable retainer, then? Was there some surveillance system in the Lullist room, and we had been watched at our most intimate, by some guffawing Yahoo?

Or had my Latin letter leaked from Hessy's house, to be the sport of Whoever with a grammar school grudge?

It was all in pieces. I couldn't make contact with Hessy to warn her, to share the horror, to face the solution. If there was one. I couldn't turn to Charles. I dreaded my uncle finding out – it would touch every paranoid nerve in his body. My maid was a suspect. My servants.

Unable to endure being in it, I couldn't yet bear to venture out of the house, lest some loathsome accuser should shove up to me and point me out.

I shut myself in my room. It was a terror, a physical pain under my heart. I was proved monstrous. Let me dash my head against some sharp point. Let me run at the window and hurl myself out. Why would not my body obey me? Was I also coward? Baseness. I should starve.

Charles called. I let it be known I was ill. He became attentive through the door. I told him he must go away. Eventually he did. They tried sending meals up. I couldn't think of eating; nothing should pass my lips. I wanted to die. It was what I deserved.

Lucy'lizabeth knocked. 'Miss Kit.'

I didn't answer. I would not answer *her* of all people.

Minutes passed.

'Miss Kit,' she whispered, 'what am I to say to Char . . . Mr Charles?'

How quickly would I die? Ah, not quickly enough, since I was so feeble of purpose.

We'd grown accustomed to this sharing of key information. My situation wouldn't resolve itself. I'd have to tell her, soon enough; supposing she wasn't the person responsible. Nobody could say when more explicit accounts of my love would reach Charles or Isaac, or the public at large, and she'd be called upon to put on a face. These wrangles! Perhaps deep down in my misery I just wanted to see someone.

'Lucy'lizabeth?'

'Yes.'

'Come in.' She slipped herself round the door.

'What's the matter?'

'I'm . . . ruined.'

'Miss! Now?'

'Oh don't be ridiculous. Please, don't be cruel. Listen. There are rumours spreading about me. Horrible malicious rumours.'

'I haven't heard anything.'

'No. But you might very soon.'

'Saying what?'

The words stuck in my throat. 'That I . . . That Miss Hessy and I . . . That we . . . '

'That you're in love with her? Everyone knows that.'

'What?'

'Of course.'

'Everyone?'

'Yes.'

'Charles?'

'No. No, he doesn't know.'

'What d'you mean, then?'

'Household people.'

'I see.' I tried not to show how appalled I was.

'You know about . . . Abbs Court?'

She fiddled with her apron-strings. 'I could make a guess.'

'I see,' I said again. 'Do you want money?'

'I beg your pardon?' It was her turn to look surprised.

'How much do you want? Or is it the estate? You want some agreement settled now?'

'I don't follow you.'

'What do you want? I presume you threaten to tell Charles.'

'No. Miss Kit. Kit. Why should I do that?'

'For advantage.'

'What good would it do me?' Her eyes, wide and engaging mine, were clear.

'Then you're not . . . ?'

'No. I am not.'

A wave of relief burst over me. Very hesitantly I embraced her. 'I'm grateful,' I said, 'for your confidence, Lucy'lizabeth. We haven't been . . . the best of friends. I want you to know, I'm grateful.'

'That's alright,' she said, lapsing back into her Oxfordshire a little.

'It don't help always being accrost, does it?' She patted me gently. 'You're quite forlorn, aren't you? What are we going to do with you?'

I realised that my authority had evaporated, and although the sensation wasn't as unpleasant as I might have expected, it could not go on. How could I function if I had not control, that curse, that need? I pulled myself up. But with my proper role came back the dread of the exposure, though it was a comfort that she knew after all, and thought nothing of what to me was so hauntingly fearful. 'But if it isn't you, there's still someone who plots my ruin. What am I to do?'

'That I can't say.' And she, too, closed back into our more customary mode.

'I'll have to stay in my room.' I turned away. 'I can't show my face. I'll have to stay here.'

'Very well. Shall I bring you something to eat?'

'No. How can I think of food? I shall starve myself. Shall I? But my body is so strong, so well. If I could ruin it; if I could be sick; if I could waste away. But it would take so long: I haven't the strength to be weak.' A thought came to me. 'Lucy'lizabeth, can you send word to Miss Pawnee? I'll give you a letter.'

'Graveling's about. I'll send him to Mrs Bellamy's.'

'Would you?'

'You're not well?' said Pawnee when I smuggled her in through my door. 'Your uncle's worried about you. He has that look of the racoon.'

I explained my predicament; indeed I explained everything. She looked at me, as you might say, very sideways, then picked up my skull, opened its old jaw and placed it to her bosom. 'Are you still my friend?' I said.

'I'm to be married,' she said. 'There is a sea captain. He's younger than I am. He's an American, but not a pirate. I have assurances of this. From reliable sources.'

'Pawnee!'

'As for this affair of your honour – ' she turned back to face me and made the skull face me too, its gape hovering melodramatically along the line of her bodice – 'there is something I can do for you.'

'Tell me, my dear. Please tell me. I feel I'm drowning.'

She stroked the bald head of the skull and set it on my dressing-

321

table next to the rosewater. Her hands were now freed. Fixing my eye, she laid them loosely down, resting them on her skirt. With imperceptible movement at first, very enigmatically I should say, she began to reef up the skirt of her gown into her working fists.

I was uneasy, taken aback, yet stayed where I was as if in an enchantment of some sort. The white expanse of petticoat between the floor and her hem grew larger, and larger, until she could catch hold of the whole ruche of it and lift it right up. Something in metal was revealed.

Grasping it without looking at it she took out from the long pocket stitched into her petticoat lace a glittering Spanish dagger, fully eighteen inches, and beautifully engraved along the blade. Then she dropped her hem back. 'Yes. It is an affair of your ultimate honour. There is only one course open to you.' She handed me the blade. I took it cautiously, as if it could skew up and bite my face with its deadly focus. I had never held a weapon.

My evening had lurched from the extremity of despair to a kind of comic self-discovery, to relief, to terrible agitation, to hope. It overplayed my scene. I could hear them laughing outside my door almost, the other people in the world. But while the reeling interlude struck on, I believed I was wedded to the tragic. I looked at her face to glean intelligence of the meaning she imputed to the dagger, and wondered why it should be that out of all the women of my acquaintance I should have summoned her to my side tonight; not Anne, not Mary Pierrepont, not Betty Germain, not Prudence Steele – I would not even have summoned Hessy if I could. Not now. No, I had asked for Pawnee, who had formed my early experiences of London, starkly, fiercely in her own way; Pawnee, who saw herself, like me, as an anomaly, an unthinkable, in this place.

I sat down. The thing lay across my lap. What kind of counsel was this? As far as I could see, the situation had closed all around me, offering no gap through which to squeeze. Honour, she insisted. Honour? Her gestures, equivocal, provocative, insulting almost – what did they import? Did she hate me for what had happened between us after all? Was she somehow calling in a debt of frustrated feeling? The weapon and its proximity made everything dubious, so that I was held in a trance, almost; I watched, in my mind's eye, the soliloquy of a troubled female upon the stage after the ravishment, yet I was too far off to hear what she was saying.

I looked down. How beautiful was the weapon. Had it been used in earnest, I wondered. Had it entered the boundary of a creature of this world in a shudder of pain and release? I stretched out and made the shape of my closure: now the blade lay along the line of my thighs pointing towards me, and my hands were loosely tangled on the pretty wired hilt, so that the steel cross-piece rested on the pale of my wrists. How would it feel to be finished with it all for good, I allowed myself to wonder. So on the stage the poor creature, weeping and bruised, her dress disordered to excite the watching citizenry, restores by one sharp deed the clarity of her honour, and erases from society, and from the text of herself, the intolerability of her suffering. I pictured, still as if from outside myself, the flashing violence of a moment, the neat slit in the pale blue outer fabric of my dress, the sudden spill of the white linen shift beneath, like the fat below the slashed skin of some unusual sea creature. Then the searing overload of pain; then the blood, and my collapse forward.

How convenient for the dramatist, the audience, and the rest of the cast! How truly tragic! How satisfactory! And how I too longed to die, to be free of it all, love, pain, memory, shame. Complicit.

My hands had not tightened noticeably in the effect of my reverie. I felt Pawnee kneel down beside me, and place her one hand next to mine on the hilt. Her other she dropped under the point – I felt the back of her fingers press close to the top of my legs through my gown. Gently she lifted the dagger's point from my belly, looping it up in an arc so that it flipped quite over and aimed away, out, into the world. I felt a faint exuberance of anger in my veins. But my fingers had grown tighter and the muscular system felt wound up. My arms, seemingly without my volition, returned the point over the top of its arc, back to its former position along my lap. Twice more she made the unspoken statement. Each time I felt the slight flush of anger, but the dagger returned. On the next attempt she unthreaded my fingers and broke my rapt state.

'Look!' she said. 'How sharp it is!' She drew the side of her index finger along the length of the blade as softly as a lover on the adored hair, or a mother upon her baby's skin. Bright drops gathered from the cut and fell on to the floor. 'Try it for yourself if you don't believe me.' She sucked the wound.

Gingerly, and not to be outdone by this cool display of American temper, I repeated the gesture for myself on the other edge of the blade. It was almost painless, a razor-sharp sincerity. My blood gathered on my finger and dripped on to my dress. I remembered a night with Charles and the wrists of Ruth.

'If it were me,' she said in her perfect English, 'I should use it for needlework. I should set the bastard up, put on my best gown, and then stitch his balls to his tongue – through the inside. It's merely a suggestion. Charles could be persuaded to help, I don't doubt, with the facilities if not in person. But we're not all the same I suppose, Kit. Indeed we are not. Still, I am going off with my new life and everything, and sometimes I weep and sometimes I'm very, very glad and so I want you to have it, in memory of me. It's a good piece, I think. Don't you?'

I couldn't let go. The dagger held such a fascination for me I couldn't put it down. I transferred it to the hand with the cut finger as I stood up to embrace her, and so let it hang down at my side, a delectable weight. Probably the drips ran all along it and on to my skirt. Well, that pleased me. I held her tight with my one arm and recalled the feel of her closeness. 'Everybody leaves, Pawnee. How can we make them stay?'

'It's a spirit gift, and so has a life of its own. Perhaps it will tell you itself when you must use it, and what you must do.' She hugged me and we rocked quietly together there, remembering the past and not looking to the future. I felt that my trouble had eased because the onus of decision had been removed. The bright, fascinating bodkin that I held at my side would tell me when, and what.

'I am hungry,' said Pawnee, 'even if you're not. Tuck it away and let's go down. Perhaps something liquid . . . '

I felt myself draw away, and the feeling of collapsing inside came back with a rush. I stood cradling my dagger.

'Come. I'll send word to keep the menfolk away. We'll sit in the parlour as we used to sit in Jermyn Street when Etta was first pregnant. Do you remember what I once said to you then? That from Etta's wings there were two drops of blood: one was me and the other you.'

'I didn't understand you.'

'I didn't understand myself. This evening is another such. We shall know when we know. Or perhaps we shall not. I am frightened too, Kit.'

'I don't want you to go.'

324

'Well, I'll ask Lucy'lizabeth to get us some supper. I shall take beef and you shall take beef tea.'

I smiled and began to allow myself to be taken down. 'But . . . What about Hessy . . . ? You see, I don't mind for myself so much. It's when someone else is used against you.'

'Has it happened yet?'

'Not exactly yet. I don't know what might have been done, or set in train.'

'Come. We can't do everything at once. One thing is sure.'

'What is that?'

'You're no good to her dead. That is a matter of honour.' We went down.

Madonnella

'It's always the first thing they say.'

We sat in Anne's saloon on the second floor in Howard Street. Through her well-taxed (thanks to my Lord) windows, large and so placed as to offer a majestic prospect, I watched the commerce on the Thames. Great wooden ships lay sweating in the morning's reflection, gilded and dazzling silhouettes. One of them was being warped along its mooring past the others. Barges and shallops fought the tide. The light off the river seemed to wrap the spars, wrap the spider lines of their rigging in a blazing coat. Optics. Angles of incidence and angles of reflection. My uncle had once seriously dented his eyeball by inserting a bodkin deep inside the corner by the bone, and compressing the jelly, to observe the effect on vision. It had made certain rings of colour, he said, which remained there for a week so that he bumped into doors and fell over his cat.

'A woman achieves anything,' Anne went on, 'and up goes the cry SAPPHO! They love to see you breeched and showing off your legs on stage, striding about the world of affairs, but at the end, my dear, you must reassure them that you'd rather be somebody's wife.'

'I was called *Madonnella*. Also *La Platonne*.' The other tea-drinker in the room was Mary Astell, whom Anne had found out and invited specially because I'd been so frightened and upset. I was touched at people being kind. The dreadful thing was beginning to feel more like a badge than a placard. And Hessy seemed to be alive. But then, every so often, in waves as it were, I'd find myself thrown back to some pit of self-abasement where the very thought of her stung me. Children. The Stone in my head, a confusion; or out, a wolf's red spike thrusting from my loins. 'They broke my heart, child.' She peered over her spectacles like a little old lady, which she wasn't. She was no more than forty-odd, but it seemed she'd withdrawn inside a wire framework stretched over with black and white clothing. Her teacup seemed to hover in front of it unsupported, so transparent was her hand. 'Not the name-calling. But the cloud of refusal. Like struggling against a mountain of wool. I was telling Mrs Bracegirdle before you came, I can't put myself through that again. Where was the harm? Where was the difficulty? You'd have thought we were asking for the moon, instead of a foundation where women could entertain ideas. I do believe they would rather we'd entertained gallants of the town. I do believe it, Mrs Bracegirdle.'

'So you see, Kit, it is almost a mark of achievement. Think nothing of it. Let them bray their worst; they are nothing but asses. Hurl it back in their teeth, or turn it round. Make something of it. You are not who you were, that charming, witty but unassertive Kit. You've made a triumph. You're a public person, who is impinging on the world. By this trial you'll have earned your spurs. When I was young I knew Mrs Behn in the theatre. Setting up for a poet! I acted in something of hers, I think. The going was very rough. For her. And I too have been branded, as if my decision not to marry was an incitement. You must call the bluff and have them do their worst. It's the only way with such people.'

'Mrs Bracegirdle is right, my dear young lady, in this matter. But I hope I may, without giving offence, make one distinction of type and another of degree. I say without giving offence ... but you will see why. The distinction of type concerns the nature of the theatre. The stage is the one sphere in which our sex have succeeded in finding a voice. I do not intend a musical pun, Mrs Barton.' She meant it kindly, no doubt, but her manner was of fine steel in everything, and I felt I was being reprimanded. Nevertheless, I listened intently. I had never heard a woman discourse like this before. She went on. 'No. I mean simply that here women have spoken in public for the first time, and been heard. This achievement is a profound one, Mrs Bracegirdle, and my admiration for you and Mrs Barry, for having become, what shall I say, established in the world, is very great. You

326

are known as yourselves, not by some common term, or by some man's name; but as yourselves. How? By *riding*, so to speak, the vehicle of the public gaze, for which Nature fitted you by appearance and temperament: by *enduring* it with fortitude, temperance and prudence. Well and good. You in particular, Mrs Bracegirdle, have eschewed the temptations that must attend a woman's journey on such a vehicle, and have brought dignity to it. The integrity of your reputation remains an example to the future, and a reproof to those who have seen fit to compromise. Our sex now has a foothold; that is undoubted. That foothold is the stage.'

'You're most kind,' said Anne.

'But the nature of the theatre is such that it attracts as many debased spectators as those with some pretension to virtue. I make no moral judgement here, please understand me. Who am I? These matters are for God. I make the point because it is this very nature of the stage that permits the wielders of authority to regard it lightly. As a froth of entertainment. Which I do not think it necessarily is. But it serves them to represent the stage as backing on to the Bagnio. This must be said. I do not wish to give offence.' She looked hard at Anne through her lenses, and continued.

'The distinction of type, then, is between the world of drama, and the seclusion of academic retirement.' She paused, in her measured way, to sip at the dish of tea which must have grown quite cold. 'I hope I've not upset you. You understand that the stage would never have wanted *me*, even if I had wanted *it*. I could never have hoped to fight that fight, as a number of admirable young women are doing now. But it is not *sour grapes*. It is merely a fact.'

'Not at all. Will you take some more tea?' said Anne.

'Thank ye.' Anne poured the pale tea from her Chinese pot. I looked out again at the river. The glare was over, the sun was higher, the day already blue and hazy.

'Do go on.'

'The difference of type. An Academy is a withdrawal; it is not public. It is not accessible to spectators, whatever their ethical status. It does not make money, rather consumes it. But note this, we had the money, so that was not the objection.' She sipped the China tea, making no comment on it. 'The distinction of degree is this. That the stage is tolerated as a *fait accompli*; its women are howled on and patronised, in both senses of the word. But the idea of an Academy, that softest, quietest, simplest, indeed seemingly most harmless of projects, meets with a fortress of silence. At every turn after I had the Princess's pledge and was known, I tired myself against these walls. At every turn, ladies. At first I thought these were accidents along the way – minor upsets. I was hurt, but I continued. In prayer and in endeavour. I considered that God for some reason might not wish what I proposed. But my meditations taught me otherwise. As did my study. I was convinced from within that what I intended could not be otherwise than religious, dutiful and admirable. I wished to serve. Nor would I oppose wilfully the ministers of His Church. I am not a hypocrite, I hope. Nor was I unaware of the specific instruction of St Paul: "Let the woman learn in silence with all subjection. But I suffer not a woman to teach, nor to usurp authority over the man, but to be in silence." I took this very much to heart. Our design was indeed to learn in silence. We had no plans for formal teaching – no whipping and chanting. Our aims were academic, in the original sense of the word. And as for usurping the authority of the man: we were in retreat, were we not?' The three of us sat quietly in the room, the two listeners, I remember, held bound by the import of the history. It was perhaps a minute before Mrs Astell took up the thread again.

'If I was scrupulous in adhering to Biblical authority, I did realise that in my wish to make academic education available to my sex I was exceeding the classical paradigms, except that attributed to Sappho herself, and who knows what form her institution took? It was certainly not a Christian foundation.' There was no flicker of a smile. It was a scholarly observation. 'But in several things our culture has indeed begun to exceed those of antiquity, and this must be the consequence and fulfilment of Christianity at last, having purged itself of the Italian error. We may contemplate freely and in our own tongue the rewards of Virtue. We do not keep slaves. We have abolished the torture of witnesses. Metals. Gunpowder. There is this steam-pump and the mathematics. These things surely are new, if rather dreadful. So there is the climate of the times, and a degree of precedent. Disallowed. To be brief, Ladies, it took me several years of the deepest frustration and disappointment of the heart to arrive at my present conclusions, beyond which I cannot go in conscience.'

'What are your conclusions, Madam?' I said.

She drank again with a tiny slurping sound and gestured to Anne as if to indicate that she had nowhere to put her saucer down. Anne got up to relieve her of it. Although they were of an age, Anne seemed almost reverential before her. I could see why. She was not quite of this world.

'My conclusions are hard ones. They are also impossible ones. Yet they are the only hypotheses which fit my experience. I will not bore you with the intricacies of the trials I have made of them. Suffice it to say that I *have* made them. I conclude in the first place that there is an unwritten, unspoken, unarticulated conspiracy against my proposal. Why? I cannot imagine. How? God perhaps knows. In the second place . . . It is very difficult for me to go on.' She collected herself. 'Bishop Burnet quoted further from Authority. It is the same passage: the First Epistle of Paul to Timothy, chapter two: "And Adam was not deceived, but the woman, being deceived, was in the transgression. Notwithstanding, she shall be saved in childbearing, if they continue in faith and charity and holiness with sobriety." When the Bishop spoke to me his final objection was on this ground; that such a withdrawal as we proposed frustrated the salvation referred to by Paul: women should not be diverted from their hope in childbearing. The pain his interpretation caused me you can only guess at. It placed my whole work in a spiritual wilderness for many months. From this wilderness I emerged with my personal experience of God intact. My sense of the holiness of my hopes burned as strongly as ever it did. I came then to my second hypothesis. That in the interests of the first hypothesis many centuries ago Scripture had been altered.'

We both drew in our breath. Anne because of the enormity of her heresy, spoken coolly and plainly by the frail assembly of clothes in one of her best chairs; I because Mrs Astell had come to the very same conclusion my uncle had reached in his unease about the doctrine of the Trinity. His researches had led him to the very same part of scripture, the letter to Timothy. He'd written an essay on that and a passage from St John. It was called "Two Notable Corruptions of Scripture" and was the product of what was probably the most extensive reading of Patristic Literature ever undertaken. He'd become in his total obscurity in Cambridge the world's leading authority on fourth-century history. This had led him to pin the blame for the fraud on Athanasius, the formulator of the Trinity. The task had taken years of his, Isaac's, withdrawal. 'I have spent the last few years,' said Mrs Astell, 'attempting to substantiate my claim – to myself at least – but I have reached a dead end. I have no more access to the necessary documentation. My hypotheses will remain unproven. I am only sure that in the proceedings of the Royal Society they will not, ever, be discussed.'

She had gone far enough, 'in conscience'. The woman who had published the critique of marriage, conceived the project of the Female Academy, now outlined the cultural psychology of unconscious denial, and the possibility of historical reconstruction of Biblical texts.

Later when she had gone, Anne said, 'I'm glad she doesn't know about me and William. I don't think she'd approve.'

Letters

I thought a good deal about Mrs Astell's conclusions. They were the deciding factor in not paying the demand for money when it eventually arrived. There was an interval, presumably designed to make me sweat in trepidation, which I did my share of, incidentally, and then came the letter:

50l. will seal my lips. A modest expense to protect loved ones, I think. Let your man carry it in a stuffed bag to The George and Dragon in Acton. Leave it behind the South hedge at four o'clock on Thursday, and let him then ride away out of sight. Your honourable discharge from your penance is in your own hands, and honourably it must be done, if it is to be safe. Be advised I have left instructions if I do not get clear of it.

I threw the letter into the kitchen fire.

On Friday I received another:

I can only hope that you will forgive me my dearest Kit for my long silence to you. Put it down to my uncertainty, my illness, my inexperience, if you will. My dearest Kit I have been so overwhelmed and so confused in myself. What can I say? I cannot write what I feel; nor continue to feel so distraught, so pulled apart. I must take the step, Kit, though it is perhaps the hardest thing I have done in my short life, to make my life at least something I know and recognise. All my familiar signs, the waymarks by which I have trotted my foolish course, I find gone. I shall be lost; I am lost. Though we are so close – but a few doors away, my dear – we must not meet. Please, if you care for me, spare my frailty by accepting this earnest request from your true friend,

Hester Vanhomrigh

I was crying in the kitchen with Lucy'lizabeth when my uncle came in, wearing his loose crimson dressing-gown and without his wig, seized me by the wrist and dragged me to his study, a little place he'd taken over on the ground floor and filled with letters and books. It was his campaign headquarters, dominated by the new Thornhill portrait of himself, which filled one wall. It seemed as though the portrait had come alive, and its spare, white- haired old occupant was going to chisel at me with its sharp nose. The violence took me by surprise. We went our separate ways emotionally, and rubbed along domestically. And he'd been only simmering for years, going about his concerns of this and that with the appearance of adjustment. Now, suddenly, I encountered the full force of his temper, and realised how much lay beneath his exterior. He really hurt my wrist. I'd not imagined he was so strong. He threw me down before him in the den, almost I swear with flames coming out of his eyes, and the veins in his forehead looking like cranial cracks; he was a sealed pot which had been left on the fire.

He thrust a letter in my face:

S,

Your woman in your house, which is to say your niece, otherwise styled Halifax's Whore, is surely a lustful Bitch. *I have two witnesses who will swear to every detail of her sinful congress with her Female Friend. Will you brazen it out as she seems inclined? True to* Nature *no doubt. Or will your scruple protect the names of friends and* Neighbours *viz. V———h; not least your own Honour, Sir. For if I receive not the 5ol. as I asked before, I shall release names and places detailing these unspeakable practices contrary to the Laws of Creation and the Ordinances of God.*

I am, Knight, a Lover of Truth and Justice

When he'd seen that I'd read it over twice, he said: 'Do you deny the contents, Catherine Barton?' And so began our disgusting argument. But at first I said nothing. He hit the side of my head. 'Speak, damn you! Refute this . . . calumny. If you can!'

331

What could I say? He hit me again. I held on to the back of a wooden chair. 'Is this how you repay me? Is this how you repay my friend? For by your silence I see the worst is true. You can't speak in your own defence, and are indeed a prey to devilish lusts. Who is your partner in this . . . enormity? Speak! Why don't you speak? Who would think that behind so fair and delicate an exterior lurked such . . . monstrosity. Was not a man . . . *sufficient* for you? A man? My friend! Charles, who is in everyone's mouth a man of absolute credit. A man of gold, who gives you money, position, security, his constant love. The ornament of his age, I think; the mirror of what it is to be a man indeed. A man of brilliance!'

I gathered up my resolution, standing up behind my chair. 'I don't deny that I've lost her who has become my life.'

'How dare you! Then it's true! Come! Who is this depraved female?'

'She is not depraved. She is our near neighbour and the daughter of *your* female friend Mrs Vanhomrigh.'

'You venom! You viper! You eat at my innards! Catherine! You turn my house into a . . . common brothel, you more than whore! Worse than a brothel. Catherine! Are you listening to me?' His anger drove him backward and forward behind his table, directing eyes of hate at me.

'How could I fail to hear you, Uncle?'

'You answer me back! You bandy words with me? Harlot? I want to know exactly what went on.'

'Ah, wouldn't you,' I said.

'Meaning?' He swept on. 'Who was the instigator? Was it you? Were you naked? Had you no shame?'

'Would you like to have observed? To analyse? Do you wish to make a theory out of it? Or now Charles's Junto is superseded, do you have another potent friend, a new one, to whom you could sell the keyhole for your next advancement?' He stopped his pacing, and picked up a heavy Bible. For a long moment I thought he was going to reach over and hit me with it. But he fought himself back. His face was white as his hair. His lips drew tight, menacing lines across his teeth. From which he spat the following:

'I have a name, Catherine. I have a place. I have a reputation that is world-wide. Why? Because the only woman I have served is the Lady Philosophy, a pure and mathematical abstraction. I have eschewed what other men have indulged in. The flesh of women. That painted corpse-flesh. That damned lisping, patched obscenity. That parcel of loose riot tricked out with tangles and ornament. That pit of uncleanness. I have kept myself off from that . . . embroilment, which reduces us to the farmyard, to beasts, lacking reason. I have kept His commandments and attempted to imitate the chaste example of His Son. Thus have I triumphed, Catherine! Triumphed! In despite of my detractors and the knavish crew of fornicators who call themselves learned! Who set up their paltry devices against mine! I have not sought publicity, distinction. It has been thrust upon me. But now I have it, and I have deserved it, I shall fight to preserve it.'

I was appalled. This was what he thought of me. He continued, his face twisted with a snarl of scorn. 'This German . . . '

'Dr Leibniz?' My heart thumped, but I sought to cool the scene, fearing for both our safety. As my hand brushed my skirt I felt the Spanish dagger now sewn into my petticoat.

'He would steal my name. My discovery. My life. My achievements. Prostituted before the public gaze.'

'It's precisely because you didn't prostitute your discoveries, as you call it, that the dispute arises. From what I can make out, Dr Leibniz's calculus is an excellent device.'

'You speak to me of mathematics?' The sneer addressed itself brutally to me. The old teeth disclosed themselves. 'Mathematics? You'll never approach the foothills of that mountain. What do you know of mathematics, you . . . faddler!'

My hand gripped the dagger. It was a reassurance. It calmed me a little.

'You taught me, Uncle!' I tried reason again. 'Anyway he acknowledges your Arithmetic of Fluxions was known to him. He has his place to keep up as well. It's his livelihood.'

'Be quiet, impudence! You're the wrecker here. You've driven everything awry.'

'If it wasn't for me you'd still be in Cambridge, you madman, playing at chemicals. You'd have blown yourself up by now, you over-witted fool. You'd be your own bloody Guy Fawkes.'

'Where's my stick?' He turned and peered up at his shelves, feeling along them for the educational implement he used to keep. He turned back empty-handed. 'You'd not look amiss at a cart's tail, witch!'

'Or in the Pillory, even? Like someone we both know? You men. Your works. Your stupid toys. Your paltry constructions. Your cutting up of animals. Your worms in the liver of a lizard. Your bottles of slugs. Your vulgar, insensitive compulsion to pull everything to pieces. All of you! You're all posturing hypocrites, with your numbers and your Latin. You are little boys. Nasty cruel little boys. Pubescents who can't talk to girls, yet long to. And you, especially, who could never even aspire to touch the hem of one of my sex. Why, anyone would think you keep your inventions standing in your breeches, you are so prim of them. And so self-righteously furtive!'

He waved his arms in absolute fury. 'You shall learn to whom you're talking, Miss! My God! What do I find within my own door? A tongue, mischievously employed. The carnal toilings of a corrupt woman. You will not comment on my activities. You aren't worthy even to . . . ' He paused to draw breath. The tempest was exhausting his lungs. 'Catherine! If I could abstain, who am a man . . . ! If I could resist female temptation through seventy devoted years; then could not you? In whom in any case the natural urge is otherwise directed, by virtue – I hesitate to use the word – of your sex . . . ?'

'By virtue of my sex? Yes, Uncle. You of all people should attest to *my* sex. For you were present when it was contrived!'

'Don't bring that up. That's all in the past. You have lived as a woman. You have the body of a woman, and the functions and motions of a woman.'

'All of which you've observed for yourself, I believe.'

His jaw dropped, but he covered his discomfiture by shouting: 'Remain silent! Do you hear? You forfeit the right to speech! By your depraved appetites! I say you are a woman, no matter how you came to be so! And you have brought shame and exposure upon a house and a life which were unspotted. Venom! You've bit the hand that fed you!'

'Well, I am a woman, whatever that means. I acknowledge it. And I am not ashamed of being anything that you're not! You talk of beasts! By God I'd not realised what a beast you had become. Yet when I think on it, I've heard how you're a petty tyrant in your little kingdom, Mister. President of the Royal Society! I've heard how you are hated. How they fear you. I thought it was idle malice. Of fools.

But now I see you for what you are. You are a spiteful, cruel, tyrannical old man. You are the monster. It is your heart which never felt the
merest breath of love. Save only for one. For one weak, low, fawning,
contemptible, perverse . . . mathematician!'

I realised I'd gone too far, and was glad. Tears stood in his eyes for
a moment. Then I sensed, rather than heard, breathy words escape
his throat, his open mouth – without its consent almost: 'Nothing. I
have no trace. No. Of me there is . . . no . . . inscription. No child
taste. I have extinguished all . . . of . . . it. What was . . . loathsome-
ness. No. No. Not to be borne.' Tiny muscles round his eyes. Then his
face hardened again. He fought back tenderness with a vicious
thrust. 'How dare you! The Vanhomrigh girl, is it? At whose house I
see daily that clerical joke Swift going a-courting.'

'Ah cruel!' I screamed. 'Why, you're not above the tittle-tattle for
all your saintly . . . scientism!'

He was still holding his Bible. He threw it at me, the great heavy
thing. I stepped aside just in time. It raffled past my ear and smashed
against the wall. He ground his old joints round to prise another
from the shelves. I thought I would come under a barrage of testaments, but he opened it and scrabbled in the pages. 'Let the woman
keep silent!' he read in a hoarse shout. It was from the Second Epistle
to Timothy:

' "This know also, that in the last days perilous times shall come.
For men shall be lovers of their own selves, covetous, boasters,
proud, blasphemers, disobedient to parents, unthankful" – note this,
Kit,' he said – ' "unholy, without natural affection, truce-breakers,
false accusers, incontinent," ' (he hurried over this one) ' "fierce,
despisers of those that are good, traitors, heady, high-minded, lovers
of pleasures more than lovers of God; having a form of godliness, but
denying the power thereof: from such turn away. For of this sort are
they which creep into houses, and lead captive silly women laden
with sins, led away with divers lusts, ever learning, and never able to
come to the knowledge of the truth."

'Catherine, I shall leave you to think upon these things. Whether
you want to be responsible for the entry of the Devil into this house
and the mind of your uncle. Think on. If possible upon your knees.'
He left.

I took the dagger from my petticoat and drove the point into
the insulting page. As I did so, he returned, having remembered, I

335

suppose, that he'd left me in his sanctum and excluded himself. 'Out!' he said, and then blenched as he saw what I had in my hand. I waved it under his nose as I swept out.

Two more letters came that day, one informing us of the death of my military brother in the wars in Canada. No hearts were touched in our house over the demise of Colonel Robert Barton.

Swift called. I sent word that I was in mourning and kept my chamber. To which the other letter was delivered. It was from Heidegger, and called me to a voyage to Dublin to give *Rinaldo* to the Irish.

I know it for a fact that on the following day my splenetic uncle loosed his hounds Professor Halley and Dr Arbuthnot down to Greenwich, to bite poor Flamsteed, the Astronomer Royal. I felt sorry for the old fellow and his life's work. Imagine spending thirty-five years under a telescope making a precision map of all the fixed stars, only to have it seized at the last few twinkles on the orders of a world-famous chemist who's had a row with his niece.

Scene Change

The successive dash of wave after wave: like minutes, I thought, or months, or years. So many, so remorseless; and we in our frail assembly of effects, heeling and creaking, and making no discernible progress. Nicolini and I, our arms round each other, stood in the forecastle, practising. We could hardly hear ourselves over the wind and the scurry of the white water whipped up at the bow. We sang to allay our terror at what lay beneath us. We sang also for professional reasons, and to remind ourselves that we were lovers of a gentle, artistic sort, friends of the electric surface.

Great wracks of grey cloud surged above us, hardly higher than our scriber masts, scratching incomprehensible diagrams into the belly of the sky, as we rolled and tossed halfway to Ireland.

Aaron's fake sea machine was stowed below. So fast my years robbed me of certainty, or love, or stability; and I pitched here forever young, beautiful and accursed by the Stone in my head. Or by the mystery of my past. Or both.

Behind me I knew at least that Hessy would be protected. Charles's reaction to his version of the blackmail letter had been to reassure me, and to send to Mrs Van advising her to monitor Hessy's letters, because some political enemy was seeking to slander his associates. He'd been magnificent. He was so used to political attack that he didn't pause for a moment to imagine whether it might be true. He brushed the whole matter off, and sent some men to apprehend whoever should pick up the bundle he had placed at the George and Dragon at Acton. I never heard any more about the business.

Thus the male. I speculated on my reaction to the sex. I knew I could never function as Charles did, confident, acquisitive – forever in the world. He lived for what was tangible and was careful of it. I thought of his collection of coins. That was his version of history, his key to the world. I depended upon him for everything, it seemed, but I couldn't love him. Perhaps the best thing I'd done for him was to give him the gift of Lucy'lizabeth. And in the giving I sought to leave him, to escape.

And my uncle, on whom I was also dependent? In what form did maleness manifest itself here? Surely he was the opposite of Charles. But it could be that the remorseless construction of engines of the mind . . . indeed these were my uncle's hallmark. How was it that I associated the masculine with grim mechanisms designed to overcome . . . ? Not so hard a conundrum after all. I remembered Nick with a shudder unrelated to the fierce Irish wind. I kept away from men as a whole, it seemed. Well, as a woman, society itself kept me away from them, so I was no different to the rest of my sex; at least the rich ones. We were saved up within walls until we reached our maximum value, then sold off. No, this wasn't true, although that was the way it felt to someone like me who was a mistress rather than a wife. In the way of marriage the same pattern operated, but in addition an opposite one: the woman's owner had, as it were, to pin money to her as part of the deal. This was why I couldn't marry Charles even if I wished. My uncle had no way of attaching sufficient financial status to my other charms to make the business socially acceptable. But either way, mistress or wife, we remained beholden to somebody.

I couldn't tell whether my love for Hessy was a condition of my original maleness, or of its violation. I mean my objection to the maleness of men might spring from underlying nature, or from my early experience of them. Either way, that would be to see my feelings for her as a distortion – since I was now a woman. Society regarded it so. But it could be another way round; according to Aristophanes's joke speech in the *Symposium*, we all search for our other half, and some were split originally from pairs of the same sex. So in the matter of 'other half' you had to take what you were given.

Or would my feelings for her fade away? Would I fall in love again, with someone else?

I gave it up. What difference there was between men and women eluded me as a rich, folded mystery. I realised why, standing on this shifting deck, I was more in control than other members of the company, who lay below, gripping the rails of their cots and vomiting into canvas buckets. I realised I'd *always* felt twenty fathoms of watery uncertainty underneath me. Whereas Charles, I reflected, had always lived in the security of a walled garden – his perpetual *hortus conclusus*. And this was why he could live now so flexibly, and with such mobility; casual under attack, tenacious in achievement. His great home in Northamptonshire; his years at Westminster School under the protection of Dr Busby; Trinity, Cambridge – a walled garden *par excellence*; and now the palaces of power, Westminster again, Hampton, Windsor, Kensington . . . and Abbs Court. I and Lucy'lizabeth were his rose.

Nicolini and I watched the ship go about. With a great shouting of commands and flapping of canvas, the old vessel strove across the wind, until the sails filled and we pointed up again as nearly as we could into the Westerly.

I gazed at the ever-extending horizon. Beyond that? It reminded me of how I'd come to think of the war. It was Out There. It occupied its own specially privileged and horrifying universe somewhere disconnected; where Marlborough went every year, where Nicolini came from, where Orpheus came from. Somewhere I couldn't go but which had its own doings that impinged inevitably on mine. And what of the future? America? Atlantis? Death? They were all out there in our direction. The future filled with progress and brotherly love: Philadelphia. A multiplicity of ideal commonwealths? Pawnee's aim? Drowning tomorrow?

Charles again: with his networks, his unmentioned brotherhoods, so many old boys, which enabled him to take care of a blackmailer at the merest drop of a note to a friend. Nothing like that for me. For Us. Tea drinking with chit-chat, and secret, pressured cabals which brought us a bad name. I dreamed of my own *hortus conclusus*. I would have walls and a wondrous roof like the bubble of miraculous engineering that covered the Church of Wisdom in Constantinople. I would be safe within its walls instead of knocking against them. And Hessy would be my rose. My hope was that one day there might be no serpent present, as there had in Trinity Garden.

Nicolini and I ran through the Augelletti love duet from *Rinaldo*. It flew from our mouths and was snatched away by the wind. Our singing: the triumph of the human spirit over life? Or just licensed screaming?

We gave *Rinaldo* in Dublin that Autumn. It was stripped of its political overtones for fear of inflaming Irish opinion. We presented it straight – as the triumph of mediaeval Christianity over the Saracens. I would never be as good as Pilotti. She was magnificent. And she was quite civil to me this time, I think because her husband Schiavonetti was with us now, and she felt soothed. It was the first Opera ever seen there, and a success.

Nicolini and I, almost without a word being said, found ourselves sharing a bed like an old staid married couple. It was as if one of us always forgot to return to his own room after the performance. Not a word was said by anyone – I believe we had some sort of artistic licence to be unconventional. We were a little like circus animals, and to be in bed with Nicolini was truly like sharing a large tent.

It was an experience safe, companionable, and gently erotic, shared by two people whose love could never find resolution; and who took care, therefore, not to overbend Cupid's bow.

'Read to me, Cara. Have you brought your Crackenthorpe? I want to hear of my Lady Simper, eh? Squire Singleton, Mr Courtall, Mrs Everchat. You bring nothing but your body this time, Cara. No Mrs Butterfly. No Mrs Shittlecock. Those were good days, Signorina Newton, eh? Can't bring them back now.' He lay on his back. He was like a huge, professional baby. 'And Isaac Bickerstaff. You don't bring Isaac.'

'He's defunct,' I said.

I had never been away so long and by such a journey. Lying beside my mountain lion, or mountain of a lion to make my meaning clearer, I cast my thoughts often to London: to Hessy even now in some teasing conversation with Swift; to Charles unable to sleep with Lucy'lizabeth because I was away in Ireland; to my uncle whose life's accumulation of wrath had begun to set him up for the angriest years of his life; to Anne, losing blind William to a Churchill; to Mary Pierrepont, hoping and not hoping that her father would sort out her marriage settlement with Wortley; to Pawnee, contemplating pregnancy; to sleep, with great soft hands holding me just intimately enough. I didn't dream for a moment of Harley's bright idea to solve the Government's financial crisis: an investment project called the South Sea Scheme. He and Defoe set it up to rival Charles's invention of the Bank of England. It was supposed to be the Tory alternative.

Observations of Restraint

To London, in the wake of my thoughts. To disallowed love, via Holyhead.

Handel, whom I've said little about because I (like the other singers) was never much more than a soundbox to him, had left England to return to the Hanoverian court. Nicolini also couldn't stay long. Hasting away all; so fast for me, as I now guessed, because I was a hostage to the Stone, which turned Nature out of its natural grammar. Time itself ran tightly round me, curving in, I felt. Caught, pressurised, driven. I thought and thought about it – how it would be to be a man, and go a-courting to Hessy in the normal way. But there were so many variables. I poked the bump under my luxuriant hair. The Stone, which, if cut from my head, would challenge me to risk everything in its lottery – who could say what would happen? I dared not do it, even for her; for at least now I had a denied closeness which might change of its own accord. Whilst if I took the chance . . . what might I become?

I saw Mary Pierrepont after Christmas and her return from dreadful captivity in the country in the bosom of her family. We met for chocolate in Bull's.

'Since you've been away, Kit, I've called it all off. It's finished – a dead letter. How glad I am. I've been caught, pressurised, driven; I can't tell you how nauseous all these manipulating men make me. Do you want to know the details?'

'Of course.'

'I can tell you more now that I'm free of it. We've had to be oh so cautious, meeting here and there like conspirators, which I suppose we have been, and always at odds. He's . . . well, he is himself. Heavens, I don't even like the man, though he is very handsome. In his wig and so on. But I should like to live single – at least until *I* chose otherwise.' We sat in a nook, feeling very assured and worldly, though I never really enjoyed this chocolate so much; Swift couldn't abide it.

'Give me your details, dear,' I said. 'I'm all ears. My uncle's all eyes.'

'How do you mean?'

'Another time. I want to know about Edward.'

'I told you there were difficulties. They started two years ago. You know. He writes to me through my friend, his sister. He dictates! He almost twists her arm as she sits at her writing-desk. I'll have none of you, Sir, was my constant breastplate. I can like, I said, but as to love . . . well, how am I expected? Love arises from contact, communication. Hardly from a page of dictation.'

'I've heard how he began.'

'But I led him on. Did I lead him on? I was polite. One may write to a friend.'

'I heard you resolved.'

'Of course. You have your spies on his side, through the family. I did resolve. I shall never write to you again, was my text. My resolutions are seldom made, I told him, and never broken. No, I said to marriage. Now burn this letter. Which of course he didn't. And I wrote again, God help me. Why?'

'Why?' I said.

'Perhaps to keep my options open. I don't know. It's flattering to have these beaux dancing attendance. I have a number. It's all very silly, yet we do it. It's almost a game. Then he's laying siege to my father, and it becomes a matter between men. And this I very much don't like, as you've heard me say. For then the game's up. Suddenly you have to be very, very serious about every move you make.'

'I remember.'

'Ah, Kit. So love didn't go so easily for you, then. Everyone says it did . . . does. Everyone says you must be Venus's expert, to hold on to Halifax for a decade.'

'So that's what the town says, is it? An athlete.'

'You're my Exemplum of the Heart, my dear. Not of the couch. I know nothing of that. I'm not sure I want to. Of the Heart.'

'Am I such, Mary?'

'You two must love indeed. And I'm only beginning – and I've already made a near disaster of the whole . . . shooting match!'

'But you've got off.'

'Wait. My father became very grasping and wilful about a financial settlement. He expected Wortley to put up some sort of entail on the first child – I wasn't told the full implications except that it was an impossible condition. Poor Wortley is all very landed but his father's still alive. Mine's just cantankerous, or has something to hide, because on paper we're the ideal couple. On paper. Wortley believed he could manage him. Ha. He doesn't know my father. Well, he didn't. He does now.' She looked penetratingly at me. She had a strong energy about her. She continued her story. 'But he writes to me.'

'Who?'

'Wortley. Asking me to let him know what I'm worth, at marriage, Kit. I can't abide this. I wrote back that I found people in my kind of way are sold like slaves, and that I couldn't tell what price my master would put on me.'

'You're brave,' I said.

'But he asked again, and I just called everything off.'

'But you were together when I opened *Rinaldo*.'

'Together! Ha! So it may have seemed. We put on confident faces and spoke of an impending agreement. In fact we scurried from rendezvous to rendezvous. The Chapel – St James's. Miscellaneous shops as if by chance, Colman's Toyshop. He kissed me in Corticelli's Warehouse. Which was something, though I was in constant fear we'd be discovered and made the butt of gossip. My father's a very immoderate man, as you've seen. Lord Somers's sister's house. We met there, by design – unbeknown to the old lady, who thought we'd each turned up by some happy coincidence of young people.'

'I thought you'd met at Prue Steele's. I saw you there.'

'Well that was the best, because she's so utterly virtuous and the whole world knows it. So my father couldn't possibly object. But he's so jealous.'

'Your father?'

'Equally, but I meant Wortley. He can't bear another man near me.

I can't keep them off, Kit. Should I be impolite? And then that old goat Wharton.'

'Not Tommy still at it?'

'Dolly Walpole and I got cornered by him and some other ancient and disgusting Baron at my father's villa in Acton. In the grounds.'

'How far did he get?'

'Far enough. I say no more about that. I didn't like it, Kit. And Wortley became fiendish, as if it were our fault.'

'So now it's all over.'

'Yes. Oh, you know.'

We paid and left. Arm in arm we rambled off beyond the old City limit, on the path across frosted Moorfields. One of the steeples behind us rang the morning hour. From nearer at hand on our left came the dinning of a handbell. Soon, the open space ahead of us was peppered with a volley of small boys, running, chasing, shouting, and forming into impromptu games. Their exuberance gave forth streamers of smoky breath on the wintry air. They were just far enough away to stir spinsterly sentiment: 'Of course, there's the prospect of children,' sighed Mary. Our skirting of the play area sent us away to the right, nearer to the Hospital: Bedlam, where a short queue of visitors was waiting at the door.

'Have you been in?' she said.

'Never.'

'You amaze me. I think you should. It's very instructive.'

I came out shocked. I'd heard some society women went to see the pretty naked men that were displayed sometimes, tied amongst the grotesques. There were none today. It was a hell of severe order, because all social and personal barriers were plainly violated. The only security lay in ropes or chains. Poor masturbating wretches, mothers with children in the filthy straw, a well-clothed man who asked me again and again the way to Aylesbury, lost souls, lost eyes. A girl told me she'd fucking kill me if I didn't give her a cup of Gineva. She reminded me of Ruth. She was chained by the wrist to the far wall and stood barefoot in the circle of her own piss. From deep within the institution came the shouts of an unseen man, growling, roaring and begging them, whoever they were, not to do it. An attendant with a spade and a brush was cleaning the cold floor round a naked man. His device of attachment was a metal collar to

343

which several chains were linked and riveted to his portion of wall. He was one of the prime money-spinners of the hospital, which partly relied on this kind of self-funding enterprise. The families of sightseers would stand just out of his range, and then entice him to run at them in whatever way they could think. When he could bear the provocation no more he would charge his tormentors, drooling and spitting voiceless rage from between his broken, mouldering sets of teeth, clawing the air with his nails. To the length of the chain appropriate to that direction. Like a dog in a run, his collar would yank him back at his most expressive moment, choking him and dumping him horribly on the hard floor. He sat scratching at himself, his lips and face, as if puzzled by his own claws. The intensity of his emotion clearly overcame each time the lesson of his pain.

But most affecting of all, for me, was the sight of a boy of about eight. I say the sight, but he was partly obscured, held with his back to us at the rear of the main chamber. Held, I say. A rope to each wrist led away so that his arms were pulled wide. This was the mode of containment deemed appropriate by his superintendents for his treatment.

'It's a useful education for well-brought-up young women on the brink of marriage, don't you think?' said Mary.

The Boy

'He can't stay here, Catherine. This house is not a common asylum.'

'Not a common one, Uncle. The common asylum is where he came from. We are his unaccustomed refuge.'

'But I have work to do. How can I deal with . . . anything? How can I think, if there's a mad boy in the spare room?'

'Does he harm you, Sir? Does he make a noise? Does he beat at the walls or bite the floorboards? No, Sir. He cannot. Because he is restrained. And because he is mute.'

My uncle threw up his arms. 'I will not have this constant insolence from you! Catherine! Listen to me! Are you listening?'

'You don't have to shout!'

'Tomorrow I have Mr Cotes coming from Cambridge. Mr Cotes puts me to the question as to the syzygies and the quadratures. Mr Cotes has doubts about Proposition Thirty-Seven.' I knew Mr Cotes.

344

He was a young mathematician from Cambridge. He and my uncle were revising the *Principia* for its new edition. 'I am pressed, Catherine, on the matter of lunar theory. Some of the fruits of my calculations remain beyond the keyhole. And I have very little time. How will it seem if I keep a lunatic at hand? Already this German,' he couldn't bear to use the name Leibniz now, 'makes . . . insinuations.'

'How's that, Uncle? What insinuations?'

'Damned insinuations, Catherine! Damned libels from his damnable ignorance!'

'Yes but what are they?'

'Damn you, woman! About the theory of attraction at a distance.'

'And what does Dr Leibniz have to say about it?'

'That it's . . . unscientific!' He blurted this most telling, most personally wounding of insults with an intensity of rage that bordered on tears. I knew further that of all the cornerstones of his gravitational theory, Isaac was least happy about the seemingly magical Attraction at a Distance. 'He calls me an enthusiast! To him I seem as a distorted fanatic, who uses the fancy more than the reason. These are the insults I must bear! He couples my name with Fludd! A Fluddist! An idle dreamer. A chymical nonsense!'

'He doesn't say these things. It's all overheated. You're both mathematicians. He can't buck the calculations, and you both know it.'

'He does say them, Madam! Don't contradict me. He does! And he means it! He overturns my name. Cartesian! Spiritist! I work from experiment. I have always worked from experiment! I draw my conclusions from what is, not from what ought to be. I observe, try, hypothesise, calculate, observe again, re-try, check and re-check, before I formulate. I am not an incontinent dreamer! The whole premise of my endeavour is that bodies both large and particular are real, hard, impenetrable and observable. Do you understand me?'

'Yes.'

'Listen! Is this not good enough for him?' He took up the pages he was working on. 'Lastly, if it universally appears, by experiments and astronomical observations, that all bodies about the earth gravitate towards the earth, and that in proportion to the quantity of matter which they severally contain; that the moon likewise, according to the quantity of its matter, gravitates towards the earth; that, on the other hand, our sea gravitates towards the moon, and all the planets, one towards another; and the comets in like manner towards the sun; we must, in consequence of this rule, universally allow that all bodies whatsoever are endowed with a principle of mutual gravitation!'

'Very good.'

'Indeed. And Mr Cotes will mention the clock. Must I be accountable for everything?' He'd promised an expensive clock for the new Observatory at Trinity College, for they were trying to set the place up as a centre of scientific activity. He'd promised the clock four years ago and had done nothing about it.

I thought his temper had spent itself, and I was about to go on my way. But I was wrong.

'So you'll take that imbecile back where he came from. Mary and Tony have already been to me and complained. And you might consider staying there for a spell yourself, for you are become a thorn in my flesh.'

I was disconcerted by his sudden burst of cruelty. In a sense I was used to the rest, although it was much worse of late. But this went home.

'You took *me* in,' I said. 'And it was a Christian act. May I not perform one?'

'You'll not cast your sophistries upon *me*, Madam. You'll take the beast away *this* morning!'

'So you didn't take me out of kindness and charity after all. But more to control me, and to prevent the secret leaking of what you had *done*! And that's why you won't let me bring this child away. Because it reminds you of what I was! And *you* can't bear that!'

'Silence! How dare you beard me! You'll do as I say in *my* house. In my house I shall have whom I choose to have, and shall exclude whom I choose to exclude!'

'As in the Royal Society, when every moneyed dullard is admitted without question, until Mr Williams of the West Indies makes an application and is refused. Because he is the descendant of slaves! Because he doesn't exist against the dark panelling! Because he is an Oroonoko!'

'A what?'

'Never you mind! You wouldn't understand what slavery is. But I do.'

I believe we were both excessive here. But we were in deep.

'Go! Strumpet! I have nothing more to say to you! Leave my chamber! Leave it now!'

'I will go, tyrant! There is a mutual attraction called feeling! Called compassion! Which you know nothing of! I will go! Watch me go!'

In fact neither of us could bear the creature in the spare room. I'd engaged that morning a capable woman, a former wet nurse, Mrs Starr. She was to have sympathetic care of it . . . him. I went from my uncle's study up to the second floor. I peered through the keyhole. Mrs Starr was feeding him by the fire. I saw his tied hands; I couldn't see his face. I didn't want to. I didn't want to see the mess of food pap around his peeling lips. I didn't want to see the sharp yellow teeth they revealed.

But I'd had enough of my uncle. What kept me here? Habit.

It occurred to me that my house was likely to be ready: the Ranger's Lodge in Bushy Park, which Charles said he'd been having restored for me, and to which I had shut my mind, because it represented an acceptance of slave mistress status, albeit a very pampered one. My mind had been in London with Hessy always, my forbidden neighbour; not with Charles's rich gift, which I regarded as an irrelevance. What did I need a house in Bushy Park for? My dealings were in the city, and I lived with my uncle. Had Hessy and I been together, that would have been a different matter. But we were not. Swift had virtually taken up residence at Hessy's mother's because he was ill with the shingles, and also terrified that he would become meat for the Mohocks, the riotous sons of Whig grandees who were reputedly terrorising the streets, on the look-out for virtually anyone they could mutilate; and, in particular, turncoat pro-Tory pamphleteers with Irish connexions. Hessy was nursing him. I knew that. I was excluded. And I didn't enjoy his calls any more, either. And Anne Long had died in Norfolk. In debt.

St Martin's Street became by all this acutely painful to me. I left. I took Lucy'lizabeth, and the boy and his keeper, and Graveling and Pet, to Bushy Park. And I stayed there living on Charles's money and delight, now that his mistress had accepted his gift and was absolutely readily available to him whenever he was at Hampton, or almost anywhere, really.

Lucy'lizabeth luxuriated. Here, we hardly needed to keep up the deception. More and more he was hers, not mine.

347

We hired more help. And I lived suddenly in a walled garden, which contained, not a rose, but a fretted, speechless boy child confined to a padded room, where he would twist and tremble until we could make some progress with him. It was a room I hardly dared go in, because it was alive with panic. He looked as though he would bite me if he were released. I wondered whether I might one day speak with him.

Home Truths

It is all a blur now. Was this beautiful house really mine?

'It's certainly a start,' said Mrs Manley. She sat smoking her mixture in the light of the great first-floor windows. My blue drapes, vast drops of finery, framed the prospect: Spring light on the deer park. 'What would the Earl of Halifax say?' She mentioned Charles's full ennoblement with a certain irony. He had been an Earl since last year. And Viscount Sunbury.

'Would he have to know? Just now?' I said. I enjoyed the smoke in the air. It reminded me of a pleasanter London. 'Supposing I had a party of women friends? They would be just that. My companions. And why not? I wouldn't have to say on the gates *Ladies' Academy*.'

'A few people and it could be managed. Otherwise you would attract . . . undesirable comment. I'm not sure you wouldn't anyway. But why *should* it be done secretly? Why should it have to be an affair of dubiousness?'

'It shouldn't, I agree. But it could be a start. Don't call it secrecy. Call it privacy.'

'You'd have to buy books. Would Julius the Earl cough up for a library in his love nest? Forgive me. He's *your* lover. I spoke as if of mine. It may be you have tender feelings for him.'

'I don't see why he shouldn't buy me some books,' I said.

She thought for a minute, gazing out at the view, sucking on her pipe. 'I'll speak frankly. I believe it may all be too much *in his pocket*. I believe I'm more realistic than you. I believe – you'll forgive me speaking frankly – that you have an idea. But that it's lost somewhere in the clouds. Your New Atalantis. Yours flies. Mine is on the ground. My concept, I mean. I believe your motives are confused. Don't be offended. I mean this kindly. When I think of Astell, single-minded, in all senses of the word, with ten thousand pounds from the Queen. And she failed. And I see you, dear, looking twenty still, a bit of an opera singer, a bit of a philosopher, and somebody's honey-pot . . . there, I've hurt you, but I believe in facing the facts.'

'No. I'm not hurt,' I lied. I was hurt to see the reflection of myself. The trouble was I could add a lot of other bits to those she'd listed. And that was me: fragments. 'I do see what you're saying,' fighting back the blushes and the all too ready tears.

'You possibly don't realise what we're up against,' she said, politely looking away so that I could deal with my discomfiture. 'It's nothing to do with education, or the right to speech as such.' She took a deep, sighing breath. 'It's that a lot of people do a lot of rather sordid things to others in private. They want to keep doing it. I'd even say they *need* to keep doing it, or the world as they know it, and as we know it come to that, would fall to pieces. To sustain that need, they will invent, lie, cheat, suborn, torture and kill. On a very large scale, witness the war and the Church; or on a very small one, very domestically. Aristophanes, in the *Symposium* of Plato, referred to three types of lovers before the gods in their wrath split them into the human race as we know it: those that were originally double male, double female, and one of each. As you'll remember, these witty spherical creations rolled and sported about with their two heads, all the livelong day. After their division, they are forever in quest of the true partner, from whom they were so cruelly and casually split. But I'd put it to you Mrs Barton, that this pretty and light-hearted proposition has its negative. That we may also be considered, as a result of I know not what division or original sin or punishment or whatever, those who are enslaved and used, those who enslave and use, and those who are both tyrannical and violated according to circumstances and occasion. From what hard, impenetrable bodies these Types might have been created I don't care to speculate. Hard, unlovely particles appearing and splitting, combining and impinging on each other, without remorse. Without ceasing. Without caring. Two paradigms then of generation and change: one of love, and the other of force, each with its capacity for multiplication – its chemistry, you might say. Each having within, its antipathies and attractions: its genders and its neuter. Each operating on us, little players, pulling us, pulling us always to choose this way, or that. The Royal Society, as we know it, is of course wedded to one side. And what you're intending to revive . . . ' – she knocked her ash out – 'is, at least in my heart, on the other.'

There was a hiatus in the room. I adjusted to what my ears had just received. My world, my universe, disclosed itself before my inward eye, laws and loves, and the popping, splitting, desiring and combining of original spheres, small and large, like a foam of bubbles. What were the ethics of my associations, my projections?

'I don't know what to say,' I said, still sniffing. There was no way that I could voice the vision her words had occasioned. I felt grounded. 'I'm useless. You're quite right. If it were easy, tougher, cleverer women than I would already have done it. I've been a fool to think of it.'

'No, darling. You're not useless. You're not a fool. Try, by all means. But you must see what's what. It's painful.'

'It is. It's very painful, when there's so much suffering; and one can do nothing. You have given me a difficult gift; I recognise it but I don't rejoice at receiving it. I wish . . . ' my voice tailed off. 'Have you seen Swift?'

'He's full of cataplasms and cures. He's a mess, and down. All Winter. And it's been so cold this year. He meets that Vanhomrigh girl at Barber's house – I mean his other ménage, not ours. They drink their coffee like a couple of virgins, which they are. Whereas we *kept* women . . . may drink whatever we like.' I took this as a request for something stronger, and poured her some mixture in which Gineva figured quite prominently. Then I poured one for myself. Ah, *lascia ch'io pianga*.

Taking advantage of the fine weather, the Londoners came down in droves to stroll under the long avenue of chestnuts in flower and to picnic in the park. Was it a dream, or did I walk naked with my shadowy backer in my private enclosure, bathed in sunlight and celebrated with the first flowers of my Dutch garden? Had my Stone-slowed heart-rate and my abstraction from normal time so sensitised me that I could partake of consummation with another world? I rehearsed for a new opera I was given: Ofelia in Gasparini's *Amleto*, an uncomfortable version of *Hamlet*. I rehearsed naked at the instrument outdoors, strummed by the intimate breeze as my backer plucked a lute. I sent my delicious stream of sound out like a transcendental bird. And did I dream it that my backer put down his lute and all his supple amorousness pressed against my spine, my shoulderblades, my buttocks, the backs of my thighs, my tendons; that his hands roved the front of my body; that his kisses stirred the flesh of my neck, so that my singing drowsed into the most sensual of whispers? What was this dazed eroticism, this languor, composed of butterfly brushes and the moistness of folded skin, the scent of flowers, the scent of humanness, the firmness of a rod of flesh, the drops of liquor on my wheaten, sun-warmed belly, like alchemical *lac virginis*?

I said: 'How can I believe what you have always tried to tell me? Where is the proof? Such things could not be concealed. I cannot believe you. Surely it would come to light. It would be in the language. It would figure in speech, in writing.' In reply he raised his fingers to his mouth and squeezed his lips shut. But I turned my regard aside.

Well. How sad I was. How fulfilled and how frustrated. Outside, the world flitted away. I had still given no name to that creature in the secure room, whom it almost hurt to look upon.

Mrs Starr told me he was making progress. I wondered what that meant.

Mary Pierrepont came down.

'My father has moved against me, Kit. It's a great betrayal. I'm to marry.'

'Not Edward.'

'Not Edward. Edward vows he'll live a bachelor. I've given him no reason to change his mind.'

'Who, then?'

'A man I hate. A horrid gawkish monster of a man. I'm absolutely wretched, Kit. What shall I do?'

'Is it anyone I know?' I put my arm round her and attempted to poke a tissue of fabric towards her eyes, where the main upset was centred.

'His name, Kit,' she drew a deep breath through her tears, 'is Clotworthy Skeffington.' She choked out the rending sobs like great guffaws. 'He has a vast deal of property in Ireland and a character entirely consistent with his name. And I must have him in three months because my father says so, and I don't know what to do.' She howled into my shoulder. 'I will not be poked about by that grotesque, that gargoyle of a man. Mrs Clotworthy Skeffington. No! I will not! Kit, I don't want to be poked about by anyone. I'm not ready, Kit. And I can't see that I ever shall be; not at this rate, Kit. Not at this rate.'

Summer. Mary Pierrepont eloped with Edward. She wrote:

Kit, what could I do? I was sent to Acton last month. My father had got the wedding clothes already ordered; fabric patterns etc awaited me. I was about to be dressed in a fait accompli. *I was desperate. What a monster he is. Who do I mean? I'm not so sure myself. Trapped, Kit. Horribly entangled. I wrote to Wortley.* Take me away! *Much more to that effect. He still thought there was some way to do it above board. He had the fond belief common to so many men that another man will join him in the rational world at the end of everything, because he is a man; so he continued to negotiate over the price. Fool! I pressed him, Kit, but what could I do? He stood to lose ground; I stood to be legally ravished at my father's behest. Do you love me after all? I wrote. Do you love me enough to take me with nothing? Are you sure you will love me for ever? Shall we never repent? He said he would do it. Very well, I wrote. My resolution is taken. Love me and use me well. I drove off with my seconds on August the seventeenth. He followed on horseback, to meet us at the agreed inn. On the way he was taken for a highwayman. I would have laughed had I not been so wrought. I can hardly laugh now. We are married. I shall not belong to Clotworthy, and Edward is the happiest man in the world. Well we all know what that is a euphemism for. When events permit us to return to London I long to see you. You are always in the thoughts of her who is now*

Mary Wortley Montagu

Anne came to stay, and while she was with me Swift flitted in for a visit, which, like the Vanhomrigh calls, he didn't record that night in his scribble to My Dears in Dublin; because, he said, Stella and Mrs Dingley would not understand his association with a couple of beautiful, notorious actresses. He wasn't convincing. He couldn't understand anything that was going on in his life at the time. I wondered if he were compelled to press his craving for sexual contact, for love, right up to a certain limit, which he'd approach more and more carefully as he got near it – almost by infinitesimal degrees – in case by going suddenly too far he found himself declared.

Compromised. In a new and threatening world, from which he'd have to escape by being cruel and puritanical and insulting.

'Absolutely harmless as *we* know between us, Ladies. We don't stroll naked in the garden, do we?'

'Break off, Swift,' I said. 'We're neither the women we were. You hurt us, though you don't know it. We're small and vulnerable. You squash us with your great, thoughtless play.' I didn't know whether to hate him for taking my darling away from me, to tease her to death for foolish love of him – or to be glad that she would never melt in his arms as she had in mine. I didn't *know* quite what I was saying, nor what I wanted to say. The words just kept coming out. 'You are a walking destruction to our sex,' I told him, meaning it seriously. But of course he took it lightly and held up his hands. 'Harmless, Kit.'

'Swift, you're not harmless. You are more cruel than a libertine. In fact you *are* a libertine; but you're a libertine of the mind.'

'Kit! Why're you so hard on the man?' said Anne. 'Oh, but I know why, of course.'

'Why, then?' Swift asked. 'I don't.'

'Nor shall you,' said Anne.

But I couldn't leave him alone. I wanted to hurt him. 'You think there's safety in numbers, don't you, Swift? Two women. Always two women.'

'What's the meaning of that, Kit? I should be very safe then with the two of you. I'd hoped you'd invite me to an excursion, not roast me today. I was looking forward to your company. In fact I believe that to drift upon the river with my two friends this afternoon would be the nearest thing to heaven that I should achieve in this world. It would be as much as I'm allowed. As much happiness as I could bear. I have a proposal, Kit.'

'Have you indeed?'

'I've written a letter to Harley – my Lord of Oxford. *A Proposal for Correcting, Improving, and Ascertaining the English Tongue.*' He pulled a printed pamphlet from his pocket. 'I'm proposing to set up an Academy for the fixing of correct English. On the model of the French Academy.' He flicked it through and read:

In order to reform our language, I conceive, my Lord, that a free judicious choice should be made of such persons, as are generally allowed to be best qualified for such a work, without any regard to quality, party, or profession. These, to a certain number at least, should assemble at some appointed time and place, and fix on rules by which they design to proceed . . . The persons who are to undertake this work will have the example of the French before them to imitate, where these have proceeded right, and to avoid their mistakes. Besides the grammar part, wherein we are allowed to be very defective, they will observe many gross improprieties, which however authorised by practice, and grown familiar, ought to be discarded. They will find many words that deserve to be utterly thrown out of our language, many more to be corrected, and perhaps not a few long since antiquated, which ought to be restored on account of their energy and sound.

I felt mortified and didn't know how to respond. Then I said quietly: 'Will there be any women eligible to contribute?'

I believe he thought I was joking. In any case he went on: 'I'm taken to task by a redoutable old Whig, no doubt still smarting from the upset in Government.' He pulled out a pamphlet from a different pocket. 'You must hear what he says, among what amounts to a scurvy personal attack:

The Doctor may as well set up a Society to find out the Grand Elixir, the Perpetual Motion, the Longitude, and other such discoveries, as to fix our language beyond their own times . . . This would be doing what was never done before, what neither Roman *nor* Greek, *which lasted the longest of any in its purity, could pretend to.*

'Don't you think it a reply of spite?'

'My God, Swift, you are a monstrous hypocrite,' I said and turned away to hide my rage. Rage I think at the fact that he could put up his stupid scheme so easily, and I could not put up mine.

'Anne?' I said.

'I'd like to go, Kit. It's a wonderful day.'

It was a beautiful September afternoon. I agreed to the little excursion. I have the memory of it. The water was thick and filmy; its surface was jealous of its drops. Swift at the oars was almost stirring it rather than rowing in it. And where the lowered sun caught the surface it was as if gold were melted upon glass. We, Anne and I, lay in the stern on cushions, holding our parasols. In his shirt and waistcoat, he sat in the middle of the little boat. Handsome when at some physical thing.

'Ain't I safe with you girls?'

'You're an Irish flirt.'

'You're safe with one of us,' said Anne.

But my words pulled me along. 'Listen, Swift, my dear. We've known each other a good while. I, who once killed a man – for you remember what I told you years ago, at our first meeting – hold you in the palm of my hand. For you can't escape now.'

'Kit?'

'You're our prisoner out here, Swift. If I did something terrible out here on the river, you couldn't run away.'

'You unnerve me, Kit. Have you something in mind? I hope not,' said Anne. But Swift was focused on me, smiling his charming smile, yet a little bleached about the eyes suddenly.

'And you, innocent Dr Scribbler, would be wrecked.'

'I could swim, Kit,' he said.

'And leave me to drown? My clothes all torn open?' I put my hand on the top of my bodice as if to rip it down. He wiped the sweat off his brow.

'The curse of Adam,' he said, half-joking.

'I've never liked being a third person,' said Anne.

I held my moment a fraction longer, then gave it up. 'You're right, dearest Anne. I've been unpleasant, and inhospitable; to you both. It's just that when the chance opens for wielding just the smallest bit of power, then it's a hard temptation to resist. And that's our function, isn't it, as women? For if we don't resist temptation, how shall the men?'

'I've done my best, Kit, to be a man who does resist temptation. Why even at the moment . . . '

'Don't go on, Swift. I should be very sad to hear what it is you might say. Let's leave it that you think you're resisting temptation, while I think you're leading someone astray.'

'But I'm not. I assure you I never . . . I have no intention . . . '

'Precisely. But we'll say no more. And Hessy . . . '

'Kit. It's none of your business,' Anne said.

'Will you marry her? And make love to her? And give her children?'

'Kit. You've hurt the man.'

'Yes,' was all I could say. For we were all caught, perhaps. And it was just cruel to hurt him so.

Later I took them to see the boy. We led him out with us into the garden, where he pulled his clothes off and climbed trees and was generally difficult and unhygienic. We helped him to eat and talked to Mrs Starr about his progress. One had to guess what he wanted, what he was thinking. Perhaps he had to guess what we thought too. Sometimes I did feel, uncannily, as though I understood his mind, and that we shared things in a reserved, non-real space, where communication was an instantaneous image. At others he was a horrible blank. He wasn't utterly voiceless. On rare occasions he babbled. 'Ba . . . Ber . . . Ba . . . Bububub . . . ' He could spend short intervals without restraint, but he didn't succeed that afternoon because Anne and Swift were strangers to him, and he couldn't trust them, I think. Even now, you see, I refer to him obliquely, as if he hardly had a place in my life at that time, which of course isn't true. He was central. He lived in the centre of the house. He took up a good deal of my attention. But he's hard to bring face-on to the eye of my memory.

So his first summer with me passed; and even his first Christmas has left no trace on my mind, it seems, though I would like to think we made an effort.

The Demon

You could almost feel the ice clouds, rare sun-stretching filaments high up in the very pale blue. The park ran off to meet it, sheep-strewn – distant whitenesses clustered on the woodland. It was a clear, cold, privileged universe; the breeze which touched our faces the only moving thing.

Charles and I turned back to the Palace's East Gate.

'That has it, Kit,' he said. 'That is the statement.'

The gate was crisp and yellow in the Winter light, being made from ton upon ton of the distinctive local stone. The wall was huge, modern, with exact lines. It could have marked the boundary of an empire. It could be the efficient wall of a confident, technological city.

Hardly an entrance, more a massive wedge of power, the gate, with its single Roman arch, awaited our return.

It was merely a return to breakfast. We didn't choose to take it yet, but stood admiring John Vanbrugh's dream. Then we turned North and began a wide circle in order to catch this clear morning's effect on the front elevation. A mere quarter of a mile away to our right there fell a steep local abyss which the River Glyme had taken centuries to wear out of the prospect. Now a colossal *Grand Bridge* was planned over this tiny stream, giving it airs to think itself a Thames.

We walked down to the site for the bridge, treading carefully the damp grazing; I lifting my Winter skirts with both hands while he steadied me with his arm. Then we gazed back along the planned Great Approach. If the Palace ever got finished and roofed over it would be unequalled in all the land. In the centre stood what looked like the temple of some god of power, with a kind of shallow double triangle above its columns – an enormous inflation of our classical façade at Abbs Court. From either side of the temple spread wings in an impressive symmetry. The mode was always imperial, but full of interest and detail in the modern taste. It was breathtaking and pleasing, yet a little frightening for the scale of its statement.

'Was Blenheim so great a victory?' I asked Charles.

'It seems to have been,' was his cautious answer. We strolled up towards the main gate and the enormous piazza which the two wings had already swept forward to embrace. One could see the concept of the plan.

'Then why has Marlborough left the country?'

'Oh, Kit, I can't talk to you about the details, you know that; and yet I'm reluctant to fob you off with the standard lines we release to the town.' He seemed on the point of further speech, but hesitated. We reached the wrought iron of the gate, and stood, looking in. He made up his mind. 'To have to be restrained about the secrets of State in front of nearly everyone – to have to guard my back even among my lords of the Junto, my co-mates in enterprise as it were; this is a great strain. It's policy and it's my oath, but it's a monstrous load to bear after all these years. And it seems to say you're nothing but a mistress – while to me you are so much more than that. More probably than a wife. There are times when I long for a confidante of the deepest heart. In my work as much as anything.'

I was touched by these words, indeed so suddenly touched that I might have started an argument, had it not been for the appearance of a solitary figure from the scaffolded West wing. It was a woman. Elegantly dressed in a fur mantle, but tiny from this distance, with her skirts sweeping the stone of the piazza, she moved from the untenanted shell of that part of the building and out across the space, heading straight for the occupied East wing where she lived. Indeed it could be none other than our hostess, for the place was deserted of everyone except our respective security staffs. There were no builders, masons, sawyers, plasterers, furnishers, decorators, nor contractors' delivery wagons. Neither were there the family and parties, the philosophers and politicians, writers and beauties who ought in the spirit of the design to have peopled this expanse on a bright Winter's morning; standing in knots and poses, perhaps; throwing up the scale of the creation with their little spots of colour and dazzle; taking the beauty of the crisp hour. I was, of course, fond in my imagining that society folk would get out of bed at this time merely to paint my scene. But the Palace was conspicuously empty. Not even Arthur Maynwaring, the Duchess's creature of information, was to be found closeted with his helpers and his lists amid the labyrinth of part-finished rooms, since he had died the previous November and left her disconnected. And the security people were discreet, as is the custom of such folk, employed more seriously by more and more people these days, since the attempt on Harley's life.

The lone woman made her way to the centre, looking neither to right nor left. Her movement was slightly constrained. We saw what it was; she was weighed down with two slim sacking bags, one in each hand.

'Well!' said Charles.

'What's she doing?'

'It looks like money.'

She continued across, and went into the East wing. Charles returned to contemplation of the Palace. 'It's an Aeneid in stone.'

I reflected that from my vague knowledge of court intrigue it was an Aeneid complicated in every respect by the figure we'd just seen, who served as an amalgam of the roles of Creusa, Dido, Lavinia, the Cumaean Sybil and, most possibly, Emperor Augustus's wife Livia.

'Why does she want *me* here?' I said to Charles.

'She wants, suddenly, to make up friends with me again,' he said.

*

'If they don't want it. If they can't be bothered to turn up for it.' Another Restoration baby, whose aliases had at one time or another been Sarah Jennings, Sarah Churchill, Lady Marlborough, and now the First Duchess of Marlborough, aged fifty-two and still handsome, dumped a further two sacks of gold coins on the heap in the East wing. Her fingers were white, and the backs of her hands were mottled red and blue from the cold outside.

Charles laid a hand on hers. 'They've all gone away, Sarah. It's too late.'

'Last night before you came I took it all over the other side to be ready in the morning. Now I've brought it all back.'

'There was no need, dear. No need.'

'You tell me of need? I never wanted the custody of this . . . bloody box. I never wanted to live in a monument. I'm not supposed to have to pay for it. It's supposed to be a gift. But I'm not having them all traipsing up to my front door with their damned boots on. I'm leaving, dear,' she said to me. 'I've done my bit. I'm going to join the King over the water.'

I must have looked aghast. I couldn't decide whether she was mad or starkly sane.

She laughed cruelly. 'No, trollop. My husband. Marlborough. He might as well be King for all that debilitated invert can do now. He might as well . . .'

'I'm sorry . . . ?' I said, not sure whether I'd just heard treason.

'What have you got to be sorry for? By God, don't expect politeness from me, girl. Don't expect me to put on a false face. I've done enough of that. I've done enough of smiling and simpering for the sake of this damned nation. It's a nation of fools. A nation that at the drop of a hat will forget everything that's advantaged them. A collection of narrow-minded wastrels and grubbers in the soil who will believe the most arrant pap. Low, pandering Tory pap. Swift pap.' She looked fiercely at me. 'Why your *friend* doesn't come out with it and admit he's a flagrant Jacobite at heart, I don't know. And they believe him! As soon as we need a hint of intellectual resolution and a grain of memory to pull us through, the British voter puts his head in his native sand, opens his eyes and sees the spark of God in the House of Stuart. What a country! Excessive religious preoccupation. You know what that's a sign of?'

'No, Madam.'

'No. I don't suppose you do. But it's not even that. This is probably the most irreligious country in the world. No. It's a preoccupation with damned mythology, with superstition and bloody King Arthur. I want to know what Charles sees in you, that keeps him obsessed, I suppose the polite word is *in love*.' She searched at Charles penetratingly. Then back to me. 'What is it you have to offer, besides a bosom and a vacuum? Oh and a voice, I suppose.'

'Sarah.' Charles attempted to soften her and protect me.

'Oh, don't touch me. I suppose you realise, *Mistress* Barton, that you have between your legs the first mind in Europe.'

I looked back at her, interested. Women didn't frighten me.

'Where did all this come from?' She gestured around the little ante-room in the East wing, as if by doing so to include the whole edifice. 'Eh?'

'From the quarry, Madam, and the labour of men,' I ventured.

'Labour of men. Two a penny. Ball through the chest. Chain-shot. Take his legs off! That's what my husband says in his sleep. He knows nothing of it. He's the most equable and conciliatory of men: rational, diplomatic, brilliant, thorough, daring. It's as if nothing touches him, by day. But at night he fills the bedroom with bloodshed, maiming and the terror of horses. Come the morning? Nothing again. I've spent my winters lying through Blenheim, Ramillies, Oudenarde and all the carnage of Malplaquet. And so I'm not the sort of Whig who'll tell you that modern warfare is relatively surgical compared to the all-out struggle in Germany fifty years ago. Nor will Charles. Will you, Charles?'

'I see no alternative to it, Sarah. But it's very regrettable. A very extreme diplomacy for extreme times.'

'As always. So don't talk to me about men, Mistress Barton. I know more about them than you do. Expendable. Replaceable in one night. One night. Less. It only takes a minute to get one. And a lifetime to lose one.' Her mood veered suddenly into what looked like pain – or painful anger. I presumed she thought of her dead son. But she turned back to me. 'Like you, dear. Replaceable in one night. Lips and a bosom are two a penny. Aren't they? Grinling Gibbons.' She seemed lost in the contemplation of something, and then drifted out of the ante-room. Charles looked at me; we felt obliged to follow.

There was some furnishing in the block. And some pictures on the walls. It seemed partially inhabited at least, although it was well

360

known that the Duchess much preferred her house at St James's, which she'd had Wren put up for a fraction of the cost of this, with despatch, and as different as possible. A servant was polishing something. She, the servant, looked small and lost.

'It came from Charles,' the Duchess shouted over her shoulder, from well ahead of us. Her voice echoed.

We caught her up in the great hall – more like a great forum, for it was open to the sky still. It was curious to find ourselves in the cold suddenly, without going out, and amongst the accumulation of builder's materials and waste.

'*I* don't know,' whispered Charles, in response to my glance of enquiry.

Sarah stood in the middle of the space. She held her arms out, like a French dancer, and looked up to the sky. Then she hugged her arms in to herself and seemed to twirl round suddenly. Dangerous, unpredictable, difficult. Electric, somehow, in her sinewy middle age.

'It came from the brain. It came from *his* brain, you idle girl. Did you know that? Do you realise whom you stand beside? Is this country not now the richest in the alliance? Why? Because we understand what you can do with money. Money is power. And what does that tribade pudding at Kensington do with it? She has an overweening ape by the name of Vanbrugh put up the biggest building in the land, in the middle of nowhere. What a Tory vision! What an idleness! And then, halfway through its edifications, she casts off the reasonable friends who've made her what she is, and pulls the damned cash. If I'm to have it I may as well have it finished, don't ye think? Eh?'

I said: 'Indeed,' but I don't think she heard. I was interested to see the special regard between Charles and her, though. I thought back to our difficult period, when he'd spent some time with her in St Albans after her mourning for her son. Had he done more than just comfort her? And she'd been so spiteful to him ever since.

Now she didn't really address us as fellow creatures. But neither would she let us go, as we discovered as the day wore on. What drove her now? What did she want from us?

After luncheon: 'So I'm going to join my husband on the Continent. You'll be glad to see me go, no doubt, Madam,' she said to me.

'Not at all, your Grace,' I replied.

'No one on our side will rejoice at your going, Sarah,' said Charles with gallantry. 'You are, and always have been, the rose on our banner. The times are all crooked. We've been out-Harleyed. To talk still of a weak peace at almost any price will be to throw away everything, and yet they come near to carrying it. People seem to be prepared to welcome in tyranny simply to lessen their taxes.'

'I speak the truth to people's faces. I don't mince and flatter. I can't abide these fawning hypocrites. If they don't like it they can get out of my way. Especially if they're brainless, unlettered, unread sycophants who are prepared to fondle and faddle their way into Britannia's bedcovers. Who have no regard for the integrity of the State. Which, Mrs Barton, you'll be aware, we call our Common-wealth, Mrs Barton, which happens to be a direct translation of the Roman word Republic, Mrs Barton, which in itself renders the Greek *Polity*. You're aware of whom I refer to, Mrs Barton?'

'No, Madam. I have no idea. I thought you spoke in the general way.'

'I refer to my cousin Mrs Hill, Harley's creature of the royal bed-chamber, whose ordinary charms have caught Her Majesty's special favour for the last years, and who has broken up, come between, two women who were the most sensitive of friends from childhood. A woman whom I, God rot me, placed. Out of my very charity. From childhood, Mistress. No, Charles, I speak what I wish now to whom I wish. I don't care for this heartless, thankless country any more. I don't care for the bloody place. Cold. Cold-hearted. Consoling her ungrateful ruin of a body with a heartless chamber-maid. A female gallant, Mrs Barton. While her wretched husband loved a sailor.'

By degrees as we went on the Duchess's preoccupations became more explicitly focused on the royal partners, as they were before Prince George died. She had firm evidence, she said, that the Prince and her brother-in-law, Admiral George Churchill, had been up to dark deeds. Her fine mind and political convictions were irremedi-ably sexualised, and something compelled her, under the guise of Party enthusiasm, to tell a story. It was a story full of intensity, full of betrayal, of power and pain.

She followed us into the bedroom even, when the evening had passed at cards and 'conversation' in front of a poor fire.

'The die's cast. So what need now for caution and policy? You are my friends. You're my political allies. Despite my sharp tongue,

Charles and I have a special alliance, Mistress Barton, which I trust you'll respect. He's much undervalued in fact by the rest of the Junto, who little realise what an intellectual giant they have among them. Charles may know that as to the Continent we aren't merely slinking off. Marlborough has gone to raise a new alliance with a new purpose.'

'Has he indeed, Sarah?' Charles could barely smother his absolute yawn.

'What d'ye think his plan is? Eh? What d'ye think Our plan is?'

'He offers his skills and service to the Emperor Leopold? Or simply Hanover? The last time I spoke with him he told me he longed to retire here and wished it were finished. Now perhaps it would make sense to become involved diplomatically with the Elector in Hanover.'

'Tame, Charles. Tame. D'you think that's all we're made of? He's going to raise an invasion force. He's going to return favour for favour to the gouty and sullen Anna, who is always indisposed to her best friend, her true friend, and sensible guide. He's going to teach this country a lesson. And when he does it, I shall be with him. I want to be sure I can count on your support. That's why I've asked you here, Charles. Pax. I want to call Pax with you.'

'Sarah. I assure you that whatever you intend to do you'll have my full support. I must beg you to excuse me. The journey. Tiredness overcoming . . . '

She only left when we'd actually started undressing.

The Platonick Lady

'Did you hear what you just said? What you agreed to?'

'No,' said Charles. 'What was it?'

The bedroom was cold. We huddled down in the bed.

'Only to support an invasion attempt to secure the Protestant succession by overthrowing the Queen.'

'Oh God. Did I? Well, never mind.'

'Never mind, Charles? It's high treason. It's death.'

'Well she's leaving in February, she says.'

'But aren't you worried? Supposing she repeats . . . '

'It's of no matter. Nothing she says has weight any more with the

Queen. She's cast her off absolutely. And I realise I needn't . . . *We* five of the Junto needn't worry about the Queen's intentions. Needn't have worried. We've all been played more than we realised. And if we'd realised we were being played by a firm, rational woman we needn't have been so excessive in our pressure on her. And so we shouldn't have needed to've been played. There we are: hindsight.'

'You mean the Queen?'

'I mean the Queen. Everybody in the country thinks she's wonderful, but of course that's what they're supposed to think. Like Elizabeth. It consists in the fabrication of a person – a *persona* – through the press, the pageantry and so on. Whereas in government . . . But I mustn't talk about it, of course. State secrets. I believe Sarah'll take all that money across again before she goes to sleep.' He said it to my ear as if he were feeling amorous.

'Do you think so? Is she mad?'

'It isn't madness as I'd imagine it. It's another thing. A compulsion. She's driven. She can also be quite different. It is true they're probably the richest couple in Europe. Or will be if the peace proves a sound thing.'

It was two years since we'd been in bed together. Despite the habit of sharing and preparation which Lucy'lizabeth and I had cultivated into a species of second nature, I was aware that his actual intimate presence was something I still felt very unsure of. I found myself wide awake and nervous. I had to move, as if by moving constantly I should be protected.

Yet I'd changed. I was aware I'd changed. Maybe my shell had hardened since I'd lost Hessy. Part of me was cynical enough, Roman enough if you like, to be prepared to try the act with him again, as a throw of some sort. At this stage of the game. I'd thought I might be able to during the day. But here, when it came to it, I couldn't. I knew I didn't love him and couldn't. I could never feel for him what I'd felt for Hessy. Possibly not for anyone.

I found myself agitated. I had to talk.

'I wish you *would* tell me these things. I'd like to know you after all this time. So much of you is your work. You say I'm almost more than a wife to you. Perhaps you'll believe at least that I'm not a French agent or intelligencer. I believe it would do you good, and bring us together. Even more.'

'Every man desires a true friend at last,' he whispered. 'I should like to unburden myself. If I were a Papist I could go to my ghostly confessor. As I'm an economist I have none such.'

'Tell me then.'

'You must not repeat.'

'I shall not. I swear. You were going to speak of the Queen.'

'Indeed. Everyone thought it was a disaster when King Billy died. A woman on the throne; and a Stuart to boot. We thought it'd be a lethal combination.'

'We?'

'The Junto. And most of the Party. Particularly as she didn't like us. We thought she'd be a pawn of the Tories, and most dangerously the Jacobite Tories. All this you know. But we had Sarah. The Queen doted on her. Through Sarah we could have Marlborough some of the time. Through husband and wife we at least knew what Godolphin was up to because of Henrietta Churchill's marriage. So even when all five of us were excluded from Cabinet we could operate to a strategy of some sort. What we dreaded was that she should be otherwise influenced.'

'Harley,' I said.

'Exactly. What was Tricky Robin up to? How much was he played by the Jacobite wing of the Tories? How much did the Queen's sex, her family background and her natural prejudices open her to the Tories through Harley?'

'And Abigail Hill.'

'And there we have the central nonsense, my dear. That our strongest voice with the Queen, our most persistent advocate, turns out to have been our most distorted ear. Sarah's insistence that the Queen was in love with Abigail played us into Harley's hands, for we had to put on so much pressure in favour of the war because we thought we couldn't trust the Queen to make rational judgements. As you know from reports, I myself have made the most aggressive speeches in the Lords. We came to seem and feel like mad dogs almost – I mean politically. Wharton's a mad dog in himself anyway. The strain is of having to play a role all the time, and men are being killed. Well perhaps the war was a necessity, and has secured the peace of the realm. But it has to be brought to proper terms, which may not happen. But I was talking of the acting. You know from the theatre, my darling, how exhausting it is to take on another person. Imagine having to do that all the time. Ah, it's such a relief to talk – I mean to be able to tell you straight out that I'm not such a strident villain in truth as I have been forced by events to become.'

'I never thought you were, Charles. But I'm glad you feel better.' And truly I was. 'So the Queen hasn't just been a cipher.'

'Things come at last into perspective. Sarah spoke of the Republic. I believe her to have taken her Plato very much to heart.'

When I grasped it, I was shaken by the audaciousness of the thought he'd just seeded in my mind. Things whirred and clicked into place. 'You don't mean Sarah saw herself as one of the . . . philosopher rulers.'

'I do. She may have seen *herself* so. What *we* see is an oligarch, almost a tyrant, though powerless for the moment. She's an aristocrat, but both she and the Duke have risen from a degree of obscurity; she may have been partly justified in seeing herself as one of Nature's promotions. She had legendary beauty, a Platonic quality. She had . . . has great intelligence. She's very well read and educated. And she prides herself on speaking the absolute truth. As she perceives it. What a laudable guide to the launch of her younger and duller friend who happens, against the odds, to become Queen. If I'd been her I should have found it hard to believe that my guardianship had not been specially ordained by some enlightened Wisdom. And when Blenheim occurred, and Europe was saved, and we were somehow almost magically central to Continental wealth and authority, could she resist the belief that she'd been right all along? Wouldn't she become increasingly bitter and furious that she was heeded less and less? How did it serve *our* Party that she should invent smears on the Queen and engineer blackmail threats against her? What no one knew was that the person who had no axe to grind was the most Platonic of all – probably having no inkling of the academic tradition.'

'You mean the Queen herself?'

'If you lose eighteen children and are still sane after your beloved husband dies, your closest friend tries to destroy your reputation and your body attacks you with acute pain year after year, then you are remarkable. She was stripped bare of all advantage; there was nothing to do except her duty as she saw it; and that's what she did, instinctively in terms of the Platonic mean. I remember it from school, dearest. Dr Busby made me learn it by heart: A man must take with him into the world below an adamantine faith in truth and right, that there too he may be undazzled by the desire of wealth or the other allurements of evil, lest, coming upon tyrannies and similar villainies, he do irremediable wrongs to others and suffer yet worse himself; but let him know how to choose the mean and avoid extremes on either side, as far as possible not only in this life but in all that which is to come. For this is the way of happiness.'

'This is what a woman has done, then. The very same woman who goes hunting in Windsor Great Park in her little one-horse wheel-chair coach. Swift told me. And she's called Mrs Morley.'

'And Sarah is Mrs Freeman. These are their homely alter egos. But Queen Anne has always been firm to the Protestant succession. Her overtures to the Jacobites were tactical. This is a thing I should like to have known.'

'But are you a Platonist in government, then Charles? How lovely it is to talk to you so fully. As if we weren't bound by man and mistress at all. This moderation is how *you* believe we should live, Charles, so very cautiously and philosophically – like modest scientists?'

'No, darling. It's perhaps how Queen Anne has been a great monarch. But I . . . I'm a politician through and through.'

I slept in his arms knowing that if I'd never been a lover to him, I had performed the office of a friend at last.

The Coup

The pages of my life flicked by. Some brought scenes that cast us in the appearance of a family.

'Come with me, Rinaldo!' It was Charles who'd named him. They went off in the park with a huntsman and an apprentice. Naldo limped off on his weak legs, grinning, and doing his best to race away with the others after the dogs. They had some errand with hares and rats and squirrels. Yes, I shall have to tell you about him, or you'll think I led an enchanted life in my bower. We did travel about, somewhat, in the course of our living – as much as you would. Occasional visiting; sometimes at Abbs Court together. Sometimes I had an engagement to sing in London, or at a country house or rich person's villa. I did go back to London to stay with Mary or with

Anne. I didn't communicate with my uncle, nor he with me. Thus by not writing we wrote each other out of our lives.

Swift left in 1713. Back to Dublin, Dean of Dublin, not Wells, disappointed, exiled or running away. Mary's father, now elevated as the Earl of Kingston for some reason, made a match whose hypocrisy took the breath away. Having looked for some time with an eager eye on Belle Bentinck, the beautiful daughter of King Billy's fancy man, he actually married her; so that Mary, disinherited, had a stepmother who was only a year older than herself. The European war clicked to a zero with the Peace of Utrecht. Though Charles grew deeply agitated and very conspiratorial with his allies concerning the state of things at home, I chose not to face the prospect of civil war which was a grim rumour on many people's lips. I had my own grim rumour to contend with, which was confirmed by a letter from Anne – that Hessy, her mother having died, had taken her sister with her in pursuit of Swift, and gone off to Ireland. Ostensibly she went to seek to secure her property there. I was surprised to find myself heartbroken. I'd thought I'd adjusted to losing her, but it was the idea of London without her that haunted my imagination and seemed to crystallise what it was she meant to me; and also why I'd found it very difficult to imagine being there, so close, for the last years. I too had run away, I realised. And Abbs Court's old roof fell.

Then the poor Queen died. Charles was made some sort of Lord Justice or Protector of the Interim – I forget this title among all his others – while everybody leaped into action to get George the First from Hanover. Thus we ensured the Protestant succession. He told me about when he'd been the special envoy to that court all those years ago. He and Lionel Cranfield had gone off to wait on the Elector and his antique mother, the Electress Sophia.

'There we were, Kit, delivering our sop about the German Prince's prospects of an English title, and all the while the Electress stood rigid with her back to the wall.'

I was sewing on to his jacket Naldo's first pulled-off button of the morning. I looked up.

'D'you know what it was, Kit?'

'No, my dear. Was she mad?'

'She looked it. Stiff as a post against the wall, like an eighty-year-old frightened rabbit, all through the proceedings. I kept on in my uneasy French, but I couldn't stop peering at her. Lionel had everything to do not to collapse with laughter. When it was all over we found an opportunity to go back to the chamber. All the time she'd been trying to cover the picture. It was a picture of her cousin the Pretender. She wanted to blot out the Jacobite, so we shouldn't see it was there. Imagine that. She must suddenly have realised what was on the wall, and what was at stake, and flattened herself against it.'

'She preferred the appearance of madness to the disclosure of what was a regrettable and painful fact,' I said.

'Exactly, Kit,' he said. I remember the boy sitting next to him, eating toast, and gazing up at his adoptive father with a sort of worship.

'Charles Papa talks to the King, Naldo,' I said. 'He and Aunt Mary Pierrepont are the only ones in all England who can talk to the King, because they know French. And that's what the King can speak. Well, I think he can also speak German because that's where he used to live. Aunt Mary has started to learn German so that she can be pretty and useful to her husband at the King's court. The King is a very funny old man with a crown. Sometimes. And he has two great Turkish servants called Mustapha and Mehmet. Would you like to go with Papa to see the King?'

Charles put a big wig on Naldo's head, and the boy squirmed and made a giggling noise in the delight of being the centre of attention. But the next moment he flew into a rage – perhaps because he couldn't express himself – and threw his bread at me. Mrs Starr remonstrated:

'Now come on, Master Naldo! Where's your manners this morning?'

He tipped his milk over and made ready to spit.

'Don't even think of it, young man,' she wagged her finger at him.

'BA! BUB! BA! BURBABAB! BUGGA! BEN! BARNABUB! BOOOO!'

Charles never minded these outbursts. He cuffed him mildly round the head and took him out to feed the chickens. I watched them from my own bedroom; because I did mind them. They drove me to a pitch of anger. I wanted to kill the boy; and hated myself for it. I wanted to hammer him into the ground with a piece of wood, so that he should cease to exist. And later when I'd overcome my rage I felt so guilty that I'd renew my efforts to play paper games with him and to try to get him to speak. I did try. And he may have profited, but I knew no way to laugh off the violent feelings he seemed to have the absolute knack of calling up in me. I found him provocative. Why did he have to go out of his way to do the very thing that would set me off? Our sessions ended so often on a note of frustration: him having flown at my breast, teeth bared, or in tears and making that high-pitched noise which was his howl; and me in a fury with his wrist in my one hand and a ruler in my other, handing him over to Mrs Starr so that I didn't execute the whole matter on him there and then. You can see why I find it hard to relate. Not only does it show me up in a light I'd prefer not to acknowledge, but it relates, of course, to my own past. Perhaps I expected him to sing.

That was 1715.

It was a year of great significance to me, because of one great event. In mid-May, late in the evening, I was helping Naldo with his meal at Bushy Park Lodge when a letter was delivered at the door and was brought up by Lucy'lizabeth. Naldo ran to her and hung about her waist. Normally they might have gone off together. Today she stood with her arm about him anxiously waiting for me to open the letter.

'What's the matter?' I said. 'Do you want something, Lucy'lizabeth?' I said it in the way that means *Go away then, if you can't tell me why you're still here*, but she stood her ground, saying nothing. Naldo yanked at her apron.

I shrugged my shoulders and opened my letter.

Madam. My Lord Halifax has been taken ill while in attendance at the house of Mynheer Duvenvoord of the Dutch Embassy. He very urgently requests that you come there at your earliest opportunity, for the inflammation in his lungs causes great concern, both to him and to the physician attending him.

It was signed by some private secretary or official at the ambassador's house.

Outside the night was dark. I looked around in that state of pre-shock which is emotionless enough to permit some sort of packing and organisation, but which always sees to it that you take the most stupid things and leave behind the most obvious. I drove the implications of the letter out of my mind and found myself pushing dresses into baskets, and having Lucy'lizabeth pack Charles's spare mirrors and scented gift washballs, as if we were to dine tomorrow at the Embassy.

Then at the door to the coach I forbade her to come with me.

'I'll manage alone, thank you, Lucy'lizabeth. He'll be in no fit state to . . . '

'But . . . ' She looked at me half bewildered and half in pure hatred. I slammed the door for myself and got the coachman to make haste. All the way up to town along that long straight moonlit road, I convinced myself that all was still in its place.

When I saw him, however, I realised the seriousness of the situation. Charles was dying. They'd taken him from where he'd collapsed, and put him in a bed on the first floor. It was the small hours of the night. He looked at me out of frightened eyes, propped up there on the red pillows. Pain from coughing seemed already to have left its mark on his face.

'Catherine,' he said in a voice made hoarse by the illness. I sent the physician away and embraced him. Charles dying? He was not yet sixty. Ready to crown his political life by seeing to the security of the succession and the triumph of Protestantism. Charles couldn't die. Why not my uncle? What would become of the boy?

'I've left you the house,' he whispered when he could speak. 'I mean the Lodge. I discover it is supposed to revert to the Crown, no matter what I will. But I've left all in the hands of my lawyers. You should be alright there – I'm not without influence; and more importantly money. The necessary backhanders. I had the attorney here not an hour ago. I told him he must see you safe there for as long as you need. You're not to be troubled about it. I've set aside more than enough to fix it absolutely. I was going to sell Abbs Court for you.'

'*Sell* it for me?'

'The family. They wouldn't have let you have it. No matter what the will said. They'd be a much harder prospect than the Crown Commissioners!' He managed a laugh, and then coughed. It was terrible to watch. I put my head against his chest for a moment. 'But it hasn't gone through. The sale. Don't expect the property. But maybe Wortley will use it in his hour of need.' He tried to laugh. The pain brought the creases to his face again.

I said. 'You'll be alright. It's not as bad as it seems, I think. You'll be better tomorrow, my dear . . . Charles.'

'I doubt it, Kit.'

'What brought it on?'

'The air? The sudden cold? A meteor? A miasma? A sudden pain across my chest, and I couldn't breathe, Kit. I struggled it seemed for hours and I couldn't breathe.'

'It's easier now,' I said.

He waited to gather his forces. 'Yes, it's easier. But it's no good, Kit. It's no good.'

'You'll be better tomorrow.'

Another spasm of pain. Then he said: 'Do you know, Kit, I'd just heard the most incredible thing.'

'What was that, my dear?' I wiped his forehead with my hand, then sat on the bed and held his wrist.

'The ambassador told me. Over dinner. The Revolution. Our Revolution. You know . . . you *knew* . . . we *all knew* for a fact that Cherry Russell and Danby and Shrewsbury and the others in '88 . . . We knew they *invited* that Dutch bastard over here to be King. To save our country from Papism. To preserve our free Parliament, our democracy. To guide our own destiny.'

'Yes, my dear.'

'I hear tonight from Duvenvoord that the Dutch forced our hand all along. There was no invitation as such. It's all a myth, all a very clever myth. It was a bloody invasion, Kit. It was a bloody conquest. That we kept anything of our bloody free Parliament was a miracle. An accident even. It's the damnedest bloody thing. Damnedest. Do you know, Kit, if I hadn't believed in all that . . . what shall I call it? That myth. What shall I label it? Roman stuff. Well, Christian and Roman. Freedom! Brotherhood! An imperial republic, if you like. If I hadn't believed in all that I'd never have . . . Well, I'd never have bothered to do anything that I did. Who would? Who'd bother with the management of a mere political football? I'd have gone abroad, maybe. I'd have . . . I don't know. I'd have gone to Hanover to work with Leibniz. But then I'd never have met you.' He held my hand. The pain across his face again. His body trying to turn itself inside out.

A Dutch servant came in, closely followed by Lucy'lizabeth in a cloak and hood. She glared at me and took Charles's hand from the other side of the bed. Then she pressed it to her lips.

Charles looked at me and then, painfully turning his head, at her. And then back to me.

An Academy of One

Since we spoke at the Abbey, my dearest Uncle, and made our peace at that sad occasion, I have been thinking deeply about the future and about what Charles would have wished me to do. I also consult my own wishes. What do I wish to do? And what do I think is the honestest course for a woman in my position? I respect your opinions about the boy. He is now well-grown – or at least grown, yet I cannot say that he is an ornament for a civilised saloon. He is himself. He misses his father very much, and that causes him to misbehave. He draws very neatly and accurately, and plays the spinet modestly, but he still cannot converse, nor give any indication as to whether the condition we find him in is the effect of some terrible mistreatment, or is some freak of nature. That you have need of help at home I understand, in view of your years and the burdens of your responsibilities at the Mint; not to mention your theoretical labours. I miss London, and have no reason now to feel ill at ease in St Martin's Street. The boy can and should be here, I think, whatever you suggest about my future. He is surrounded by my staff, people who understand him and whom he has come to trust. It would be a shame to disrupt his world any further at the moment, and I could with ease make visits to him as and when was convenient. To put the matter very bluntly, Uncle, I desire to know whether you would have me wait here at the Lodge where indeed I am comfortable enough, or come home to your house and take up where I left off. I remain, my dear Uncle,

> *Your Obedient Niece*
> *and Humble Servant*
> *C. Barton*

Kit. For heaven's sake, come home.

> *Your very Loving Uncle*
> *Is. Newton*

But when it came to it I couldn't do it. I dispatched Lucy'lizabeth in deep mourning to St Martin's Street. We'd reached an agreement. She'd be a good niece to him: she knew enough of my life to carry it off. She knew me like a glove in fact, and at least had the decency to grow older, which I was prevented from doing by the Stone. She would be a better niece, indeed, and would be protected by mourning from having to receive my circle of acquaintances – those not in the know – for as long as she wished. And after that she could take them up or build up her own circle. She was very skilled at being me. She could have Abbs Court, if she could hold it from the Montagus, so long as I held the Lodge and my annuity. As for the rest: there was ample willed to me to provide for every eventuality within reason.

I gave my time to the boy, trying to make some kind of relationship with him. In the afternoons when he was out with the men for his ride or working in the stables, or in the evenings when he'd gone to bed, I devoted myself to my project at last. Was this pride? Was it retreat? Disgust? Fear? Ungratefulness? I didn't want to be with people. Not now. I couldn't bear people. I didn't want to be touched any more. Not even to risk it.

I got out the notebook, in which over the years I'd made so many scribblings and attempts to understand things, and opened it at the front at my *Quaestiones Quaedam*.

How far now was I in a position to answer them? The first:

'1) Jesus said, *I come not to bring peace but a sword.*
    Is this the razor of the anatomist?'

In my petticoat I still kept the Spanish dagger.

'2) Is God well pleased? Has He indeed come down again? Is that Him? Downstairs?'

I was sure enough by now that my uncle had missed the riddle of the universe, even if he'd solved, like Aaron Hill, the mechanism of the tides and a good many other bits of celestial and terrestrial clockwork. Brilliantly. But downstairs as I read there was the boy. Not God. But a human being. Just now being cleaned because he'd soiled himself and he stank. I knew by intuition, by our special bond of shared thought, when he was going to do it. I took care to be out of the way. Not well pleased, most of the time. But a transcendent mystery.

'3) *If the Son therefore shall make you free, ye shall be free indeed.*'

I thought with anger of Bishop Burnet. He was someone's son.

374

'4) Is it a bold thing for a woman to devote herself to study and experiment? Is it an unattempted thing? Am I the first?'

No, I was not the first. But it was a very bold thing.

'5) If motion in this age of progress and wonders is determined as my uncle has shown, how shall Christ intervene to bring comfort to the tormented? Are we but bodies ceaselessly continuing in our right lines? What forces are impressed on us? Hunger? Disease? Lust? Blows? Blades? Have we in us *inherent* forces? What is Love?'

I left that one. And the next:

'6) These lovers sport in the public eye. But in private, when there is no one to see, what is it they say and do? What feel?
'7) Why will not my passion discharge? Is a woman's body inferior to a man's in this? Is a woman's *mind* capable of discharge?'

No on the first count. Yes on the second. As to my own body, I didn't know the reason why it wouldn't, but it was extremely frustrating.

'8) Why does my time hasten away, faster than my uncle's clock, so that I am always afraid? Are these the last days?'

My time appeared to be affected by the Stone, whose quintessence, I imagined, was permeating my frame more and more substantially. I didn't know why I was always afraid. As to the Last Days. We were still here despite Fatio and the Camisards. And my uncle's revised calculations based on his code key to the Book of Daniel put the date some time in the twentieth century.

'9) Why am I so frightened of my words?'

I thought again of Naldo. Perhaps I was frightened of what might come out of its own accord. What might blurt. Here, locked away in my Lodge, I would produce them – but perhaps only the safe ones.

'10) What forces have I reacted to, so that I should once have been of a lupine disposition?'

And was still. I pressed my ribs through my steel-stiffened stays. I pressed my legs to contact the hardness of the wolf-creature's sinews. I sighed, and turned to a vacant section of the notebook to begin. But did not. For something still delayed me from commitment to it. I went to bed.

Finally, though, I did send even my shadowy backer away, when next I found him with me, touching the back of my neck with his sweet lips, feathery, parting with his hands the cleft of my buttocks. I put aside that passingly precious temptation of an entry into the other world. I would live, as it were, in a bottle, waiting. I would wait for something to end of its own accord, partially anaesthetised from all that; and I would surrender myself to my studies.

I wanted to consider the subject of value. Since Mary's marriage it had begun to interest me greatly. She who had been worth so much, was now worth nothing in her own right, yet Wortley saw her nothing as everything. I who still held myself as of no value had been worth this house to Charles – and much more. What were we females to these males? What did they really know of us? Nothing. They said it was love. Could one talk of true partners? I doubted it. What were we to them, then: mobile openings, intelligent *vaginae*, unusual in that we could both speak Latin somewhat? But this wasn't a regular requirement. Quite the contrary – or the country would have been dense with female academies.

We were ourselves. However, by the arousal of nearby males we were mathematicised. The erection of a *one* turned our *zeros* into *infinities*. Financially, in my case, a very great bequest. We became their estate, their universe, their *all the world*, so they said. So their actions proved.

My treatise was a way of making my tribute to him, and my goodbye to him: the ultimate economist of his day. It was also a farewell to my irascible uncle, the ultimate computer of his day. I couldn't hope to equal them. Nevertheless, my work was to be the great synthesis of all my odd bits of thought, and a unification of all the points and theories that I'd come across. My *Principia*. Or perhaps my *Essay on Woman*, since my experience as a woman was to be centrally significant.

I knew where I would begin. I'd begin with a riddle: why was it that £1 invested in the South Sea Scheme would increase in value year on year, and pay off the country's war debt?

I sat in my garden in pleasant shade from the midsummer sun. I'd had a writing-desk moved out of doors. I chewed at the quill stalk of my pen. I tried to think as Charles would, with World Trade and Profits and Losses. But I couldn't do it that way. I had to start from very first principles. What is a commodity worth? It's worth what someone will give, trade, swap, pay for it. That is a market-place of two. And then as the market-place increases, and the commodities, let us say, duplicate, then the value goes down, until the customers, with their desires and needs and their convertible currency, exceed the supply. Then the value goes up.

I envisaged, I don't know why, the woollen cap in which my Lord was buried in the Abbey at Westminster. The commodity was the wool on the sheep's back. Then washed and bleached by someone. Combed and bundled by someone. Passed on from transaction to transaction. Value added at the distaff or wheel. Value added at the loom, at the making up, at the presentation and dressing of the corpse. There was a net of micro-markets, for the folk involved were all tied into constant exchange by their needs, not just content with producing Charles's cap as a life's work and then dying. Charles had believed in the network of markets. But if you were the landowner who owned the sheep and the workers anyway, you just told them to get on with it for loyalty's sake or you'd take away their subsistence and throw them out of their houses; then value was as nothing. Either you had everything or you had nothing. To Charles that was the old way, the feudal way, the Jacobite way, the Tory way. Being a younger son, he'd not had the landowner mentality. He believed in industry and the facilitation of trade. But if he ended up owning the market itself, which was possibly an exaggeration, was that so different? And now I had the property. I could vote in my own right, now. But I couldn't feel comfortable about either of their parties, any more. They both entirely missed *my* point of view, anyway. I didn't recall having been consulted over exactly how the less fortunate were plundered, bought, raped or sold.

Thoughts started to come haphazard, swarming up and falling like the dance of gnats at the corner of my bed of trefoils: why a woman increased in value according to her face and her age, up to a certain point, and then decreased. How that point could be shifted by presentation and adornment, a species of advertising. Why was it that if the membrane of her virginity were *accounted* intact, then her

377

value was consistent with regular tables? It didn't matter whether it was *actually* intact, as long as it was thought to be. What was important was the theoretical integrity, the Virtue, which she, the person perhaps least able and empowered to control it, was required to preserve: her *virtual* integrity. And if the membrane was *known* to be broken, the woman's value *might* slump to zero. But *might* not, depending on a whole range of variables. Such as her birth and breeding, and the attitudes of customers. And these variables were not just variables, but bordered on anomaly. The laws of female value weren't universal laws; they could be thrown aside by imponderable quirks of behaviour, such as the old Duke of York who became King James marrying Anne Hyde, a relative commoner, and producing the baby who eventually became our Queen Anne. And here value was immediately conferred on the lady, the mother, by ennoblement, so that the laws of female value should *seem* to have been followed, even though everyone *knew* they had not been. But then the female value might sink again to zero according to fertility – not necessarily hers, but possibly her husband's. I reflected on the fact that the concept of zero itself, the cipher, had emerged in a country where, on the death of a husband of status, a woman's value might sink so utterly that they threw her on the fire. A tragic zero.

Why was it then that Mary Pierrepont's father, Evelyn, had required Wortley to play that guessing game about her total worth? It grew incomprehensible, like alchemy, and drew me on.

Then again, I considered Ruth. Ruth assigned value to her women precisely on the basis that their openings were available and *known* to be so. This was the only case in which proof of the membrane might be physically required as an incentive to extra payment. Whereas in the culture of the new King's two Turkish valets, this proof was a requirement of marriage.

Value was clearly a function of the market-place. But one market-place was not the same as another, and when women were given the status of commodities, then commodities started to behave in an anomalous way. So that anyone who contemplated making a great thesis on the subject of value and the market-place had better take into account the view from behind the corset before drawing any conclusions. Because of the instant anomalous tendency introduced by our gender.

Then I considered the anomaly of *my* own gender – such that gender itself became an imponderable, and the tendency to make universal laws insecure and uncertain leaked into the male as well.

My project, beginning its fulfilment at last, showed signs of excessive proliferation. It was becoming a drug, by removing me to a speculative world of humour and dry possibility. I was becoming bitter and satirical. Good. We were all horseflesh and were traded by dealers. My project was working: I was spared feeling. I should have matter here for years. I scribbled on in the warm afternoon.

About ethics and the rule of law. Our markets were governed by principles of decency and fairness. Such was Mary's world. She was at least legally married. I occupied the under-market. I had no rights, but relied upon the decency of my protector. I was a liaison. Ruth was the pirate world – there was no love, no decency in her market. She was from the stripped world, and was the victim of forces. Then came the market in children, differing by sex only in virtue of one penetrable orifice.

Only the first of the market-places was actually admitted to; the others were masked over and denied. They were short cuts between the ethical walks, without which, I thought, the official system could not run. I thought of Naldo. *It's a world where only the strong survive*, Charles had said to me in the carriage after he'd hit me. Dog eat dog. The survival of the fittest, the most ruthless. It was the consequence of the market-place. I couldn't believe that Nature reflected herself from our financial imperatives. I forgave him. He must be wrong. There must be some other way, I thought. It is all corruption. Yet I would catalogue it. I would expose the paperings and paintings over. Perhaps I should reveal Sophia standing rigid against the wall hiding a frightful picture. A Testament of Gaps. Fourteen wolf years were missing from my memory.

I see myself writing, then getting up to do a little weeding in my garden. I see through the glass of memory how that year of Charles's death drove on. The civil war flashed up but was quickly put out. They called it the Jacobite Rebellion. In December Mary caught smallpox. It pitted and scarred the lovely value of her cheeks and she was left without eyelashes, despite the best endeavours of Dr Sloane.

The Message

Naldo, my young gentleman, and I got down from our horses. There was a seat before Charles's ornamental pond. We tied the beasts behind us. I gave him the stale bread from the morning, and then sat with my piece of paper on my knee, jotting the fragments of sentences down with the stub of a pencil as they occurred to me, crosswriting and steering the point round the blob of sealing-wax which was in my way. Naldo fed the ducks. They came fanning in to mill around, quacking and fighting, where he teased them with his providence. Behind me I could hear the steady, greedy, munch-munch of the grazing mares. He and I had just had one of our rows. I had screamed at him for his disobedience in not bothering to air his bed properly or bring his clothes down. His room was such a mess that the servant wouldn't go in. The place stank. He needn't think I was going in there to clean it out. Did he want to live like an animal? Why wouldn't he try just a little harder at his speech lessons?

'Why must you provoke me so, you horrible boy! Does it please you to see me upset? Do you really wish to make me cry? Why, Naldo? What do you get out of it? Alright! If you won't do what I ask – something quite reasonable ... You agree that it's reasonable to ask someone to take a little responsibility for the place we both have to live in? It's not a cruel thing I ask? It isn't, is it, Naldo? Then why in hell won't you do it when I ask you! You'll not ride for a week , then.'

Naldo had stamped and made that high-pitched sound as the tears ran down his cheeks. He'd stamped very loudly up the stairs, and stamped for fifteen solid minutes in his room until I thought the ceilings were going to come down.

When the bread was finished and the ducks had gone away I put my work aside and went to stand next to him; for I'd got down what had occurred to me on the ride, and needed to rest a little from the obsession of my thought. We put our arms round each other. I looked down at our reflection. He was neater in his appearance than I was. My hair straggled. Well, I didn't care for I had no one to please with my appearance. In market-value terms I looked like someone aspiring to an honest zero. My comfortable woollen dress which I wore day after day was inky and stained with coffee or other dribs.

I believe my *air* might have been noticeable in a London salon, but I suited myself. I bathed every now and then, especially if I started to itch. Occasionally someone from the Crown Commissioners called about their claim on the property, but I always referred them to Charles's attorney. This seemed to be a ritual code for keeping up the necessary bribes.

The work was well on its way, nearly finished in fact, but I was wrestling with the most difficult part: the economics and politics of amnesia. I'd been on this at least a year, probably longer; probably since the Bubble had burst and everyone had gone broke. That was the only piece of news from the outside world which had interested me. I'd studied and anatomised it from all the sources I could get hold of. It wasn't only the Government's South Sea Scheme, of course; in the burst of that porcupine a thousand little verminous sub-schemes had been exposed to wriggle and lie about in their own corruption. I could have pointed the finger and said: 'Well, Harley started it!' But it was more than a Party thing – it was an emblem of the disease of the whole system, and I found it a very convenient indicator for my project.

I brought Naldo back to the seat. 'Would you like me to read you the little book Aunt Mary's made up for you? Well I shall, anyway.' I looked inside the cover for the few sewn sheets of her charming story, for I'd been writing my notes on the letter in which she'd enclosed the gift. 'Bother. I've left it back at the house. Very well, I shall tell you about it now, and we'll have it later. It's a very pretty story with pictures, all about you. Well, it's about her really, when she and Uncle Wortley were in Constantinople. But it's about *your* health, Naldo. You know there's an epidemic?'

He looked at me. I never knew how to pitch my language to him – whether he responded only to baby talk or could grasp more demanding concepts. Our mental link didn't seem to operate in words. He wouldn't confirm or deny his reception. I struggled on. 'Lots of poor little children have been very ill, and lots have died since Winter. It's called the smallpox. Big people can get it too. I had it a long time ago. Mary had it. That's why her face is damaged. It's a very nasty disease. Not everybody gets better. But Aunt Mary is a very special woman. When she was far away beyond the sea in the land of Turkey with Uncle Wortley and the children she dressed in long silk robes and floppy pyjamas. She wore no stays and covered her face except for a slot for her eyes. With her funny hat she was free to go anywhere and saw lots of wonderful things, like magic carpets with tobacco pipes that bubble; like steaming pools that bubble where the beautiful ladies swim naked; and a magic bubble of wisdom which used to be a church.'

He stared at me, but was at least still.

'She found an old Greek lady who had a special way of stopping people getting the smallpox. She had it done to *her* little boy, so that he'd be safe from the illness. It's only a scratch on the arm. It's called an engraftment. Only the old lady used a nasty rusty needle and hurt his right arm, so Aunt Mary told her not to be silly and gave her a clean needle and told her to use the other arm. And that didn't hurt hardly at all. And there he was. Well, he was a little bit ill afterwards. But then he was safe.'

Naldo looked back at the ducks.

'We want you to be safe, Naldo. Mary's having the engraftment done to her little girl now. The little book is a story to tell you all about it. She's written other little books. Poems and stories. And some of them are to teach the grown-up Doctors about the engraftment. So that they'll save the children from the smallpox. Do you think that's a good thing?'

Naldo looked back to me. 'Bugg Bar Boy Buggaboo,' he said. I sighed.

'Mr Pope from Twitenham is in love with Aunt Mary and writes her naughty letters and sad poems. And,' I muttered under my breath, 'some stupid churchman is already preaching against interfering with God's disease to punish sin and how they should all be left to die.'

We rode back then, because I was anxious to get to my desk to write up and develop the latest of my notes. But as I did so I had the strangest feeling. It was as if there occurred a hiatus in the continuity of things, and this was filled almost by a voice, so clearly did it impress itself upon my inward sensation. Hessy's voice. Hessy was in distress.

I tried to put it from me once we'd got back to the stables and untacked our mounts. I tried to bustle it away in the effort of carrying the heavy saddle and stowing it on its peg in the tack-room, in the busy-ness of talking with the groom, in the smell of horse and oil and tobacco, of checking this or ordering a new that. I heard Naldo babbling. For once he made sense of something. He said his first words:

'Bababen Barnabas Ben Boys Bugger Bugger Boy BaBenjamin Beast Bugger . . . '

'Naldo!' Preoccupied and worried I didn't think to congratulate him on his moment of triumph. It would have to be obscene, was my first, callous reaction. How like him to choose now!

When I sat at my desk in my riding boots, I tried to tell myself that Hessy's voice had been a phantasm – I'd been the victim of no more than a trick of the ear or brain. I settled to my notebook and quill, with Mary's letter in front of me bearing all my semi-legible scribbles. But the conviction grew instead of falling back. It grew and grew throughout the night. In the small hours I got up and paced about. I went down in the murk to make myself a drink, but the fire was too far down, and my mug of lukewarm milk failed to reassure. I heard her cry out again. It was almost as though she were in the next room. I even went looking and bumping into things about the dark house – to see if there was someone there. No one, of course. But Hessy was dying. I knew it; the conviction wouldn't release me.

Just before dawn I formed a resolution. I dressed myself up somewhat as my old self and, shaking the grumbling household out of its sleep, I managed to get my coach put to. I set off for London in the chill grey light.

I drew up in front of my uncle's house in St Martin's Street. The smoky air carried a spittle of rain, which just touched my face as I stood at the main door waiting for Mary or Tony to answer. It was Tony, much gone on in years. I pushed past him with hardly an apology. A young man in expensive clothes lounged in the parlour reading a newspaper.

'Where's Sir Isaac?' I said, without the courtesies of introduction.

The young man looked up in surprise. 'I believe he's in his study. But . . . '

I left the room abruptly and went to the hall again. My uncle was at work on some papers in his den. His activity and occupation was exactly as I remembered him, but he was now eighty-odd and looking what might have been thin and frail compared with his fuller times, but could equally have been described as tenacious and wiry. It startled me to see him thus. I'd lost sight of other people's subjection to time. I'd come here preoccupied, as I had to Charles when he lay dying; I hadn't thought.

My uncle looked up. 'Catherine. But where's John? And Kitty? I'd not expected you.' My face must have been a blank. 'I thought you were staying at Cranbourne two more months. Is something wrong? Is Kitty unwell?'

I realised at length who he was talking about. Lucy'lizabeth had married John Conduitt, of Cranbourne Park, near Winchester. They had a little girl named Catherine, who would be about four or five now. I thought fast. I did something terrible, so great was my sense of need; of Hessy's need; that inner certainty which had taken hold of me the previous afternoon and now wouldn't let me drop.

I said: 'My dearest Uncle. I am distraught; I've come up expressly. Kitty is ill with the . . . At least we fear the worst. It could be another thing at this stage. Scarlet fever. Measles. Our physician cannot be certain. I came at once myself. I was so distressed, Uncle.'

'I'm deeply saddened, my dear. How did the contagion possibly come there? It is an agony. But why did you come to me? Shouldn't you have written? Shouldn't you be with your child?'

'Uncle. The Stone. It's our only hope.'

He looked at me with his still keen eyes. How strong he was for his age. How hale – all his faculties still about him. His face was still comparatively unlined. His skin very good; his cheeks even softish. A woman might have been pleased with such a complexion at such an age. Truly he was an exceptional man and would have been in any age; exceptional in mind and constitution. Once again he held my destiny in his hands, I thought. I remembered now how much he'd invested in the South Sea project. He could have lost up to £20,000, but he seemed to have weathered the storm. He seemed to have weathered everything very well. 'But my dear, I don't have it.' His face twisted slightly as if there were some pain or difficulty called up from long ago by its mention. 'I don't have it, Catherine. Your journey is fruitless.'

'But you told Pawnee . . . all those years ago . . . your letter to Woodstock.' I felt desperate. He looked shocked.

'I no longer have any of it. It's been used, my dearest Catherine. Or lost.'

'Couldn't you search? Please!'

By way of answer he went to the small walnut case on his little

384

study sideboard. It unlocked with a key from the window-ledge. He opened a tiny drawer, and from its velvet plucked out a glass bottle. He held it up to the light for me. It was completely empty.

'But how? Where did it go? Who did you give it to?'

'I'm not at liberty to say, Catherine. I'm very sorry in this, believe me, but there is none.'

I took, almost snatched the bottle from his hand. 'Then I must go back. It's very desperate. I had hoped . . . so much. Pawnee had some . . . but she's in America. Let me go up to my old room. I must . . . rest a moment for the journey back.'

'You must rest more than that. And you must eat. You must stay at least tonight.'

'I can't. I must go back. Let me just go up and draw breath. Perhaps a bite to eat, though I'm not hungry. Who's that young man in the parlour?'

'Don't you know him? No, perhaps you don't. Perhaps you've missed crossing him. It's the young Smith boy. My step-nephew, if that's the name of the degree. I fail at genealogical niceties. Benjamin's son. Your cousin. My stepfather's grandson.'

'I see. What does he do here?'

'He's a very wild boy. Inured to profligacy, and at so young an age. He's been farmed on me. On my charity, for the moment. It's a testimony to the true state of the Church of England that he is one of its ornaments.'

'He's in orders?'

'He's in disgrace, but yes. I'll call Mary.'

'Thank you. In a moment.'

I left and ran upstairs. It was much the same – the big bed that Charles had bought me – us. Somewhat redecorated, new cloths and hangings, different knick-knacks, but the portrait of Charles still hung over the amours of Catherine Conduitt and her husband when they stayed in London. My old dressing-table and mirror still did service for Lucy'lizabeth's toilette.

I felt for the Spanish dagger in my petticoat, and drew it out. It was always with me, as Nick's skull was always at my house. How bright it was. Such excellent steel that, nested in its pocket in the folds of my underwear for so long, it had lost nothing of its sheen nor its edge. I pressed the fierce razor-keen point to my finger. Blood. Immediately blood. Hardly a touch and almost no pain. Yet it had made its incision.

Carefully, seated at the mirror, I turned it towards myself. For all its lightness and balance its considerable length made it hard to hold, and hard to manoeuvre. I ran the risk of cutting my fingers on the blade if I held it anywhere else but by the hilt, and that would cripple the intensity of my purpose.

Gingerly, supporting the handle with my right hand on the dressing-table and propping my left so that I could grip the flat of the blade between fingers and thumb, I brought the point towards my face. It seemed to stare back at me with its own concentration. Using the mirror, I guided it like a scalpel to the bump in my hairline and leant into the cut.

It was surpassingly difficult. I forced myself on as the blood streamed down my nose and chin, all over my bodice and into my lap. When it ran in my eyes I was compelled to desist and turned to rip the fabric hanging from the corner of the bed so as to mop and stem the flow. Then I tried again, fighting back the urge to cry out.

Eventually I saw, through the gashes, what I was looking for. The Stone had seated itself deeply in the tissues, but I could get hold of it with my nails. Summoning all my resolve, I gave a sudden yank. In that extremity of pain it seemed for a moment as if half my head had come away. The mirror showed a Cyclops drenched with the putting out of its own eye, and holding the emblem of a bloody nut of flesh.

When I'd recovered from my sick faintness, I tried to wash my trophy clean in the washbowl. But the blood wouldn't stop. It soaked the cloth I held up to my forehead and spilled down over me once more. I tore off another piece of material and used that screwed up as a wadding for the hole. It quickly flooded again, so I took a larger piece and had to keep one hand always at the wound, while I dabbled the little relic in the crimson water with the other, scratching off the tissuey traces with my fingernail until it was clean.

The Stone was a jagged scrap of crystal, but as you turned it about there was an instant rainbow effect, as the light from outside was split into its spectrum in a hundred magical ways. My arm ached from holding up the stanch. I changed hands to place the bright fragment in the bottle, and then hunted for paper to write its instructions on. I could almost have written in blood. But did not. I knew where she was from Swift's occasional letter. I knew how he'd kept her at arm's length. I'd gathered what a fool she'd made of herself. I knew her sister Moll was dead. I knew that now she occupied her large lonely house at Celbridge, beyond Dublin, hoping against obsessive hope for some return of her feeling; when she was not cursing God, or one in particular of his Ministers. Yes, there was some ink. I went briefly to work.

In my frightful state I left the house without a word. I knew where to go. Yes, the shop at the corner of St Martin's Street was still as it had been. I was aware of people staring at me as I made my way towards it. How I must have appeared – a lady's shape half-running distractedly along the sidewalk, pressing her brow with the one arm and clutching tightly to a little paper parcel with the other. And her face and body drenched from the top with a renewing red stain. I could feel it still trickling past my nose. I licked it automatically from my lip as I went. But I didn't care what I might look like. I had one thought only.

The young man behind the counter didn't recognise me. He'd been virtually a boy the last time I'd entered the place. I frightened him terribly. He must have thought the survivor of some dreadful highway accident had risen from beneath the horses' hoofs. But I put good money in front of him, and he promised in a tremulous voice that he would see immediately to the despatch of my parcel. I made him tie it up and wipe it and seal it properly. I gave him more money and made him shut up the shop and take it immediately to the postal agent. Tasting blood, I made him promise again to see to its sudden despatch. I stood outside the shop, watching him go as I changed my aching arm over at holding the wad. I watched him to the turn of Charing Cross Road, at which he disappeared.

Transmutation

What can I say? The rest is a dream. I think of my uncle's calculation for the Last Days. Thankfully, we have just escaped that date. I see myself who was once Kit suddenly the victim of an enormous curvature around the revealed Stone and now forever accelerated towards the present; while to myself who am the observer of this phenomenon she is held unmoving in an infinitely prolonged trance. Or is it I who am in the trance?

Could it be that, following the Disclosure, there occurred an alignment of Wormholes at the interface of two rippling n-dimensional energy systems? By the popping of one bubble I was whisked, discontinuously, into the development of another – it is an informed suggestion, as feasible as any. Thus I wandered into the wrong century ten years ago like a ghost, to haunt the vicinity of Abbs Court, until I was taken to Kingston General Hospital as a case of amnesia. No record survives of any comment on the strangeness of my clothes, nor my preoccupation with the Arithmetic of Infinites, nor the fact that I held two skulls clutched to me.

Having committed my account of myself to paper, having recovered myself . . . but how ludicrous seem the circumstances I've come to regard as normal: I mean the way I've passed this last decade. How marginal am I by comparison to my former self, who once lived closely caught up in great and formative times, and now must eke out my days under the terms of their faded legacy.

At the General Hospital, when I offered no sign of dying, but equally no clue as to my identity, nor showed up on any missing persons register, they were kind enough to fake their books, and pass me out as a certain Jacob . . . but I will not reveal his last name – a reclusive mathematics teacher from a school in Sunbury – a suicide – an emergency whom they'd lost just as I was admitted. It was a kind act – I mean the fake – supremely ethical in its unethicality.

It enabled me, after a decent interval, to convalesce, and then to slip into a new role. I took on the daily routine of work; I became reluctantly accustomed to cars, trains and supermarkets with the help of a kindly nurse who showed an interest in my case. And eventually, as I've told you, I changed my job, pitting myself aggressively against the challenge of the mental hospital, rather than submit any longer to the drudgery and humiliation of the classroom. That is how I found myself working with Seco. That is how I came to be overtaken by panic and to experience the recall of my past – as I've told you – and which I said you would not believe.

As for the other skull, which I believe to be Nicholas Fatio's own: did I pause on my journey to snatch it from his corpse? As I passed? I cannot tell; it is a fact but its mystery is beyond me.

And maybe she received the Stone, whose effects we cannot predict, for it would obey no law. And perhaps I shall see her as she was. Once upon a time. For which I wait. Truly.

Notes on people and places

* Smallpox was the killer disease of the eighteenth century. The practice of inoculation against it involved introducing actual smallpox infection into the body. This practice was also called variolation or engraftment. Its use in the Near East was known to the Royal Society as early as 1714. Lady Mary Wortley Montagu's encounter with it in Turkey, her experiments with it on her own children, and her campaign to publicise its use have been marginalised in most reference sources – in favour of Jenner. Edward Jenner FRS advocated 'vaccination', which used infected material from the related disease cowpox (hence the name), nearly a hundred years after Mary's work.

The successful inoculation of Mary's daughter took place in England observed by several leading doctors. The method was subsequently tested on volunteers from Newgate prison. Thereafter the procedure was widely used. (There was a fashion for some years of making a cut instead of a scratch. This placed the patient at much greater risk from infection, of course, and was discontinued; although in an unregulated medical system there were always opportunities for abuse and profiteering.)

In America, Cotton Mather, the Boston witch-persecutor and Presbyterian writer, learned the technique from a black slave, and sought to popularise it. Other interested parties disseminated the method from England, so that its use was to a degree world-wide.

Although vaccination was made the compulsory system in England in the mid nineteenth century, and inoculation prohibited, the older form can be shown to have had great and possibly equal success despite its virtual obliteration from history.

Mary Wortley Montagu became, by her rejection of Pope's love, the lifelong target of his vitriol. He insulted her publicly as 'Sappho' in a series of poems, and alleged that she'd profited out of her allowance for the care of her disturbed sister. She fought back in print but eventually left the country and her husband to live in Italy, without bothering to look or behave fashionably. On being shown

Richardson's novel *Clarissa* she agreed that the heroine's elopement under pressure seemed to mirror uncannily the earlier circumstances of her own life. She died in 1762.

* Mrs Astell died some years after the events described here of an operation for cancer of the breast.

* Mrs Manley also died of cancer.

* The establishment of a women's Academy took until the late nineteenth century.

* Anne Bracegirdle lived to a very good age.

* William Congreve was kind enough to leave her an annuity after his activities with Henrietta Churchill-Godolphin, the Second Duchess of Marlborough, who had a wax image made of his dead body including the details of his gouty leg. She kept this effigy sitting at table with her when she ate.

* Wortley grew incredibly rich, but not as rich as the Churchills, who may well have been at one stage the richest family in Europe. Sarah lived to be eighty-four.

* A 'Life' of Charles Montagu was brought out shortly after his death, consisting mainly of his parliamentary speeches. Commissioned by his family, its attempt to minimise his relationship with Catherine Barton is undermined by the publication of his will at the end, including the gift of Bushy Park Lodge and Abbs Court. Kit's total inheritance, estimated by the Astronomer Royal at the time, came to over £25,000 – equivalent to at least £5 million in modern terms. Charles had just bought another estate – Sandown.

* Abbs Court was reduced in the nineteenth century, and then demolished. The name now survives as a large gravel extraction site under the name of Apps Court.

* Hester Vanhomrigh is alleged to have died in Ireland in 1723, still desperately seeking some emotional commitment from Swift.

* Having written *Gulliver's Travels* and been investigated by the Lunacy Commission, Jonathan Swift suffered greatly from his Ménière's syndrome and various infections of the blood. He died, very distressed, in the Autumn of 1745. His meetings with Catherine Barton are recorded in his *Journal to Stella* (Esther Johnson), whilst he reveals his attempt to gain control over his feelings for Hessy Vanhomrigh in his poem *Cadenus and Vanessa*. The *Isaac Bickerstaff* pamphlets are only one example of his satirical indignation at religious Enthusiasm, or what we might call 'New Age Cultism'. In

his fragment 'Concerning the Mechanical Operation of the Spirit' there is a biting portrait of contemporary ecstatic hummers, their headgear, their swaying, and their other attempts, both yogic and erotic, to set loose the spirit.

In his will Swift left all his money towards the construction of a 'Hospital for idiots and lunatics' in Dublin. His other monument was a set of public toilets, divided by gender, at Market Hill, near Armagh, but it is not certain that he invented the concept. The exact spirit in which both bequests were intended is also unclear.

* The sycophantic Conduitt wrote Isaac Newton's biography soon after 1726. Conduitt got all sorts of information from his wife, including the apple-on-the-head story.

* Everyone knows of Handel and his *Messiah*. Deciding to stay in England, he moved on to oratorios after a blazing success at opera. The religious dramas, which needed no staging and no writer, proved a great deal cheaper and more viable when tastes changed, following the rival company's down-market *Beggar's Opera*. Swift approved the *Beggar's Opera* because it wasn't foreign and 'effeminate' like the proper form. Here he shows his populist Toryism rather than his taste.

* Women who fulfilled the property qualifications, or held 'freeman' status, lost their voting rights in the great Reform Act of 1832.

* One of the spin-offs of the Peace of Utrecht in 1713 was that it guaranteed Britain's establishment of control over the Spanish American slave trade: part of the 'South Sea' venture. Sugar, coffee, rum, chocolate, tobacco, domestic servants – so many evidences of modern luxury, and so much sheer British wealth, came from the silent transport of people selected on racial grounds from one far-off country to another.

* Millbank became the site of the first Panopticon – a prison with a central watchtower designed so that the prisoners didn't know whether it was occupied or not. Feeling that they were spied upon was supposed to make them police themselves, and saved money on staff. It was later knocked down, and part was rebuilt as the Tate Gallery. Sugar again.

* The typewriter was invented in 1714, but failed to work.

Acknowledgements

Grateful thanks are due to Keith Gregory, Bill Hamilton, Peter Lamb, and Leslie Wilson for their readiness to talk over several of the problems of construction and historical detail. I am much indebted to Nicholas Pearson, practically, and Ann Bartholomew, intangibly, for helping me to realise the novel. Stephen Cox's detailed comments and suggestions have proved invaluable. Thanks also to Franco Antinoro for support with my Italian. The extracts from Newton's notebooks, some of his comments, some elements of his correspondence with his niece and her replies are as quoted in Richard S. Westfall's excellent biography of Isaac Newton, *Never at Rest*.